Truthfully, Yours

Caden Armstrong

Author's note

Truthfully, Yours is an adult romance, but it is also a story about the disabled identity. When I set out to write this book, I was in a place of rage; I was angry at the world. I wanted to write a character who had faced some of my struggles, while still having her happy ending.

I think books that highlight queer and disabled joy are so incredibly important, and in my mind, this book is one. However, it is also a book that delves into darker subjects such as queerphobia, sexism, and ableism. I wanted to write a book that showed disabled and queer joy, but I found that to tell Charlie, and Page's, story I needed to also discuss the hardships that they face in their lives. So, I urge you to check the content warnings included in this book before reading; please take care of yourself and your own mental health first and foremost.

For Charlie, it was important to me to use the autistic and bisexual label. Where some find labels constricting, I find joy in my queer and disabled labels. Personally, I consider my autism a disability; Charlie does as well. Please know that not all neurodivergent people consider themselves disabled and that some autistic people might prefer to use the neurodivergent label instead. This is a very personal choice. It is important to remind people who are not a part of the queer and disabled communities that neither community is a monolith. Therefore, my experience, and Charlie and Page's experiences do not represent the disabled, autistic, bisexual, or queer communities.

My hope, when writing this book, is Charlie and Page's story will resonate with some of you. Through romance fiction, I discovered my own neurodivergence and queer identities. Other books, for which I am forever thankful for, helped show me that I deserve to be loved and deserve happiness. For the disabled community, I believe stories that show disabled people overcoming ableism while finding love and happiness is inherently radical. My hope is this book can show people with similar experiences as myself, that they deserve the self-love, romantic love, and happiness that Charlie and Page find.

Happy reading!
Caden

To my sensitivity readers

This book would not be here without the help of my lovely and amazing sensitivity readers. Before you begin reading *Truthfully, Yours*, I want to take a moment to acknowledge and thank the sensitivity readers who helped make this book the best it could be. To me, it is very important to work with and acknowledge the sensitivity readers that made sure I not only checked my internal biases but also made sure the representation I included in this book is respectful to the communities included in the story.

Thank you to Jess, Swati, Joel and Sukhi, for their work and contribution towards sensitivity reading for BIPOC representation.

Thank you to Bethany, Chloe, and Joel for their work and contribution towards sensitivity reading for disability and neurodivergent representation.

Thank you to Bethany, Joel, and Theresa for their work and contribution towards sensitivity reading for queer representation.

And finally, thank you Theresa and Joel for their work and contribution towards sensitivity reading for the British and Scottish representation.

I am forever thankful for your time, effort, and work you put into this project.

Content Warnings

Ableism (on page and in the past), more specific ableism against the autistic community (on page and in the past),

Death of a parent and sibling (twin) (both in the past by almost twenty years, off page, only mentioned and in a scene discussing how the MC handles his grief) (from brother's perspective),

Discussions of queerphobia and racism in the workplace (not detailed, brief),

Explicit sexual content (on page, all consensual),

Misogyny (on page),

Mention of past emotional abuse from a partner (mentioned, brief snippets of past emotional abuse on the page as flashbacks or thoughts),

Sexism (on page).

Playlist

Brutal — Olivia Rodrigo

I've Just Seen a Face — The Beatles

There She Goes — The La's

Out of My League — Fitz and the Tantrums

I Think We're Alone Now — Tiffany

Apartment — Young the Giant

Electric Touch —Taylor Swift and Fall Out Boy

Tightrope — Young the Giant

Heat of the Summer — Young the Giant

Ways to Go — GROUPLOVE

California Friends — The Regrettes

Would That I — Hozier

Where You Lead — Carole King

Cruel Summer — Taylor Swift

Say You Love Me — Fleetwood Mac

The Ballad of John and Yoko — The Beatles

Happiness — Taylor Swift

Go Your Own Way — Fleetwood Mac

Until I Found You —Stephen Sanchez and Em Beihold

Dreams — The Cranberries

To neurodivergent people still learning to love themselves; I hear you, I see you, I am you. May Charlie and Page's story give you the comfort it gave me to write it.

And to the neurodivergent people in my life that showed me how strong, brilliant, kind, and creative we can be.

PART I

Prologue

Excerpt from *STARVERSE*: Season 2, Episode 5

INT. SPACESHIP BRIDGE — DAY

Car Brandon walks onto the bridge. Asmor is in the navigation chair.

CAR
As—

ASMOR
I didn't do anything wrong. If she'd done her job, then the spaceport wouldn't have blown up.

CAR
I think we both know that isn't the case, asshole.

Asmor turns around. Stands.

CAR
You do one more thing that puts my crew in danger and you're out, you hear me?

ASMOR
Loud and clear, captain.

Charlie

"He is a disgrace to all Spiderman fans. Everyone knows that Spider Gwen should totally count under that sign," Ripley said, her hands flying around her. Charlie looked back forlornly at the coffee shop, the 'Free coffee for anyone dressed as Spiderman' sign still blinking, and the angry barista who kept on sending glares at their backs as she tried to hurry them back into the convention's endless crowds. "You could even argue that, because of the multiverse and the absence of Peter Parker in Spider

Gwen's AU, she is Spiderman!" Ripley's body always showed her emotions. It was something Charlie had always loved about her friend because it made reading Ripley's body language so much easier.

Charlie tried not to laugh at her loud outrage and nodded instead, taking in the scenery around them and silently lamenting over the fact that neither of them had gotten the caffeine they'd been craving—Ripley because she had stormed off, and Charlie because she'd run off after her friend, and was too scared of the pissed off employee to order anything. She wondered if he was already starting to hate working during StarCon, one of the biggest nerd events of the year… Probably.

Charlie could still remember the first time she'd gone to the con. To her parents' horror, Ripley's dad had gotten them tickets as a surprise for their fifteenth birthdays and had taken them to their first con that summer. They'd been coming back every year since. StarCon felt like coming home: walking into a space where she instantly felt relaxed, somewhere she could completely turn off her masking. Here, it was totally fine for an adult to squeal at fan-art or an amazing cosplay. It was more than feeling seen—it was a place where she didn't have to pretend, and she was so fucking tired of pretending.

"Come on," Charlie adjusted the wig on the top of her head irritably, wishing Ripley hadn't talked her into doing a cosplay that involved one. She felt as if each one of the wig's threads was a needle poking her skin. She wanted to take it off …but to quote Ripley, "then her cosplay wouldn't be authentic." She'd spent hours on her Spider Gwen cosplay, while Charlie was currently dressed as Mary Jane, Spiderman heart T-shirt and all. It was one of her simpler cosplays, but after the month she'd been having, she hadn't had the energy to really put her all into something more complicated. She scratched her head, adjusted the wig yet again, and scowled. "We need to get in line now for the StarVerse panel if we want to be able to get into the room."

Ripley simply grinned, adjusted her tote bag and took off. Charlie let herself be pulled along, reaching into her bag to take out her signature green headphones. She'd spent most of the morning hyped up on caffeine able to take in all the noises and lights, but her brain was now, starting to tire as sensory overload took over. She needed some quiet, especially if her brain was going to be bored out of its mind sitting in line for four hours.

They sat down in the small line already forming against one of the walls upstairs in the convention hall. The scratchy floor and pretzel-scented air might have been uncomfortable for most, but for Charlie it was comforting. No matter how many people came, or how many times they updated the inside of the convention center, two things stayed the same: the smell and the carpet's texture.

"We're going to see Killian Glass up close and personal in a few hours," Charlie said with a grin. She laughed quietly as Ripley sighed and then pulled out their snacks and bottles of water from her backpack. Ripley even had a little foldable seat tucked away. How she could fit anything in it at this point, Charlie would never know, but Ripley had always been like that. Even when they'd both been in college, Ripley had been labeled the 'mom friend', always taking care of everyone and always being prepared for anything.

"He's fine, I guess," Ripley made a face, which made Charlie laugh. "I really can't believe they have the panel this year," Ripley said, pulling out her own headphones. StarVerse was one of the largest growing television franchises of the past decade, and Killian Glass was one of the main characters—or would villain suit him best? To be honest, Charlie wasn't sure the fandom even knew. Killian played a very morally grey alien from the planet of Var called Asmor, and the entire fandom, Charlie included, was in love with him. Or at least the small corner of the fandom who wasn't obsessed with Car Brandon, the ship's human captain played by the hot Scotsman, Jamie Mahone.

"Hey, we both know my type in fiction is tall, dark, and brooding," Charlie said, feeling the need to defend her fictional crush.

"And bad," Ripley joked. She sighed, leaning back on her

hands. "But man will I swoon when Jamie Mahone starts talking."

Charlie rolled her eyes. She had to admit that, even if she was mainly coming to see Glass in person, she was excited to see the rest of the cast speak—even Jamie Mahone, who played her least favorite character on the show. It wasn't that she didn't like the guy—she didn't *know* him—Charlie simply didn't like his character: a stereotypical blond, toxic man in need of an ego fix.

"Okay, fine," she admitted, grinning at her friend who had the biggest celebrity crush on him. "It will be nice when he opens his mouth."

Jamie Mahone was admittedly nice to look at, even if his character sucked. He was a tall white man in his mid-twenties, his blond hair cut short, and his body built but lean. From the fan-wiki page that Ripley loved to stalk, they'd found out that he'd grown up in Scotland and was three years older than them. *StarVerse* had been his first large acting role. Other than that, the fans didn't know much about him because 1. he never did solo-interviews, and 2. he never talked about his personal life. The rest of the cast was amazing and that was one of the reasons why *StarVerse* was so popular; the fans invested in not only the show but the actors behind their favorite characters. The creators had put money and time into the show and were now announcing the third season—a season that fans had been waiting the past year for.

"I knew you secretly had a thing for his character," Ripley teased. "It's impossible to always fall for the bad ones." The joke shouldn't have hit home, but Charlie saw the moment Ripley's face matched her own. "Char, I'm sorry, you know I didn't mean it like that."

Charlie tried to brush it off, but knew every expression showed on her face as clear as day. Even though they'd only been dating for a few months, it had been a mess of a breakup—Jacob deciding that dating someone on the autism spectrum, someone he just couldn't connect with, was too much for him. He couldn't deal with her anymore. His words. Not hers.

Charlie took a deep breath. Every time she thought she finally had her feet back underneath her, she would hear his name and there it was: this feeling of being tackled to the ground by a tsunami, and being back in his living room, hearing those words in person again. These past six months, Charlie might as well have been walking through fog. Autistic burnout had hit her hard; struggling to get out of bed, appetite completely gone, unable to even shower some days because water on her skin felt too overstimulating, and not able to communicate it all because talking was simply too hard. She was *just* starting to crawl her way out of it.

Charlie felt herself zoning out, sending Ripley a small smile to reassure her that she was okay, and pulled her headphones back over her ears.

By the time they were let into the ballroom, Charlie's butt was asleep. At least, with her audiobook playing, the wait time had gone by quickly. Even though her back was hurting and she could see that Ripley's joints were bothering her, both of them were glad they'd gotten in line when they did, hundreds of people now shuffling into the ballroom behind them.

The lights dimmed and the announcements started—the sound blasting around them as the actors' names were declared one by one as they walked out onto the stage, the directors by their side. She was suddenly glad they hadn't sat near one of the speakers. From their vantage point, she could make out all of the actors' faces as they sat above them, their bodies outlined with the light focusing on the stage. They announced Jamie Mahone and then Sandhya Vaughn, who gave Mahone a roll of her eyes and a playful shove on his shoulder as she sat. Charlie felt herself smiling nonstop, and when the moderation came to an end, she hurried to get into the line for questions, which was forming in the middle of the room.

She was startled to find a boy standing in front of her. He looked to be around ten, his brown hair covered by a large pair of headphones. Someone in front of them was asking when people would hear about the new trailer drop for season three. The question wound down, and the boy stepped up to the mic.

"Hi, my name is Aiden," he said, pausing for a moment of silence. She saw the panel shift in their seats. Finally, Jamie Mahone smiled.

"Hiya, what is your question for us?" She almost rolled her eyes. His accent was perfect. But *why*, God, *why* did such a pretty human being have to have such a boring ass character?

"My question is actually for Killian." Killian straightened in his chair, preparing for the question. During the panel, he had been short, succinct, and flirty with a few of the cast members. Nothing drastic or new for a young film star.

"Hit me, little man."

"Well, um, I'm autistic, and a lot of people online have been speculating about how your character, Asmor, could be on the spectrum and represent the autism spectrum in science-fiction. I was just wondering what you thought of this?"

Damn, Charlie thought, looking out at the crowd who had gone silent. This kid was brave. She'd never felt comfortable asking questions about her disability in relation to more mainstream media because it usually wasn't well-received at all. Charlie stepped a bit closer to the kid to show her support. Their images were being shown across the lecture hall on big screens behind the panel and around the room.

Killian's character was clearly autism-coded. Charlie had spotted it from a mile away. And even though she knew it was a problem that the one autistic character was an alien and not human, on top of the fact that they never actually labeled him as autistic, she still liked his character. She'd seen and participated in a ton of conversations about the autism-coding online since the show had come out, but she was surprised that this kid was asking the panel about it.

"Well, little dude, I get what you mean but I guess I've never seen Asmor's character that way. I've always read him as normal." Charlie saw a few other cast members, including Jamie Mahone, wince at the harsh statement but all she could hear in her ears was static.

Why can't you just be normal, Charlie? Everything is so difficult with you.

Her hands curled into fists at her side as she glimpsed the sad but determined face of Aiden up on the jumbo screens. She saw Jamie Mahone lean back away from his mic, trying to stop Killian from talking, but he went on.

"I mean, I have nothing against people with autism." Yep, mistake two. "But I had to make sure I connected with the character I was representing, so I never saw him as having autism."

And it just got *worse.*

Aiden was silent when the woman standing next to the microphone ushered him back to his seat. His shoulders were slumped slightly and, when she looked back, she saw his mother glaring up at the panel seats. The question that she'd prepared for weeks in her head flew out the window.

The microphone lady held the mic out to her, but she couldn't find it in her to give the woman a small smile of thanks. Her hands were shaking, her breath short. She knew, on a logical level, that ableism existed. Of course, it existed. But just because she knew that didn't mean it still didn't affect her. The crowd clapped around her, the sound roaring in her head, and she stood up to the little yellow X made of tape on the floor.

"Um, hi," she said, cleared her throat. Her voice shook more than she would've liked, but in that moment, she wasn't even embarrassed. Anger swept through her, so overwhelming that it stopped her from fully thinking. "My name is Charlie James. I had a question for the entire cast, but I thought I would just ask Mr. Glass a question first." The image of Aiden standing in front of her, his shoulders drooping, his body going stiff, flashed in her head again. "I've loved your character in the past, but as someone who is also autistic, not someone with autism, I thought I would just state what that boy couldn't." The entire room seemed to pause, as if in that one moment, they had all taken a breath with her, and were all waiting for the bomb to drop. So, she dropped it. "What you just said is ableist. Especially in how you described autistic people as other." She saw her words slowly registering on the actor's face. First shock, then confusion, finally anger. She kept going. Honestly, she wasn't sure if she could stop herself now. The words seemed to flow right out of her. Her hands shook, and she gripped the mic so hard her knuckles turned white. "There is *nothing* wrong with people who are autistic, we are normal and calling us not normal is disgusting. Especially to that small boy who looked up to you and your character. So, I hope you realize your mistakes because you should be ashamed of yourself."

She looked at the other actors, some were shocked and some, like Jamie Mahone, were trying to hold in their smile. Her gaze met Mahone's briefly, and she smiled bitterly. "Thanks for your time."

She handed the mic back to the lady whose face was white with fear in the darkness, and a part of her felt slightly guilty that this woman would probably get in trouble because of her. She stood there for a moment, but then she grabbed the mic back, ignoring the lady's protests and glared back at the panel. "Actually, I take that back. Fuck you." She heard the gasps in the crowd, but her entire body was full on shaking now. She could even feel tears in her eyes, but the last thing she wanted was to cry in front of them. Another part of her was too angry to care.

She had no idea that, within the day, she would be as famous as the entire cast of *StarVerse*.

FilmVerseNow Exclusive Interview Transcript

Marie Clark: Now, there was a little bit of controversy recently when a fan verbally harassed you at StarCon just a few weeks ago. Here, we can show the clip. Do you have anything to say to that? Let me just say how sorry I am that you had to endure this.

Killian Glass: Well, first, thank you, Marie. The woman in question is known to have some mental illnesses. I just feel bad for her and her family. She shouldn't have been allowed into the event in the first place. I just hope that, now, she's getting the help she needs.

2 months later...

Chapter 1
Charlie

"This was a bad idea."

Charlie silently repeated the words to herself in her head as she stood on the tarmac of Edinburgh airport, her backpack slung over her shoulder.

Ripley groaned in Charlie's ear, her voice staticky on the phone. Charlie hadn't quite figured out how she was going to keep on using her phone without international charges. To be honest, Charlie hadn't really thought out any part of this trip at all. It had all been very last minute, and she rarely did anything last minute. Which was why she had called her best friend in a panic.

"You know that this is what you need," Ripley said for the thousandth time since StarCon. Ever since that fateful day when she had called out Killian Glass in public, her world had turned upside down. The videos of her laying into him had gone viral later that day. Then she had been fired from her job at the bookstore because, and she quoted, "We cannot support your abhorrent behavior of attacking a poor man that way and, honestly, we just don't have the budget to support an employee's disabled needs." Apparently, they'd had an issue with her not notifying them about her being autistic when she'd applied for the job. When they'd asked her why, she had snorted and said, "Maybe for this exact reason."

They hadn't appreciated that.

Four weeks later, Charlie found herself moping on her and Ripley's couch, chocolate ice cream in hand, hate-watching all the episodes of *Friends* and monologuing about how outdated the show was and how it was impossible for the characters to own an apartment like that on their salaries. Ripley had decided she'd had enough.

"You will love this job, Charlie. You know you will," Ripley said, pulling Charlie out of her own head and back into the present. She wasn't back in their apartment in SoCal. No, she was in another country, across the world and across a fucking ocean. She was alone, about to start a new job for the summer. She needed to get away from the bad press that hadn't gone away since she'd "attacked" the poor actor. Yes, most of the Internet, especially the #ActuallyAutistic side, had supported her, and the praise and numbers behind her had been amazing... but she wasn't exactly shocked to see how many Killian Glass fans—a large amount of them old, cis, straight, white, male sci-fi fans who complained about anything with a woman in it—attacked her validity as an autistic person. They'd started calling her all sorts of ableist and misogynistic bullshit online shortly after. She'd even gotten hate mail. How they'd found her address, she had no idea.

Then there was the hashtag.

#AngryCharlie

That was when she'd deleted all of her social media.

So, here she was, recently fired, single (though that had happened months before, not due to Killian Glass... but *still* single), and in a foreign country about to embark on a journey she was not sure she was prepared for. Actually, she knew she was one hundred percent NOT prepared for it.

It was Ripley who had found the job offer. Working in media management, she'd always been good at finding small, unique job offers around the world. She had a few friends who worked

bookish quotes from old novels painted above the entryways that led into smaller sitting spaces or other rooms.

"Oh my gosh, you must be Charlie!" a voice sounded as a young Black woman around Charlie's age jumped up from where she was crouching behind the counter.

She was petite, her black, curly hair framing her face. "I'm so glad you were able to make it before we closed the store down for the day." She came over and instantly pulled Charlie in for a hug. Hugs were not always her thing, depending on the day and if she wasn't too overwhelmed. And today, well, overwhelmed seemed to be an understatement. But she hugged the woman back, terrified at being labeled rude on her first day here. "So good to finally see you. And you came on the most perfect day. We aren't that busy, and after we close, I can take you out for tea."

Charlie had no idea why they would have tea before dinner but stayed quiet. Usually, people who were this happy made Charlie want *to* hide, but there was nowhere to hide, so Charlie fit a grin onto her face—one she hoped didn't looked too pained.

"Um, sorry, but you seem to know who I am, and I don't know who you are," Charlie said, clearing her throat. She always hated introductions.

"My goodness, sorry." The woman laughed, grabbing one of Charlie's bags in one hand and signaling Charlie to follow her with the other. "You must be so confused. You've been talking with Lilian online, yes?" At Charlie's hesitant nod, she continued. "I'm Layla. I've been working the store since I was sixteen. I'll be working half the week and showing you everything you need to know."

"Will Lilian be here soon?" Charlie asked, taking the time to look more closely at the store. The space was small, but it wasn't overwhelming. She'd been in bookstores before that had been so packed with books that she'd been scared a stack would fall on her and she'd be buried alive. Here, however, the shelves were filled with books of all ages and genres, a good selection at first glance, but there was still space to... breathe.

"Oh," Layla stopped, a deer-caught-in-headlights look on her face. "Lilian is staying up north with her mother, that's why you're here. Did she not—"

"I probably should have put two and two together," Charlie interrupted, knowing for a fact that she'd only skimmed over the information that Lilian McAllister had sent over by email a few days ago. She'd never been so unprepared for anything in her life.

"You must be exhausted." Charlie, who was now near the check-out-counter, set her bag down, and leaned against it. Layla paused next to her, her eyes shaded a dark purple that matched the beautiful tone of her sweater. She had elegant features; thin brows, cheerful eyes, lips that always seemed to be tipped upwards in a smile. She was gorgeous, and if Charlie weren't so tired, she had a feeling she would have been stumbling over her words a bit more. "Jet lag is a bitch," Charlie said, chuckling. She was just glad that she'd gotten some sleep on the plane. The flight had been fine, but she could feel herself starting to get irritable. The less sleep she got, the more susceptible she became to sensory overload. She tried her best to give Layla a smile, but she could tell the other woman saw her exhaustion.

"Well then, the best thing to do would be to get you settled, wouldn't it?" She smiled a bright smile that lit up her face. "Follow me."

Charlie grabbed her bags, following Layla around the counter and to a small back door that Layla opened to show a small stairway. Before she started up, Charlie couldn't help but look back, taking in the store again. The smell of books and honeysuckle wafted through the air.

She steadied herself, taking in a breath. Even if she never got back on her feet again—never felt back to herself as she worked here—she had a feeling that, at least, it would give her the escape she needed.

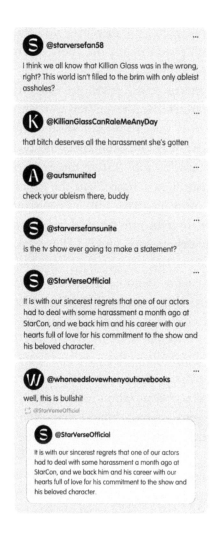

Chapter 2
Page

"I don't want to see any news about any of you."

Page's stomach was in knots. He was in his hotel room in LA, the group call open on his computer in front of him. It was a mix of the different actors on *StarVerse* and their managers, a few of the show execs, the directors, and the producers. Jim Valencia, the main producer for the show, cleared his throat on the call.

"What Mark means to say, is that we don't want any news to surface that we aren't already sending out with our marketing team." And there it was. Page had always known how shifty the movie industry was, but sometimes he really hated all the bureaucracy around his job. "After the StarCon fiasco," Page had not really seen it as a fiasco, but the execs really did, "we don't want any more negative publicity surrounding our new season. Take this three-month break to relax, not to go out and party, not to date new people, and NOT to make some political statements."

"So, you want us to become hermits," Sandhya, the actress who played Valeri—his character's childhood best friend turned lover—said, her voice flat. He could hear the annoyance in it and couldn't even imagine how angry she was. Sandhya and he had become close friends in the past two years of filming, and he knew that, at twenty-six, she was about done with the politics of acting. She was someone who loved to speak out and protest, and with Pride month coming up, he knew she had plans to go to New York Pride with her girlfriend—if she was allowed to go without being fired from the show. Page, who had his group chat with Theo and Sandhya pulled up on his computer beside the video call, had to hold in his reaction when Sandhya's next text came through a few moments later.

Sandhya

> I'm a queer Indian woman, I can't NOT be political, jackass.

Theo

> *angry devil face emoji* I want to hit him over the head with a clapperboard.

"No, no," Mark said, his voice sounding as tired as Page felt.

"We just need you to not make any news that would hurt the show in any way."

Page knew that "news that would hurt the show" was a very broad spectrum. It was also something that really depended on someone's point of view. *He* hadn't seen supporting the woman at StarCon as a bad idea, but Mark? Well, Mark's point of view of the situation was not in line with his.

A voice cleared and then spoke the words that they'd all been waiting for. "To be fair, Mark, what's happened with Killian was not news that should've negatively impacted the show. Only him." Theodore Marcus, who would kill anyone who called him anything other than Theo, had been Page's best friend since the first day of filming. They all heard his other unspoken words. *Or it wouldn't have if the show had not decided to publicly back Killian Glass.*

Page felt a familiar wave of anger surge within his chest as he heard Mark start on another rant about how "that woman" was "mentally ill." The past month had been the worst. In all of their contracts, there was a clause stating that they couldn't publicly speak out against *StarVerse*, or any of the behind-the-scenes action, until they were either fired or the show ended. If they did, they would be fired and sued… and with the way the film industry worked, probably never work again. But Page had just about had enough, same with Theo and Sandhya. He didn't know how he could stay silent when they were being misogynistic, ableist fucks, and basically harassing the woman in question until she had finally gone silent on social media.

How the producers and media team thought that supporting Killian was a good move, he would never know.

"I don't want to hear any news about any of you," Mark repeated, his voice firm. Page was currently imagining Mark's face on the wall in front of him, prime distance for throwing darts at, like he'd grown up doing in the pub across from his house. He, Theo, and Sandhya, along with Carmen Becket and Bodega Jones—the other two main actors of the intimate cast of *StarVerse*—all stayed silent. Unsurprisingly, Killian was absent from their weekly meeting. With a fast round of goodbyes and a click, the call ended.

Two seconds later, his phone was ringing, and he answered to see Sandhya and Theo on his screen. Sandhya had her wavy black hair tied up in a large topknot on the top of her head. Her skin had tanned in the past month of being on break in Florida with her dad's family. And right now, her usually kind, wide brown eyes were dark and narrowed, her brows furrowed. She leaned forward, elbows resting on her chair's armrests, her presence already making Page feel more settled.

"Well, that was bullshit." She had an American accent, but some words or phrases sounded British to him. He knew she'd grown up on the East Coast of the US but had UK citizenship through her Welsh grandfather. This allowed her to live in London, where she'd moved after finishing up her uni studies at the Royal Academy of Dramatic Arts.

"You look like you're planning on murdering someone, Sunni," Theo said to Sandhya, using the nickname reserved for her family and closest friends, his voice tired as he leaned back in his chair. He and Sandhya had known each other for almost a decade now, rooming together at uni and then, by chance, getting roles together on *StarVerse*. Theo always joked with Sandhya that she would never be able to get rid of him. The man in question grinned at the screen, sending a pang of yearning to see his friends in person again through Page's chest. He hadn't seen them since StarCon, their busy schedules broken up by midnight texts and last-minute group calls.

Theo was Page's opposite in almost every way. He was muscled from his days in the gym lifting weights and had an energy that matched a creative and energetic ten-year-old at Disneyland. He was one of the most empathetic people Page had ever met and, at least to Page, was the heart of their small friend group. Pushing back his shoulder-length brown hair, his pale skin scattered with freckles, he sighed. "Honestly, I'll join in with you on that. What they're doing is ridiculous." Other than Page, he was the only other member of the cast who'd grown up in the UK, his voice strictly representing his London upbringing. He moved out of the screen for a moment, falling onto what Page recognized as his couch. Theo was always moving—his knees jumping, foot tapping, fingers playing the piano on the table in front of him. Even now, in his own living room, he got up to start pacing, throwing a small tennis ball between his hands.

"If murder becomes legal tomorrow, I just might," Sandhya said, her voice angry. She was the kind of person who expressed her emotions in subtle ways, but she never *hid* them, and right now… well, she was angry. After a million scenes with her over the past two years, he had learned how to read the small crease between her brows and her nose scrunching up as tells of her anger. Her hands waved in front of her face in exasperation, finally coming to rest over her face as she groaned. "This is disgusting. I cannot believe that the first major acting role we all get is led by some ableist fucks and we can't even say a word."

Theo shook his head in annoyance. "Yep, and you know if we do, we'll never work again."

"Did we hear what happened to the woman?" Page finally asked, moving back to lean against the hotel bed's massive collection of puffy pillows. That was one thing he had always loved about traveling for work—the beds and pillows were always super soft and comfortable.

Sandhya shook her head. "She went silent after that asshole posted her address on the Internet." Even though they hadn't been able to say anything, Sandhya, Theo, and Page had been trying to track the news about the woman as much as possible from their personal twitter accounts. Well, Sandhya and Theo's twitter accounts. Page had a strict no-social media policy, which would not budge even if he was curious about her. "I tried to do a bit of social media stalking, and even the other woman who first defended her—I assume she's a friend because they follow one another—went silent as well. I can't even imagine what it's been like." Sandhya bit the inside of her cheek. "Usually, these things die out, but with the blatant support that the execs have been giving Killian, this entire scandal doesn't seem to be dying."

"Hopefully she's safe," he said, opening a bottle of water.

The woman in question, whom he knew as Charlie from when she'd introduced herself at the con, had been in the back of his mind for the past couple of months. Maybe it was the way her anger had physically run through her body, or her eyes, or her *voice*, or maybe it had been the way she'd knocked down Killian with no more than a paragraph of words. When she'd spoken at the con, he had wanted to get up and cheer, but he had seen the look of horror on the producers' faces and his anxiety had stopped him from doing anything.

He felt a tug in his stomach. Guilt. He should have said something that day.

"Oh, look, the famous Jamie Mahone is interested in a woman. Finally," Theo said with a smirk. Sandhya hid her laugh. Page almost choked on his drink.

"I'm not interested in her," he insisted through his coughing. "I just admire what she did. But I am not being creepy, looking her up on the Internet or messaging her or stalking her on social media."

"Mhm," Sandhya said, humor firing in her dark brown eyes. They knew he wasn't doing that, but they also knew he had been thinking about her. Non-stop. Like an obsessed teenager. "You're just using us to do it."

"Shut it," he said, and at Theo and Sandhya's laughs, chuckled under his breath. "It's not like I'm ever going to see her again. I am just worried. What happened after that con was super sad. I would be an emotionless human being if I didn't, at the very least, worry."

"That's funny, I thought you *were* an emotionless human being," Theo said with a smile. Page rolled his eyes. Theo knew all too well that Page was anything but. He cried when they watched any movie—he'd even cried during *Star Wars*. Then again, so did Theo, but his friend always insisted it was because George Lucas had never come out and admitted that Luke was gay. But sometimes, his emotions shut down fully when he was anxious, making it seem like he didn't care… when in fact, he cared deeply.

Sandhya and Theo were some of the only people he had told about his anxiety and how hard it was for him to receive all the public attention at cons, in crowds, or having to speak in interviews. The only way he dealt with that was by putting on his persona and shutting off his emotions. Jamie Mahone, TV star and rising Scottish actor, could handle the spotlight. Page McAllister? He would have a panic attack before he stepped out on the stage. Even now, a part of him was shocked at how close he was with Sandhya and Theo, but when they'd met, their small friendship had clicked into place, whether it had been from the need to have someone on their side on set other than their agents, or just that he had been lucky enough to find his people by chance.

"I swear to God, though, I don't know how much longer I can stay quiet. They want us to be people to look up to, but then they ask us to act in ways that make us not deserving of the spotlight."

He had to agree with Sandhya there. He just wished they could do something... His eyes caught on the clock at the top of his phone and widened.

"Hey, got to get going, my flight is at 8 am tomorrow."

"You going home, mate?" Theo asked.

Page nodded. "Yeah, decided to head home and surprise my sister. She's been super busy lately, so it should be good to see her. Plus, I have to check up on the construction." Page had bought a small beach house only last year and had started a full renovation of the inside a few months back. Even thinking those words made something in him pause. He and his family had never had the money growing up that they had now, and the fact that he had enough to build a home... "Hopefully you can come up and join me for a bit. We'll go grab a pint at the pub."

Sandhya rolled her eyes. "Brits, with your pints and your mates and your corgis."

"I'm Scottish," Page mumbled, and Sandhya rolled her eyes again.

"Wow, we had no idea, mate. Really?" Theo's eyes were filled with laughter as he snorted at Page's glare.

Laughs and rushed goodbyes and a few minutes later, he was sitting in silence. He leaned back against the headboard of the bed, rolling his tight shoulders. After a year of constant filming, auditions for other jobs, and traveling for the publicity of the new season, he was finally going home. And he didn't quite know what home would now look like.

Excerpt from *STARVERSE*: Season 3, Episode 1

INT. SPACESHIP BRIDGE — NIGHT

VALERI
Car, we don't even know where we are—

CAR
It doesn't matter, Val. We'll be okay.

VALERI
You don't know that.

CAR
Of course, I know that. We have each other. If we
were alone… well, then I'd worry.

VALERI
If I were alone, I wouldn't be in this situation
to begin with.

CAR
You're saying this is my fault?

VALERI
Yes.

Chapter 3
Charlie

"So," Layla said matter-of-factly as she set Charlie's cup of coffee in front of her, sitting down with a sigh. They'd woken up extra early this morning to fit in some time at the coffee house down the street before they opened shop. Layla had arrived bright and early at the apartment door to drag Charlie out of bed. And Charlie, who had been up at the crack of dawn due to jet lag— yes, she was still not used to the time difference… it seemed to be taking her forever to adjust—had been wondering if she should crawl back into bed and pretend the sun hadn't come out.

It had been a week since Charlie had arrived in Scotland and already, she was slowly falling in love with everything the country had to offer. Entirely against her will, she might add. The last thing she wanted was to enjoy being here, a part of her convinced that, if she hated it, she could stay in her small bubble of misery. But no, this place had insisted she like it. Not that she had left the town that much. She had barely set foot outside of her two-bedroom apartment above the bookstore, her only company Layla and the apartment's cat named Gandalf the White. But she was already in love with how calm everything was. It didn't hurt that she and Layla had hit it off immediately, bonding over their love of bodice-ripper romances.

Layla had given Charlie a few days to get over her jet lag before she'd dragged her out of the apartment and down to the store. Two days later, Charlie was confident in using the inventory and check-out system and was starting to understand the organization of the shelves. Even though a part of her brain still wanted to be curled up in bed, she was glad that Layla had pulled her out of the apartment. Charlie knew that, if she'd been left alone, she might've not come out for a week, her system needing a bit longer than others to adjust to new spaces.

Layla paused mid-sentence to down half of her cup of coffee. Charlie sent her an amused glance. "Yes?"

"Sorry," she said, her voice light and warm. "Got to get my caffeine fix before we open." Her makeup was a mix of dark nude tones, her brown skin glowing, her lips painted a bright shade of pink that matched the dress she had thrown on under a white, puffy sweater. Charlie had put on the first thing she'd seen in her suitcase, not having unpacked yet. It was a light blue sweater and jeans, her dark hair pulled into a messy topknot on the top of her head. "Now that you have the layout of the shop figured out, it's my turn to pass on the magic of running a bookstore to you since you'll be alone for the rest of the week."

Charlie felt anxiety rise in her chest, but she did her best to shove it down. It was only a few days until the end of the week. She'd taken notes in her small notebook as Layla had walked her through the store. She was ready.

Or at least she hoped she was. Even though she knew that the small voice in the back of her head telling her all the ways she was going to fail was wrong, she couldn't quite seem to block it out completely. No matter how long it had been since her first job at sixteen, she still got nervous when starting something new.

"Of course, I'll only be a call away if you need anything." Layla must have seen the panic on Charlie's face because she reached over to pat her hand and gave her a small smile that seemed to say, "You got this."

Instead of voicing her anxiety, Charlie sipped at the hot drink that was currently warming her cold fingers. It was supposed to be early June here in Scotland, but where June meant warm weather interspersed with foggy mornings, which LA people considered 'June Gloom', Scotland had missed the memo. Instead, their days sometimes reached fifty degrees Fahrenheit if they were lucky, and she had been forced to purchase a few new sweaters from the small local clothing shop in order not to freeze. She had to wonder if this was normal or not. And if it was, well, clearly, this was one more reason why she should not travel on a whim. No matter what Ripley said.

"Of course, we are a small town, so I doubt you'll get swarmed with customers. So really, you shouldn't have too much trouble." Taking a large sip of her coffee, Layla silently motioned for Charlie to grab her drink and bag. Within minutes, they were walking down the small main street, through a large courtyard and turning down an even smaller street to the left where the bookstore resided. Charlie looked up from her feet and around at the grey stone buildings, a cold breeze sweeping her bangs into a frenzy around her face. She swiped them behind her ears, pulling her sleeves farther down onto her hands. Stonehaven was all symmetrical grey stone buildings, accented with stone filigree that spoke to its history. The main square had never been full since she'd arrived, only a few cars and groups of people mulling about at all hours. The only tourists she'd seen had been waiting for the bus for the castle nearby, the town just one stop on their epic travels.

"I'll be okay, Layla," Charlie said, pushing the door to the store open with her shoulder. It'd been a short walk, but Charlie hadn't realized how stuck in her head she'd been until she saw the bookstore's sign above their heads.

Holding the door open for Layla, she let herself pause and take in a deep breath. In just a few short days, the store's building had become a second home. Her apartment above was small, but just large enough for two or three people to live comfortably. She'd even been lucky enough to have a washing machine, so she didn't have to find a laundromat. And the store… it was a dream. The next time she saw Ripley, she would crown her the queen of all Charlie's life-decisions-making team. Ripley would have the final say from now on. Charlie let that thought float around in her head for a hot second and held back a shudder. She loved Ripley with her entire being, but she would never allow her to make all decisions for her.

"Really," she said, her gaze focusing back on Layla, who was already organizing a few stacks of books on one of their three display tables. "I've done a few jobs in retail before, even worked at a large bookstore for a bit. Selling books is way more fun than selling women's underwear."

"Oh, just wait until one of those moms comes in," Layla gave her a look that made Charlie a bit hesitant. It felt like there was some inside joke that Charlie should have understood but didn't. Or at least right away. Sometimes, it just took her a bit longer to figure out what Layla, and others, were *not* saying. Charlie forced a small smile, feeling Layla's gaze on her, and moved farther into the store, dropping her bag behind the small checkout counter. It was awkward and there was nothing she could do about it.

It was moments like these that Charlie hated most: when she knew people wanted her to say or do something, but she didn't know *what*. Layla was aware Charlie was autistic, and she hadn't said anything *bad*; but even though Charlie really liked Layla, it took a bit longer than a week for Charlie to know if someone was actually *safe*. Too many times, she'd jumped into a friendship headfirst and been burned when people didn't want to understand her autism.

Thankfully, though, Layla just gave Charlie a small smile, as if she understood—though what she understood, Charlie wasn't sure—and got started on her daily routine.

Layla reminded her of a gust of wind; sometimes calm and soft, and other times a complete ball of energy when she set her mind on a task, her energy whipping through the space with gusto. Her aura filled up the space with light laughter and gave the bookstore life. In her short amount of time working here, Charlie had seen how much Layla and the owner, Lilian, seemed to have created a community around the bookstore. The town was so small this was the only bookstore that existed unless someone wanted to go to one of the larger cities by train or bus. This made the store, and the coffee shop down the street (*Joe's Coffee*), a hub for people walking by when they needed to get out of the fog or rain. And it didn't take a lot to see that Lilian and Layla were at the heart of that community.

Charlie just hoped she wouldn't be too much of a change. She hoped she would be able to fit into the slot that needed to be filled while Lilian was away.

Her text tone sounded, pulling Charlie out of her thoughts. She'd been ignoring everyone but Ripley, and at the image of the text, she scowled down at her phone. Unfortunately, it was not Ripley, but her mother.

Mother

> I heard from your father that you
> have moved to Scotland.

Charlie tried not to roll her eyes at the text. She might not be good at reading subtext in conversations with other people, but over the years she *had* learned how to read her mother's passive aggressive messages crystal clear. Charlie's relationship with her mother had always been tense at best—Charlie being closer to her father. But ever since her diagnosis, things had become... worse. Her brother and mother had been a pain, not being willing to learn, listen, or accept Charlie's disability. She knew it was a lack of knowledge about autism that made them act the way they did, but it was hard to move past their snide comments about her being lazy or weird when, in fact, she was dealing with overstimulation or autistic burnout.

Charlie pursed her lips, sliding her phone back into her jeans pocket. She knew that, eventually, she'd have to respond—eventually being when her dad texted her telling her to do so—but today was not that day. Charlie had come here to get away, and not just from the show drama, she now realized. She'd needed to get away from everything. Her job in LA had felt stifling, the breakup with Jacob had thrown her off, and being so close to her family, yet so far from them emotionally, had made Charlie feel like she was trapped in a box with no exit.

Even though this apartment and store were small, Stonehaven had been the escape she desperately needed. She knew she didn't have long here, but she would take these three months day by day, basking in her new-found anonymity. Relishing in a place where no one had preconceived notions about who Charlie was, or how Charlie needed to act.

"I have a few things to work out quickly in the backroom and then I'll leave you to it, okay?" Layla asked, dropping a large stack of books onto the counter. It was a stack of newly published romances, small pink stickers with the word "New Reads" shining on the covers. Charlie simply nodded, needing to not be vocal. And when Layla moved past her and into the small backroom behind the checkout counter, Charlie pushed away the anxiety and lifted her chin up. Even though no one was in the store, she looked around, forcing her attention on her surroundings instead of letting herself get caught up in her head.

This was going to be her new job; it was her new home for the next three months. She was determined to make this work. She owed herself that much.

Unexpectedly, the next few days went by smoothly, lacking any major hiccups. It hadn't taken Charlie long to pick up how to use the cash register without help, and she surprisingly loved interacting with customers. She had her headphones by her station behind the register if she ever needed a moment of pure quiet, but she found that the space around her was calming enough to her senses. Sometimes, when Charlie moved into a space, made it her own with small adjustments here or there, she could relax—be busy without the feelings of sensory overload starting to wear at her mind. The bookstore was now one of those places.

But she wasn't shocked by this because she'd always felt safe in bookstores, surrounded by stories and beautiful covers, the smell of books and ink filling her senses.

This had always been her dream. That was why it had been so easy to say yes when Ripley had signed her up for it. She'd known she couldn't say no.

Layla, coming out of the backroom with a large stack of books, let out a breath. Charlie quickly moved to take part of the stack. "Thanks," Layla said, a small grin on her face. "We just got these in, and Lilian always likes us to shelve the new releases as quickly as possible."

The book in question was a new Young Adult Fantasy she'd heard about and had been meaning to add to her never-ending reading pile.

"You can yell out for me if you need help carrying any books," Charlie said, sending Layla a grin.

Layla rolled her eyes, bringing her arms up to check her muscles. "I might be short, but my arms are mighty."

"Who needs to work out when you work in a bookstore."

Layla giggled. "I mean, unless you want to go work out and also see some hot people."

Charlie snorted. "There is that." Her mind flashed back to Jacob, the last gym fanatic she'd known, and her smile fell.

"What, don't like the gym?"

Charlie almost winced. "More like, I don't like the memories of someone who did like the gym and didn't like that I didn't?"

Layla scowled. "People are awful sometimes."

"That," Charlie said, picking up one of the new books and shaking it, "is why I read."

Charlie's love for books had been an ongoing relationship since she had turned thirteen and discovered YA Paranormal Romance, the stories filling her mind and making her feel safe in the confines of high school. She had felt so lost then, and those books had been the only things to get her through the week sometimes. After her diagnosis, she'd laughed with Ripley about how she'd learned how to socialize through reading fiction. That deep connection with literature had been one of the reasons she'd studied publishing and writing in college. The only issue was that she'd been so lost with what she wanted to do with her degree once school was over that the last year had been a whirlwind of autistic burnout, depression, and living off the savings she'd made while working at her paid internship during college. It hadn't helped when Jacob had broken up with her a few months ago.

"Okay, yes, but books don't give you orgasms."

"But books and a vibrator do." The words were out of Charlie's mouth before she could think them through, and there was a moment of silence before they both burst into laughter.

"Okay," Layla said through her laughs, "fair. I will give you that." She smiled, her gaze somewhere else. "But don't you always leave a book looking for that feeling in your actual life?" The words made Charlie pause. She had an answer, it was just a bit pathetic—she did, every time she put down a book, especially a romance. But she had learned early on that people never acted how she expected them to, and in the end, they always left. Charlie had once had the romantic look that Layla had in her eyes, but now, after everything?

Successful career? Successful dating life?

What was that?

When she'd gone into college, she'd had direction. Her plan had been to get her degree, write, publish, maybe work in the industry. Finally, in her third year, her diagnosis had taken up so much space in her mind that writing and romance had seemed so far away. But now? She was lost. And writing… she loved writing, but she had soon realized how she needed more than the solitary existence of having a relationship with only her computer. Starting her own bookstore had been in the back of her mind for the past two years; she just didn't have the courage to do it. How could she have the time to run a business when she barely had the time to take care of herself?

But now, she was proving Jacob and her family wrong. Not that she was running a business, but something about stepping away and working at *Turn the Page* made it seem like she was finally stepping in the right direction. She was working full time in a place she loved, and she had the confidence to say that she was thriving.

Which she was. Charlie couldn't stop smiling. Even though she had been alone the entire time, she hadn't been *lonely*. Or maybe she just wanted to pretend she wasn't lonely. She wanted to say that she was okay being alone, sometimes she even needed it. But there was a part of her that knew she missed having someone.

Layla was a romantic—Charlie wished she could be.

"And have you ever found that feeling?" Charlie asked, moving to shelve a few more books and place another stack on one of their tables. She looked up to find Layla blushing and she couldn't help but smile.

"My boyfriend is up in Aberdeen right now, but aye, I've found it." Her eyes seemed to light up, and Charlie couldn't help but feel a twinge of jealousy. But she shoved that away. This trip wasn't about finding romance, or even finding sex. It was about healing from a romantic relationship and more. It was about her.

"At least some people can."

"Ohhh," Layla said, a conspiratorial look falling into place. "Do we have a non-romantic in the house?"

"No, we have a realist," Charlie said, mock-glaring at the other woman and moving to sit back behind the counter.

Layla smirked. "I bet that, by the time you leave, I can prove you wrong."

"I will take that bet," Charlie said. "The last thing I need in my life right now is romance."

"Everyone needs a bit of romance, Charlie," Layla said. The bell rung above the front door, and she flashed a grin before going to help the new customer.

The good thing was that the day wasn't too long and, after a few hours, Charlie realized her shift was over. Layla had left an hour earlier, off to her babysitting job that she did three times a week, leaving Charlie alone to her thoughts and the books around her.

After the long day at work, it took her about thirty minutes to decide she would walk to the small café near the beach, another hour to grab food at the pub and nurse a vodka lemonade alone at a table, and then another fifteen minutes to walk along the beach and then cut into town on her way back to the store. Her residence had a separate entrance in the back, along with a stairwell inside the store that led up to the same landing. Since she had already locked up for the night, she made her way to the back stairs. Because it was summer, the sun was still up even though it was almost nine, the light blue sky melting into the brownish-grey brick of her new building. Fishing out her keys, Charlie pushed her way into the apartment, shutting the door behind her softly and, within a minute, was sighing at the warm temperature of the apartment.

Her only issue with Scotland so far was the weather.

The people were nice—coming from a city like LA, almost *too* nice. The food was good, the nature was beautiful, and there were tons of dogs around. One could never go wrong with a town that loved dogs.

The weather? It was starting to irritate her.

Gandalf the White, the white, fluffy Persian cat, meowed at her from his spot on the kitchen counter. His squished face glared at her, and she sighed, going to fill his bowl with food. Their relationship had been tense since she'd arrived, Gandalf the White already staking his territory on the couch and in the other bedroom.

She looked at the cat as he started eating, not even attempting to pet him. She'd learned that lesson within the first hour, the scratches still visible on her hands. Over the past couple of days, since that debacle, they'd come to a stalemate. It hadn't taken Charlie long to figure out that he never scratched her if she fed him regularly. The cat had a feisty personality, and he roamed around the apartment, and the store when Layla was there, like he owned the ground he walked on.

Gandalf looked up at her, his gaze seeming to say, *you look tired*.

She narrowed her eyes at him. "It's been a long day, give me a break," she said, and then paused because now she was talking to a cat.

What she needed was a bath. And a good book. Then, *maybe then*, she would allow herself to think more about how her life was going nowhere, even though she'd promised herself she would relax. But if she were being honest, Charlie knew her brain would turn off and on when it wanted and not when she wanted. And even though she couldn't stop smiling when she'd been out and about, the small, empty apartment was making her face the real world. Because despite her love for this bookstore… it wasn't hers. This life here in Stonehaven, which she had only just begun, was a borrowed life. In two months, she would be getting onto a plane to fly back to LA and reality.

Surviving Alone Together
CarBrandonIsLife

Thank you so much to everyone who has liked and commented on this fanfic. I honestly didn't think anyone would ever read it. The support I've gotten is astounding, so here's the next chapter. I'm so sorry it took so long to upload. I was so busy with finals and then I moved to college and didn't have internet for like a month. Ah, the issues with being in college. Oh well, here is the next installment. Enjoy!

Even though the wind howled outside of their room, Car was calm. In fact, he was always calm. Especially when Valeri was by his side.

But tonight, he wasn't thinking of Valeri, even though her body warmed his in their bed.

No.

He was thinking about the one person he shouldn't be thinking of, his rival, whose species wanted Car's gone from their planet.

Asmor.

The only issue was that Car had no idea why he was thinking of him. Of his stupid face, dark hair, bright purple eyes. It annoyed him.

So, here he was awake instead of asleep, with his lover beside him.

Charlie

Charlie had always hated silence. Because even when it was quiet around her, it was never truly silent. It hadn't been silent when she'd tried falling asleep in middle school in her friend's bedroom, the air-conditioning keeping her up because the sound was new and strange. It hadn't been silent when she'd had her first kiss under the stars on the beach near her parents' house. Even though she'd been trying her best to focus on Karla Spier's lips or her beautiful blond hair, her brain had instead decided to focus on a bird chirping too high-pitched and too regularly. It hadn't been silent when she'd come out as bisexual to her parents, even though they'd been dead-quiet for around ten minutes before her dad had said, "Okay, cool," and the conversation had moved on. The silence had been interrupted by her mom's finger tapping against the wooden dining room chair. It hadn't been silent then, and it wasn't now. Because true silence, the silence her brain *needed*, didn't exist. But she'd learned long ago that white noise was her downfall, and it always became her nemesis at night because she hated the feeling of falling asleep with earplugs in, even if her noise-canceling ones were saviors during the day.

As usual, Charlie's idea of getting to bed early after reading a book did not go as planned. Instead, she was still awake at midnight, her reading glasses barely staying on her nose, her screen open to the newest fanfic for *StarVerse*. She might refuse to watch the show, but she couldn't give up her fanfiction when it helped her out of burnout.

She was still adjusting to the apartment, the heater either too hot or too cold. Tonight, it had been the sheets. They were too scratchy, to the point that she had changed her pajamas and pulled on socks, so the sheets didn't touch her bare skin. But still, as she had tried to fall asleep, her mind had been restless.

It was because of this reason, and only this reason, that she heard the door rattle. Or more accurately, the sound of someone cursing on the other side of her door at midnight.

She knew this was a small town, but there was no other apartment on her landing, let alone in her building. She had scouted it and made sure for this exact reason—so that if she heard a noise, she could distinguish if it was dangerous or something to ignore.

But because of that, she knew that whoever was trying to get into the apartment at midnight was not supposed to be there. Setting down her book, Charlie frantically looked around her room. Her heartbeat was loud in her ears, and her hands were shaking. She clenched her fists at her side. Yes, she was in a foreign country. Yes, she was not in her home, and yes, she was alone. But she would be damned if she was helpless.

Charlie's eyes landed on the bag of old wooden golf clubs that leaned against one corner of the room. When she'd first arrived, she'd laughed at the sticky note on them that read: *These were my great grandpa's, so please take care. They are for you if you play golf, but if you do, we probably won't ever get along.*

Charlie had never understood people's fascination with golf. She probably shouldn't have decided to stay in a country that seemed to be built on the sport. Now, though, she was thankful for the set of clubs in her room as she heard the door opening and closing with a loud slam.

"Lil?" a voice called, rough, low, and tired.

She grabbed the nearest golf club she could see by the clubhead and cracked her door open. A shadow moved, and before she let her fear overtake her, she lunged out, a yell leaving her body, and brought the club down on the tall figure that had moved into the living room outside her door. She hit them in-between their shoulders on the first swing. With a curse followed by a grunt and Charlie's second swing, the figure fell.

Charlie let out a large breath, her body shaking as she reached to flip the switch on the wall next to her. She was reaching for her phone, which she had shoved into her hoodie's pocket, when she heard a deep groan. Her eyes, panicked, swung back to the man on the floor.

It took her a moment, her body frozen, before the image in front of her registered.

Blond hair.

Tall, swimmer's body.

Black flannel and blue jeans and work boots.

Light skin, sharp cheekbones, light stubble, thick brows.

"Holy shit." The words came out with a breath. Instead of trying to find the equivalent for 911 in the UK, which she probably should have done the moment she'd arrived, her fingers hit the speed dial for Ripley's number.

It answered on the second ring.

"Do you know what time it is?" her friend answered, her voice filled with joking annoyance. At Charlie's stunned silence, Ripley sighed. "I was kidding, Char, it's only the afternoon—" But before she could say anything else, Charlie let out the words she had been thinking.

"I'm so fucked." Ripley stopped talking on the other end of the phone. "I think I just knocked out Jamie Mahone."

There was a pause. And then a high pitched, "What!"

Excerpt from *STARVERSE*: Season 1, Episode 3

TRAINING ROOM — DAY

Car and Valeri are in the middle of the room, sparring. The tension from their argument the other day hangs in the air. Valeri moves, hitting Car in the face.

                         CAR
  Do you always solve your issues with violence?

                       VALERI
                       Yes.

Chapter 5

Page

Page woke to a severe headache. He blinked rapidly and winced when light hit his eyes.

What *the fuck* had happened?

The last thing he remembered was fumbling for his keys outside of Lilian's flat and then—

He sat up fast and immediately regretted it, dizziness hitting him like a crashing wave. He raised one hand to his head, the other steadying him on the couch.

"Oh, gosh, please don't move. I didn't know who to call, so I just put some ice where I hit you..." Page slowly turned his head to the left to find a woman sitting next to him, her hands frantically waving in the air, an icepack in one hand. His gaze swept upwards from the pink PJ pants covered in cats to the deep grey UCLA sweatshirt, to a long, elegant neck, her skin pale and covered in freckles. High, round cheekbones, brown eyes, and dark wavy brown hair pulled up into a sloppy topknot on the top of her head completed the look.

He was so out of it that he might've stopped breathing.

He knew her. How did he know her?

"I'm so sorry, I thought you were a burglar. I mean, in a way, you kind of were. I called Lilian, and after she stopped laughing, she said you were her brother? But she also said you weren't scheduled to come at all. And not to call the police but to get some ice? Then she said your favorite tea was chamomile, so I made some. Here—"

A large mug of tea was shoved into his face. He reached out slowly and took it. The cup was warm to the touch, centering his mind for a second before it scrambled again as the woman started talking even faster.

"But I couldn't help researching how to help. I know I shouldn't have checked Google, but, you know, I was *panicking*, so I did. And then it took me down a black hole of nonsense about how you could have a concussion, and I could have killed you—which with my luck I would, can you imagine the headlines then, seriously—so I stayed here in case you stopped breathing—"

He held up a hand, and she cut off. His head was pounding, his heart beating in his ears, and the only words he could get out of his mouth were, "You're *her*."

The woman, whom he assumed was Charlie James, winced. "So, you do remember." She turned from him, picking up her phone and scooting away. He could've sworn she muttered something like "*Should've hit him harder*" under her breath as she moved towards the kitchen. He watched her silently as she rummaged through one of the cabinets for a wine glass, grabbed a bottle of rosé from the fridge, and poured herself a generous amount. She downed it, her back turned to him, and then poured herself another. He knew he was probably staring, but he couldn't help but watch her in fascination. The woman who had been on his mind for the past two months was now standing in front of him *in his sister's flat*. If Page's head hadn't been pounding, letting him know that he was, very much so, alive, then he would have pinched himself to make sure he wasn't dreaming.

She reached into the fridge, pulled out a small ice pack, and finally turned back to him.

"Here, more ice." He took it, looking up at her. He did not

want to know what look was on his face right now. Confusion. Astonishment. Probably a bit of both.

"Um, how are you here?" he asked. He set the tea on the table next to the couch before holding the ice between his shoulder blades. He let his hand come up to check where it hurt, the pain mostly sharp between his shoulders, and when it came back clean of blood, he sighed in relief. The fog from his head was starting to clear, pain sweeping it away as he pressed the ice to the spot that hurt the most.

How hard had she hit him?

Charlie winced again. "Um, yeah. Hi, I'm Charlie James. I, uh, your sister put out a notice for a work stay thing where I stay here and work at the store downstairs while she's away for three months. I was the one who took the job!" The fake enthusiasm in her voice let him know she was probably panicking as much as he was right now. He just stared at her, taking in the way her shoulders hunched slightly when he just sat there, stunned. Her words were still floating around in his head, and before he could respond, she started talking again.

"Your sister said this was your only place to stay." She paused, and her next words made his stomach flip. "Looks like we're roommates?"

Transcript of Behind-the-Scenes footage on YouTube of the first season of *StarVerse*

Theodore Marcus: Hey everyone! Welcome to Theo's Vlogs, or whatever we are now calling this special behind the scenes segment, because what else would we call it?

Sandhya Vaughn: Can your ego get any bigger?

TM: *grins* *screen cuts to black, then comes back with Sandhya in charge of filming*

SV: And now you can see the wild Scot, Jamie Mahone, in all his glory! *a shot of Jamie Mahone coming out of his trailer in a black fluffy robe and slippers, a green facemask on his face* *laughter from Sandhya and Theo in the background*

TM: Mate, you look fabulous.

JM: You know, just preparing for that steamy scene. *He wiggles his eyebrows at Sandhya* Self-care is the best care.

SV: *snorts* Dork.

Chapter 6
Page

"What do you mean, you know her?" Lilian asked, her eyes wide and defiant as her face popped up on FaceTime on his phone. Four hours had passed since he'd woken up on the couch of his sister's flat. With his help, Charlie had called Dr. John, the local doctor who took care of in-house emergencies and such. He'd arrived thirty minutes later, breaking into the tense and awkward silence they'd been sitting in, and had checked out Page's vitals. Miraculously, Page didn't have a concussion, and Dr. John, with a shake of his head, had told him to take some ibuprofen and to call him if he got dizzy. Once he'd left, Page had immediately bolted out of the living room to lock himself in his sister's bedroom and text her. Page knew damn well that he had run away, and he was perfectly fine owning up to it.

Now, he was sitting on the edge of the bed, one hand desperately trying to hold a new ice pack between his shoulder and the other holding up his phone. Lilian was sitting in what looked to be their mother's house. Her feet were tucked underneath her, her blue pajamas dark in the barely lit room. He was also sitting in darkness, or as much darkness as he could get in the room during the summer morning. He'd only been knocked out for around thirty minutes. But he hadn't been able to sleep so instead, he'd been staring at his ceiling waiting for his sister to wake up and call him back.

His head was still pounding, however. Just how hard had she hit him?

"She's the one I told you about. The one from the con." The words seemed to spill out of him. Not that he usually kept anything from his sister, but he realized then how long it had actually been since he and Lil had been in the same room and had taken the time to just... talk.

"*No*," his sister said, shock filling her voice. He wasn't surprised that she hadn't known who Charlie was when she'd hired her. Lilian rarely went on social media, her Instagram holding maybe two photos—one of the bookshop and the other of Gandalf the White. They had both stayed away from the public eye after what had happened when he was four. But he assumed that Lilian kept away because she hated social media platforms in general, not because she feared the spotlight. When Lil didn't like something, she had no problem letting others know about it, and she had been on an anti-social media campaign ever since secondary school.

"Yes," he said, drawing out the word just like Lilian had. His head fell forward onto his arm, and he let out a groan.

"So, you've been worrying about this woman, who your TV show has completely screwed over, for months, and she just happens to be the woman who applies for our abroad visa employee program that we've just reopened?"

Page groaned. "This is bad."

The words had been repeating non-stop in his head since

Doc had left. But this was the first time he had said them out loud. For some reason, it seemed to make everything worse. Because it meant that this situation was *real*.

"Why?"

The question almost made Page turn his head and glare at his sister. But his body hurt too much to move. He rubbed a hand over his face and explained what the last call with the showrunners had been about. He wished he'd been recording Lilian's face as her expressions changed. Shock, humor, anger. Lilian had always shown her emotions clearly on her face. He and his mother, on the other hand, had learned early on to keep their emotions close to their chests. Sometimes, he wondered how Lilian had grown up to be the person she was when they had been so messed up when she'd been a baby. It just proved how amazing his stepdad, Steve, was. He had held them together after the accident and had pieced back their broken bits so they could be a family again. There was no doubt that Steve and Lilian both had healed his mum and him.

"God, I can't even imagine how furious Theo and Sandhya are." Lilian's words shook Page out of the past, and he froze.

What the hell were Theo and Sandhya going to think of all of this?

He didn't even need to think too long to answer his own question. Theo would tell him to stay away as much as possible. Keep it professional and on the downlow. Sandhya would tell him to hit that. Those exact words.

He groaned again at Lilian's silence.

"Well, we might have a bit of an issue," his sister said, her voice semi-amused.

"Aye."

"It's a good thing, though, that the store has never been publicized with your stage name," she wiggled her eyebrows when she said the last part, causing him to roll his eyes.

Page groaned. "We're lucky that the press hasn't connected the store to me yet." He hated that she called it his stage name. It sounded way too dramatic.

59

"That's what a good stage name, a great agent, and a good manager will get you."

Page couldn't help but agree. He was more than thankful for Angie and Jake. He had signed with Angie right after college, and Jake soon after. Telling them about his history, at his mother's request, had been one of the best decisions he'd ever made. It kept his family safe and his mind calm. Or as calm as possible when his face was being plastered on billboards for the show's new season. He hadn't quite been prepared for how big the show would become. And now, it wasn't like he could get out of it. No one would understand. He already knew what they would say: this is what came with his job, what he loved to do. Anonymity wasn't a part of success. He would just have to deal with it.

It didn't mean he had to like it, though.

Page huffed out a laugh. It sounded rough and fake to his own ears. "With all the heat around the show, I'm not sure how much longer we'll be lucky with that. And it would have been nice to know that you were taking a vacation at Mum's?" he said, annoyance filling his voice.

Lilian glared at him from the other side of the phone. "I would have told you if you'd called me in the last month and didn't just assume I stay in the same place all the time."

"To be fair, even if you were here, I was not expecting the flat to be filled." There was a pause and then, "When did you start up the program again, anyways?"

It was then that he realized, with a severe amount of guilt, just how long it had been since he'd been home. With the show, traveling and filming, he hadn't been back in almost a year. His mum had originally run the store when they were kids, and the work stay program had been her idea. But when Lilian had taken over two years ago, she had dropped it to focus more on hiring locals—people she knew from school who needed the job. The fact that he hadn't even known she'd changed her mind made him feel sick. It wasn't like he hadn't been checking in when he could. He texted and called his family almost every week. But texting her and talking with her were different.

He heard his sister sigh and opened his eyes to look at her. Her red hair was pulled away from her face with a headband, the curls framing her round, pale features. There were bags underneath her green eyes, and she was worrying her lip. He and Lilian didn't look much alike, her taking more after her parents and Page after his own, but Lilian's mother had green eyes, similar to his and his mum's. Growing up, they'd always said that, even if Lilian was born to different parents, they were always meant to be siblings because they had the same eyes. Those green eyes were now looking tired with worry.

"What's going on, Lilian?" he asked, his tone serious.

"Nothing, really," she said, and he knew the cheery tone of her voice was fake. "I just needed to get away from the store for a while. Mum offered to have me stay with her for a few months, and she told me about the program she used to do when she ran the store, and I decided it was a good idea, instead of leaving it all on Layla's shoulders."

Page knew for a fact that his sister did not just need to 'get away' but he saw the look in her eyes. Recognized it. He knew that the last thing she needed right now was to talk about whatever it was that was bothering her. He and Lilian were similar like that. They always needed to work through their emotions on their own before sharing with others.

"When you're ready, call me?" he asked, and when she nodded, the tightness in his chest eased. When his mum had married Lilian's dad, he hadn't been a happy camper. At four, the last thing he wanted was a new dad. And after what he had gone through, when he'd found out his new dad came with a one-year-old baby sister, he hadn't really known how to handle the news. Why would he need a new sister when he'd had Anna?

But when he'd seen Lilian for the first time, she had crawled over to where he stood and hugged his legs with pure joy on her face, and he'd instantly known that he would love her. His older-brother-ness, as Lilian called it, had engaged, and they had been close for most of their lives after that. It had been killing him a bit every day, being so far away from his family, first from going off to college in the US and then getting the job on *StarVerse*. They'd been too far from one another. But even when he had thought of quitting, they'd encouraged him to keep going and to finally take the time to focus on what he wanted.

Now, though, he was starting to wonder if this had been a good idea. If, maybe, he had been thinking about himself a bit too much lately.

Lilian looked at Page, her expression schooling into calm attention. "Page, in all seriousness, why keep the store and our family so separate from your career still?"

He met her gaze. "You know why," he said. "You know I don't like press around the family. Not after everything with Anna and my father."

Lilian looked like she'd just sucked on sour candy. They didn't really talk much about Anna. Their da had married his mum after his twin and father had died when he was four. Lilian had only been one at the time. She hadn't been aware of the press and media craze he and his mum had gone through when his father had taken Anna, or when their car had crashed and they both hadn't made it. It had taken years of therapy for him not to flinch when he heard a camera go off. He still needed to prep himself when he had to deal with the media now.

But Lilian had been brought into a family, or at least half of a family, that was still trying its hardest to heal. She'd been born to a mother who had left and had found a mother who loved her but also looked at her and still saw her other daughter, and a brother who loved her but was still dealing with trauma. Things had settled after a few years, yet he knew that Lilian and their mum had a loving but rocky relationship. One of the things that they had bonded over the most was the bookshop. That's why Page refused to be responsible for the media or fans disrupting his sister and mother's dream.

It had been one of the first things he had insisted on when he signed with Angie, his agent. Only she and his manager, Jake, and a few other chosen people, his family, and friends, like Theo and Sandhya, knew his real name. In the film world, he was Jamie

Mahone and not his real name, Jamie Page McAllister. Not even the whole cast new his real name.

He liked to keep his private life just that. Private.

"I get all of that. But I guess I thought…" she cut off, shaking her head.

"What?"

"You don't know how hard it is to keep this shop running nowadays. It was easier back when Mum was running it. Bookshops weren't in as much danger. Waterstones and other larger corporations weren't slowly taking over the industry. And it's especially harder for small bookshops that aren't in the bigger cities, like Edinburgh or Glasgow, or even Aberdeen." Page opened his mouth to jut in, say what, he wasn't even sure, but before he did, Lilian stopped him with a hand. "The shop is hurting, Page. And I know your reservations behind keeping your name separate from the bookshop, but as a business owner, there is a part of me that can't help but think that the press you'd bring in might benefit the store. Layla helped me start an Instagram—" at Page's dubious look, she paused, rolled her eyes, and continued, "you know that we need a social media presence. It wouldn't hurt… if we could have some more… support."

Page let out a breath and ran a hand over his face. Tension was filling his shoulders once again. "I have to think it over, Lil."

She pursed her lips. "I know. But I need you to *actually* think about it." He nodded. "On another note, don't think I didn't realize how you totally and completely changed the subject from our Charlie."

Our Charlie. Kill him now, please.

If Lilian was already calling the woman theirs, then she was attached and there would be no getting rid of her. It had been a common occurrence when they were little, Lilian bringing home stray puppies, bunnies, once a sheep she had seen hurt on the side of the road. They'd returned it back to its owner once they found out it was from a farm right outside of town, and Lilian had cried for days. How she had attached herself to a person she hadn't even met yet, he didn't know, but he assumed they had been conversing over phone and email since Charlie had arrived in Stonehaven.

Getting rid of her was never an option, a voice said in the back of his mind. He pushed that thought away. The last thing he needed was to bring that kind of media attention down on himself, Charlie, or the store.

He set down his cup of tea on the floor, right in front of him, and ran his hands over his face. "I don't know what to do about Charlie. The woman probably hates my guts."

Lilian made a sound between a grunt and a hmm. "I will talk with her tomorrow. But I suggest maybe leaving her be for a few days? Just try to give her as much space as you can?"

Page snorted. "That was my plan before you suggested it. But there is one issue," he said, glaring at his sister. "We're living in the same fucking flat."

His sister gave him a mischievous smile and he was tempted to hang up on her. "That's my brother, the courageous one that never hides away in his gilded tower." Page noted the sarcasm in her voice and sent her a glare that had zero weight behind it.

"Not everyone can barrel into every situation with confidence like you do, Lil."

"I know," she agreed, giving him one of her bright smiles that he had learned early on in their childhood meant mischief and love all wrapped into one. "But we love your nerdy, quiet, tall, and brooding self. Because that's the side you show to your family. Not the all-American, tall, jock man you show to the rest of the world."

"You of all people should know I'm not American."

Lilian rolled her eyes. "You get the fucking point." With a sigh, she rolled her neck and rested her chin on her fist. "It's early and I need to start breakfast. But just realize, Page, she's probably as scared as you are right now, okay?"

When he nodded, she sent him an air kiss and hung up. Lilian always hated saying goodbye. The phone went black as he turned it off, leaving him alone again in his room. He stared at the door, and when another wave of dizziness hit him, he decided that this whole thing would have to wait until tomorrow. His jetlag and headache were hitting him, and the bed was calling his name.

Chapter 7

Charlie

Charlie didn't know what to do.

She didn't know what to do when he had winced, said something about needing a second, and then had shut himself in the other bedroom across from hers.

She didn't know what to do when he hadn't proceeded to come out.

She didn't know what to do at all.

How had she gotten herself into this situation of living with a movie star, let alone a movie star on the show whose new marketing strategy was one hundred percent to discredit her?

He didn't come out of the room all day. She was starting to wonder how he was surviving, but then remembered that he must have jet lag, and that the other bedroom had a separate bathroom attached.

He was one hundred percent avoiding her. She knew it, he knew it. Even Gandalf the White knew it… and it pissed her off.

If anyone should be avoiding anyone, it should be her avoiding him.

Charlie decided that, if he wanted to avoid her, she would leave him alone. Because the last thing she wanted was to be in the same room as him. Instead, she grabbed a few snacks, a bottle of wine, along with some water—staying hydrated was always key—and burrowed into her bed for the rest of the day and night. Her kindle was her only companion.

When Charlie woke up the next morning, it took her a good fifteen minutes of brushing her teeth and waiting for the first pot of chai to steep before she remembered Jamie *Page* Mahone—or whatever his real name was—was in the other room.

With a groan, she sat on one of the two seats situated around the wooden kitchen counter and glared out the window. It was a surprisingly sunny day here, the first since she had arrived, and she was tempted to glare and shake her fist at the sky for smiting her with such pretty weather on such a depressing and stressful day.

What a shitshow.

It took her another forty minutes of choosing an outfit, getting her hair into a reasonable enough ponytail, putting everything she needed for the day into a book bag, and convincing herself that going to work was better than waiting for the man in the other room to appear.

Then she got angry that she was waiting on him in the first place.

The front door was open, even though the closed sign hadn't been flipped over yet. Layla was behind the cash register, her cat-eye eyeglasses low on her nose, her head stuffed into a large mass-market paperback romance that looked to have a shirtless pirate on the cover.

When the bell sounded above Charlie, Layla didn't look up. She just waved, pointed to the book in front of her and held up five fingers. Universal reader language for "Hi, give me five more minutes of reading."

Charlie shuffled herself past Layla and into the back room, shoved her bag into her cubby and slowly removed her headphones, making sure they were turned off so the battery wouldn't die during the day. She had a feeling she would need help with managing sensory input today.

She made herself busy, cleaning up the backroom a bit, giving Layla her much beloved reading time before they opened, and then made her way back to the front. She leaned against the counter, opposite the other woman.

"Hi."

Layla marked her page with a bookmark made from a leftover receipt paper and smiled softly at Charlie. "Hiya, Charlie. How did you sleep?"

Charlie blinked at the question and a look of subtle amusement flitted onto Layla's face. Though Charlie had never been good at reading expressions, she did find herself better at reading them than distinguishing tones when someone was speaking. It was one of the reasons she always insisted on calling people on FaceTime and never just calling them. It was harder for her to talk to people on the phone.

"I slept averagely okay."

"Averagely okay? Is averagely even a word?"

Charlie shrugged.

"Okay, look," Layla reached out and set her hand over Charlie's. For some reason, this little touch made her feel more present. It helped her understand Layla's words as she spoke them. "Lilian and I have been friends since we were kids, and we text often."

Charlie couldn't hold back her wince.

"Just how hard did you hit him?" Layla's eyes shone with amusement.

Charlie scowled. "He was out for a while."

"And you didn't call a doctor?"

"Lilian told me not to! I was panicking!"

Layla laughed. "Damn, you must have a good swing."

"I blame it all on the golf club."

"Golf club," Layla let out a snort and didn't stop giggling. "Lilian did not tell me about the golf club." Charlie opened her mouth to speak, but stopped when Lilian laughed again, her head falling back.

"I didn't hit him with the bottom but the stick part—"

"You hit him with the shaft?" Layla said through her giggles.

"Excuse me, it's called a shaft?"

Layla burst into laughter again. "I would've killed to see Page's face!"

"Okay, that!" Charlie said, jumping in. "Why is everyone

calling him Page? Isn't his name Jamie Mahone? And how is it he is related to Lilian if her last name is McAllister? Do they have different last names?"

Layla seemed to think her confusion and frustration were a bit funny. She grinned as she answered. "I've grown up here most of my life, so I went to school with Lilian. Her dad married Page's mum when he was around four and Lilian was one, I believe. He goes by Page here at home, but because he doesn't like the spotlight, he uses another name for his acting."

"And no one knows this?" Charlie said, disbelief filling her voice.

Layla shrugged. "He has a good agent and manager; they keep everything he doesn't want in the press out of it. And this is a small town. The community is tight-knit. We respect others' privacy and we're far enough away from the other big cities that, if we get tourists, it's not many."

Charlie guessed it made sense. But it was such a different life than the one she'd known growing up in LA that it still shocked her.

"I heard you're living together for the time he's home?" Layla asked, raising a dark brow at Charlie.

Charlie rolled her eyes. "From what I know, yes. And I think there's been a mutual, undiscussed agreement to stay the hell away from one another."

"Hmm," Layla said, giving Charlie a look that she did not know the meaning of. Charlie knew Layla could hear the undisguised anger in Charlie's voice, but she chose not to address it.

Before Charlie could ask her anything else, though, she spoke. "Well, enough gossip for now, we have nerds to convert, and readers who will worship the ground we walk on." She walked around the counter, slinging her arm through Charlie's. "Let's get working."

Charlie poured all her attention and discomfort into the bookstore. The store had a mix of hours, something Charlie knew was not uncommon for a small-town, independent business, and today was her last day of work until Tuesday. Friday ended with the end of week stragglers, some faces finally becoming familiar. There was the old woman, Mrs. Thompson, who ran the convenience store on the far corner of the square. Timothy and his mom, Sarah, who came in after school on Fridays. Then there was Johnny, an older man who still dressed like it was the 50s, and who had a distinct love for horror and crime fiction.

Stonehaven was a small town, not as big as the cities to the north and south, but it did get some foot traffic during this time of year, either from tourists or people taking the train between Aberdeen and Edinburgh. She had dealt with a few tourists from the States, one group from France, and a small family from Brighton, all that just today and she had thirty minutes before she closed for the day.

Charlie watched the small clock above the store entrance, the blue hands clicking annoyingly every second. If there was one thing Charlie hated more than anything in this world, it was useless ticking noises. They made her brain want to scream. Because of the one customer in the store, she couldn't even pull her snug headphones that were hanging around her neck over her ears to drown out the white noise. Not that she wanted her workday to end—in fact, today of all days, she wanted to stay in the store as long as she possibly could.

A *ding* sounded above the door and her eyes met with the tall figure in the entryway. He was a white man who looked to be in his late twenties, his flannel shirt covering broad and muscled shoulders. Dark brown hair fell around his shoulders in loose waves, framing a face meant to be on a romance book cover. He walked in with such confidence, as if he knew exactly what he wanted, so she let her attention move back to the status of a new book order she'd been checking on. But once again, she found herself sitting there, the computer mouse not moving, her thoughts on the man upstairs. Or she assumed he was upstairs. He hadn't exited the apartment from the store entrance, and she had heard light footsteps above her as the day moved on.

Not that she was paying much attention.

Charlie let out a deep breath. Who was she kidding? Of course, she had been paying attention. She hadn't been able to focus at all on anything else the entire week. Honestly, she was surprised she hadn't messed up any orders or checkouts with how distracted she'd been lately.

It had been a few days since he had walked in at midnight, and she had only seen him for one panicked second when she was leaving for work. She had let out a squealed hello before bounding out of the apartment.

Charlie was starting to think the man was a ghost, or maybe a figment of her imagination… Honestly, at this point she wouldn't be surprised—a part of her kind of hoped he was.

A throat cleared and Charlie looked up. The new man who had walked in was hovering.

"Do you need any help?" Charlie asked from her seat. The man paused, then looked over at her, a smile, more like a grimace, covering his face. He had a brown beard that covered the bottom half of his face, and thick dark brows that hung over his blue eyes. He was the epitome of a burly Scottish small-town man.

"No, just looking for something for my daughter." He stuck his hands in his front pockets, rocking back on his heels. "She's five."

"Are you a regular?" Charlie asked, moving from behind the counter.

He nodded, "Yeah, but Lil usually helps with the choosing." His accent was thick, his voice low and gruff. He didn't look at her, but around the store. Even though his eyes glanced around with familiarity, he looked a little… lost. "She always seems to know what Flora wants."

At the name, her eyes lit up. "Give me one moment," she said before rushing into the back where she found a small pile of books with a sticky note that read *for Flora if Callum comes in* and grabbed the books before shouldering the door open. She found the man, who she could only assume was Callum, standing at the counter where she had left him. She almost smiled at the sight. He was so tall and broad that he looked like a giant next to the small display tables; a tall, awkward giant who was currently studying a bodice-ripper-romance as if it were an alien substance. She wondered what his facial expression would be when he saw the alien romance on the other table…

"I'm going to take a good guess and say these are for you," she held out the sticky note to him, and as he looked down at the slip of paper, his lips tipped up in a small smile. A pained smile.

"I would say so."

She started ringing up the books for him. She could feel his eyes on her. But it wasn't uncomfortable, more like he was looking for something. When he spoke, she almost jumped, not expecting his voice.

"Do you know where Lilian is? She didn't mention she was leaving the shop."

Charlie looked up, surprised at the tone of his voice. He sounded… concerned. Charlie had assumed everyone knew that Lilian had taken a holiday, but—

"No, but I'm here looking over the shop with Layla and I'm staying upstairs for three months. She said it was while she went on vacation." Callum nodded, but his gaze wasn't focused on her anymore. He was looking behind her, his eyes unfocused.

"I'm sure she's okay, though!" she said, sending him a smile. It took him a moment, as if her smile shocked him, and then he smiled back but it didn't quite reach his eyes. She handed over the stack of books. "Do you need a bag?" she asked, and at the shake of his head, pulled her hands back. They landed in her lap awkwardly.

"Enjoy Stonehaven," he said and paused, as if he were wondering if he should wave or not, before realizing the books were in his hands. He turned and headed for the door. Charlie couldn't help but smile slightly at his back as he pushed open the door, barely making it through without bending down.

Her phone pinged. Picking it up, she frowned when she saw it was a long UK number she hadn't added yet. She could have sworn she had put Layla and Lilian's numbers in her contacts.

[Unknown Number]
> I'm going out for groceries. Do you have any allergies?

It took her a good five minutes of staring at the text to realize who it was and that the text was real.

Charlie
> Who is this?

[Unknown Number]
> Page. Allergies?

Charlie scoffed at her phone. "Okay…" she muttered under her breath.

Charlie
> None.

Then—

Charlie
> How did you get this number?

She then added the number to her contacts under Page with a Scottish flag and set down her phone. It wasn't long before it pinged again.

Page
> Lilian gave it to me. I wanted to make sure I didn't get anything that you were allergic to.

Charlie didn't respond. To be honest, she didn't know what to say. All she knew was that she was slightly annoyed and relieved at the same time. Annoyed because he had gotten her number from someone else and had texted her before talking to her, and relieved because the interaction had been over text and not in person.

Her heart was beating a million times a minute as she set her phone down on the counter. Now she was annoyed at her reaction. She was acting like a middle-schooler with a crush. Her hands raised to her flushed cheeks as she remembered the night he'd arrived. When he had woken up, his stare had been so direct, so deep in shock she hadn't been able to look away. Then he had looked at her—really *looked* at her.

She hadn't really known what to do then.

Fuck, no, Charlie thought to herself, frowning down at the counter. It was wooden but had a bunch of bookish stickers stuck to it on the side of the cash register. One corner of the purple sticker with the words "Read More" on it in white was peeling away. She reached forward to pick at it. There was no way in hell she was going to let herself think about Page being… hot. Objectively, she could acknowledge it. But thinking about him?

She loved herself too much to have a mini crush on an actor who was part of such an ableist franchise. Especially when she was now living with him.

The other customer checked out and, once they were gone and the clock chimed five pm, she locked up, falling into her new routine of cleaning and re-organizing the books before she left for the day.

Her mind couldn't help but move back to Page. Ripley was the one who found him attractive. She didn't normally like guys like him—guys who seemed to ooze confidence and had girls lined up out the door to fall at their feet. Or at least she assumed so. He was a world-famous actor… and the person he was on TV or on stage oozed charisma. Maybe he wasn't her regular *type*, but there was… *something* about him.

And now he was living in the same apartment and picking up food for her.

Like she couldn't pick up food for her goddamn self.

She didn't even know him, let alone know how she was

supposed to interact with him. Did him picking up food mean their week of silence and avoidance was over? If so, what did that mean?

God, she needed to call Ripley soon. Charlie looked down at her phone and bit the inside of her cheek. One thing she always struggled with was keeping in contact with people who weren't physically around her all the time. She got so focused and overwhelmed by everything directly around her, that thinking of people outside of that bubble made her want to cry. But she knew she needed to.

She also needed to call her mother and father…who she had yet to text back. It wasn't like she talked to her parents that often anyway. She had a close enough relationship with them, especially her father, but they gave her space. Right now, though, she was the one creating space as big as the Grand Canyon. She'd been slowly widening that gap since college.

Probably too much space, she thought. Her parents had always had a hands-off type of parenting. When she'd been living with them, it had been great, but once she moved out, it had become lonely. Adding to that her struggling relationship with her mother since her diagnosis, and Charlie had become excellent at avoiding any interaction. She felt bad, especially for avoiding her father, who she deeply missed. But when she thought about calling and remembered her mother's subtle ableist comments, or the comparisons between her career and her brother's… she wanted to throw up. Charlie had never been the type of person to avoid situations, she had never really seen the point and would rather deal with the issue head on, but sometimes, if she became overwhelmed, she needed space. And her parents were a unique issue.

Just like the man upstairs was.

Charlie turned off all the lights, grabbed her stuff and looked at the stairwell that led up to the apartment. Her hands rested on her hips, and she glared at the first step in defiance.

Come on, Charlie. Just go upstairs. Get it over with.

Charlie took a deep breath and started up the stairs.

Excerpt from *STARVERSE*: Season 2, Episode 6

INT. SPACESHIP BRIDGE — NIGHT

THOREN pulls CAR aside to discuss something as everyone else walks back to their rooms.

                        THOREN
            You're avoiding her—

                         CAR
                No, I'm not.

                        THOREN
    Don't be a bigger idiot than we both already know
                    you are, Car.

                         CAR
      I just don't know what to say to her, Ren.
    Everything was… it can't happen again. I'm her
                 captain and this—

                        THOREN
            Don't be an idiot.

Chapter 8
Charlie

Page wasn't home when she got upstairs. So, she did the only thing that could stop her from falling into a panic spiral. She called Ripley.

"What do you mean you're living with him?" Ripley asked, her voice rising with incredulity over the phone. Charlie winced slightly, the sound sharp in her ears.

"I mean just that, Ripley. His family owns the store, and apparently, his house is under construction, so the only place he can stay is at his sister's apartment."

"Your apartment."

Charlie felt herself nodding. She was curled up on the couch, her feet tucked underneath her, a wool blanket over her legs, a cup of tea in one hand and her phone in the other. She had called Ripley during one of her "burrowing" moments, as she liked to call it. Usually, around this time of the day, after or around dinner, her brain decided she'd had enough and just shut down. She either listened to a podcast or pulled out a good fantasy romance to zone out to. Sometimes, she would go out with Ripley and Ripley's other friends, but most of the time, Charlie liked being at home in the afternoon and night-time. Ripley usually knew to leave her alone when she was like this, but it wasn't her fault she was in another country, and this was the only time they could call. She would, however, have preferred to go back to her book.

Charlie could feel her brain's exhaustion starting to take over. Words were hard to come by, and it felt like, every time she talked, she was pulling the syllables out of her mouth with a wrench. She just wanted to burrow under her blankets and block out the world. Hence why she called it "burrowing." But her anxiety wouldn't let her. She knew that she would have a panic attack if she didn't talk to someone about Page. She hated panic attacks.

Ripley burst into what Charlie assumed was incredulous laughter. The sound made the right corner of her mouth tip up in a small smile, drawing comfort from the sound of her friend who had stayed by her side when a lot of other people had slowly left.

Her entire life had been a bit confusing up until she'd been diagnosed a few years ago with autism spectrum disorder. Before the diagnosis, she had never had the words to explain her feelings, which had led to a lot of misunderstandings and ended friendships. At sixteen, she had been diagnosed with OCD and anxiety, put on medication, and sent on her merry way. It wasn't until later, when she'd been exposed to the Actually Autistic community online and in literature, that she'd realized her other diagnoses had been wrong. She'd talked to her therapist about it and after almost a year of struggling to get an appointment, had gotten tested. Finally, she'd been able to put words to feelings, unable to do so for so long before that moment. How did you tell your mother that her touch seemed to physically hurt, even though five minutes ago it was fine? How did you explain that your brain seemed to shut down, words hard to form, after a five-minute call? Or how you always felt like you were on the outside of a group conversation, looking in like a spectator? How did you describe why you couldn't sleep because of a small (yet extremely annoying) noise or because of the texture of the sheets felt wrong? How did you put into words how you felt as if there was something seriously wrong with you?

Especially when Charlie and the people she loved around her all had internalized ableism to work through. It had taken time, and she still found herself dealing with the ableism and self-hatred that had developed over her life.

The hardest part was the guilt. Guilt and shame… she was still working through those. Probably would be for a while. She had to watch herself and catch the invasive thoughts when they popped up. But even though it had felt lonely at times, she had been lucky enough to have a friend like Ripley, someone who was willing to deal with her monster moments and stay by her side.

"I cannot believe you're going to be living with Jamie Mahone," Ripley said, her voice rising even farther into squeal territory. Charlie could picture her friend in her head so clearly, Ripley's straight pink hair, recently cut to a short bob, falling into her blue eyes, bright with excitement. Her pale skin was covered in freckles, which would now be multiplying as Ripley had been going to sunbathe on the beach. Ripley was beautiful, ethereal, and at the beginning of their friendship, Charlie had felt that twinge of a crush, the slight race of her heartbeat when Ripley smiled. But two weeks in, ice cream cones in hand and both of them fawning after Hercules and Meg from the Disney film after first coming out to each other as bi, she had seen clearly how Ripley, no matter how pretty, was more like a sister to her.

"Yeah, such a dream," she said, sarcasm lacing her voice. "I thought you didn't like him anymore," Charlie added with a smile. After the whole StarCon fiasco, Ripley had sworn off anything *StarVerse*, even though she'd been obsessing over the show since it had first aired last year. That was one of the things that Charlie loved most about Ripley. She was loyal and would support Charlie, even if it meant not bringing up the show and shit-talking Jamie Mahone and the other actors on their couch with ice cream and wine. Charlie winced at that memory. Now, with everything going on, she wasn't sure if that had been her best moment.

"Well, just because he works on a TV show run by ableist fuckers doesn't automatically mean he is as well." She knew Ripley was right, but there was still a part of her that was hesitant. Not only would she be crashing with an unknown man, but he also worked with some pretty bad people. And there had been too many instances over the years where she had given people the benefit of the doubt and had gotten burned. Badly. Ripley heard Charlie's silence and knew exactly what to say, slipping into a terrible impression of a Scottish accent. "'Do you have the star charts, lass? We need them for our voyage.'" Charlie found herself giggling.

"Okay, okay," she said through her laughter. "Stop. Your accent is like nails on a chalkboard."

"That accent is fucking sexy," Ripley replied, her voice firm and filled with teasing humor. "It would make anyone in a mile radius drop their panties."

Charlie hummed, her face flushing at the image of Page speaking low to her, the way she'd seen him talk to the love interests on the show. "They don't have miles here, Ripley."

Or at least, Charlie didn't think they used miles here?

Ripley fake gasped on the other side of the phone. "Do I have myself a Jamie Mahone convert? Have you finally decided that his blond hair and green eyes are just as dreamy, even if his character is a bit flat?" Charlie snorted out a laugh at that, forcefully pushing away the vivid image of Page now in her head, his body close to her, his lips at her ear.

She needed to get that image out of her mind immediately.

"God, no, Ripley. I refuse to be the person who falls for a movie star, let alone her boss."

"His sister is your boss, technically."

Charlie huffed out a breath. "Technicalities don't matter when the man is famous. His family owns the place I'm working at; therefore, he is, in my mind, my boss," she said, her voice flat and serious. Deep down, she knew that this time away was good for her. She tended to get stuck in routines... and people. Sometimes, she became too reliant and found it was good for her to go off on her own, every once in a while, to remind herself that she was strong. Otherwise, she would smother herself and her loved ones.

"Bull. Shit."

God, she missed Ripley. She wished she could create a device to teleport her friend across the ocean and to her.

"Why the hell are we even talking about this?" she said, annoyance rising. "It's fucking Jamie Mahone, who never said anything when asked about the showrunners and the shit at StarCon. For all I know, I'm going to be living with an ableist, ignorant asshole for the next month."

"I'm just saying it's been a while since your pussy last saw some action, and you have one of the world's most gorgeous men in your direct vicinity. I'd hit that."

Charlie almost choked on her tea. "Ripley!"

"What? There is nothing wrong with giving in to your sexual needs. And hate sex? Mmhmm."

Charlie rolled her eyes. "I *know* that," she said, her voice straining a bit. "But I will not give in to my sexual needs with Jamie Mahone, no matter how sexy his accent and body are."

"Oh, so you think his body is sexy now, do you?" She could almost imagine Ripley's smirk on the other end of the phone. "Wait... have you *seen* his body?" She could have sworn that her friend's voice went up a few octaves.

"No! No, of course, I haven't... But I have seen the show... and even I can admit when someone has a nice body that is attractive to me."

"I don't know, for the past year, you've been saying he isn't sexy. I think you're behind on the times if it's taken seeing him in person to realize he actually is." Her friend's voice was suddenly low. "But in all seriousness, Charlie, do you feel comfortable? I know we're joking and everything, but he's a stranger, and I want to make sure you feel safe."

And this was another reason why she loved Ripley so much. She found her lips curling up in a small smile. "I get what you mean, Ri, but other than the first night of terror, I haven't felt unsafe once. He's staying away from me, and I'm staying away from him. If any boundaries are crossed, or I don't feel comfortable, you know I'll say something."

She heard Ripley hum in agreement. "It might still be a good idea to set some ground rules, though," she said.

"I don't need ground rules. He's just a tall, dumb blond man with a sexy accent who I don't find attractive whatsoever."

"Lies."

She shook her head and was about to respond when a knock sounded on her door.

"Hold on," she said, "let me just see who's at the door."

"What time is it for you?" Ripley asked, her voice skeptical.

"Only six, but the heater stopped working and it's fucking cold, even though it's June here, so Lilian said she was going to send someone over to fix it."

"Oooh, maybe your pussy will get some hot handy-man action."

"You seem to be very obsessed with my pussy today."

"I am just looking out for it because you don't."

Charlie laughed under her breath and peeked through the small peephole in the door. Her breath caught when she saw blond hair and a sharp jaw on the other side. She pulled back, her voice lowering. "Shit."

"What? Who is it?"

"It's Page," she hissed into her phone, quickly moving her friend off speakerphone so that Page wouldn't hear Ripley as she squealed loudly. "Or Jamie, or whatever he wants to be called."

Why was he just standing out there? Didn't he have a set of keys?

"Charlie?" Page called from the other side of the door. "Are you going to let me in? I forgot my keys when I went out. I can hear you, you know." She heard the laughter in his voice and winced.

Screw the front door and its lack of soundproofing. Actually, screw him for laughing.

Keeping her hand to her ear and whispering a hold on, she used her other hand to switch the locks and open the door, sending Page a smile mixed with a wince.

"Lilian said the heater is broken?" he asked, holding up a toolbox in one hand, his other arm full of two brown grocery bags. His glasses were pushed up on his head, keeping his blond hair away from his face, his green eyes shining with laughter. "I would come back another time," he said, clearing his throat, his eyes raking over her. Her shoulders stiffened. "But I do live here. Are you busy? Heard another voice." He walked past her.

Charlie shook her head and pointed to the phone, suddenly wishing she had not decided to change her outfit when she'd gotten home. She was in her comfiest pair of sweatpants, her huge UCLA sweatshirt hanging off her shoulders. Her feet were covered in bright, fluffy socks with sheep covering them. She pushed her hair away from her face and motioned for him to come in. "No, my best friend is on the phone."

"Yes, I am! Switch over to FaceTime, you bitch! I want to see this man in real time this second." She winced as her friend's yell sounded in her ear and glanced up at Page, who was grinning at the phone. Charlie was ninety-eight percent sure then that he could hear Ripley, even though she wasn't on speaker.

"Best friend, huh?"

Charlie sighed, shutting the door behind her. "Give me a moment, Ri," she said, watching as Page moved past her. He smelled like wood and oranges. All citrusy and… Charlie froze. Why was she smelling him?

He moved to the kitchen, dumping the bags on the counter

before moving over to the heater and dropping the toolbox at his feet. Charlie watched him warily, her body frozen in the spot near the door. She didn't know what to do. Should she offer to help him? Probably not the best idea, considering she would be completely lost with what to do with the heater. Should she talk to him? That was maybe a good idea? Maybe being the keyword. Should she get him some tea? That's what people did when they were hosting someone, right—get them a drink? But... he lived here.

Anxiety started crawling up her throat. She moved a bit closer to him, hovering a few feet away from where he was bent down in front of the heater. He seemed to stiffen slightly when he noticed her standing there.

"You going to help? Or just watch?" he asked, looking over his shoulder and raising a brow.

Charlie narrowed her eyes. "I'm not sure how much help you'll be. I tried everything I could think of, but Lilian was sure that whoever she was sending could help."

Would've been helpful if Lilian had told her Page was that person. Though Charlie shouldn't have been surprised. He was her brother, and he did live here.

"Yeah, this heater's been acting up for ages but has had no need to be replaced." He chuckled at her look of skepticism. "Really, it's been fine. Maybe it just doesn't like you. I mean, who turns it up to thirty-five degrees Celsius?"

"To be fair, I am not used to Celsius. I just turned it up. *And* it is not normal to be needing sweaters in June." Like this was her fault. He had just said the damn thing was faulty, yet he had the audacity to say it was her fault?

Page shook his head, "Americans and your sweaters and Fahrenheit."

Charlie narrowed her eyes at him again, her lips pursing. "Scots and your cold-ass weather."

He snorted and knelt in front of the heater, opening his toolbox. "I believe Americans have cold weather as well. Give me ten, and I'll see what you did to the poor thing. Would you put away the food? I bought some frozens."

"*Americans have cold weather as well*," she muttered under her breath, annoyed as she stalked over to the food. She rolled her eyes and moved to the kitchen, pulling her phone out of her pocket and switching it to FaceTime. Ripley's image popped up. She was sitting in bed, her hair pulled back with a headband, an Avatar the Last Airbender sweatshirt, which Charlie had gotten her for her birthday last year, pulled over her hands as if she were cold.

"Hello," she said, drawing out the word and raising a brow. The small piercing on her right brow glinted from the light streaming in from her friend's New York apartment.

Charlie fought back a smile. She glanced over her shoulder and tried not to stare at how Page's shoulders were tensed underneath the tight, dark green Henley he was wearing. Charlie moved the phone to sit on the counter, leaning back against the blender so Ripley could see her and the apartment behind her.

"Do you want coffee after I put away all of these frozens?" she asked, raising her voice so he'd know she was talking to him. Or so she hoped.

He raised his head, pushing back his hair from where it had fallen into his eyes. "I'm Scottish, we don't drink coffee. We only consume tea. Tea for breakfast, lunch, and then we drink more tea for tea," he said, his voice serious. That's right, they called dinner tea here. It had taken her a while to get that into her brain, and she still found herself getting annoyed over it. Why would you do that?

Charlie looked at him. "Okay," she said, turning back. She heard his huff of disbelief. She started pulling the groceries out of the bag, opening the fridge to her right.

"Sarcasm, woman," he said, and she turned back to find him grinning at her. "Coffee with two sugars will do just fine."

But before she could snap at him not to call her *woman* ever again, Ripley joined in, an evil smile on her face.

"My Charlie doesn't do sarcasm that well," Ripley said loudly. "It really is a tragedy. I was practically raised on the stuff."

Charlie snorted. "It's not as if you stopped using sarcasm. I just found out how to figure you out after a while."

"Name is Ripley, by the way," she said, smiling from where she was on Charlie's phone, even though she knew for a fact that Page had no way of seeing her from where he was laboring over the heater.

"Nice to meet you, Ripley. My name is—"

"Page McAllister, a.k.a. Blond jackass, a.k.a. Tall, Blond, Hot Scot, a.k.a. Jamie Mahone in hiding."

Charlie almost choked on air. "Ripley!"

"What?"

Page laughed from behind her, Ripley's words not seeming to annoy him at all. "I see you've heard of me," he said, sending a knowing grin Charlie's way. She turned back to the coffee before he could spot the flush on her cheeks.

"Well, I did have a stalker Pinterest dedicated to you for a while up until StarCon. So yes."

Charlie shook her head as Page laughed again, this time softer, as if the laugh shocked him just as much as Ripley had. That was Ripley. Brutally honest, a woman who did not understand the words, *I'm embarrassed.*

"Okay, you've met. Ripley, I'm going to hang up now."

"Make good choices," Ripley yelled as Charlie shook her head, pressing the hang up button before Ripley could say anything else. She focused on the coffee, not the deep chuckle that was low behind her. When it was done, she grabbed the milk from the fridge, sugar from the pantry, and mixed the two coffees until hers was light and sugary and his was dark with two sugars. She took a deep breath, grabbing both mugs in her hands before turning his way.

Page was focused back on the heater, his tools on the floor. His glasses were settled on his nose, his eyebrows scrunched together in concentration as he turned one of the valves in the back. She took a moment to study him. A five o'clock shadow covered his jaw, which was clenched in concentration, the skin between his brows furrowed. She really hoped he knew what he was doing.

"Here," she said, handing him out the coffee mug as she sipped at her own. He turned, wiping a sleeve over his forehead before grabbing it. He took a long sip. She did not glance at the long lines of his throat as he swallowed. She did not tense at the sound of his groan—which honestly, should be made illegal—as he gulped down the coffee, and did not stare when his tongue licked his top lip.

She did not.

Charlie cleared her throat.

"Sorry about Ripley," she said, her voice cracking. She coughed. "She can be—"

"A lot?" he asked, sending a light smirk her way.

"I was going to say very outgoing," she replied, her hands tightening on her coffee mug as she sat down on the couch.

Page shrugged his shoulders. "She reminds me of Lilian, honestly."

"Yeah," Charlie said. "They have very similar personalities. It's probably why I felt so comfortable with your sister when we first met over FaceTime when I arrived."

"She has that quality about her."

They stared at each other for a moment, Charlie's eyes not knowing where to land and finally focusing on the small drop of coffee clinging to his bottom lip. His tongue wiped it away, and she realized then she'd been staring… at his lips. Her face flushed as she quickly looked at the heater, avoiding his gaze.

"So, what's the consensus?" she asked, motioning towards the heater. "Is it broken? Or is it actually an AI who has human feelings and decided to hate me?"

Page stared at her for a moment, as if he were trying to figure her out, a small amount of amusement highlighting his face, one eyebrow raised. Or she thought it was amusement. His gaze ran over her hair, which was pulled up into a floppy bun on the top of her head, and her small strawberry earrings she had forgotten to take out.

"Unfortunately, you don't have a magical AI machine that is

taking root in the flat," he said, shaking his head. "This thing is broken and more than ready to be retired. I was able to turn it off, though."

Charlie let out a sigh. "Double blankets tonight it is, then."

"It is not that cold," he said, giving her a look.

She pointed a finger at him playfully. "Do not judge my sensitive Southern California body, mister movie-star-handyman-bookstore-owner... or whatever your job is."

With a raise of his brows, he collected his tools, putting them back into the box neatly, every object having its specific place. Charlie watched him silently as he walked, putting his coffee mug, which was now empty, into the sink and dumping the toolbox on the counter. He moved naturally, as if he had lived here all his life. And maybe he had, Charlie thought to herself. She had no idea if the apartment had belonged to the family for a long time or not. It was scarcely decorated as if to give whichever tenant was staying there some room to make it their own. All except for Lilian's room, Charlie mused as she remembered the first time she had walked in to be attacked by the bright colors and patterns.

"I'll run by the specs of the heater tomorrow with a family friend. His company does construction and house maintenance all over town, and he's been in business with his family for years. There really is no one better. He should be able to get this fixed for you before the end of the month."

Two weeks. That wasn't *terrible*.

"Just try not to turn it up to an ungodly temperature again, and we should be fine."

And there went her mood.

"Oh, so this is my fault?" she asked, her voice cold.

"Well, it was fine until you got here. That and my back."

Now she was full-on glaring. But instead of being petty, she set her mug on the small table next to the couch, pushing to her feet as he moved from the kitchen into the living room, grabbing his jean jacket that he'd laid on the couch when he came in.

"Your back is fine," she said, trying not to roll her eyes. She had double checked—tripled checked with the doctor when he had been here to make sure she wasn't going to be responsible for killing Jamie Mahone.

He stopped by the couch and smiled down at the mass-market paperback that was open on the cushion. It was the bodice ripper romance she'd been reading before Ripley had called. She quickly grabbed it, shoving it under her blanket. He gave her an amused look and moved to the door. That was when she heard him mutter "predictable" under his breath. She stopped.

"Excuse me?" she asked, turning slowly.

He had paused, looking back at her with a raised brow and a small smirk. "Yes?"

"Predictable?" she asked again, holding up her romance in her hand and shaking the book.

He shrugged, as if he didn't understand her raised voice. "Yes…"

Charlie huffed out a breath. "Is that all you can say?" she demanded, her hands coming to her hips.

"No," he said, his voice going flat. At her glare, he continued. "Even though I'm a tall, dumb, blonde I know many words." Charlie, who now knew he'd overheard her earlier when she'd been talking with Ripley, had the decency to blush in embarrassment. Instead of commenting and explaining that she had not meant for him to overhear it and she—even though she didn't want to admit it—had totally been lying to get Ripley off her case, she pushed forward.

"Romance is a great genre," she said. Usually, when people found out she read romance, they laughed at her. Which she found stupid. Just because the books included sex, didn't mean they were any less literary than Charles Dickens. The guy's name literally had the word dick in it, and yet people who liked "higher literature" refused to read anything that had an actual dick in it. Unless it had been written by a man, of course.

"I never said it wasn't," he said, crossing his arms over his chest and leaning against the wall.

"Yes, but you implied that me reading it was predictable, I can only guess because I'm a woman."

He looked at her, opened his mouth, and shut it again. His brow furrowed. He moved, hanging up his jacket and toeing off his shoes. He pushed the long-sleeved Henley up his arms. Charlie caught the glimpse of black lettering and numbers along the inside of his wrist. But from where she was standing, she couldn't make out the tattoo. "You do know that I grew up with a mother and sister who own a bookstore with a very popular romance section, right?"

"Oh, yes, and that totally excuses you from being sexist."

Page scoffed at that one. "I never said that there is anything wrong with romance as a genre," he said, moving back into the kitchen, reaching up to get some pots and pans. He turned back to send her a wide grin. "In fact, it can be very educational."

There's Only One Bed... On The Ship
Calerilslife

Hi everyone! Here is the new chapter you have been awaiting all week. This took me wayyyy too long to write. Thank you to my beta readers @caleriisawesome and @ ValeriStarVerseFandomQueen for their time and edits. Now, on to reading! Enjoy!

"All men are idiots," Valeri muttered to herself as she stepped into her room. It was just another day, another week, another month of being Car's first in command. Another day in hell. Because how was she supposed to get any work done when he just walked around the ship... with no shirt on?

A knock sounded at her door, and she hit the button that made it slide open. But she stopped what she was doing when she saw Car standing outside.

"Can I come in?" he asked, his hand on the back of his neck. He looked almost nervous. Why the hell would he be nervous? At her nod, he stepped inside. The door shut behind them, and suddenly they were alone. "I'm sorry, for what I said."

She hadn't expected the apology, so for a moment she couldn't find the right words. "The nav computer said it would be best to go—"

"Yes, I know." At that, she almost rolled her eyes. "I'm not apologizing for my decision. I'm trying to apologize for how I said it." He moved forward, grabbed her waist, pulling her into him. "I didn't think it would be so hard to fight these feelings, but just one taste of you and—"

"And?"

"I can't stay away."

Chapter 9
Page

"It can be educational?" Page muttered to himself. He shook his head. "Idiot."

Page looked down at Gandalf the White, who was now curling himself at his feet. He and Lilian had named the cat when they'd gotten him in secondary school, insisting that he be Gandalf the White as their last cat, who was grey, had been named Gandalf the Grey. And even though their mother had thought it was ridiculous, it had stuck.

The cat looked up at him as if to say, *you really need to fix this.* He glared back. Judgmental demon.

Page looked out at Main Street, his hands tucked into his trouser pockets, a tea towel over his shoulder as he stood in front of the stove. He wondered if he should get a muzzle for himself, so that he didn't keep puking out words in front of Charlie. After their awkward and heated encounter around the heater and the romance novel, she had stalked off to her room, the only word she'd given him being "ridiculous" before shutting herself away. And then, suddenly, he had been alone in the flat once again. Alone and frustrated.

Well... not completely alone. There was a naked woman taking a shower a few walls away from him. But he had been trying his hardest *not* to think about Charlie ever since he'd arrived, and now was not an exception. Because it wasn't okay for him to be thinking about her in the shower. Naked. Especially when she had made him that annoyed that quickly. If Page was ever annoyed by one thing, it was when people jumped to conclusions—specifically about him. Though he supposed it was partly his own fault for keeping his life so ambiguous to the public.

Page glared down at the food he was cooking. As the pasta and veggies simmered in the tomato sauce, he pointedly moved his gaze to take in the scenery outside of the flat's window. Stonehaven wasn't a large town. It consisted of two main streets in a T shape, the other streets that branched off filled with small businesses and residences. However, even though there wasn't much to do here, his favorite part about the town was how close it was to the beach, the buildings stopping right along the sand. The beachfront was lined with homes and small coffee shops, catering to the locals and tourists who stopped by for the famous ice-cream and fish and chips, or stopped into town because they were hungry after voyaging to the nearby Dunnottar Castle.

He wondered if Charlie had been there yet. If not, maybe

he—

He cut off the thought before it could settle in his chest. There would be no taking Charlie anywhere. There would be no more weird flirting with her. Especially when she looked so ruffled and comfortable, her hair tied up, her cheeks flushed, and her lips—

No more thinking of Charlie like that, period.

He could almost imagine the look of horror on both his manager and agent's faces if they ever found out Charlie was working at his family store, let alone living in the flat that he was staying at. It would be a nightmare, and if the press found out... Shit.

Page's whole body froze in panic. That *would* be a nightmare. The press would have a field day if they knew the lead actor of *StarVerse* was living with the woman the show had publicly gone against. Page felt the familiar sense of panic rise in his chest, constricting his breathing, so he closed his eyes, trying to regulate his breathing as he let the dinner on the stove simmer. When he opened them again, he saw the bright blue sky, white and grey clouds blowing slowly past. He wondered if he should go for a beach run or a swim before heading to bed. Maybe it would help him get rid of the tension in his shoulders that had been there since he had arrived back in Scotland. This was supposed to be a holiday. A break. But since he had set down in Edinburgh, he hadn't been able to get the weight of guilt off his shoulders. Then with Charlie...

His phone sounded in his back pocket, pulling him out of his anxiety. He pulled open the group chat titled "Queer Sluts and Page" reading the last few texts.

Sandhya

Did you make it home ok, P?

Theo

For all we know, you're in a ditch somewhere dead.

Sandhya

You have a very dark mind,
Theodore.

Theo

angry emoji face don't call me
that.

Theo

You're still on my bad side, S after
the Dessert Debacle!

Page snorted.

Page

Dessert Debacle?

Sandhya

He's alive!

Sandhya

Now you've awoken the monster,
P.

Theo

Sunni almost killed me, Page

Sandhya

I DID NOT ALMOST KILL YOU

Sandhya

DRAMA QUEEN

Theo

LIES.

Theo

I went over to S's house this
weekend and we decided to be
ADULTS and make Gulab Jamun
from scratch because S had
bought the packet and she SAID
she had MADE IT BEFORE.

Sandhya
Which I have, you ass

Theo
AND WE WERE BOILING THE
OIL, AND SHE FORGOT TO HEAT
UP THE METAL STRAINER WITH
THE OIL AND WENT TO SCOOP
THE DOUGH BALL OUT WITH
THE STRAINER, AND THE OIL
REACTED TO THE METAL
STRAINER AND BOOM.

Page

Boom...?

Sandhya
Cold metal and hot oil do not mix
it seems

Theo
DO NOT MIX?

Sandhya
The oil and metal... reacted.

Sandhya
The oil exploded and went up in
the air

Theo
Almost killing me.

Sandhya
IT DID NOT ALMOST KILL YOU

Theo
If I had been an inch closer, my
beautiful face loved by millions
would be no longer.

Sandhya
The millions would be fine

Sandhya
You were fine

Theo
EVEN YOUR MOTHER SAID YOU
ALMOST KILLED ME.

Page

Kavita was there?

Theo
If the smart and wonderful Kavita
had been there, I would not have
almost been killed.

Sandhya
YOU WERE NOT ALMOST KILLED

Sandhya
I might have called my mother to
ask why that happened… and she
might have called me an idiot for
not remembering to heat up the
metal strainer with the hot oil or
use something that isn't metal to
scoop them out of the oil

Sandhya
Now we know

Theo
You still owe me.

Sandhya
rolling eyes emoji I DO NOT
owe you. This isn't worse than that
time you convinced me you could
make croissants just because
you're half-French and you almost
burned my kitchen down because
they caught on fire in the oven.

Theo
You promised me that we would
never speak of that.

> Maybe we should just assume that
> baking and frying isn't both of
> your best skills? Or at least keep
> 999 on speed dial when you're
> cooking?

Page held back a laugh and was about to send another message when his phone started ringing. He scowled down at the phone when he saw who it was, swiping to answer and putting the phone to his ear.

"Lilian," he said, his annoyance filling his voice now that his sister sat on the other side of the phone.

"Jamie Page Alexander McAllister."

He rolled his eyes at his full name. She only called him that when she was either mad at him or teasing him.

"I know what you're up to," he said seriously. "And you need to fuckin' stop."

"I have no idea what you mean," she replied, her voice full of fake innocence.

"You could've called Callum and his family first without having me check up on the heater. Hell, we both know Callum would love to talk to you. But no, you forced me to interact with Charlie instead of letting us pretend the other doesn't exist."

"I didn't force you or anyone in this situation. If I remember correctly, you were near ecstatic to help."

He had not been ecstatic. He hadn't been. He wasn't a damn puppy.

"We both know Cal would've been happy enough to answer your call," he repeated. Callum Ferguson's family owned a construction company that had been a presence in the community for years. Callum and Page had been in the same year growing up and friendly enough up until Page had moved to the States to go to Julliard and Callum had gone to uni locally in Aberdeen. But Page wasn't naïve enough not to notice the way Callum's gaze had always tracked Lilian's movements at parties in the last few years, or how he'd tried to casually ask him about her when they'd gotten coffee together over holiday breaks. The man was more smitten with her than Lilian was with romance books.

"I'm not speaking to *Callum* currently," Lilian said with a huff. He knew they'd been friends for years, but he'd also been absent from the town for a long time.

"What happened?" he asked, his voice deepening and feeling his protective, older brother nature rise. After everything with Anna, he had always been a bit overbearing with Lilian. She'd given him lots of shit about it in the years past, but she knew where the anxiety came from.

He could almost hear how she rolled her eyes at the question. "Nothing you need to concern yourself with, Pagey."

He rolled *his* eyes at the nickname she'd given him when she was two and had finally been able to say his name.

"You know I'm here if you need to talk, Lil," he said, his voice softening. He knew why she was so closed off when it came to relationships. He knew her weaknesses and strengths, just as much as she knew his.

"I know, older brother, I know." She let out a breath and he heard her scuffle around, the sound of dishes clanking filling the background. "How is our dear Charlie?" she asked, her voice taking up its usual mischievous tilt.

"Fine." He heard Lil's snort at his annoyed tone but chose to ignore it. "The heater is broken as fuck, so I am going to do what you should've done in the first place and call Callum."

"Good, she'll need that heater if this cold front keeps coming. If it doesn't get fixed soon, she might even need another body to warm her up."

He shook his head again, grinning as he turned off the stove. "None of that made any sense, Lil."

"Didn't it?"

He chuckled. "I'm starting to think you broke the heater on purpose with your mastermind matchmaking powers."

Lilian gasped on the other side of the phone. "Me? No, I would never do that."

He rolled his eyes, "Night, Lil."

When she hung up, he checked the pasta and put it into bowls once it was done. He paused, wondering if he should knock on Charlie's door or if he should text her and, after a few minutes of silent debate, pulled out his phone again.

Page

Dinner's ready. I can leave it on the counter.

He paused after he sent it. Then he sent the next text without thinking it through.

Page

I'll be out here if you're brave enough to interact with me.

He turned off his phone quickly before he could get a response.

Two seconds later, her door opened. More like it was thrust open. She was wearing the same outfit, but her hair was now dripping down her back.

"Brave enough?" was the only thing she asked as she moved into the shared space, one hand on her hip, the other reaching for the bowl on the counter, a scowl on her face. He had moved from the kitchen and was now sitting at one of the three bar stools next to the counter on the side of the living room.

Charlie leaned against one end of the makeshift breakfast counter, choosing to stand and eat instead of sitting next to him. She glared at him over her bowl of pasta.

Page decided then and there that her glare was kind of cute.

He shrugged his shoulders, and her glare deepened. He tried not to grin. Her gaze was hesitant, as if he made her nervous, and suddenly a bad taste formed in his mouth. He set down his food. The last thing he wanted was to make her uncomfortable. Maybe...

"I am not the only one avoiding here," she said, pointing her fork at him. "You've been avoiding me just as much as I have."

"True," he said, and met her gaze with a small smirk. "But I'm the one who made you dinner."

She narrowed her eyes at him. A mix of anger and... not fear but hesitance. "Oh, yes, and that really fixes everything. Fine, you want to stop avoiding each other, we can stop avoiding each other. But that doesn't mean I'm going to be nice or like you."

She stabbed her pasta with her fork and took a bite. He raised his brows.

"A thank you would suffice. Who said I needed you to like me?" Before she could respond, he continued. "You don't know me. What have I ever done to you?" He had a feeling that he knew where this conversation was going, but he wanted her to mention the show's mess. He didn't want to bring it up if she wasn't comfortable talking about it.

"Thank you," she grumbled. And then, "Oh, I don't know. You work on a show that has practically disrupted my life. You work with quite a few ableist assholes. You barged in on my few months to get away from the mess with your actor, famous, manly presence, and you're probably just as bad as the other men you work with because you refused to speak on the matter when asked by the press."

He looked at her, taking a sip of his water before choosing his next words carefully. He had never been one to just jump into a conversation, but he could tell that his silence was annoying her. Honestly, he didn't care. He understood her anger but hated being judged so harshly for not even doing anything. Page knew he could explain himself to her, but as he sat under her glare, a part of him started to glare back.

"Yes, because me *probably* believing something is not an assumption."

"I have every right to assume things about you when you associate with shitty people." She stabbed at her pasta again. Then, quieter, "I cannot believe I have to live here with you."

He just sipped his drink, a scoff slipping out. "Oh, trust me, if I'd known you were here, I'd never have come home." He let out a breath, trying to ease the tension in his shoulders. He rubbed his temples, a headache starting to pound.

Silence fell over the table, and Page, once again, knew he had said something wrong. But this time, he didn't really care. He had come into this situation trying to make things better. She had come at him guns blazing. He glanced up, catching her studying him. Her eyes tracked his movements, the way his shoulders tensed.

"Why?" she asked finally, moving to the cabinets and pulling down a bottle of rosé and two glasses. She poured them and brought them over, setting them between them. He didn't care much for rosé, but he welcomed any bit of alcohol, so he took the glass. The wine didn't feel like a truce, more like a stalemate.

He let out a sigh before answering her, his hands coming up to rub his temples. He guessed she had every right to know about the situation since it had to do with her. "Ever since StarCon, they want the cast to stay under the radar until filming starts again and the new season premieres at the end of the summer. They basically threatened that if we made the press, there would be consequences, and somehow, I have a feeling that if the press found out I was living with the woman my show decided to publicly hate, it would be a shit show."

She took a sip of her wine. "So go stay somewhere else," she shrugged.

He grinned sideways at her. "Not that simple. Most of my money is sent back to my mother, and if it isn't, it's going into the renovation of the beach house. I don't have enough to stay somewhere else, and this is the only place I can crash." He saw her look of skepticism and rolled his eyes. "I'm a new up-and-coming actor on a TV show only two seasons in. I'm making a lot, but not enough to pay everything I mentioned."

He could see the moment she understood. Charlie let her emotions show on her face, through the tip of her lips, the scrunch of her nose, or the energy behind her eyes. Every gesture or movement was a signal to what she was thinking. Not that he had been staring at her. Because the last thing he was supposed to be doing was staring at Charlie.

"Are you worried about the press finding you here?" she asked, sipping her wine, leaning on the counter with her elbows.

He shook his head. "Stonehaven is small, and it's a tight-knit community. Everyone who knows me knows I like my privacy. I'd be more worried if I went to Edinburgh. I would have to be careful if I went to London. But that doesn't mean I don't have to be cautious."

What was this, a conversation that wasn't going down the drain?

She nodded and then sighed. "You know, Ripley believes we need ground rules."

He raised a brow. "Ground rules? What are we, twelve?"

Charlie lifted a shoulder. "I'm living with an adult man I've never met; she wanted me to ask for some apartment rules."

Page paused. "Yeah, like rules will actually help with anything." At her look, he sighed. "Fine." Whatever made her the most comfortable. The last thing he wanted was for her to feel unsafe.

"Fine," she said, mocking his bored tone and moving to grab a piece of paper and pen from one of the drawers in the kitchen. She set it between them and, at the top, wrote in clear block letters—

CHARLIE AND PAGE/JAMIE'S ROOMMATE RULES

He scoffed at the title. "You can call me Page. Jamie's my first name, but everyone outside the film world calls me Page."

Charlie shrugged and then squeaked when he grabbed the pen out of her hand and drew a sharp line through the slash and Jamie. He thought about it for a second and crossed out "roommate", replacing it by "flatmate".

"You ruined it!" she said, her voice high.

He laughed. "I think it's more authentic this way."

She glared, grabbing the pen back. His breath caught in his throat as her fingers touched his. Her hand was cold where his was warm, her skin soft. Page brought his hand back around his wine glass, his fingers flexing.

He swallowed the lump that formed in his throat. He hated

how, with just that small touch, his skin felt like it was on fire. It had been a while since he'd been with someone, but it hadn't been that long... He didn't know what it was about her—

"Number one," Charlie said, writing a one on the page. He moved to the seat closest to her to get a better vantage of the page. His shoulder bumped hers, and he saw her tense before speaking. She shuffled away, sending him a side glare. "The apartment stays clean, and we stay out of each other's respective rooms. That way, we each have our own space."

He nodded. "Should be fine since we have different bathrooms."

He saw her slowly look at him. "What, you don't think a woman can keep a bathroom clean?" she asked, her gaze narrowed.

He looked at her and rolled his eyes. "That's not what I said," he said as he grabbed the pen and wrote down a number two before she could respond. "If one of us feels uncomfortable, then we need to tell each other. Open communication is key."

He didn't look up at her but instead grabbed his wine, taking a long sip. She had such low opinions of him, and Page had learned very early on in his career that no matter what you did, there would always be someone who didn't like you. He knew his own morals: 1. what the showrunners were doing was wrong and 2. he would respect Charlie. And even though he should probably make that clearer, the way she was judging him was really pissing him the hell off.

He looked up, grinning at her. "Do I need to put, 'No more physical harm when angry or terrified?'" Her glare made him chuckle. "I'll take that as a maybe."

Then something popped into his head, and, with a grin, he wrote down number three. It was a bit out there, but he blamed it on the wine. Charlie looked at the page, read it, looked at him, and then looked back down at the page.

"Flatmates don't fall for flatmates?" she asked.

He knew that it was probably weird for him to put that down... at least to her. The rule made perfect sense to him. But then she glared at him, her lips pursing, and he couldn't help but grin. Honestly, it was worth it just to make her annoyed.

Her next words were ones he did not expect. "Who says I'm attracted to you?" she asked, her hands falling to her hips. He almost choked on his pasta.

"I'm not trying to make any assumptions, but," he sent her a cheeky grin, "just saying, you need to keep your hands to yourself. If we," he paused at her raised brows and coughed, "*got together...* it would be a nightmare."

Charlie rolled her eyes and scoffed. She pursed her lips and then nodded. "Agreed."

Page paused at the comment, wanting to ask her why *she* thought that them getting together would be a nightmare, but then thought better of it.

"Are there enough rules for you?" he asked, capping the pen, and leaning back in his chair.

She nodded, and her hand reached out between them. He paused. It was the first time she had extended any sort of olive branch since the night he'd gotten home. He took it slowly, his skin hot against hers. Her hand was soft, where his was calloused and rough, his hand engulfing hers. There was a moment where he forgot to pull away, but Charlie broke it when she pulled her hand from his, tearing her gaze away and shuffling back. Taking the paper, she took a magnet and stuck the rules on the front of the fridge. Gandalf the White meowed loudly at his feet, as if approving. Three rules and a grumpy cat to rule them all, Page thought, nothing could go wrong.

"There," she said, looking back at him with a hesitant smile. "As long as you follow the rules, this should all be fine."

"Yeah," he said, hopping off the stool. "Because I'm the only one who could possibly break those rules." Her annoyed huff made him smirk.

"Ass," she said, stalking out of the room with her glass of wine and shutting her door loudly behind her. Page let out a breath, glaring at her door. He would have to stay very patient over the next few months. Everything would be fine. He would not be thinking of Charlie excessively, and he would not be going against any of those rules. Actually, the best idea was to just keep avoiding her.

It didn't matter what she thought of him. After she left Scotland, he probably would never see her again.

But even though he repeated that in his head over and over again, there was a small twinge in his chest at the thought of possibly hurting her. But he hadn't started this... feud... she had, and Charlie didn't know him well enough to know that Page liked a challenge. He would damn well play to win this feud, even if it went on for the entire time she was in Scotland.

YouTube Transcript of an Interview with the cast of *StarVerse*

Marcy Davis: Hello, world! Today, we have the infamous cast of the new hit show *StarVerse*, which has taken fans around the world by storm since its premiere a few months ago. Welcome to my channel, and thank you so much for taking the time to sit down with me. I know our viewers have been super excited about your show.

Sandhya Vaughn: Thank you for having us here today, Marcy!

Jamie Mahone: Aye, thank you!

Skips to time code 34:38

MD: Now, Jamie, there has been a lot of speculation about you ever since the premiere. This is your acting on-screen debut, and since the trailer, fans have been obsessed. However, there is nothing about you online, so can you tell us a bit about yourself? Are you trying to excite fans by being tall, handsome, and mysterious?

JM: Aye, well, Marcy, I'm a very private person. I know my job comes with the expectation of being in the public eye, but I try to keep as much of my life private as possible. It's just a personal choice—

Chapter 10

Charlie

With the rules set in stone and residing on their fridge, the two of them got into a somewhat comfortable routine of trying their best to ignore one another. Charlie and Page would pretend the other didn't exist until Charlie was off work. Then, they would share a small, albeit awkward, conversation over dinner that usually resulted in Charlie being angry and annoyed in her room. It wasn't that Page was mean... in fact, he rarely said more than a few words here or there. It was just that everything about him and his presence seemed to get underneath her skin.

Maybe it was the fact that they hadn't really brought up the issue of StarCon or that he hadn't ever apologized for what happened. Or that she couldn't get a clear read on his emotions or facial expressions at all. Or that every time he looked at her, it seemed like her presence either confused or annoyed him. All she knew was that she had just started feeling comfortable in Scotland—like maybe this trip wasn't the worst idea ever. And now? Now, she was tempted to look up the cheapest flight home and run out on the bookstore.

But she couldn't do that. No, she wouldn't *let* Page ruin *her* getaway. She would just have to continue to avoid him and their apartment at all costs.

Of course, avoiding each other completely was out of the question. There had been a few awkward moments when he'd come back from swimming as she'd been heading out for a walk. She'd almost run into him in the stairwell, his hair dripping into his eyes, his body still covered by a dark wetsuit that did not leave anything to the imagination. Her breath had caught, his hands coming up to hold her on her upper arms to make sure they didn't fall. His hands had been *freezing*. The feeling had jolted her, and she had scurried away with a light, "Sorry!"

Or there'd been the moment when she had caught him staring at her while she read on the couch. She'd looked up from laughing at a funny moment in her novel to find him, eyes wide, looking at her from where he'd been sitting with his laptop open. He'd jolted and looked down so quickly that she'd wondered if she'd imagined it. She'd also seen him outside the shop a few times, running to help someone with their bags or crossing the street to head to the coffee shop. His broad shoulders had been hugged by his jacket, his blond hair blowing in the wind. She hadn't been staring, really. He'd just walked into her line of vision. Layla had caught her looking and had nudged her with her elbow, Charlie turning to hide her red cheeks.

When avoiding looking at him hadn't seemed to work, she'd allowed herself to look, but *only* look. She needed to put more effort into avoiding him.

That was why, when she got off work, she found herself walking around the small town, going into the numerous small shops that held way-too-touristy and expensive merchandise, and walking along the beach. She had grown up in LA, her parents' house in Malibu having been passed down from her great-grandparents to her parents. They'd been lucky, all things considered: the real estate on Point Dume getting more expensive each year, and the fires threatening the bluff every fall and summer now. But they refused to sell or move. She couldn't blame them. Whenever she went back to visit or took a drive around the area to clear her mind, she was reminded of *why*. The California coast was one of the most beautiful places she'd ever seen.

But she had to admit, even if the weather was a bit grey here, the beaches along the eastern coast of Scotland had captured her heart after a few weeks of living there. They were full of rugged cliffs and rocky, sandy beaches with dark blue water and soft waves. The bay in which Stonehaven was situated had some of the calmest water she'd seen, and once again, she was reminded of how she wanted to ask Lilian or Layla where she could rent a wetsuit and paddle board. If the day was clear, the sun high, the wind soft, and the water not beyond freezing as it hit her bare feet, she could see herself enjoying the water in the morning or late afternoon—especially since the sun had decided to take up most of the day and night, not setting until ten or eleven. She liked to think that her body had started adapting to the colder weather, but she couldn't help but feel a little embarrassed when she was the only one with a sweatshirt on when she walked along the beach. It wasn't as if the air around her was cold, no—it was the damn wind.

Brushing off her feet and slipping them back into her sneakers, Charlie made her way to the concrete boardwalk that lined the bay. It was later in the day, with people finally getting out of work. The boardwalk was a mix of residential on one end, but as you walked north, businesses and cafes started popping up more frequently. She passed a few elderly couples, a group of old men chatting around a chess board on one of the small tables, and a few families with younger children. Stonehaven didn't seem to have a large population of people Charlie's age or younger, and if it did, Layla had mentioned a lot of them worked in Aberdeen or took the train to Edinburgh and came back on the weekends. It was a town to settle down in—something Charlie had thought might make her feel restless. But even though she found herself at a loss with what to do some days, a part of her welcomed the slow nature. It was so different from where she'd grown up, but this time, different wasn't necessarily a bad thing.

She passed the small road leading up to the main street that would take her back to the shop, and instead followed the boardwalk further, stopping when she reached a small ice cream shop. There were people of all ages milling about, cones and pots of colorful ice cream in their hands. Layla had mentioned that the ice cream here was popular, but with taking care of the shop and Page's arrival, she had completely forgotten to stop by.

She hopped in line, taking in the people around her. An image of a tall blonde pushing up his glasses with one hand, a cone in the other, his tongue flicking out to lick at the dripping ice cream, popped into her mind. She tried her hardest to shake it away. He had mentioned the shop yesterday when they'd had dinner. Something about how maybe if she was so cold to people she barely knew and had just met, ice cream would be the best snack for her to try. She had almost thrown her salad at him but had restrained herself, just barely. Instead, she'd responded with, "Oh, then it must be your favorite place to eat at, right?" and had walked off.

She had seen the shocked amusement mixed with anger on his face. She hadn't cared. Not really. She knew they were acting immature... but couldn't make herself care.

And going here had nothing to do with him... she was here on *Layla's* recommendation.

Charlie frowned at the ice cream sign that held a list of close to thirty flavors to choose from. Even though she had plenty to keep her busy, her mind had been following a thread back to Page ever since he had arrived. He had been on her mind constantly—so much so that she was starting to worry she was hyper-fixating on him, or at least the idea of him and who he was. To her, he didn't quite make sense. Here was this man she had thought would fit into a clean, perfectly shaped box of "so far out of reach and not even that interesting". And now… now he was breaking down that box and asking her to put him into a murky grey pool of "what the fuck is this now".

She hated the box of "what the fuck is this now". It always stressed her out.

Yes, he was handsome, but he had always been handsome. And it shouldn't even be bothering her because he had never been her type. And he was… annoying. He always had some comment to say back to her, or some way to shift the conversation in a direction she didn't want it to go.

She usually went for the nerdy guys, not the tall, blond Adonis types. Not that she had dated *that* much. She had dated a few people in high school, feeling almost obligated to date someone since all her friends had found partners after sophomore year. A part of her had wanted to know what dating felt like, wanted to see what everyone else seemed to be so obsessed with. She had liked meeting new people, even if it had given her a ton of anxiety, which didn't seem to have an explanation before her diagnosis. But she hadn't had an easy time getting used to physical touches. Jacob was the perfect example of how, even with her diagnosis, dating someone who didn't want to understand her was… hard.

Looking back, Charlie understood why she had been so confusing to her family and friends for such a long time. Sometimes, she wanted to interact and be on, and then she just felt the need to completely shut down and zone out—whether it be by watching a movie, reading a book, or reading fanfiction.

It had taken her a long time to figure out that it was okay if she needed to pull away. Before she had been diagnosed, everyone had been hurt by her actions, but afterwards, her parents had taken time to understand everything. To realize that her need to pull away wasn't because she didn't want to spend time with them or be around them. They'd tried.

Not her brother, though. He hadn't cared. Neither had Jacob.

But none of that mattered because Page didn't fit into the dating box. Actually, he fit farthest away from the dating box.

Yes, he was attractive. Yes, she couldn't help but track his movements as he moved around the apartment, almost as if he were a magnet. Yes—

Charlie shook her head, handed over the pounds and grabbed her ice cream. The last thing she needed was to think of Jamie Mahone this way. That was territory she couldn't enter. She was just interested because of how confusing he was. When she thought he'd want to get as far away from her as possible, she found him cooking them dinner or pushing a cup of tea at her as he sat in the chair by the couch, pulling out a book to read with her. When she thought that maybe their conversation was about to reach a comfortable territory, she found him getting flustered and leaving, ignoring her for the next two days.

She had promised herself that, after her brother and Jacob, she wouldn't allow herself to be thrown around by someone who thought differently of her because of her disability. She had *promised* herself. And now, she was living with someone whose beliefs she didn't exactly know, yes, but could assume weren't great based on who he worked with. Or… she *had* to assume. She needed her guard up, especially now, especially against Page, of all people.

I just don't get why you pull away.

I can't deal with your drama, Charlie.

Can you just act normal for once?

She hadn't seen her brother since her last year of college, two years ago. Their parents had forced him to go to her graduation, even though she hadn't really wanted him there in the first place.

You know he needs to be there, Charlie. What would people in the neighborhood think if he didn't show up?

Charlie bit the inside of her cheek as the memory of her mom's face popped up. She had been horrified when Charlie suggested that Patrick not come. But that was her mom. Always worried about other people's perceptions. Charlie had learned early on that other people would almost always misjudge or misread her and her actions. It was best to just… not care.

Those moments still hurt, though.

If they all expected her to understand them, why couldn't neurotypical people, especially her own family, try to understand her?

Ripley tried to get her to go out with her on the weekends, but she'd found herself needing to hole up in their apartment with a good book instead. Now, getting space away from their life in LA and being able to look back, she wasn't sure if it had been something she needed or if she'd just been scared.

But in her experience, it was better to assume the worst about someone and be surprised than to assume the best and be hurt again.

Charlie headed outside, the night air and wind nipping at her face. She didn't even know why she was entertaining the idea of getting to know Page. It wasn't like there was any possibility of *that* happening.

That is a lie, and you know it, a voice said in the back of her mind. The voice scarily sounded like Ripley.

She groaned to herself, pulling her jacket tighter around her. She knew why these thoughts were coming up. It was because of the way his stare made her breath catch in her throat or how she couldn't take her eyes away from the skin above his jeans when he stretched. Because no matter how much he annoyed her, he was still attractive. Charlie frowned at the ground as she walked. Her feet moved at a steady pace, hitting the ground in a motion and tempo that slowed the breaths in her chest. She could feel the wind on her face and her heartbeat in her ears, but no matter how overwhelming the world got around her, her feet on the boardwalk stayed steady.

It was just attraction. It had to be. Because anything else, and… well, that would just be a recipe for disaster.

When she made her way back from her walk along the beach, she stopped as she saw the bookstore's lights on. Charlie frowned, pulling out her keys from her jacket pocket and fumbling for them in the dim light. There were no streetlights, not that she needed them. Even though it was almost nine—she hadn't realized how late her walk had gone until she'd gotten a text from Ripley—the sun was just starting to set and bathed the town in a mix of soft yellows and darkening blue hues. Her plan had been to sneak into her room and take a shower without even seeing Page, but the light stopped her. She knew for a fact that she'd locked up before she'd left. She opened the front door, the bell ringing softly above her. Locking it behind her, she pulled out her phone, preparing to call for help, nerves coursing through her.

"Hello?" she raised her voice into the dark bookstore.

"Back here," came a deep voice, tired and rugged. Even though she hadn't heard his voice that much since he'd arrived, Charlie felt as if she'd know it anywhere.

She let out a breath full of anxiety and felt her shoulders relax. Page must have come down through their back stairs. But what was he doing in the store? To her knowledge, he hadn't stepped foot in it since he'd arrived, and Lilian and Layla hadn't mentioned that he worked or helped in here at all. Adjusting her purse on her shoulder, she moved to the backroom, the hardwood floor creaking underneath her steps.

She found Page sitting behind Lilian's small desk in the corner. The room was small—just big enough for a series of cubbies to line the right wall, a small drink and coffee station beside it, and a table and chairs in the middle. A large armchair covered in purple velvet sat in one corner, and the desk Page sat at took up a small portion of the room. He looked almost comical, his large shoulders and long legs stuffed awkwardly behind a desk that was obviously built for someone shorter than him.

His laptop was open, a few of their retail books and financial papers she'd seen Layla tend to spread haphazardly across the desk. He was leaning on his elbows, his hands in his blond hair. The fluorescent light of the room made his green eyes shine through the blurry image of the screen, reflected in his brown glasses that were so low they were almost falling off his nose.

not drastically so. I would say this is normal for an independent business in a small town. But I'm not sure if our daily sales are enough..."

He gave her a boyish grin. "You seem to know what you're doing, too."

"I took a few business classes myself in college," she said, shrugging, her voice already on the defense. But when she glanced at Page, she realized he hadn't said it in a way that implied he was shocked. He sounded almost relieved. So she relaxed her shoulders and continued. "I always wanted to open a store like this one, but it's tough to do so in a city like LA. And... I never really thought of moving."

Looking back now, she didn't really know why that was. She guessed she had just gotten... stuck. Her life back in LA, living with Ripley, was good. But the more she stayed here in Scotland, the more she wondered if LA was really the best place for her.

"You might be right, though..." Page moved his chair again, this time closer, pulling the laptop towards him. "I'm not sure our daily sales would be enough to keep us afloat in the long run. We'll be fine for a few months, but the store might be in danger if we don't hit the Christmas sales quota."

He ran a hand over his face and groaned. The room had been so quiet with just the two of them that the sound startled Charlie, making her move back and look at him. He had bags under his eyes, and his gaze was full of worry and... anxiety?

It was situations like this, with people like Page—new acquaintances she was getting to know and understand—where it was extremely hard for her to read expressions.

"Lilian might be right," he said under his breath, his eyes flitting between the screen and her face. His voice pulled her out of her head. She had been studying him intently, so much so she had zoned out. She felt her cheeks heat up and hoped she wasn't blushing.

"Right about what?" she asked, breathless and suddenly aware of their position. Her hip was against the desk, her calf touching his shin. He was sitting in the chair, looking up at her, their bodies so close that they were breathing the same air.

Charlie's eyes swept down, catching on the muscles of his throat. He swallowed, the action moving her gaze to his chin, to his lips and then finally to his eyes. Charlie always had mixed feelings about looking people in the eyes. Sometimes, it helped her understand someone's thoughts better, but other times, it was just… too much. She often found herself confused, wondering if she was staring too hard or what eye to look at—because it was stupid how people used the phrase, "look into my eyes," when one could really only look at one eye, not both.

But Page's eyes, a stark moss green, made her pause.

He wasn't looking at her eyes or studying her like she was studying him. He was looking down—

At her mouth.

Charlie's palms felt sweaty, her chest tightening as their gaze met again. The air seemed to still around her. She felt as if her entire body was on fire, heat—

Page let out a breath and then—

He moved back.

The movement broke whatever spell had pulled them closer. Charlie felt her fingers start to tap unconsciously against the table, her eyes trying to focus on anything but him—falling on the small scar above his eyebrow as she looked at him from the corner of her eyes. She turned sideways, looking back at the computer, her gaze unfocused. She didn't think she could look into his eyes in this moment. She didn't want to.

What the hell had just happened?

Page cleared his throat, the sound pulling her out of her head. When he spoke, it was as if the last moment hadn't happened. She didn't know how he could do that—move from one thing to another so quickly.

"My sister said that it would be a good idea to do a media coverage of the store," he said, his voice strained.

Had that moment *actually* happened? Or had she imagined it?

Was she finding something in the moment that wasn't there? Was she misreading him? Or had he been about to lean in? Had he been just as close to pulling her mouth to his as she was?

She wasn't sure if she wanted to know. She needed to create space.

Charlie pushed away from the table, moving across the room and pushing herself up to sit on the staff's lunch table instead. She forced her brain to go back to the conversation at hand, her legs swinging underneath her. The movement helped her focus on his words.

"I mean," she said, weighing her words as she spoke, watching for his reaction. "I don't think it would hurt." At her words, his shoulders fell, almost in defeat. She felt her annoyance rise. "Oh, yes, it must be so hard to be famous and share some of that success with others—"

"It's not that I don't want to do it to help the store, but my family and I try our hardest to stay out of the press," he said, his voice heavy with another layer of meaning she had no context to. It made her next comment freeze before she said it. "Putting the store in the paper or asking for media coverage would just pull the press here. It wouldn't be long before they connected it to me, and then they would be swarming the town. It would be good for the store, but—"

"Not good for you," she finished. She saw his shoulders tense.

"Go on, tell me how I'm selfish—"

She hadn't meant for the comment to come out that way. But she understood why he thought she'd meant that. It was something she would imply about him. But something in his voice told her it wasn't really about him, and if it was, it wasn't coming from a selfish place.

"No—I," she paused when he looked up at her, raising a brow. She blew out an annoyed breath. "I didn't mean it that way."

She supposed if anyone near him right now understood the fear and anxiety and need to get away from the press, it was her. Not that Charlie was famous, but since StarCon, she now had a decent idea of how shitty and invasive being in the spotlight could be.

He nodded, the gesture small and sharp, and fell silent, his eyes unfocused on the desk in front of him.

"I'm going to head up," she said, and then, because he looked so small—so... not lonely, but *fragile*, she paused. Since he had arrived, Page had been a pain in her ass; he'd been rude, had interrupted her quiet time, and had completely invaded her alone space, careening into her plans that she had made for these next few months and changing *everything*. But she had never seen him look like this. This Page didn't fit the Jamie Mahone image she had seen in the media and the news.

She almost wanted to stay down here and help—in what way she wasn't sure. But she realized that it wasn't her job to help him. And he hadn't actually done anything to deserve her help.

Charlie was suddenly annoyed with herself. She knew, even if she didn't really want to admit it to herself out loud, that Page was someone who, if she understood him like she wanted to, would never leave her mind—be that good or bad.

Seeing him down here, seeing that fear of recognition, had strangely eaten away at the idea that he was untouchable, and that made her want to run.

She nodded, sending him a small smile before heading upstairs. But something made her stay awake in her room until she heard the front door close around midnight and knew he had gone to sleep.

Excerpt from *STARVERSE*: Season 3, Episode 1

CAR BRANDON'S ROOM — NIGHT

CAR sits alone on his bed. The lights are dim. The room is silent. Something is wrong, but he doesn't speak. There is a knock on his door. He waits, hesitates.

> THOREN
> Car… are you alright?

Car doesn't respond. He looks at the door, looks back down. We hear Thoren move away from the door.

> CAR
> (TO HIMSELF)
> Confused, Ren, I'm confused.

Chapter 11
Page

What the fuck was that? Page thought to himself as he lay in bed.

After Charlie had left him alone in the back room, he had spent the next three hours looking deeper at the store's finances. But he hadn't gotten any work done. Instead, he had been doing the one thing he knew he shouldn't—thinking about Charlie.

Gandalf the White jumped up on the bed, curling up on his chest and pulling Page out of his head and into the moment. He had been lying awake for the past hour, and even though he had things to do in the morning, he knew he wouldn't be getting much sleep tonight.

There was no way. Not after what had happened—

Almost happened. In the back room.

Gandalf meowed, nudging his head against Page's chest.

He sighed. "Yeah, buddy." He scratched the cat's ears. "I know, I'm screwed." When the cat started to purr, he spoke to the dark room again and said the one thing he had been replaying in his head for the past few hours. "Do *you* know why I almost kissed her tonight, GW?" he asked, looking at the cat with narrowed eyes. "She's the last woman I should kiss." At the cat's blank, happy look, he sighed. "Yeah, she is pretty interesting though." Because even if she got under his skin, jumped to conclusions, and assumed the worst about him, there still was a part of him that was attracted to her. Annoyingly.

His mind went to the call at the beginning of summer. He had one job in the next few months. Stay out of the press. No stories. Say what they want, do what they want. Stay away from anyone or anything that could bring the show some bad press.

He knew that the showrunners had been talking to the entire cast during the call, but a part of him knew there was extra pressure on him. He was the lead, the show's "golden boy". He hated that they called him that, knowing that the show's story would be lost without all the other cast members. But he also knew there was always more pressure on him and Sandhya because their characters were the two leads. People expected him to be just as perfect as his character was on screen.

He almost rolled his eyes at the thought. He was so far away from the character he played. He found it sad how so many people around the world thought that he and his character were so similar. But then again… he supposed that it was his fault. Jamie Mahone was close to Car Brandon. Jamie Mahone, the actor that the world knew… was a part he had created, a façade to get away from the anxiety caused by the press, the anxiety of showing his true self to millions who would judge him.

Page remembered when he had gotten the job. It had been out of the blue, an audition he hadn't even thought he would get a callback for. But somehow, they had loved him. When they cast him, it'd been a whirlwind. And when his first paycheck came in, it'd been a relief. His mother and stepfather weren't bad with money, but he could now make them comfortable. He wouldn't have to worry about them or Lilian. He could help Lilian pay for her school, even if it was much cheaper than the one he had gone to years earlier in the States. He had finally felt like he was helping his family. Not just reminding them of his twin. Not just reminding them of all the pain that had happened *before*.

But now… he didn't want to stay under the radar. Honestly, the last couple of weeks before he came home had felt stifling. He was sick of how much weight seemed to be on his shoulders at all times—how he was always scared that his manager and agent wouldn't do their jobs and the press would start to hound him. He loved acting, loved film, loved his job, loved working with his fellow actors… well, not everyone, but most of them. He loved the feeling that came over him when he stepped onto a set, loved the feeling of success and magic he felt when he got his lines right or when the chemistry between him and another actor just *clicked*.

But the life that came along with it? It was a life he'd never thought he would have after Anna had died, not since the press had hounded him and his mother after his dad had stolen Anna away in a rage one night and their car had crashed on one of the bridges north of Stonehaven.

Local journalists had called it the story of the year. He could still remember the loud sounds outside their home, shouts and sounds he hadn't understood. He'd been so young. It wasn't until later, after he'd been in therapy for a few years, that he had understood. His life, his grief and pain, had become their possible success. All they needed was one picture, one statement, one moment with him. Because he was the son. The son of the man who had killed himself and his daughter. He was the *twin brother*.

It had taken him way too long to get over the panic attacks that started every time he heard a camera click. Or the panic that settled in his chest when he had to push through a crowd. It had gotten better in secondary school, but he'd still hated things that seemed simple to others—grad and prom photos, social media, personal questions, and introductions. The only thing that made everything better was how the town had rallied around him and his mother. They'd supported and taken care of them both.

So, when he'd gotten the job, it had been an easy decision to try and stay out of the press as much as possible, even though his career usually called for the opposite. But now... with everything going on at the store and with... with Charlie...

He no longer wanted to play it safe. And *that* was what scared him.

He wanted to know what made her laugh, what she wanted to do, how she liked her coffee, and why she took walks on the beach. Page wanted to get to *know* her. Even if it seemed like she wanted nothing to do with him. Though, after tonight, maybe he was wrong. When they'd been downstairs, she hadn't immediately assumed the worst of him. He didn't know why, but maybe she was just as intrigued by him as he was by her.

But he couldn't risk it. Not just because of his anxiety, not because he still didn't even know if she wanted to get to know *him*—but because of the show. He still needed the show. What would he be without the person he had created through *StarVerse*? Where would he be now? Where would his family be? He knew that StarVerse was successful, but there was never a guarantee that he would get another job as secure as this one.

Page needed to stay out of trouble for the next few months.

He needed to stay away from *her*... which now seemed impossible.

He groaned and held up the cat, glaring into Gandalf's knowing face. "How am I supposed to stay away when she is literally in the other room?" he asked before rolling his eyes at the look the cat shot him.

"I know, GW, I know... We're screwed."

Chapter 12
Charlie

Charlie woke up early. She always tried to wake up around eight, but some days were just harder than others, especially if she was dealing with burnout. However, since leaving the States, she had felt her burnout regressing. It pulled away from her mind slowly, and she was now functioning a bit better than she had after StarCon. But she still found herself having days that were hard; days where her bed seemed better than the real world.

Today was a good day. She could feel it. When Layla had offered to take her to the castle, she'd been wary at first. Her emotional state had not exactly been stable since Page had showed up, but she knew that, in theory, she needed to get out more. And now that she was out of her bed, out of her room, she couldn't help but be excited. She had just been shocked when Layla had suggested that they go together.

That was one thing she'd always had trouble with—discerning whether or not someone thought of her as a friend. When she was younger, she'd considered someone a friend after one conversation. However, after a few years in school, she had learned very quickly that was not normal for people. Learning all the subtle social cues and rules had given her so much anxiety that she hadn't talked to anyone other than the teachers inside and outside of classes for a good six months. It was something that so many people took for granted, and something that she always worried about. She wasn't naturally shy, but she had become shy in high school just so that she wouldn't come off wrong or get stared at and labeled the "weird one".

That anxiety always came back when she met new people.

She wasn't quite sure where her new friendship with Layla fell, but she knew that she wanted to get to know her better. She'd been spending most of her time with her and Page, and she had discovered that Layla was someone who liked to stay busy. When she wasn't working at the bookstore, she was babysitting for families in the town, visiting her boyfriend in Aberdeen, setting time aside to call her younger brother who had just started uni at Durham University in Physics. Charlie had found out after she'd caught Layla on the phone with her brother, Austin, that Layla was a hidden science genius, having majored in Chemistry and Physics before graduating last year. She'd also found out that she liked to tutor at the local secondary school whenever students needed help before the end of year exams. She was present in the community, which was evident whenever a local customer came in and lit up with joy when they saw her.

But Layla wasn't the only relationship that was causing her anxiety.

She had gathered that Page liked to rise early in the morning. He seemed to be out of the apartment before she headed to work at nine, and only came back after she had already gone upstairs. But today, even though she assumed he would be ready to go as usual, his coffee cup wasn't sitting in the sink like it normally was. Instead, she heard the distinct sound of scratching against his door, and instantly knew he had slept through his alarm and forgotten to let Gandalf out of his room.

Charlie walked over to his door, turning the handle slowly as to make as little noise as possible, and pushed it open. Gandalf streaked by her, a white blur with a loud and unhappy *meoooow* as he made his way over to his food and water bowls in the kitchen.

The room was still dark as she peered her head in to see if Page was still asleep. He was, his body contorted around a pillow, the comforter twisted between his legs. She flushed as she saw his body in the low light. He was sleeping in his boxers and T-shirt, his arms curled around his head and face. His bicep bulged, the muscles in his back shifting as he groaned in his sleep and moved to cover his eyes. He was relaxed, still asleep. And...

And now Charlie felt like a stalker.

Charlie quickly backed up and closed the door. Flashes of last night came back to her as she walked into the kitchen. The way his eyes had tracked her lips, the brush of his blond hair against his forehead and glasses. His jaw tightening as he had moved away.

Gandalf meowed at her again, and she glared at him. "Give me one second, you tiny monster. I need to make myself some coffee before I give you your food."

He sent her a look that told her he was not impressed and curled up on the armrest of one of the leather armchairs. Thirty minutes later, she had fed Gandalf, downed a cup of coffee, and gone out to get some breakfast from one of the local coffee shop, Joe's, down the street. Layla was supposed to pick her up around ten, so she still had a bit of time. Today was their day off, the store being closed once a week on Sundays. When she got back, noise in the kitchen filtered to their front door, letting her know Page was finally awake.

"Oh, you're up," she said, dropping her bag by the front door and hanging up her coat. "I got some food from Joe—"

She cut off as she took him in. He had obviously just woken up, his hair standing up in different directions. He was in boxer briefs and a tight shirt with the *StarVerse* logo on it. His glasses were low on his nose, a cup of coffee in his hand.

Charlie almost choked on her own spit. He looked like every nerd's sexy dream. Her eyes traveled down and—

Why were men's thighs so sexy? And—

127

God, she needed to look away.

"Oh, good, you got food," he said, yawning and pushing his hair back with his free hand. "Give me five, and then we can get going."

Charlie, finally pulling out of her lust-filled stupor, froze.

"What?" she asked, looking at him as if he had just suggested they take off their clothes and run naked in the street.

Page paused, looking at her, and then his eyes widened, a small smirk forming on his lips. She hated those lips.

No, she didn't. But right now, she hated them.

"Did you not check your phone?" he asked, and then, without another word, went back into his room.

Charlie quickly shuffled to drop the small bags of pastries on the counter, pulling her phone out of her back pocket to find a string of text messages.

Layla
Hey love! I woke up with a sore throat, so Idk if I'll be able to make it today!

Layla
But you should still go without me!

Layla
Just checked with Page, and he said he was free! I hope you two have fun! *winky face emoji*

Then there was a text from Lilian.

Lilian
Have fun at the castle today! Side note, Page hates taking photos, so... give him hell.

Charlie couldn't help but wonder if they'd planned this. She leaned against the counter, her hands falling at her sides. She was alone, all except for Gandalf, who was looking at her from where he sat on the kitchen counter. This was supposed to be her day *away* from Page. And now, he was, what... her tour guide? Charlie flushed as an image of Page in the living room moments before flashed in her brain.

"Rule three, Gandalf," she whisper-hissed at him. "You're supposed to remind me of rule three."

The cat stared back at her blankly.

The Rivals
ThisBisexualLovesStarVerse

Hello there. Here is the next chapter in my *STARVERSE* AU, where they are all in high school! We left off with Asmor and Car fighting for the attention of Valeri in their lacrosse game. Rivals... the tension! Let's see where we are now. Just a reminder that Asmor, in my fanfic, is autistic, and Thoren has ADHD, Valeri is also nonbinary. So be respectful in the comments, please! Also, I have a petition in my bio to get Killian Glass to publicly apologize to Charlie James because how he's been acting is complete and utter shit. Okay... see you next week! Enjoy!

"You're going down, Brandon," Asmor said, sweat dripping from his forehead. He was exhausted, his lacrosse uniform was too tight, and the lights from the field were making his eyes hurt. But all that mattered, in this very moment, was the game.

All that mattered was Brandon. If he couldn't beat Brandon here, why would Valeri choose him off the field?

"We'll see, Asmor," Brandon said, rolling his eyes. Fury sparked in Asmor's gut, making him grit his teeth. This man was the worst of them—showy, perfect teeth, blond hair, an asshole. Except, of course, you had to add the perfect accent from his boarding school in the UK. No wonder all the girls were floundering at his feet.

Chapter 13
Page

After a rushed breakfast and another twenty minutes spent in his room getting ready and wondering why the fuck he was doing this, they grabbed the bus from the middle of town. Charlie, who was usually put together perfectly, with her confidence and comfortability shining in the bookstore, was more subdued today, her smile more cautious. Since he'd woken up, he'd noticed she seemed off. But instead of saying anything, because he didn't quite think they were at that stage in their... relationship... he bought their tickets and followed her to their seats at the back of the bus.

He was off today, too, because all his plans—he had hoped to go and spend the day helping Callum at the house—had been changed last minute when his sister and Layla had forced him to take Charlie to the castle.

Well, not forced. But basically. Lilian knew he couldn't say no to her, and Layla had taken advantage of this. And maybe, just maybe, there was a small part of him (very small) that wanted to spend time with Charlie after last night, just to see if their dynamic was changing for the better.

They were lucky that they had decided to go on a Sunday. Saturdays, he knew, especially during the summer, were busy. Dunnottar Castle was just far enough from Aberdeen and Edinburgh that it might not get packed with tourists, but it still drew a lot of people, either brave enough to rent a car or smart enough to take the train along the east coast.

From their seats in the back, Page watched the other people. There was a young couple up front, a few solo travelers, a group of fifteen-year-old girls, and a small family of four—the two kids playing with their iPads while their dads talked animatedly, their eyes never leaving their children. Charlie, who had taken the window seat to his right, had her headphones over her ears, her eyes distractedly watching the landscape out of the window. He had seen her scrunch up her nose at the noise when they'd started driving, not commenting when she dug out her headphones.

And since they had barely spoken a full sentence to each other since they'd left, he had decidedly kept his questions to himself.

Page would like to say that he was knowledgeable about autism and its traits, but he wasn't. No one in his family was autistic, but his younger cousin had been diagnosed with ADHD when he was fifteen. Since his parents' marriage, he had always been close with Lilian's side of the family, their cousins, aunts and uncles always spending Christmas with them. He remembered how relieved and scared his cousin had seemed after his diagnosis. And now, just a few years later, he was thriving. John's diagnosis had not only been good for him but for their entire family. It had opened up so many discussions about neurodivergence and ableism in their family, home life, and society in general. It hadn't been smooth sailing, but now, he couldn't help but see his family as being all the better for it—being better at communicating with one another.

Since the StarCon fiasco, he'd been doing research online and instantly picked up on the divide between the broader psychological field and the Actually Autistic community—made of public speakers, influencers, and online and in-person educators. But being around Charlie—*living* with Charlie—he had started to pick up on her routines. Because no matter how much he tried to pretend she wasn't there, there was something about her that called his attention whenever she walked into a room.

He noticed when a noise was bothering her and she needed her headphones. He noticed how routine before bed seemed to be something that calmed her. He noticed how, sometimes, when she was stressed, her OCD became overwhelming and she turned her lights off and on multiple times. He noticed how she would pull on a jacket, scrunch up her nose slightly and then change it because of the feeling of the fabric against her arms.

He noticed everything.

They were small things. Small things that sometimes impacted him, and sometimes didn't at all. Once he had started recognizing them, however, he'd made sure to make a mental log, changing his actions if they seemed to trigger her. All of society asked her to change for them. The very least he could do was give her a space where he was the one who would change to help accommodate her needs.

Especially after everything that had happened.

Taking his sunglasses off, he pulled the ball cap lower on his face and burrowed into his jacket. He could feel where his arm was touching hers; could feel her tense slightly but not pull away. He knew there wasn't a lot of space for her to move, but she hadn't even shifted. Page was hyperaware of her as he tried to shut off his brain. Charlie's anxiety hadn't been the only thing joining them on their journey today. His own anxiety had decided this was a good day for adventure, a common occurrence whenever he went outside or left Stonehaven.

What if someone recognized him today? What if someone took a picture of him? Or worse, what if they recognized Charlie and took a picture of them together?

These were all valid anxieties that had been plaguing him since he'd gotten home and found her in his sister's apartment. But this morning, when he'd seen the pure, naïve excitement on her face, all mixed with the anxiety of going out on her own to a new place, Page had known he couldn't let her down. Before his sister had convinced him, more like coerced him, there had been a small part of him ready to tell Charlie that he wasn't feeling well. But she'd already been up and dressed, so ready to go out and go on her adventure that he hadn't been able to get the words out of his mouth. It had nothing to do with how the morning light had fallen into her eyes or how the freckles on her face had made him want to spend an hour counting them. For some reason, even if she hated him, a small part of him wanted to prove to Charlie that she was wrong about her original sentiments towards him.

He didn't like that he was feeling this way.

Page sighed, his mind going back, once again, to the first time he had seen her. She'd been wearing a monstrous red wig, her tight white shirt with a heart and Spiderman in the middle making her cosplay obvious. Looking back, he wasn't sure what drew him to Charlie. But since that first sighting, there had been something about her that stuck in his brain.

He slipped his earphones into his ears and hit play on the playlist Sandhya had made him soon after they had become friends. She was obsessed with making Spotify playlists for every occasion and every friend, which he quickly found out was one of Sandhya's true talents—understanding a person through music. Sometimes, when he was writing, he would have her make a playlist for whatever project he was working on.

Page scoffed to himself. Not that he was working on anything lately. Since college, Page had loved writing. Mostly scripts. He'd known from a young age that he loved film; he'd known the industry was where he wanted to pursue work. However, it had taken him a while to figure out which avenue he wanted to work in.

Acting had, surprisingly, been his last choice, his first being screenwriting. But when he got the job on *StarVerse*, an audition his roommate had suggested he go on, his free time had gone completely out the window. The job was challenging—he had to be in a specific fit shape, learn the fight choreography, and work directly with a personal trainer. Then there were the premieres, the cons, the shows, *all* of the publicity. When he got home after being on set all day, sometimes all he could do was fall into bed.

Not that he didn't have a project going. He always had a project going. But he hadn't been able to sit and write for long enough periods of time to get anything concrete down on the page. Maybe this break was an opportunity for him to do that. If he had time when he wasn't helping Callum on the house.

Young the Giant started playing in his ears, and he focused on the words, willing his mind to calm for the rest of the drive. The song reminded him of the time Sandhya had forced him to listen to the band's entire first album during one of their slow days on set, and he couldn't help but feel a small smile slip onto his face as he closed his eyes.

Celebrity Talk Show Excerpt
A Year Ago

Host #1: You know, Karen, it's just so sad to see a man like him, you know what I mean, without a good girl on his arm at those premieres. Jamie Mahone is just too pretty for his own good, it seems.

Host #2: Well, at least until then, his fans and us married women can have our own fantasies without him being taken.

Host #1: Yes, but I know we, as well as some other fans, do wonder if there is more to our new favorite Scottish Hottie than just his looks. The man is tight-lipped about his personal life, something that makes the fans even more ravenous for more information on him.

Chapter 14

Charlie

The bus ride lasted about fifteen minutes. Fifteen minutes of pure torture.

Maybe it was the sound of the engine or the bouncing rhythm of the bus on the small winding roads, but Charlie's senses were overwhelmed within seconds. She was glad that Page seemed to be in his own small bubble for the ride. If he had wanted to talk, she would have sorely disappointed him. That, and she wasn't quite sure how to talk to him today. It was a rare moment—especially with someone she had recently met—where there was a period of silence that her brain didn't feel like she needed to fill. But she could tell she wasn't the only one who had been a bit off since their journey had begun.

When they stepped off the bus and onto the small roadside bus stop, she exhaled a sigh of relief, stuffing her headphones into her backpack and pulling out a stick of mint gum. Gum *always* helped. It was a stim that seemed to keep her mind and anxiety on track and wasn't as obvious as pulling out a small stim toy—even though she had brought one with her just in case she needed it. And right now, surrounded by strangers getting off the bus and by Page, who was the weirdest combination of a stranger and... not a *friend*, but an acquaintance, she didn't feel like stimming in a way that was obvious.

Page had been silent since they had stepped on the bus. He had sent her a cautious smile, his sunglasses sliding down his nose a bit. Without seeing his eyes, she couldn't tell if the smile was genuine, but his body language seemed tense. He had changed the moment they'd left the apartment, she realized. It was like he put a filter over himself when he went out. Yet this was not the movie star mask that made people fall at his feet. Instead, it felt like he was actively trying to disappear.

She instantly hated it and wanted to do anything she could to make him feel safe enough to rip the mask off and throw it in the trash.

It was a feeling that came out of nowhere. One she needed to squash.

She scowled and pulled her beanie lower on her head as she rushed to catch up with Page. His legs were much longer than hers, and she had to quicken her pace to keep up with him.

"Okay, you promised me a castle and," she glanced around them, her hands sweeping around her, "there is no castle in sight. All I see is the sea and lots of green fields." There were fields as far as her eyes could see, bracketing the small road in green parentheses made of grass and weeds. A small road wound off the main highway—or what Page insisted was a highway, though, to Charlie's knowledge, it was one of the smallest two-way streets she had ever seen—winding its way to their right and towards the coast. "And sheep," she added, pointing at the multiple white fluff balls that moved slowly in the tall glass around them. "There seems to always be sheep in Scotland, though."

Page huffed out a laugh. "There are actually more sheep than people."

Charlie's laugh startled out of her. "No way," she said, and at Page's loose grin, she felt a sense of triumph.

He lowered his gaze, tipping his sunglasses down his nose so their eyes could meet. In the midday sun, his eyes shone a bright moss green. "Do you doubt the Scottish-born man standing next to you? Somehow, I doubt your American knowledge of my country wins against my own."

Charlie pointedly looked out at the sheep, ignoring him, and wondered if she and Page could go ten minutes without getting annoyed with each other.

When Page headed towards the small road, she followed, their feet slapping the pavement in tandem. It was cold today, but not so much that Charlie found herself shivering. The sun was out, the clouds disappearing for the first time in a week, and a harsh breeze blew around them, lifting her hair around her shoulders as they walked. They passed a small house, a mother and a young boy playing by the swing set. She couldn't imagine growing up in a small cottage like this, right on the coast, next to a castle.

It might even sound foolish, but this was really the first moment she'd acknowledged she was living in another country. Even though the apartment, town and bookstore were all so different from her life back home, going out to the coast, to this new place, made her brain center enough to acknowledge that she had taken that jump to *live in another country* for a few months. Something she never thought she would do.

It took a few more minutes of walking along the road, a car passing them, before she saw the sign. Not even the castle, but the small sign pointing to the tiny parking lot for castle tourism.

Charlie clapped her hands and tried to ignore how the deep chuckle that emanated from Page's chest affected her. Butterflies flapped their wings in her chest, excitement filling her bones and pushing her body forward. Passing a small coffee cart and picnic tables, they made their way to a long dirt walkway. It wasn't long before she saw it.

The castle, which Page informed her had been built as early as the 1300s, sat precariously on the cliff edge. The ruins were tall, the stone reflecting a brownish grey in the misty landscape. It looked like something out of a fantasy novel. Charlie couldn't keep the smile off her face. Her family had never really had the money to spend on traveling, and sometimes it was easy for her to get caught up in everyday life, falling into the comfort of staying in her apartment. But moments like this one reminded her of why she needed to travel. Why she needed to see the world. It was for moments, for views, like this one. The path led them to a long set of stairs that sloped downwards towards a cove and then arched upwards onto the cliff and into the castle.

They took their time, heading to the castle first. Page paid the small fee for them to enter, and they spent the next hour exploring every crevice of the remaining castle. As they walked, the wind started to blow around them, and the irritated feeling Charlie had been trying to suppress rose up inside her.

"Are you okay?" Page asked, looking at her from where he was standing. Charlie paused, realizing they had stopped to look at the castle and that she'd been shaking her hands and bouncing on the soles of her feet. She stopped immediately, her smile shutting down.

"Yeah."

"Did I say something—"

"No, it's fine."

"Obviously, it's not."

Charlie sighed, her arms crossing over her chest. "I was stimming. I do that when I'm excited or nervous. Clearly, it bothers you, so—"

"Woah, hey, I never said it bothers me." His voice had turned low, serious. But not... not angry.

Charlie frowned at the ground and started to walk away. "You didn't need to."

Page blew out an exasperated breath. But Charlie was already running. Not physically, but in her mind. Running as far away as she possibly could, away from the possibility—from the probable moment of realization where Page would say something offensive, and she wouldn't be able to forget it. She would no longer have the possibility of being safe around him. Or, at least, it would take a while to feel safe around him again.

Charlie paused at the cliff, leaning against the wooden fence that lined the edge. She looked out at the castle, trying to calm herself, her blood rushing in her ears. Before this moment, she hadn't realized just how much Page's opinion of her, of autism, mattered to her. And now that she saw her reaction, a reaction that very clearly meant he did matter to her in some way—that he had some kind of power over her emotions—she wanted to crawl in a hole and never come out.

"Hey." He jogged to catch up with her, his voice cutting into her panic. He paused next to her, his body close and facing her instead of the view. She could feel his eyes on her, the weight heavy and hot. His hand came up to touch her wrist, but he paused at the last moment, as if his brain thought better of it, before finally lightly grabbing her wrist. The pads of his fingers were rough, his fingers a harsh contrast of heat compared to the cold wind around them. She looked over finally. Charlie had to fight the urge to cover his hand with hers, to try and soak in the warmth from where his fingers touched her. He let go.

She caught a glimpse of his finger and thumb rubbing together before he shoved his hands in his pockets.

"I'm sorry if I upset you. The bouncing didn't bother me. I just didn't know if you were stressed or not." He waited a moment, studying her as if awaiting her reaction. Charlie wasn't sure what was on her face because she didn't know what she was feeling. He continued. "You can, you know, do it around me if you want."

A darkly amused grin flitted onto her face and then disappeared. "I know that I can stim wherever I want. I don't need your seal of approval."

"Shit," Page said under his breath before stepping closer. "That's not what I meant. I just—I..." He paused, as if struggling to find the right words. "I have panic attacks. I deal with anxiety, and you're safe here. I don't know everything, but I'm... willing to learn."

Charlie wanted to believe him. The last person she had trusted, though, had been Jacob. And Jacob had stomped all over her trust. Before that, her previous girlfriend had *tried* to understand. But they'd broken up before they'd gotten deeply

141

into the emotional side of their relationship.

Charlie did her best to study him. She could see a small crack in his mask now. And even though she was going to be hesitant, she didn't want to be someone who couldn't trust again. Because then people like Jacob would win.

Charlie nodded and tried for a smile. A few seconds later, Page's answering smile melted the rest of the frost between them.

They'd been walking around in a comfortable silence until she took the camera out of her bag. Charlie had brought her old canon that used film instead of digital. She swore she saw Page's entire body tense.

"No," he said, as she brought the camera up to her eye, grinning. Before she could take a photo, his hand came up to stop her, ruining the shot. She let the camera drop, raising a brow at him. The air around them was misty, the morning's fog still receding from the coastline. Little drops of dew had fallen into Page's hair and forehead, and Charlie watched as one drop moved from his forehead, down his nose, and onto his cheek.

She forcibly looked away and waved at the landscape around them. "It's beautiful here. Please, let me take some photos?" A part of her had been scared to pick up a camera in the past six months, her burnout taking hold, and this was the first time she had felt that small spark of *something* asking her to put a lens up to her eyes.

"Oh, you can take photos," Page said, shoving his hands into his jean pockets. He had pulled on a light grey sweater over his jeans and a white button-down, the collar just peeking through the wool around his neck. "Just not of me." His scowl almost rivaled her own.

She could almost hear Ripley in her head commenting on how their stubbornness matched one another's.

Charlie held back a sigh. She saw his hesitance and paused, looking over at him, trying to read his expression, which was near impossible. "I promise these photos won't go anywhere. It's film, not digital." She gave him her best puppy dog eyes, and she saw his glare, his look of disbelief, and then the very moment she had cracked him. His hand came up to push back his hair, a laugh breaking out of his chest before he conceded.

"Fine. But I have every right to delete them when you're done."

Charlie held up the camera, a smirk on her face. "Film camera."

His eyes narrowed, but a small smile stayed on his lips. "Burn, then."

At her horrified expression, he laughed, turning to walk one of the other paths closest to them. Charlie jogged forward, grabbing his wrist. Page froze, and she tried her best to give him a look of seriousness. "I promise that the photos won't go anywhere, and if you really aren't comfortable, I won't take any photos of you."

Page looked her in the eyes, and she did her best not to look away and hold his gaze, to let him know that he could trust her. Finally, he nodded. "Okay," he said and grinned softly when she let out a *whoop* of joy.

With a few groans and whining when she told him to stop for a moment while she lined up a shot, she was able to get a few pictures of Page, his hat off, his hair blowing around in the wind. There was one of him leaning against a stone wall, looking off at the sea, another where he walked away from her, and one on the bench, leaning forward as he stared at his hands. As they got closer to seeing all that was left of the castle, the wind became fiercer, and Charlie could feel her cheeks starting to get windburned. In the photos that Page took of her, she was sure her cheeks would be bright red, her curly hair blowing around her head and face, her hands burrowed into the pockets of the new fleece she had gotten online the week she'd arrived.

Page stood at one of the broken walls, the wind blowing his hair, and she raised her camera, lining up a portrait shot, but she paused before taking the photo. She felt her breath stop in her chest when he looked her way and smiled. She snapped the photo.

"Come on," he said, turning back to her. "The best part is the actual ruins." And with that, he walked off. She hurried after him, taking in the old stonework. They moved up into the old rooms formerly used by the owners, the ceiling now gone. An older couple stood to their left, a family to their right. She moved out of the way as two kids ran by her, the rest of the family calling out and following. She raised her camera again.

"Do you want me to take a photo of you both?" Charlie paused, looking to see the older woman. She had a smile on her face as she looked between them. "You two are such a lovely couple." Charlie knew Page mirrored her look of awkward panic.

"Oh, we aren't—" Page started, but the woman just clucked her tongue and shook her head.

"Couple or not, let me take a photo."

Charlie grinned and handed over the camera but froze at Page's scowl. Was he mad? Should she stop this? Should—Page rolled his eyes and turned to the woman.

"That would be lovely, thank you."

Charlie felt a little bit of warmth seep into her limbs. She looked over at the woman, "Do you know—"

"I used one of these cameras when I was your age," the woman said, lifting an eyebrow. "I think I know how to use this better than one of your video phones."

Charlie held back a laugh at Page's raised brows. He still had his hat and sunglasses on. As she moved closer to him, she could feel his eyes on her.

"Just suck it up, she's nice," she said under her breath.

"Get closer, you two," the woman sent a grin that looked way too similar to the one Ripley gave her when she was scheming. Charlie made a note to tell Ri that she looked like a scheming old woman the next time she saw her. She had a feeling Ripley would take it as a compliment. She could feel Page's annoyance coming off him in waves as they scooted a bit closer.

"*Closer*," the woman said, waving a hand at this. She had a thick, southern American accent that sounded out of place in the Scottish castle ruins. "This isn't the sixteenth century."

Charlie failed at holding in her giggle, especially when Page grumbled something about how he wished he were in a different century or anywhere else. He moved, his arm sliding around her waist. She tried not to jump when his fingers brushed against her lower back. His touch was electric, even through the layered fleece and sweater. When he pulled her in, she stumbled a bit, her hands coming up to stop on his chest. His hand rested on the top of her hip, and she tried not to squirm.

"Sorry," she said quietly. He radiated body heat, and when she looked up, she could feel his eyes on her, even though she couldn't see them through the glasses.

A small grin appeared on his face, and she almost scowled but covered it. "It's fine, she's nice."

Charlie looked up at him, studying his face. She felt him pull her a bit closer.

"Smile, dears!" She heard the camera click.

Charlie pulled herself away, turning to thank the women, and after she said her goodbyes, she turned to find Page gone. She stood still for a moment, frowning. He had run off.

Excerpt from *STARVERSE*: Season 2, Episode 10

SHIP'S OBSERVATION DECK — NIGHT

VALERI sits with CARYS. She's just joined the ship, and the men left the room after a fight.

VALERI
I've learned that no matter if they are alien or human, men are always idiots.

CARYS
You can say that again.

Chapter 15
Page

He knew he had run away. He could at least admit that to himself. But he also knew that, if he'd had her in his arms for one more second, he would have done something extremely stupid.

They were in public, for fuck's sake. And Charlie was right, he had been a bit of an asshole to the older woman, but—

But...

His brain had malfunctioned when his arm had wrapped around her, his hand gliding over her lower back, resting on her hip. Even through the layers of jumper and fleece, he had felt her curves as he'd stupidly pulled her against him. Her body against his, the way her curves felt against the side of his body— he could still feel the heat of her on him as he walked.

He had run. Because, of course, that was what he did best.

Page cursed under his breath and froze when a mother and child walked by. The mother glared at him, and he did his best not to wince.

Again, he reminded himself, you are in public. Act like it. He took off his ball cap and ran his hands through his hair. In the dungeons, where he had escaped to, the wind wasn't as fierce, but it still seeped in through the age-old cracks and tiny

147

windows.

He stood there, his hands in his pockets, rocking back on his heels, and frowned, taking the moment to get his thoughts in order. Boundaries. They had established boundaries and he needed to follow them. Because whatever had happened back in the office last night, and in that… that *moment*, could not happen again.

Page turned, moving towards the doorway, but as he stepped through, a small body smacked into him. His hands came forward to catch the person. Brown curls, the smell of vanilla.

Charlie.

He hated that he knew what she smelled like. But how could he not? The entire flat smelled like her. Which made sense since she'd been living there for a few weeks before his arrival. But the fact still bothered him. Because how could he relax, even in a flat he called a second home, when it constantly smelled like her?

"Oh," she said, sounding almost out of breath. He did not need to know what she sounded like when she was winded. "There you are," she said, looking up at him with a wry grin. "I was starting to think you'd been abducted by aliens."

The statement made him pause. "Abducted… by aliens?"

She shrugged. "Weirder things have happened."

"Have they?" He realized then that his hands were still on her waist, just as she seemed to realize that her hands were on his chest. The air between them stilled. He froze. How did this keep on happening? Was the universe playing one big joke on him?

He let her go, pushing himself back quickly, almost tripping over one of the large stones that made up the floor beneath them. They both looked somewhere else, and he cleared his throat.

"Well," she said, breaking the silence. He looked at her then and noticed a small flush on her cheeks and neck. He had put that there. When it slowly faded, he realized he wanted to put that flush in her cheeks again and see how far down her body it went—

No, Page. He almost yelled the words. No. No. NO.

He thought of anything else. The castle. The wind. Sheep. The look on his agent and manager's faces when he told them about Charlie—

That threw him out of his funk. He felt his shoulders stiffen and did his best to fit a calm smile onto his face. "Come on, there's a lot more to see."

He saw her hesitate, but he was already moving out of the room before she responded.

"I'd like to see all of it if we can," she said, and for some reason, the words made something in him relax a bit. He wasn't sure how she did it.

"Me too."

Chapter 16
Charlie

After they'd seen all of the castle, Page insisted on taking her down to the beach. It was rocky, nowhere near the sandy, bright beaches of LA. Rocks and harsh cliffside, mixed with a few nesting birds and dark opaque water, made for a picturesque landscape that took her breath away. They climbed the rocks, checking the small pools for crabs before walking down to the far edge of the beach so they could have lunch. Laying out a long towel, Charlie pulled out the makeshift sandwiches they'd made, along with the bottles of water they'd brought from home.

They had fallen into a nice silence, Charlie staring over the water, her brain hyper-fixating on the food, when Page spoke.

"So," he said, pulling her out of her head. "Who are we going to be angry at first? Layla or Lilian? Because we both know that Layla is not sick, and this was totally a scheme to get us to get along."

Charlie's hand came up to her chest, and she said in a mocking tone, "Why, Page, we don't get along?" His look said he didn't find it amusing. Charlie held in a snort. "I would say this is totally your sister's fault, but I've seen the scheming glint Layla gets in her eyes when she wants to match a customer with a book. She has matchmaking dreams."

"Personally, I think they're both guilty," he said, staring out at the ocean. There was a moment of silence, followed by, "I'm sorry."

The words were so unexpected that she almost choked on her

sandwich, and Page looked at her with concern. She swallowed and took a sip of water.

"Why?" she asked. She could guess one of many reasons why he was apologizing, but she needed to know exactly why this was happening out of the blue.

Page shrugged. "I should have said that to you the minute I woke up from my mini coma." He ignored the exasperated glare she sent his way. "No, I'm not going to let you forget that," he added before she could interrupt. "But... I guess *things* got in the way."

"Things?" she asked, sputtering. "You mean your asshole personality?"

He looked at her as if he found her amusing. It made her shoulders rise in annoyance. "I was going to say your jerk reaction to assume the worst about me, but sure, we can go with that."

"Oh, so now this entire," she waved her hands around, looking for the right word because 'relationship' seemed too strange to say, "... *thing* is my fault?"

He grinned. "You said it."

Charlie scoffed.

"Getting back to what I was trying to say," he continued and gave her a pointed look that she decided to ignore. They were good at that, ignoring each other's pointed glances. "I'm sorry about what Mark, Jim and Killian did to you. It... it isn't okay. And I guess I'm sorry that I've pissed you off and have been an asshole to you since you arrived," he said, trying to catch her eyes. But she couldn't meet his eyes right now, so she looked out at the ocean instead. He sighed. "I just... well—"

"How do you even work for those assholes?" she asked before the nerve left her. "I don't know if I'd be able to work with them after what they did. Better yet, I really don't understand how someone can say 'no comment' when asked about it all in an interview." She saw Page wince at that. The interview had been short and brief, only a few weeks after the con. To be fair, he had said no comment to all the questions that weren't directly about the new season, but still. No comment. Two words that had been stuck in her chest since she had read them. Stuck and crystalized there with weeks full of anger and resentment. She knew that what had happened was close and emotional to her, but even looking at the entire fiasco from a faraway distance, she couldn't imagine working on the show anymore. The showrunners had played their hand, showing their ableism as clear as day. "And honestly, thanks for the apology, but before you started living with me, against my will, I might add, I didn't even care about your acting, let alone your opinion, so."

She could see the annoyance on his face, maybe even a smidge of anger. But Charlie didn't want to hold back the truth with anyone, and Page was no different.

"One, yeah, I work with those assholes, but since I did sign a contract with them two years ago, I don't really have a choice if I still want a leading role or to make money." His voice was hoarse, filled with a stern determination to get her to listen. But he didn't have to try too hard. She wanted to hear what he had to say. They'd been dancing around, no, fighting around this conversation since he'd arrived. "Two, I can't help that you don't like my job or my acting. Three, I didn't know you were going to be here. If I had known, trust me, I wouldn't have come, and me staying was not *against your will*. If you had said you didn't feel comfortable, I would have left. Four, I always decline to speak to the press. Always. I don't need to tell you why. And *five*, I doubt me saying I'm not an ableist asshole like my co-worker and bosses will appease your feelings, so I guess I'll just have to show you, but no, I do not agree with the way my show handled the situation at all. And for the record, I'm not the only one on the cast who thinks that way."

"Then why—"

He cut her off, knowing exactly what she was going to say. "There are things called NDAs and contracts. We aren't allowed to speak on it. Plus, as I said," he met her gaze, "I never speak to the press unless it's a joint cast interview."

"Hmm," she hummed, staring down at her hands while he went back to his food. It wasn't uncomfortable. It seemed as if they'd gotten the heat of the conversation over with, and now, they were both just sitting in silence… together. She felt the mood change from one of conflict to one of a stalemate. Because she was listening. She knew that, realistically, he seemed to have his reasons. And… she could admit, even if it annoyed her, that they were good reasons. They were still strangers, but not strangers with perceived hatred of one another. Or, really, one-sided perceived hatred.

"Okay," she said. When he looked at her with confusion, she continued. "Okay, I understand why you said, 'no comment'. And I guess I can't exactly hold anything against you for working on the show… It was just… It's been hard to separate you and the show. I've had so much anger because of the things they've said, and it wasn't fair for me to put that on to you. *And*," she said, drawing out the word as if it was painful, "I'm sorry for jumping to conclusions about you and… saying your acting was terrible."

"You said you didn't care about it, not that it was terrible."

"Semantics," she said and then winced when she heard how that came out. What she wasn't expecting was for him to laugh. It started as a chuckle and then developed into a loud belly laugh. He leaned back on his hands, his head falling back. She watched as his shoulders bounced with the movement, his hair falling into his eyes, and his glasses sliding down his nose. She resisted the urge to push them back up.

"You are… definitely different," Page said through his chuckles. "Not in a bad way," he said and paused, thinking over his words. She could almost see the panic turning the wheels of his brain as he thought of what he should say. She decided to throw him a lifeline.

"Calling me different is fine," she said, shrugging. "I know you didn't mean it in a mean way, and," she scrunched up her nose, "there's nothing wrong with being different. I know that now."

"You're right." Page was looking at her intently now, his green eyes stuck on her face. She wrinkled her nose again.

"Stop," she said, and at his raised brow, rolled her eyes and moved so she could grab one of the water bottles. Nerves bounced around in her stomach, moving up and down between her belly and her chest. Maybe this was why she had put off their conversation for so long. It had been a wall between them—a tense wall, but a needed one. Because now that all of it was out in the air, now that they'd both said their piece, the way Page looked at her felt more... real. More present. And that couldn't happen. What she was feeling right now couldn't happen.

It just wasn't smart.

"When were you diagnosed?" His voice pulled her out of her head, and she turned to look at him. It was a question that she hadn't expected but didn't mind. When they'd first *met*—although Charlie wasn't sure if she could call their experience at StarCon a meeting—she'd been an oddity. But now that she knew his stance on everything, she found she felt safe talking about everything with him. There was something calming about his presence that made her shoulders and her mind relax. The way he asked the question, too, made her pause and look at him. There wasn't a hint of judgment in his voice, only pure, innocent curiosity. She could tell he wanted to know so he could know more about *her*.

She finished chewing on her food and then took a drink of water before she answered. "I was nineteen."

"That late?" The shock in his voice made her giggle a bit. She didn't know why it was funny. Maybe it was the dark humor that had bubbled up inside of her. So many people didn't know anything about autism and the diagnosis process, especially when it pertained to femme-presenting people.

"Yeah," she said, scooting closer and facing towards him, her arms wrapping around her knees. "Though it isn't that late, it's actually pretty early. It's normal for femme-presenting people to be diagnosed later in life. Then there is the issue that they didn't really think women could be autistic until recently, and the fact that the traits show up a bit differently in different people because of how we learn to mask and so on."

Page nodded, not in a way that made her seem like he knew everything, but one that told her he was listening. She scratched the back of her neck, suddenly feeling awkward. "But yeah. I was diagnosed halfway through college, and it was a really long process. I self-diagnosed myself first. I read a book, and the experience was written by an autistic author, and I really related to it, and I just knew." She laughed, subconsciously. "I just *knew* that it was right, and then so much around me suddenly made sense, so I reached out to a few different people and got my diagnosis a few months later."

"My cousin has ADHD," he said, taking off his glasses so she could see his whole face. "And he told me something similar. Like, it was always there but was suddenly revealed because he had a name to put to those feelings he couldn't really explain most of his life."

She nodded enthusiastically. "Exactly. But as I'm sure your cousin can tell you, it's not exactly smooth sailing afterwards. There's a ton of shit to work through. Suddenly, you have to explain yourself, and then you deal with how so many people aren't educated about your disability and how shitty society is for people like you. Then, you have to work through your own internalized ableism because we *all* have it. It's a lot to go through after being diagnosed, and I hope your cousin was lucky enough to have his family there because it sucks going through it alone."

Page was silent for a moment, but the weight of his gaze was heavy. Then, "He was lucky. Were you not?"

She shook her head. Her throat felt like it clogged when she tried to look for the right words. But were there even words to describe how hard it had been to deal with her brother? To not have the unquestioned support that she'd desperately needed from her mom?

"No," she said finally, looking out at the water. She knew that if she looked at Page, his gaze would be too much. Too many feelings. "My parents didn't really understand. They saw how I had been *functioning* without my diagnosis and told me it was wrong to call myself disabled when so many other people had it much worse." She heard Page's sound of disgust but pushed on. "My brother…" she shrugged. "We've never been close. He's seven years older than I am, and he always kind of looked down on me. He used to tease me a lot, and my parents would just write it off as brotherly affection, but it got cruel at times. Nothing physical," she added when she noticed Page's clenched jaw. "But still pretty bad. He got worse after my diagnosis, his taunts getting super ableist."

She tried to shrug it off. She hated the emotions that were spilling up and over. She needed to take the attention off her, but she couldn't think of something to ask Page, so she just looked out at the ocean in front of them.

Charlie started when she felt fingertips against her hand. She looked over to find that Page had reached out and covered her hand in his grip. She wondered if he knew that a strong grip was better than a soft touch for her. But she didn't ask him, and she just squeezed back before he pulled his hand away. He seemed to understand that she didn't want more than this in that moment. Most people would have tried to hug her.

But then again, Page wasn't most people, and she wasn't even sure if they were friendly enough to hug one another.

Were they?

God, she hated navigating new relationships.

Not that this was a relationship…

Charlie had learned early on that whenever she put herself out there too early with friendships or relationships, she always ended up screwing them up somehow. She always ended up alone in the end. Ripley was the only exception. Why wouldn't she be scared to put herself out there when she knew that, at some point, whoever she came to love would hurt her? It wasn't like many people understood autism and her, let alone wanted *to* take the time to understand everything. Putting herself out there again made her want to throw up. She wasn't sure how many times she could deal with the rejections.

She knew that she and Page weren't *friends*, but maybe they could call a truce.

"I'm sorry," he said, his voice gruff. "That isn't okay." She thought he was done, but before she could say anything, he resumed. "That's... What happened at StarCon... What people were saying... It was disgusting. You should be proud of who you are. You're strong, resilient, bright, funny, beautiful—" Page cut himself off, and Charlie could have sworn that he was blushing. *Beautiful*. He'd called her beautiful. "I mean, I know I don't know you that well, but...." Page huffed out a laugh, looking off again.

"Thanks," she said, feeling her cheeks flush. She turned her gaze back to the ocean and tried to ignore the heat she felt in her body. "I was lucky enough to have Ripley, though. She always tried to understand and listen." She shrugged. "Sometimes, there are things that neurotypical people can't understand fully, and that's when you just need someone to listen to you."

Page nodded. "I get that. It... I don't know... It sounds like there are similarities with anxiety." Charlie tried her hardest to keep the curiosity off her face, but Page's small grin told her she'd failed. "I was diagnosed with severe anxiety when I was eight. We had some... trauma in the family, and it really impacted me. I was getting anxiety attacks every time I left the house, and I was put on medication. Been on it since. With anxiety, a lot of it isn't rational, so sometimes all you need is someone to listen and *not* tell you how your anxiety isn't making sense to them."

She nodded. She had dealt with anxiety most of her life as well. When she'd been in high school, she'd been diagnosed with anxiety and OCD—a common dual diagnosis that many undiagnosed autistic people were accidentally misdiagnosed with.

Page shrugged. "I was pretty lucky, though, with my mum and stepdad. Lilian, too. They all tried to understand the way my brain works. They didn't coddle my anxiety, but they were always there to comfort me and not push me if I needed to take a step away from things."

Charlie felt a small bit of jealousy light up in her stomach. The only person she had been able to connect with about this before was Ripley. Her father had been good with listening, but he hadn't been that good at learning. She had always been closer to her father, their shared interests in nerd culture and movies pulling them together. Her mother, on the other hand? Charlie winced. They had always had a rocky relationship at best, but they hadn't really spoken ever since her ex had broken up with her. Her mother had been a huge fan of Jacob, and when they'd broken up, she had just been... disappointed. Charlie didn't need her mother to say the words. She had seen them, plain as day, on her face when they'd video-called afterwards.

Looking out at the water she spotted someone on a paddle board out by the rocks. Page caught her looking, smiling. "Theo, Sandhya and I did that once." He said, making her look at him. He so rarely gave up information, and Charlie felt like this moment on the beach was rare. He was showing her that he was willing to share things with her, since she had opened up as well. "Last summer. Theo loves water sports and so does Sandhya." He laughed a little. She knew from the press and news that Theo, Sandhya, and he were close. But she also knew how wrong the tabloids were sometimes; how fabricated. "Sandhya's grandpa is Welsh and moved to the US when her dad was around twelve, but they have a summer home up here and a family home outside of Cardiff. In the summer, her parents usually come up here and spend their holiday with mine. Last summer, we all rented paddle boards and went around the castle." His eyes were distant as he almost laughed softly at a memory. It was almost strange hearing about Sandhya Vaughn from Page's perspective. For the longest time, she, and the other actors that Page was so intimately connected with, had been distant public figures. But the more Page talked, the more they became grounded people in her mind. To Page, Sandhya and Theo weren't just friends. They were his family. Charlie vaguely knew about Sandhya's family, knew the facts that the internet told her; that Sandhya was biracial, her dad from Massachusetts and her mother from Mumbai. A few years ago, Sandhya had discussed in an interview how her parents had met at Yale, then had gotten married and had her a few years after graduating. For Theo, she knew his parents were rich, his mom French and his dad English. Charlie knew they worked in business but that was about it. She was aware that Theodore Marcus liked the press just as much as she liked her kindle, his photo in gossip magazines almost every weekend. She wondered how a man who had his image splashed across every magazine could be such close friends with a someone like Page. But those were facts. It wasn't the truth or their individual stories. Page, he was telling her his story. He was showing her how they all fit together like a jigsaw puzzle. "Sandhya's Da forgot to put sunscreen on because it was kind of overcast, and when they came back, her mum gave him the biggest scolding. The man was as red as a tomato for the rest of the week."

"You seem really close with Theo and Sandhya," she said, looking at him. He was pulled out of the memory, sending her a small grin. So small, but so bright. Charlie felt her cheeks heat.

"They're my best mates. I know it sounds strange, but they're my family outside of Lilian, my Da and my mum. Well, and Callum."

"That isn't strange at all. Ripley is that for me. She found me," she almost rolled her eyes. "Kind of adopted me, really. And well, we all have a *chosen* family eventually. Ripley is mine. They're yours."

"Chosen family, yeah," Page whispered, studying her. It was too intense. Charlie needed his attention to move away.

"Have you always wanted to act?" she asked, needing to pull the conversation away from her family or anything remotely personal. She looked at Page's profile. She'd been living with him for almost two weeks, and yet she still knew so little about him. She had looked him up on Google the moment he arrived, but as Ripley had pointed out, there had been barely any information there. Just that he had been born in Inverness, his family moving to Stonehaven when he was a baby. He had gone to Julliard, graduating with honors, and had gotten the job on *StarVerse* right after. It was his first big acting role. Other than the fact that he was a Gemini, his birthday being in early June, there wasn't much else to find online.

Page McAllister was an enigma to the entire world. She couldn't help that a part of her wanted to pull the mask that he showed everyone else away. She knew that she had seen glimpses of the real him over the past week. But they'd been tinged with annoyance, and now that they were starting to break through the wall of being strangers, she felt comfortable enough to ask those questions she desperately wanted answers to.

Page rubbed the back of his neck, taking off the ball cap and running a hand through his hair. It was longer than it had been when they'd both been at the con, the tips curling slightly as they fell into his face. His forearms came to rest on his bent knees, his hands twirling the cap in his hands. "Actually, no. I knew I wanted to go into film, but for a while, I was pretty interested in screenwriting. But then acting just kind of came into my life."

Charlie studied him. He raised a brow. "What?"

Her lips tipped up in a small smile. "I can see it. Kind of ironic that your name is Page, and you want to be a writer."

His laugh was startled out of him, and she saw some of the tension leave his shoulders. "Aye, it is."

"Do you still write?"

He shrugged and sent a hesitant look her way when she scooted a bit closer, gesturing for him to continue. He sighed. "But nothing I would share with anyone."

"Well, you're never going to get out there as a screenwriter if you never share your work with anyone," she said, and at his surprised look, she thought back over her words, wincing at her harshness. But before she could apologize, he spoke.

"You're right. You're absolutely right." He sent her an amused look. "We'll see… Maybe one day, soon, I'll share it with someone."

"Well, I look forward to the day I can watch a film written by one Page McAllister." They shared a smile, and Charlie felt some of her anxiety left over from being around someone new ease. "Maybe it will be better than your acting."

He laughed again, and she knew then that she liked making

him laugh.

They stayed on the beach for another hour, soaking up the sun before it slipped back into a foggy, cloudy day that seemed to threaten rain. But, of course, it was normal. Or at least Page said it was normal, while Charlie was too busy sending up a small frown to the sky.

But even though the sky threatened rain, the later hours of the day seemed to call more and more people to the castle. Groups upon groups passed them as they went up the stairs, and Charlie could almost feel Page's anxiety rise. From their conversation and discussions around the show, it wasn't hard to figure out that he didn't like the public attention, but she hadn't had a clue about how much it seemed to eat at him.

Before they caught their bus, Charlie went in line to get them water from the coffee stand while Page sat at one of the many coffee tables. She ordered, waited for their water and the croissant she'd gotten, and turned to head back to him and... stopped.

Two teenage girls were standing around him. She saw his tense shoulders and the forced smile as one of them spoke. She could only guess that they watched the show and recognized him, especially when they pulled out their phones.

And suddenly, she perfectly understood the anxiety that Page had been feeling all day. It rooted itself inside of her chest.

What if they saw her and knew who she was?

What if they saw them together? Or *had* seen them together today?

What would that mean for Page? Or her?

Page slipped on the star smile that he had on in all his red-carpet shots. She felt her stomach flip.

God, she thought to herself as she walked around to stand on the other side of the coffee cart. She was so, so stupid.

She had gone and gotten a ridiculous little crush on Page

McAllister. The last thing she needed was to start crushing on her roommate, who happened to be an internationally known actor. It was the worst idea her brain had come up with in the last decade.

Charlie remembered the rules on the fridge.

Flatmates don't fall for flatmates.

At first, she had scoffed at that rule. Now, she was thankful Page had written it down. It seemed so frivolous, but then again, here she was, thinking about having a stupid crush. As if she didn't have more important things to worry about—like what she was supposed to do when this trip was over. Because even though she loved the work, and loved Scotland, that was all this was... a glorified vacation. A vacation she had uprooted her entire life for.

Flatmates don't fall for flatmates.

Charlie stared down the image of the list in her head, daring it almost. If there was one thing Charlie was good at, it was coming out on top when it came to stubbornness.

What would even happen if they got together? To Page, or his job?

In Charlie's mind, the only possible outcome was their respective worlds imploding. Logically, she knew they would make it out okay—

Why was she even thinking this? They wouldn't get together. She wasn't even sure if Page saw her that way. She was actually pretty sure he didn't.

She would not break those rules. Not even if Page was nice, hot, and sexy...

Maybe it wasn't a crush, she thought, nodding to herself as she thought it. Maybe it was just... he was handsome, and honestly, anyone in her position would be attracted to him.

She still had a good glimpse of where he was sitting, taking a selfie with the girls before they left. After they did, she walked towards him, taking a quick look at the people around them. Thankfully, no one else seemed too interested in them as he stood and followed her.

"Are you okay?" she asked as they made their way onto the road that led back to the bus stop. She glanced over at him, but not wanting to draw attention to them, she kept her distance.

He nodded but didn't reply. They got onto the bus, Page guiding them once more to the back. And when they pulled away from the bus stop, he sighed a bit. She remembered how he had grabbed her hand on the beach. His palm against her own, warm and rough. She reached out, her hand squeezing his. It was the only way she knew how to help.

"Yeah," he finally said, his voice soft. "I'm okay."

She was surprised when he squeezed her hand in return. He didn't let go until they exited the bus to head home. She didn't question what it meant.

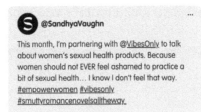

Chapter 17

Charlie

Charlie did the only thing she could do after that day: shut herself in her room alone before she made a mistake.

Although she was really starting to think making a mistake might be worth it.

No, Charlie. Rule Three… *Rule Three.*

She muttered the words to herself as she got ready for bed, her mind wandering to their day and going over their different conversations. It was something she always found herself doing at the end of the day. Maybe it was a mix of OCD, anxiety, or just her own brain, but she always analyzed the different conversations she'd had that day to see how she would respond now or if she could have responded differently.

She remembered the first time she'd mentioned this to her therapist. The woman had laughed softly, told her she wasn't crazy, and had explained that it was probably something she did as a form of masking and trying to better understand the social cues she'd experienced during the day. It was her brain's way of learning and making sense of the world.

And after today, the way their conversation and… *moments…* had completely uprooted her feelings for Page, crumpled them together and thrown them around, she *needed* to go over everything and every moment. She didn't know where he *fit*. And surprisingly, the anxiety she usually experienced when it came to not being able to read someone felt… different this time.

She still had trouble reading him fully and probably would for a while. But today had helped her get a tighter grasp on how he reacted to things. Page knew how to mask his emotions when he wanted to.

He was a good actor. But she wasn't surprised by that, obviously.

When she was finally ready for bed, she found herself restless.

Her brain couldn't stop thinking about Page. Every time she closed her eyes, there he was. An image of him this morning with his coffee, him fixing their heater, him working on the papers in the bookshop. Him smiling at her, the wind whipping his hair into his eyes.

Charlie groaned, her hands coming up to rub her face. She just needed to distract herself. She would reach for a romance novel, but her eyes were tired from the wind today, so instead, she reached for her vibrator.

It was small but mighty, so when she'd gotten it as a present from Ripley for her birthday one year—it had been a joke between them that Charlie needed one—she had named it Ant-Man when she'd gotten drunk on eggnog. It had stuck.

She turned it on, having cleaned it after the last time she'd used it, and felt the vibrations start. She was so tense, and the moment she closed her eyes and let sensations take over, she felt her shoulders start to relax. The tension in her neck eased.

She had never been able to get off if a guy went down on her immediately. For her, it had always taken more. More teasing, more kissing, more time spent getting to know one another. Fast and hard had never been good for her. It was the same story when she got herself off. She teased herself, her hand dragging up her side, along the curve of her breast underneath her shirt.

Sex was an area of interest for Charlie. Maybe it was because she'd had a lot of trouble fully understanding it when she was a teen, or maybe it was because she loved romance novels. She needed to know how it worked. How it felt. But her own experiences had been rocky. It'd taken her a long time to get comfortable with sex, the new sensations and feelings—the brush of someone else's skin against hers or their lips—making her skin uncomfortable. She'd never felt comfortable asking for what she needed, so… she'd avoided sex. It wasn't until college and finding friends who were comfortable *talking* about sex, along with her own diagnosis, that she started understanding how sex worked for her and her body.

Charlie felt herself relax, her heart starting to race. She needed, *wanted* release. With her eyes closed, she could almost imagine that her hands weren't her own. She could feel the calluses that her hands didn't have, feel the hint of open-mouth kisses on her neck and chest that weren't there. Feel the brush of stubble against her chest. She was close, and she felt it, her hand moving down, the vibrator moving against her clit right where she needed it—

—his eyes looked down at her, his gaze heated and filled with lust. Green eyes that she'd been thinking about for weeks. Those lips smirked before moving to her breast—

Charlie gasped, her body rocking with shocks as she came, his name gasping out of her mouth as her body collapsed back into her bed. The vibrator was still on where she'd let go of it when she'd come, her body moving through the aftershocks, one hand thrown above her head.

"Fuck," she whispered to herself. Because she knew exactly whose eyes she had pictured, whose lips had touched her body in her mind and whose hands she had imagined getting her off. She knew exactly whose name she had gasped as she came.

Page *fucking* McAllister.

The one man she should not be imagining while she came. The one man who had surprised her more in the past couple of weeks than any man had. When he had arrived, she had been so nervous. Not because he was there but because of what he meant. She had seen what being involved with that show meant, even if she had only been a disgruntled fan. Charlie could see the pressure that Page felt when he talked about his job and the possibility of publicizing the bookstore. That wasn't a life she wanted—her business everywhere for anyone to see.

It had been a while since she'd been with someone.

The thought almost took her out of the moment because Jacob was the last person she'd been with. Looking back, she wasn't sure what had drawn her to him. Maybe it had been his smile because when he wasn't an ass, it had been beautiful... charming. But now, Charlie suspected she had been with him because she had wanted to feel wanted. His charisma, his attention, made her feel something other than the numb confusion she'd been struggling with when she'd met him. And now... the idea that he had been her last interaction with sex... It made her sick to her stomach. Jacob hadn't loved her... He hadn't even respected her. He had just used her.

Charlie paused, taking in a deep breath and opening her eyes. She stared upwards, reigning in her emotions. Her hands shook at her side. She glared at the ceiling, a light blue color that matched the walls of her room.

Fuck Jacob. Charlie almost laughed at the thought. Fuck him. She deserved to be able to love herself, to move on without thinking of him constantly. He had been like a shadow looming over her since they had broken up—a shadow she'd been running from, unwilling to face. And then... with what happened at StarCon...

Even though she loved herself, loved her brain and her body, what happened at StarCon had made her doubt a lot. It had made her wonder if maybe Jacob was a little bit right.

Why can't you just be normal, Charlie? Everything is so difficult with you.

Think of something else, Charlie...

Her mind went back to the trip earlier that day. She couldn't help it. The image of being on the beach helped calm her thoughts.

You should be proud of who you are. You're strong, resilient, bright, funny, beautiful—

Page... God, her brain was getting ahead of itself even now. There was no way he looked at her and saw the same things she saw in him. He was probably just being nice to appease his sister and make sure she didn't leave the bookstore unattended. He had told her when he arrived that they couldn't be seen together because of the show. He had *told* her. *He* had been the one to put that rule on the fridge.

Not that she was falling for him.

She wasn't. That would be ridiculous. She was just attracted to him. Being forced to be around him all the time would make any woman remotely attracted to him feel breathless. Yes, they had almost kissed in the backroom… and at the castle… Or she thought they'd almost kissed. Looking back, those had just been moments of… comfort. They had both opened themselves up, and that was all it had been—two people leaning towards each other, looking for a moment of comfort. It meant nothing.

What she was feeling was completely normal and nothing to trouble herself over, or so she told herself. Turning off the vibrator, cleaning it and shutting it in her bedside table drawer, she let out a sigh.

Then why did she feel like she'd just had a realization she couldn't ignore? Why did she feel like seeing him, imagining him, was just the beginning?

Only You
ValeriForLife

Hellooooo there. We all know this is the best scene in season one. SO here is a small one-shot of the battle scene but from Car Brandon's POV since the scene is mostly from Valeri's. Hope you enjoy!

Car saw her fall. He saw it, and his heart almost fell out of his chest.

He ran. His feet pounded over the moon's surface, the only sound his blood rushing, his heart pumping. He could hear his ragged breath in his helmet.

No.

She couldn't be.

"Val!" He yelled through their com, but all he heard was static. "Come on, Val, let me know you're okay? I need you to be okay!" He was almost to her now. Almost. "Only you, remember? Only you!"

Chapter 18
Page

Page truly hadn't meant to listen to Charlie as he passed her room.

Really... he hadn't.

It wasn't like he had stood outside her door, put his ear to it, and hoped he would hear her masturbating. He had been getting a snack. He had woken up, realized it wasn't even that late, and had gone to the kitchen to get a snack and some water.

He had heard his name as he walked past the door. Flats like this one—built long ago and renovated recently—usually lacked one important thing. Insulation. They were stone, which blocked a lot of sounds, but not everything. That was why the flat got so cold and was also why he could hear her as she gasped his name.

The sound made him stop cold where he was, halfway between her room, the kitchen, and his bedroom door.

Then he had heard the soft, "Fuck." And his brain short-circuited.

It had taken a few moments for his brain to catch up and realize that Charlie was getting herself off and calling his name while doing it.

After a few moments of silence, he shut himself in his room, his mind stuck on the thought of Charlie.

Setting his piece of toast and glass of water on the side table, he fell onto his bed, groaning. A part of him felt guilty for hearing her. It wasn't as if she had consented to him hearing.

But he *had* heard.

And now he couldn't think of anything else… and he was fucking hard.

He had been trying his best *not* to think about Charlie since he had gotten to know her over the past couple of weeks. And to be completely honest, he had been doing a pretty bad job of it. He knew he needed to stay away… but something about her made him want to do just the opposite.

He had been drawn to her since StarCon. He had seen her stand there, her hands on her hips, her eyes filled with fierce protectiveness, and he had known then that she was someone he wanted to know.

Then he had showed up here and there she was, living with him. It had been like the universe was laughing at him.

But Charlie was more than what he had seen at StarCon.

She was fierce and strong but also so much more. She had so many layers, and he had only glimpsed a few of them. She was kind, and quirky. She read romance unabashedly and wore clothes with nerdy sayings with those damn short pajama shorts and her long hoodies and the socks… She loved wearing the long socks with her shorts, an image he had been trying his hardest to get out of his brain. And even if it had driven him up the wall, he admired her stubbornness and sense of justice.

Today, when she mentioned her family and had opened up to him about her diagnosis, he had been blown away by her strength. But he saw the cracks in that façade, a glimpse at how hurt she'd been over the years. Instead of making him want to back away, he had felt the opposite. He had never wanted to get to know and understand a person more.

And that scared him.

A part of him acknowledged the feelings that had been growing in him. But the other part knocked them off with a scoff.

But *hearing* her. Hearing her coming to *his* name…

Page groaned, his arms coming up to cover his face.

God, he didn't know what to do. If he were different—if he didn't have the job on *StarVerse* and didn't want to keep his job—he wouldn't hesitate. He would be knocking on her door right now, asking her if he could kiss her until they were both breathless and moaning each other's names.

But he wasn't. He couldn't ask her to. Because he knew what his job entailed. Not only would it be a mess with the showrunners, but he wouldn't want to pull Charlie into that mess. He had seen what the press did to people who weren't prepared for it. He didn't—*couldn't*—pull her into that.

It wasn't fair.

But when were the hard things in life ever fair? At least for Page, fairness had never been part of the big decisions in his life.

He would have to forget Charlie James. He would have to pretend that he wasn't craving her in more ways than one.

Page stood, heading to the bathroom. All he needed was a cold shower and to desperately stop thinking about her. But as the cold water hit his skin, his wet hair falling into his eyes, he simply knew it would be harder to get rid of the new image of her from his mind.

Excerpt from *STARVERSE*: Season 3, Episode 3

CAR BRANDON'S ROOM — NIGHT

CAR and THOREN are in Car's room. They are playing cards. A knock sounds, and Car stands up to open the door to find Asmor on the other side.

> CAR
> What do you want, Asmor?

Asmor walks into the room uninvited. Car raises a brow. Thoren snickers.

> ASMOR
> What is the game you're playing?

> THOREN
> Just regular old poker, mate… alien.

> ASMOR
> (Ignoring the awkwardness)
> I have not played that before.

> CAR
> I'm not surprised. It's an old game from before the federation was created. It's really only played among people on earth now.

> CAR
> (Hesitantly, almost reluctantly)
> We can… teach you if you want.

> ASMOR
> I do want. Teach me your… earth… game.

> THOREN
> How do you always find a way to make earth sound disgusting in everything you say Asmor?

> ASMOR
> It's a gift.

> ASMOR
> (Hesitantly)
> And call me Az. At least when we are not on the bridge.It would be against protocol there, of course.

> CAR
> (Laughs under his breath)
> Of course, it's not like we haven't gone against protocol before.

<pre>
                    ASMOR
This time, I know you're using sarcasm because
 you break protocol all the time, Captain. It is
               like a hobby for you.

                   THOREN
 I can't tell if that's a compliment or not.

                    CAR
            I'll take it as one.
</pre>

Chapter 19

Charlie

"How are things working out with Page?" Layla asked, pulling Charlie out of her categorization of the numbers on her sheet. They had just opened the store, and today, Charlie was extra thankful to have Layla working with her.

Maybe their conversation would help her keep her mind off Page.

Well, Charlie's idea would have worked in theory, but Layla seemed to have other plans. Maybe it was the fact that Layla was in a long-term relationship, but she was very invested in love.

Yes, Charlie loved romance, but romantics? They believed that romance, that *love*, fixed everything. And that just wasn't the case.

It hadn't fixed her relationship with her mom, her brother, or Jacob.

At first, it had been small, innocent questions, but then... well, Charlie wasn't an idiot. She knew what Layla was doing. She could see the mischievous glint in her friend's eyes.

"Fine," she said, pulling her gaze back to the sheet in her hand and pointedly not looking at the woman across from her. "Let's talk about how you're feeling today, huh, Layla? Is the cough gone?"

Layla had the decency to look somewhat guilty. "Okay, so

maybe I was sick of hearing you complain about Page all the time." She wiggled her fingers at Charlie showing her now bright lilac nails. "I went to the salon and had a personal day."

"I was not complaining about him that much," she scoffed. "And I wish I could've gone to the salon." Charlie cocked her head to the side. "Actually, the salon sucks and is way too overstimulating, so I take that back."

"Fine, huh?" Layla sent her a smile. It took a minute for Charlie to follow the conversation back to yesterday's trip. She scowled. "Just fine?"

Charlie narrowed her eyes, noting the change in subject, and set down the sheet of paper on the desk in front of her. "I know what you're doing."

Layla smirked, moving to put the stickers that were in her hands on the stack of books in front of her. They had just gotten a huge shipment of books the day before yesterday, just as they were about to close, and the inventory before them was going to take days, if not the entire week. For such a small store, Lilian sure liked to have it stocked with new releases, as well as making sure they had popular older books in stock for new fans. Charlie frowned at the boxes in front of them. She knew that the store was doing okay, but after her conversation with Page, she couldn't help but worry about Lilian buying so much stock right now. Not that it was her business on how the woman ran her bookstore. Charlie would only be here for the summer. A fact she had been reminding herself of repeatedly over the past couple of days.

"I have no idea what you're talking about, love," Layla said, sticking a bright orange half-priced sticker onto an old thriller novel Charlie had seen around a lot. She made a note to herself to look it up and see if she would like it. She didn't pick up a lot of thrillers, but whenever she did, she found herself enjoying the genre.

"You think that if you hint enough, I will tell you that Page and I made out and had steamy sex."

"*You made out and had steamy sex?*" Layla practically screamed her question, turning to look at Charlie. Suddenly, she was glad that there was no one in the store.

"No," she hissed at her friend. "I was trying to say that's what you want to happen."

Layla didn't hide the disappointment on her face. "*Dammit.* And of course, I do. I know we haven't known each other long, but we've been working together almost every day for the past month, and I really like you, Charlie. I consider both of you friends who might need to get laid, and I don't see why you can't use one another." She said it so calmly that Charlie had to fight the blush on her cheeks. Layla grinned at her expression. "I mean, come on, if I weren't head over heels in love with Fred, I would shag him."

Charlie's blush deepened. "I am not going to have sex with Page."

"Why the fuck not?" Charlie almost laughed at Layla's exclamation, not able to hide her smile.

"Seriously, Layla?" she asked, moving from behind the desk to start unpacking one of the other boxes. "So many reasons. One, the press. Two, his job. Three, the press. Four, the fact that I'm leaving in a month—"

"I'm not saying you should start dating," Layla said, walking to help Charlie move the books so she could break down the box. "I'm saying you should have sex. Big difference." Layla studied her for a moment. Her look was hesitant, but her eyes were kind. "You've only done relationships, haven't you?" she asked, her eyes widening.

Charlie shrugged, suddenly feeling shy. "I don't know. Sex is weird for me. I need to feel comfortable around someone before doing it with them. So, one-night stands aren't really my thing."

Layla nodded, her hand resting on Charlie's arm. Charlie usually didn't like these small touches, but since she had met Layla, she had learned that this was how her new friend showed affection. Layla loved to hug her or touch Charlie's cheek or her arm in comfort. And even if, sometimes, the touch felt uncomfortable, she appreciated Layla's own personal form of affection. "I didn't mean it to come off so judgmental, sorry. But all I'm saying is that giving into those looks you both send one another when the other isn't looking *might* not be such a bad thing."

Charlie shook her head. "He doesn't look at me."

She couldn't find it in herself to lie about how she wasn't looking at him. She had a feeling that would make Layla laugh at her.

Layla shrugged. "When he was down here the other day, he was definitely looking at you."

The day before yesterday had been the only time Page had come down to the store during the day since Charlie had started working. He had spent the day looking through their financials again and had been there to help them move all the new orders into their backroom when they'd arrived. But that had been before she'd found him down here at night... Before their day out at the castle.

"There's just no outcome where it would end well," she said finally, giving in to the conversation. It wasn't as if she had been thinking about anything else, herself.

"So, you *have* been thinking about it," Layla said, her look of triumph making Charlie shake her head. Layla lifted one of the books and did a small happy dance, making Charlie laugh. "I knew I was right."

"Of course, I have. I mean, I'm a grown woman attracted to men." Charlie frowned down at the books in front of her. "Abs and boobs are my weakness."

Layla laughed. "He does have nice abs." At Charlie's raised brows, Layla laughed, her own cheeks turned a bit red. "I grew up with him. He did swimming as a sport in secondary school, and all my friends had a crush on him." Since starting work, Charlie had been slowly getting to know Layla. And she wanted to know more. She knew that Layla's mom had grown up in Edinburgh, staying there for university, and that was where she met her husband. She'd fallen in love and had moved to Stonehaven to be with him. She learned that Layla liked her coffee with copious amounts of milk and caramel drizzle, and she was fiercely dedicated to the town library where she tutored kids after school. And, to Charlie's chagrin, the hopelessly romantic gene ran through every bone in her body.

"God, swimmers are so hot," Charlie said, sighing. "Of course, he was a swimmer. So unfair."

Now, all she could picture was Page in a speedo.

She needed to stop thinking of that immediately.

Charlie forced her mind to sober, her smile falling. "Like I said, though, this wouldn't end well. It's best for both of us if we just stay clear of each other and stay friendly."

"Friendly, huh?" She saw Layla's small, knowing smile out of the corner of her eyes as she started shelving the books Layla had put stickers on.

"*Platonically* friendly," Charlie said, her glare not holding much weight behind it as Layla laughed. She liked Layla a lot. Over the past couple of weeks, she had become a fixture in her life. But Layla, like everyone, was… complicated. She had seen glimpses of her friend, of happiness—like when she teased Charlie, or when she talked about Fred. But then there were days when Layla was shut off… far away. Layla was busy outside of the store going on her free weekends to visit her boyfriend. They hadn't really had any time outside of work to hang out. And for Charlie… well, she never knew when asking questions was good or when it was overstepping. So, most of the time, she just let others tell her things when they were ready. Didn't mean she wasn't curious, though.

"I get it," Layla said, pulling Charlie out of her head. At Charlie's look, she sighed. "Okay, I don't think I can really get it. You know I love a happy ending. But I just think that giving into your… *urges*… isn't necessarily a bad thing."

"I wish I had your rose-colored glasses when it comes to love."

"You will when you're in love," Layla said, sending her an innocent grin. For a second, her eyes seemed far away, as if she were somewhere else.

Love. Charlie tasted the word in her head. Looking back at her relationships, she knew she had never been in love or even said the words to someone. All her life, she had seen declarations of love in movies or in books, and they had seemed so... grand. But in her own life, her relationships had been nothing like that. Saying the words "I love you" seemed so final. In books and movies, the couple always said the words and then the story ended. It was a finality she'd never wanted to put into her past relationships. What if she said the words and it didn't work out? Then, when things ended, it would just hurt more.

Why would she put herself in the position to be even more hurt by a breakup than she had to be?

A few of her past partners, including Jacob, had called her cold whenever she had tried to explain these feelings to them. And maybe she was... but she simply didn't see the point in saying those words when she didn't feel them or when she didn't see these relationships going anywhere. Lying to please them had seemed pointless.

It wasn't like she didn't want love. She did. But maybe she had too high of expectations for love. Perhaps she just needed to realize that finding someone who gave her what she needed while still challenging her and respecting all her quirks was impossible.

The thought just seemed depressing.

Charlie frowned down at the book in her hands. The cover showed a happy couple dancing in the rain. She'd read this book and loved it. But in this moment, the cover felt like it was mocking her. Because even though she was skeptical, even though she liked to be pessimistic—after all, it kept her heart safe—another part of her, a part that was still naïve and giddy every time she re-watched a movie or read a book like this one, hoped that it wasn't true.

Snippet of an online news article about the crew of *StarVerse*

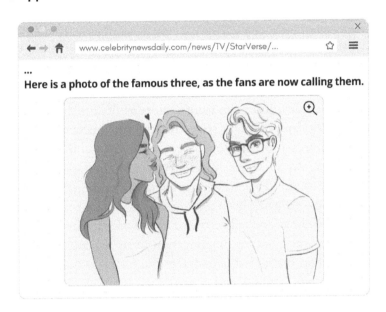

...
Here is a photo of the famous three, as the fans are now calling them.

Chapter 20

Page

Page knew he should be at the house, helping Callum and the crew with putting the hardwood floors into the upstairs rooms. He wasn't as handy as Callum, but he'd worked with the Ferguson family all through his teenage years and tried his best to help out with the house when he could. But today was different. He had promised himself he would take the day off. He had also promised himself he would get some writing done.

So far, that had been a lie.

He had gone to one of the coffee shops that sat on the beach's boardwalk, grabbing his usual coffee and croissant, and sitting at one of the corner tables, away from people and conversation. But when he had opened his laptop, he had gone straight to work, answering a few emails from his manager and agent about upcoming publicity and scheduling for the premiere of the new season, plus new filming schedule possibilities. Then, he had fallen down the rabbit hole of messaging with Sandhya and Theo.

Both were back in London for the summer, staying in their separate places. But he knew they both spent most of their time together. Sandhya and Theo were as close as siblings, having met before work, and Theo insisting that the two queer people on the show needed to stick together. Sandhya had come out well before being on the show, around uni, while Theo was only out to his close friends. Page still remembered when he had come out to him as bi—they had been leaving the first season's wrap party, and his friend had looked terrified. Page had just said, "Thanks for trusting me" before hugging him. The tension in Theo's shoulders had dissipated, and a few moments later, they were both laughing. Sandhya had shared with him later that where her parents had been accepting, wanting to learn everything they could about how to support her and the queer community at large, Theo, however, was still not out to his parents. They'd been about to meet the Marcuses for dinner, and she hadn't wanted him to say anything accidentally. Not that he would have... Page hated talking to Theo's parents and usually put up the same social front he did when talking to them as when he talked to his producers.

Page knew that Sandhya and Theo had become one another's rock when it came to dealing with queerphobia on set, even huddling together to speak French during breaks, or making their own small queer book club together. He just tried to help as much as he could—calling out or asking to change lines that continued stereotypes or talking to the directors of the episodes if he had to.

He just wanted his two best friends to feel as safe as possible.

Page grinned at the photo Theo sent through of Sandhya with Theo's corgi, Han Solo. Sandhya was tall, almost as tall as Page, her long legs folded underneath her as she sat on her living room rug. The beige and white Corgi was cuddling into her arms. Sandhya's hair was in two braids, a yellow handkerchief folded and tied around her head like a headband. Her high, sharp cheekbones were softer as she laughed, her mouth wide and open mid-laugh, her eyes scrunched up as Han Solo licked her face.

Solo's back with his favourite parent.

Page liked the photo with a heart.

Page
That dog loves her more than he loves you.

Theo
The little traitor.

Theo
Now they're both telling me to tell you to get back to writing so that you can sell the next great Hollywood film and cast both of us as your lead actors and make us all millions.

With a roll of his eyes, he shut off his phone and looked at the opened Word document on his laptop, his grin fading. He'd been looking at the blank page for the past thirty minutes. He was about ready to pull his hair out.

This was the reason why he hadn't written in almost a year. He didn't have any ideas.

At Julliard, ideas had seemed to spill out of him. Maybe it was his naïve view of the industry or the pressure-free environment he had been in. But now, every time he sat down to write, he was too aware of how his ideas would be perceived by the world and the industry. So much so that even typing the first words felt like the hardest thing in the world.

He groaned, rubbing his eyes with the heels of his hands. He adjusted his glasses and wrote "Concept, Title, and Synopsis" on the Word doc. Maybe going back to the basics he had learned in one of his intro screenwriting classes would help him. He doubted it, though.

He couldn't help but think back to Charlie's excitement when he said he liked to write. He supposed he shouldn't be surprised. He knew that she loved to read. But there had been something about that look, the pure belief in his ability even though she hadn't read any of his work, that had made him set aside this day to write.

Page scoffed. If he ended up writing at all.

Think, think, think…. He thought and almost sighed in relief when the text tone on his phone sounded. He frowned at the text when he saw it was from Callum.

Callum
Has Lil texted you?

Page
No…

Page
Why?

Callum
No reason.

Page frowned down at his phone. He almost texted something back but stopped himself. He had learned early on not to put himself in Lilian's business. And he was smart enough to know that Callum had always been Lilian's business. He knew that she… well, he knew what he meant to her, even if she never told him. And Callum had been through enough in the past ten years. He deserved better than what he had gone through with Flora and her mother. Those two seriously needed to settle whatever was going on between them. But there was nothing *he* could do about it, even if he wanted to lock them both in a room until they saw some sense.

Something about the conversation lit a spark in his mind, and he bit his lip in concentration, trying to follow the wisp of an idea that breezed past him. It was small, only an image, but it was there.

He set his hands on the keys and started typing. He just needed to get something on the page. Then he could work from there.

By the time Page got home, it was just getting dark. He had zoned out at the coffee shop, falling into writing so much that he had been forced out of the cafe by Claire, the owner, when they'd been closing. He hadn't had a writing day that solid in… well, months.

In fact, he was still so much in his head walking back home that he didn't realize where he was until he slammed into a body on the stairwell up to the flat.

"Shit," he exclaimed, reaching out for the stairwell railing, his other hand coming up to stabilize Charlie, who was wobbling and leaning sideways. His feet stumbled, and he pulled her closer, and before he knew it, he was falling forward, pulling her on top of him so that his body would cushion their fall. He winced as his shoulder hit the edge of the steps and thanked whatever was out there that he'd fallen forward instead of backwards.

"Oh my God, Page," Charlie, currently on top of him, her hands on either side of his shoulders, was looking down at him, worry clear in her brown eyes. "Are you okay? I'm so sorry."

"Fuck," he said, "we really need to stop running into each other like this," he hissed under his breath, trying his best to sit up, but his body was at an awkward angle on the stairs, the edges of the stone digging into his back, Charlie's body on top of him—

Charlie was lying on top of him. Suddenly, all pain was forgotten as his entire existence zeroed in to where his hands were grasping her hips and where her legs tangled with his, her hips pressing against him and her chest…

Her chest was way too close to his face. Or not close enough. He sucked in a breath. He clocked the minute that Charlie noticed their position as well. She froze mid-sentence, and whatever she had been saying, which Page was too distracted to remember, died. Their eyes met, hers bright, and he could feel her heart beating against his.

For a moment, he thought of leaning up, of pulling her closer, because she wasn't close enough. No, he wanted to pull her into him, to feel his hands slide up under the jumper she had on. His hands gripped her hips tighter, and he heard her breath stutter. Her eyes slid to his lips, and this time he knew he wasn't making it up. But then again, maybe he had fallen and hit his head because this moment simply couldn't be real.

That thought was like a bucket of cold water splashed on top of them.

"Are you okay?" he asked, and it was like a wall materialized between them, Charlie scrambling off him and pushing to a stand, her hands gripping the railing. Page groaned as he stood up, his hand coming up to rub his shoulder.

"Yes," she said, and her voice sounded rough. Page wondered briefly if it was due to realizing how bad their fall could've been or if… he affected her as much as she affected him. He looked anywhere but at her and he could feel her gaze on him. Heavy, hot. Then it was gone.

"Is your shoulder okay?" She blew out an exasperated breath. "I cannot believe you took the fall—"

"For once, could you just accept that I saved your life?" he said. He had meant it to come out jokingly, but the moment before had rattled him, completely broken through whatever self-resolve he had been trying to build up around her, and instead the words came out harsh. "Shit, sorry—" he said. "Are you okay? Ignore me, I'm in pain."

Charlie looked at him, and he tried to ignore how closely she was studying his face. "Thanks for, you know, helping me not die by falling down the stairs." He nodded. "You're going to need an ice pack."

"I think I'm going to need to invest in ice packs for the duration of your stay."

Charlie huffed out a breath and turned a small glare on him. There it was, he thought as he followed her back up the stairs. There was the fire that had first annoyed him, and now... now it didn't. He sighed. "I will admit, that was mostly my fault. I was... in my head." He looked her up and down. Nice jeans and a jumper that accented her breasts and eyes. She even had makeup on... "Where were you going?"

Charlie raised a brow at him, pulling an ice pack from the freezer and walking over to him. "I'm meeting Layla for drinks."

Page cleared his throat. "Ah," he said, shifting as he moved the pack to where he felt the most pain, trying not to wince.

"Or at least I was before a big blonde oaf almost threw me down the stairs." He saw her small smirk and tried not to roll his eyes.

"Sorry about that—"

"It's fine," Charlie said, waving him off. "It was bound to happen, we're both a bit clumsy," she said, smiling. She grabbed her bag, which she had dumped onto the couch on their way in, and sent him a small smile. "But I am now running late." She paused as if unsure what she was going to say next. "Will you be okay?"

"If I'm not, I'll call Dr. John."

She nodded, paused again as if she were going to say something, but then seemed to change her mind and turned to the door. "I'll be back later!" she called out, and then she was gone.

Page felt his shoulders tense when she left. The past fifteen minutes had been such a whirlwind that he felt like he'd been knocked on his ass. Page grinned to himself. Technically, Charlie had literally knocked him on his ass. He clenched his hands into fists as he tried not to think about how her body had felt against his. How right—

His eyes slid to the rules on the fridge in front of him. He glared at them.

That night, he tried not to think of Charlie at the pub. He tried not to think of her meeting someone else. Because it wasn't his place to think that way. And when she came home, alone, he hadn't realized that he was waiting for her to be back before falling asleep. But when he heard the door close and lock, when he heard her soft footsteps sound outside his door, he finally relaxed.

PART II

Lovers Always Interrupted
SVFanQueen

Okay, so we had the one-shot, where they were going at it *winks* in the kitchen, the weapons room, their room, and the storage closet. Now, it is time for *drum roll* the showers.

Car stumbled as he was pushed back into the wall. The water from the shower fell down his back, over his chest and thighs. Asmor kissed under his chin, finding the spot he loved.

He gritted his teeth. "Right there," he said, hissing out a breath.

"Right there?" God, Car thought. Sometimes, he hated how cheeky Asmor got when they were together.

Asmor kissed him, pushing his tongue between his lips, his hands gripping his waist. Car was reminded how much he didn't hate this man.

"Car?" A voice called from the doorway. They froze when they heard the door to the showers open. Thoren. Shit.

Asmor's head fell forward onto Car's shoulder, his body already shaking with laughter. He heard him curse in his language. God, Car loved it when Asmor spoke his own language. He found it so beautiful.

"Thoren, I'm in the shower."

"Oh, is that what they're calling it nowadays?"

Chapter 21

Charlie

The bathroom had turned into a sauna. And it had nothing to do with her shower or her sink. The toilet was currently steaming.

"Page?" she yelled. They had the rule that they wouldn't walk into each other's spaces, but as she backed out of her bathroom and rushed to his bedroom door, she started to think that breaking this specific rule might be a good idea.

It wasn't there for emergencies… He wouldn't be too mad, would he?

When she heard a gurgling sound come from her bathroom, she made up her mind.

Raising her hand, she banged on his door. The doors and walls were made of thick wood, so she couldn't hear much coming from his room. She banged on the door again.

"Page? Do you have a minute? I need your help!"

No answer.

Charlie let out a huff of annoyance and pushed open the door. Privacy be damned when her toilet was starting to look like a middle-school volcano science project gone wrong. She hadn't stepped foot in his room since the first day she'd arrived. She had explored every inch of the apartment then, choosing the bedroom with the notes from Lilian as her own and assuming it was where she was supposed to sleep. But that didn't mean she hadn't at least peeked at the other room.

She now assumed it was Lilian's room. It was a mix of dark and bright colors, the walls a deep plum, the sheets a dark teal with orange flowers. The blend of bright colors made her a bit dizzy. There was music playing loudly, and the bathroom door was shut, steam flowing out from beneath the door.

"Page?" she yelled, staying in the doorway, not letting herself move any farther into the room. A small suitcase was stuffed into one corner, a large copy of *Crime and Punishment* sitting on the bedside table with a pencil marking the reader's place. "Page? I'm sorry to interrupt, but my toilet is—"

She cut off when the door opened, and steam billowed out. She didn't know what she'd been expecting, but it was not for Page to walk out in a towel.

And nothing else.

He must have just come out of the shower because his skin was still wet. She'd seen him with his shirt on and in short-sleeved shirts that showed off the muscles of his arms. But this, *him*, was so much more. His chest and body were sculpted, his abs like concrete, and as her gaze swept down, she felt the heat flood to her cheeks and neck and… lower.

God, he was beautiful. Her gaze caught on a tiny freckle

above where the towel hung low on his hips, a bit of dark hair showing just above the bulge in the towel.

"Charlie?" When he said her name, her eyes snapped up to his, and she caught the smirk on his face as he took her in. She was in her pajama shorts, a pair that should have been retired years ago because of how small they were, and an oversized StarCon T-shirt.

Page reached up, pushing his wet hair away from his face, the rivulets of water dripping down his features and throat.

Charlie wished she could catch those drips of water with her tongue.

The thought pushed her out of her own head, and she flushed, backing away quickly with a yelp and turning away from him. "God, sorry! I knocked, but you didn't answer—"

There was laughter in his voice when he interrupted her. "I was in the shower."

"Yes," she said, scowling at the floor. "I can see that."

"I noticed you saw that," he said, more laughter in his voice. She held back a groan. God, she was in so much trouble. "Why did you decide to try and catch me in the nude?" he asked, and chuckled when she turned around to glare at him.

Her eyes met his. "I wasn't trying to—" and then she took him in again and shrieked. "Oh my God, put some pants on!"

"To be fair, you are in my room—"

Charlie slammed the door, falling back against it. "Put some pants on, and then come help me? My toilet has turned into a volcano," she said, her voice rough as she leaned her head back against the door and tried to get the image of him, all of him, out of her mind.

It was an image she knew would live rent-free in her head.

Honestly, she didn't really want it to disappear.

He chuckled from the other side of the door, and a few seconds later, the door opened. Charlie stumbled, squeaking as she fell back and straight into Page's hard chest.

Now, thankfully, covered by a T-shirt.

Her hands came up to his chest as he reached out to steady

her, his palm sitting firmly on her hip. Her skin heated where his hands touched her body.

"I think I'm going to need to get you a pair of training wheels. You seem to stumble around way too much." At her scowl, he sent her a cheeky smile. Then he raised a brow. "Now, what is so important that you needed to interrupt my shower?"

"Again, I'm sorry—" she said, pushing away from him.

"I'm just teasing you," he replied, his voice low. "You're welcome," he smirked. "I know seeing me almost naked was the highlight of your day."

She rolled her eyes at him instead of letting out the small squeak that seemed to get stuck in her throat and then sent him a serious look before wincing. "My toilet seems to be a volcano."

Page's eyes widened in alarm, and he pushed past her into her room, opening the door she had shut to look into the bathroom.

"Shit," he said, his voice muffled by the doors and walls, and she stood outside her room, slightly scared to go anywhere near the bathroom. "Will you grab my phone for me?" he asked, walking into the bathroom to open the small window in the shower stall and let out some of the steam.

She walked back into his room, and finally, after flipping over the blankets, she found it, rushing back to her room to hand it to him. He dialed a number, and then a man answered on speaker.

"Callum?"

"Yeah?"

"We might have a steaming toilet in Lilian's flat."

"Shit, what the fuck did you do?"

"I don't fucking know, mate."

Charlie smiled to herself as she watched him talk to his friend on the phone. His accent, which she realized he must be softening for her, got thicker as he spoke. His voice was low, and she quietly laughed when she heard Callum curse up a storm on the other end of the phone.

"Open up the window, then turn off the water for the flat. We don't need the steam hurting the walls or the ceiling, and I'll be over in a few," she heard him say.

"Aye, sounds good," Page said, hanging up just as Callum muttered something like, 'I told that damn woman to fix the plumbing ages ago.' Page opened the main window, moved into the hall closet, and cursed. She heard a click, and then the water seemed to stop running from her bathroom. She stood there awkwardly as Page moved back to the bathroom. There was a long sigh and then silence.

Page looked back at her and, to her complete amazement, didn't get angry but suddenly started…

Laughing.

"Are you laughing?" she asked, her voice incredulous.

"What else," he kept on laughing, "am I supposed to do in this situation? How the fuck did this happen?" She couldn't help but giggle at his laughter, her eyes entrapped by his face. His features lit up as he smiled, the tension leaving his body as he leaned against the door-jam and rested his hands on his knees to keep himself from falling over. His shirt was damp from the shower and stuck to his body in a few places while his blond hair fell onto his face and stuck to his forehead.

Charlie knew that the last thing she needed to do was get involved, emotionally or physically, with this man, but… fuck… she didn't see how she could stop herself when he looked like this. He was stoically beautiful when he wasn't smiling, but then he laughed or smirked or sent her a blazing smile, and she felt like she did now—

Her knees were fucking weak.

She looked up to find that Page had caught her looking at him, and her cheeks flushed.

"You know, sometimes you're hard to read," he said, moving out of the bathroom and closing the door behind him. The hardwood shut out the sound of the fiasco that was in there, and since her room was large and the window in the bathroom was now open, the air around them was no longer foggy. Page, whose face had been lit up a moment ago, looked at her, his eyes glinting with a look she couldn't quite decipher.

"Oh really?" she asked, moving back to lean against the wall behind her. She crossed her arms over her chest, her T-shirt riding up her legs slightly. The shorts were so short that they were practically underwear, and the T-shirt... It was more of a nightgown than a sleep shirt, really. Charlie suddenly realized that she was barely dressed. After she'd woken up to find her the bathroom fiasco, she had gone straight into fixing mode, not even thinking to put some real clothes on.

"Yeah," he said, moving towards her slowly. She sucked in some air as he moved closer. "One moment, I swear the last thing you want is to be around me, and the very next, you're looking at me with those big brown eyes."

"So, now looking at you needs to be regulated and put on our rule list?" she asked with a grin.

He rolled his eyes, and to her dismay, his smirk deepened.

"You're deflecting," he said, shaking his head and taking another step closer. He was in front of her, his chest a couple of inches from hers. She felt her breath catch. He was so much taller than she was, and it was something she'd never realized until he was right in her personal space. He towered over her, heat radiating off him.

He was right, Charlie thought to herself as she looked up, her gaze meeting his own. She had been going back and forth, but so had he. One moment, he looked as if he wanted to run away, and the next—

The next, he was looking at her as he was now. Like he *needed* her.

"Just how am I looking at you?" she asked, trying to keep her voice from shaking.

She didn't think it was possible, but he moved even closer, leaning forward, his forearm on the wall behind her, tilting his head down and whispering into her ear. "Like you want me," he said, his voice low and rough. His breath hit her ear and the skin behind it when she shifted; she shivered. "As much as I've been wanting you." She felt the whisper of his touch on her wrist. "Like you want me to fuck you, Charlie. Fuck you like I want to."

When he'd moved closer, her eyes had closed on their own

accord, but now she opened them. She looked at him and met his gaze unapologetically. The heat she saw there matched her own. Heat that had been building up since the moment they had met. It was a deep and raw feeling that she hadn't felt before. A feeling she had been pushing down for all sorts of reasons.

But when one pushed something down like that over and over, it began to build up. And now, those feelings were spilling over.

"This… isn't a good idea…" she finally said, her voice breathless. She hated how much he affected her, how much her body was rebelling against her mind.

"Fuck good ideas." His tongue came out and brushed his lower lip, a lip she had been looking at—dreaming about. God, she really wanted to kiss him.

He leaned forward as if he could hear her thoughts, his lips hovering above hers. His hand came up to rest above her hip, but he didn't touch her. Her mind flashed back to their conversation the other day about how touch was such a sensitive subject for her. She knew automatically that he was waiting for her, waiting to see if he could touch her.

"Can I touch you?" His words rang through her mind, shocking her system. "Charlie?" His voice sounded almost… pained. "Tell me I can touch you."

"Yes," she said, her voice breathy. His hand went to her hip, sliding down her thigh, and she sighed when his rough palms and fingers touched her bare skin. Slid underneath the T-shirt. "Yes."

His face was close to hers, but her eyes were now shut. She'd shut them when his hand had touched her. Her skin felt like it was on fire, even though he hadn't kissed her yet. The air between them was thick with tension and heat as he opened his mouth to ask another question.

"Can I kiss you—"

A knock sounded on the front door. "Page?" a deep voice called, interrupting them and forcibly pulling them out of the moment. Page's forehead came down to lean against the wall at her back. He muttered a soft, *"fucking hell"* before he pulled himself away and went to the front door.

The moment he was gone, she felt her breath leave her body in a whoosh. But she didn't have time to collapse into her bed like she wanted to or to take a moment to wonder what had just happened before Page and Callum walked from the front door and into her space.

The other man, clad in his work clothes, rough jeans, a green Henley, and orange work boots, paused when he saw her, blinked slowly, and then looked past her.

"Hi, Callum," she said, pulling on her best smile. "I'm Charlie." She stuck out her hand and let it fall when she saw his were full of tools. "We met the other day at Lilian's bookstore."

His confused but polite look darkened when she mentioned Lilian's name, but it was gone in a moment, making Charlie wonder if she had imagined it. "Oh, aye, I remember, hello," he said, pushing past her. "In here, right?" Then he paused, looking at her with a small frown before shuffling past. "You have some sweat on your brow. Sorry, I would have come by faster if I'd known it was that hot in here."

Charlie felt her cheeks flush and wiped at her forehead, knowing full well it wasn't sweat but drops of water from where Page's wet hair had touched her skin.

"Yeah," Page said, pushing past her as well. But she didn't miss the smirk he sent her way. Then the scowl he sent at Callum's back, "Good thing you got here so fast."

Charlie almost laughed. Almost.

She stood there a moment before realizing she really was more in the way than anything else. She might know how to change a tire and fix a lot of stuff in her own apartment, but plumbing was not her area of expertise. Instead, she grabbed her kindle and headed to the couch to read.

What had just happened in the other room, before Callum had barged in, was...

Lust. Pure lust.

The only question she kept asking herself was, what was she

going to do about it?

It was about half an hour before both men came out of her room and a few more minutes before Callum left. Charlie looked up from her book, which she'd been one hundred percent pretending to read, cringing when she realized that Callum had left before she'd said goodbye. The only thing she'd been able to think about was Page's hands on her body, how close they'd been, how—

"Is everything fixed?" she asked as Page walked into the living room, making his way into the kitchen.

"Yep, fixed and ready for use." Page paused in front of the fridge, and if she didn't know better, she would say he was looking at their list.

Not that she was looking at him.

Page pulled out some milk, pouring a glass before shutting the fridge and leaning against the counter.

They stared at each other across the room, silence filling the air.

"So… that happened."

Charlie scoffed, then laughed hoarsely. "Yeah, that happened."

Page nodded, biting his lip and then taking a sip from his glass. Her body was still buzzing, her head still in a fog. Page opened his mouth to say something, but Charlie beat him to it.

"Shit, what is the time?" she asked, jumping up from the couch and looking for her phone. With the toilet and then the almost kiss, she had completely zoned out from overstimulation, and she had to get to work.

"Almost nine—"

"Shit!" She ran into her room, slamming the door behind her. She couldn't help but think about his hands on her body, skin against skin, all day long.

To say she'd been a mess at work that day would be an understatement.

Chapter 22
Page

Page wanted to murder Callum—in a kind way that totally did not involve Callum dead and Flora without a father, of course. But he wanted to steal a time watch from his show and use it to prevent Callum from banging on his door at the very exact, perfectly wrong moment.

So instead of calling his friend to yell at him, "WHY?", he called Theo, whom he'd been meaning to call anyway.

"What do you mean, Charlie James is living in your demon of a sister's flat?" Theo asked once Page had updated him on all the information from the past couple of weeks. To say he was bad at communicating when overwhelmed was an understatement.

"I mean just that."

"The fuck..." Theo said. A bark sounded from the other side of the phone. "Yeah, buddy, Page is fucked."

Page rolled his eyes at his friend's theatrics. "Oh, and you missed the best part."

"What else happened?"

"I almost kissed her. Multiple times."

The curse on the other side of the phone made Page pull it away from his ear. Once Theo had calmed down, the first thing he said was, "Sandhya is going to kill you if you don't tell her right now."

Page already knew that. But he appreciated Theo reminding him of his impending doom.

"And she's working downstairs?" he asked and, at Page's confirmation, went silent. His next words made Page relax. "How do you really feel about it all?"

He hadn't told him to fuck off, he hadn't brought up the *show*. And maybe it should worry Page because he should be thinking of those things. But in this moment, he had wanted— no, needed—to just be a normal man with his mate talking about a woman he liked with no abnormal repercussions.

"I don't know," he said finally, letting out a breath.

"Not good enough, Page." At that, Page glared at the wall since he couldn't glare at his friend.

"I know."

"Well, at least you know something."

Page almost growled. Almost. "I know it's a bad idea, but I just... I don't know. Truly. I feel like, if I move in one direction, I'm going to fuck up everything, but if I move in the other, it... won't fuck up everything. And then I wonder if fucking up everything would lead to not having everything fucked up, but actually fucked in a good way."

"You just said fucked way too many times, Page."

Page let out a sigh.

"Look," Theo said. He heard his friend shuffle around, a dog whine, and then a door close. "I think we both know what you *should* do. But if anyone knows you, it's Sandhya and I, and I know what she would say, we both do." Yeah, that was one of the reasons why Page had called Theo and not Sandhya. Sandhya would tell him to go for it without thinking about the consequences. But Theo took more time when reacting to things, and he had needed that side of his friend today. "But you live so much of your life worrying about what others will think and do, or worrying about the ones you love, and Page... I think it's time to just do something for yourself. If that's letting her go, let her go. If that's *not*... well. You know Sandhya and I will support you in whatever you do. Unless it's unintelligent and foolish."

"This might be unintelligent and foolish."

He could almost see Theo's shrug. "I don't think it is. Not if she makes you smile the way you did every time you've said her name. Even I can hear it in your voice."

Page spent the entire day thinking over Theo's words, even though he knew he already had his answer. He needed to tell Charlie that they would go their separate ways, that yes, he was attracted to her, but he was attracted to a lot of people. He could stay away from one person if it meant keeping his career and family safe from prying eyes and bad attention.

He had planned it all out. Make her dinner, sit down, say the words, go to his room. But when she walked through the door, dumping her bag on the couch, all his thoughts went out the window. Her hair was down, cascading around her shoulders instead of up in a ponytail or a bun. She was still in her work clothes, leggings, and a long wool jumper the color of the clouds on a sunny day. Her cheeks were flushed, her freckles scattered across her nose, cheeks and down her neck. A neck he wanted to lick—

"We need to talk," she said, her words making him meet her gaze. He hadn't realized just how hazel brown her eyes were until they'd been sitting at the beach the other day. The sun had hit them at just the right angle to make them shine. In the shadow, her eyes were a dark brown, but in the sun… they were golden. Right now, he could see the determination shining in them.

"I agree—"

"Let me get this out first," she said, and he stopped talking. Because, of course, he did. No matter what he had planned all day, the look she sent him, the way she stood there, her hands on her hips, her chin high—well, he'd honestly have done anything she asked. "I've been thinking all day about what happened earlier or almost happened. Or—"

"The almost kiss. My hands on your body. Me telling you that I want to fu—"

"Yes, that," she glared at him, but it didn't hold too much

weight. "And the thing is, this is a bad idea." Page felt his shoulders fall a bit, but he let her continue. He didn't know why he was so disappointed. This was exactly what he was going to suggest. It was a *good* thing. "We know this is a bad idea," she continued. "But the truth is, it's only a bad idea if other people find out. So," she said, with a small shrug, "other people won't find out."

"Define other people," he said, moving from where he'd been leaning against the counter as he stepped closer to her. Step by step. He could hear his heart beating loudly in his ears.

"I don't know," she said, her gaze tracking his movements. Her hands came up to push through her hair. "Like—well, Ripley obviously already knows."

"Obviously," he said, trying to hide back a smile. "So does a friend of mine."

She looked at him in surprise. "Really?" He almost chuckled at the shock in her voice.

"Yes," he said, finally standing in front of her. His arms crossed over his chest. "I was a bit… confused today."

He caught the small smile on her face before she lifted her chin to look him right in the eyes. "We keep this between us and whoever we might want to tell. No one else."

"Okay." He knew it was stupid. He knew this was, somehow, someway, going to come back and bite him in the ass, but when she looked at him like that, with that grin, that *knowing grin*—

"Wait," she said, pushing back against his chest. He hadn't realized he had moved even closer to her until her hands touched him. He seemed to be gravitating towards her, caught in her orbit. Her heart was beating fast, her body already moving back towards him. He looked at her skeptically, but she smiled, letting him know they were okay. "What about the rules?" she asked, her hands still resting on his chest as she spoke.

His eyes glinted as he remembered their third rule. "We never mentioned sex," he said, grinning at her mischievously.

She laughed, the sound cut off as his hand on her hip started moving. "God," she said, her voice breathless. "You're right," she agreed, her eyes meeting his. She breathed in and then out. "Just sex."

Before she could take a step back, he pulled her into him. His breath caught when her chest touched his. "Just sex...then we aren't... breaking any of the rules."

They stared at each other for a moment, the only sound their erratic breathing.

"Ask me again," she said, her voice hoarse.

He didn't need to confirm what she meant. He already knew.

Chapter 23
Charlie

"Can I kiss you?"

She let out a shaky breath. "Yes."

He did, his mouth kissing behind her ear, sucking on the soft skin there. The feeling made her moan instantly.

"Can I fuck you?" he asked, his voice hoarse.

"*Please—*"

He cut her off, his lips covering hers. The kiss wasn't gentle. His lips were hard against hers, and she let out another moan as his tongue pushed into her mouth, caressing hers.

The rules. Rule Three.

Who the hell in their right mind cared about rules right now? Charlie didn't. Not when Page was kissing her as if she were air itself. Not when his hand touched her right where she needed it, not when he found the spot on her neck just below her ear and he kissed her there, a gasp leaving her mouth as her head fell back and her eyes closed.

Page hummed, the sound deep in his chest, at the noise she made, and he kissed her there again, his palm pushing against her back and moving her body against his.

It felt amazing, but it wasn't enough. She needed more.

Charlie reached down, grabbed her sweater, and pulled it over her head. Page pulled back enough to give her room, and when the sweater fell on the floor, she saw the searing heat in his gaze. His eyes drank her in, taking in the curve of her waist, her small breasts, the birthmark underneath her belly button. She hadn't worn a bra today—hadn't been able to stand the texture of it. And now, for the first time in her life, she was thanking overstimulation and sensory overload.

"You are so beautiful," he said in awe, his voice rough and deep as he dragged her by the hand into her room. He stepped forward into her, his hands settling on her hips, pausing at the top of her jeans.

"Can I?" he asked.

"Yes," she said, barely gasping out the word as he kissed the top of her shoulder, and only pulled away when he leaned back, dragging her jeans down her legs until she was standing in front of him in only her underwear. His hands came back to rest on her hips, pulling her in, his mouth capturing hers for another long, heated kiss. His clothes were still on, but she could feel the heat radiating off his skin as her hands slipped under his shirt. She dragged her hands up, and he broke their kiss to grab the back of his shirt and pull it over his head.

She took a moment to look at him. She had seen him shirtless in the apartment, and once or twice in the TV show, but she hadn't let herself look. She hadn't imagined that she would even get to look, at least not like this. Charlie had tried to picture what he would look like, at night, when she'd wanted him beside her, inside her. But her imagination had not done him justice. Page was gorgeous. His shoulders were broad and strong, his waist and hips leaner. Her eyes dragged down body, paused on the bit of dark hair curling around where his pants hung low on his hips. God, she wanted to touch him.

"Can I… can I touch you?" she asked, her voice hoarse. The look he gave her nearly melted her.

"Touch me," he said as a plea.

So she did. Her hands came up, dragging along his chest, her mouth settling above his heart as her hands graced the tattoo on his wrist.

She wanted to ask him about it, but she stopped herself, instead pulling back to look at him.

"So are you," she said, an answer to his own earlier description of her.

Page kissed her up against the wall, her body stuck between his and the hard surface for… Charlie couldn't tell how long. Time seemed to be irrelevant when he nipped at her lip, drawing a groan out of her. He grabbed her under her thighs, her legs wrapping around his body and walked them sideways, his legs hitting the bed. They both fell, a mix of tangled limbs and laughs that soon turned into groans as she straddled his waist and let herself grind down against him. He still had his pants on, and her hands came down to undo the zipper and button, her knuckles brushing against him. Page let out a stream of curses underneath her and lifted his hips, helping her take off his pants.

He hadn't been wearing underwear. She stared at him, taking all of him in.

His hands rested on her hips—no, gripped her hips, his fingers digging into her skin fiercely. She let out a gasp as he moved her hips against him, her hands scrabbling for purchase and settling on his thighs behind her.

"I need to get these pants off you," he said, gripping her underwear.

She let out a huff. "You mean my underwear?" she teased, raising a brow at him.

He shook his head, sitting up and bending down so he could scatter kisses along her chest. He dragged her breast into his mouth, his tongue swirling the bud. She gasped. "You Americans, calling things by the wrong name."

"You Scots—" she cut off as a moan left her as he moved his hips and sucked her other breast into his mouth.

He pulled back, sending her a cheeky grin. "Yes?"

"Oh, shut up," she said and pulled him in for a kiss. He pushed her back onto the bed, moving so he hovered over her. As he kissed down, her hands went into his hair, her fingers tangling in the blond strands. It was softer than she had imagined it would be.

She couldn't quite believe she was here, with him in her arms and her in his. With his tongue touching hers, caressing her lips, his hands moving along her skin.

He went down, and down, his tongue darting out to run against her birthmark, next along the top of her underwear.

Then he kissed her thighs, his hands cupping her hips, his fingers gripping her as if he were afraid she would disappear. Her hands grabbed the sheet as his breath hit her right where she wanted him to be. When she gasped, her hands pulling him closer, she heard his soft chuckle and—

"Fuck."

With one hand, he grasped her underwear, pulling it to the side as he kissed her inner thigh. "Do you need something, love?" he asked, and she lifted her head to catch the cheeky grin he sent her way. It was more a smirk, his eyes looking up at her.

"Yes," she said, her voice breathy. She couldn't seem to catch her breath. She wondered if she had taken a real breath since he had first kissed her. When he bit down on the soft flesh of her thigh, nipping at her skin, she gasped. "God, kiss me, Page…"

"Kiss you where?" he asked, his voice low and gravely. He hovered over her, moving her legs around his shoulders, locking him right where she wanted him.

"Here?" he continued, kissing her above her underwear, just above her clit. She groaned. "Or here?" he asked, moving lower and pushing her underwear aside, giving her a chaste kiss right where she wanted him.

"…right there."

He chuckled when she pulled on his hair, urging him closer. The vibrations ricocheted through her body. She had been waiting for this longer than she had thought, probably since the moment she'd seen him, fixing that damn heater—

She gasped when he kissed her, his tongue—

God, *his tongue.*

"Page," she gasped.

"God, you taste just like I'd imagined…"

She couldn't control herself, her hips moving against his face. His hands came up to hold her hips still as he worked her higher and higher, and it wasn't long before shocks moved through her as she collapsed back into the pillows. She came, her hands gripping his hair between her fingers.

When she opened her eyes, her body still coming down, he was standing at the foot of the bed, completely naked, his body caught in a stream of light coming in from the window to her right.

She leaned over, reaching into her bedside table for a condom. Their eyes met.

"Are you sure?" he asked, moving back onto his knees on the bed. She sighed a bit when his hands grabbed her calves, massaging the muscles, the rough calluses of his hands harsh against her skin.

"Yes," she said, her voice calm and sure. She hadn't ever been *more* sure. She wanted this. Wanted him. And she loved that he wanted to check.

"I want you," she said, sitting up, ripping the condom open, and reaching forward to grab him in her hands. His eyes heated as he bit back a groan. She rolled the condom onto him, her eyes never leaving his. "But I—" she cut herself off. Maybe now wasn't the time—

"What? Is something wrong?" She looked up at him, into his eyes, and what she saw almost made her melt..

"No, I mean, I don't think so." She covered her face with her hands, chuckling. He slowly grabbed her wrists, pulling her hands down so they sat in his, looking at her patiently. So patiently. She took a deep breath. "It's just, sometimes, I can't come as much as other partners during sex," she admitted, pulling out the words. "With my sensory issues, sometimes, things just become too much. And when they do, I can't help but need a bit of space and time. Sometimes, after I come, I can't come again, or I need a small break before continuing." She let out an unamused laugh, afraid to look at him.

She sucked in a breath when his hand gripped her chin lightly. "Can you look me in the eyes right now?" he asked, and when she nodded, he shifted her gaze to his. "It's okay if it's too much. Charlie, I don't pretend to understand everything you go through," he said softly, his hands coming up to cup her cheeks. "But this is you and me, and the communication doesn't stop here. If you need to stop, we stop. If something is too much, we stop. If you want more, you tell me. I want to bring you pleasure," he said, moving to kiss her. When he pulled away, she almost groaned.

"Same," she said, her voice wobbly. "For all of that. I just... don't want you to be disappointed."

Page's gaze roamed over her, over her body, lingering on her breasts until she flushed, up her neck, over her face. What she saw there was pure lust and maybe—no, just sex, they had said just sex. But whatever she saw, even if she couldn't acknowledge it, made her feel a bit stronger. "I want to fuck you, Charlie. I want to make you come again, this time on my cock. Do you want me to?"

They were kneeling in front of one another, and even on their knees, he was taller than her, her head reaching his shoulder. But she didn't feel small in this moment. Maybe it was the way he was looking at her, a bit in awe, heat scorching her skin and making her flush, want so clear in his green eyes. Or maybe it was the way he touched her without any hesitancy. He knew she wasn't fragile, had known that right away, and had never treated her so.

"Yes," she said, her voice breathy.

His hands gripped her waist, pulling her closer and her breath caught in her throat. "I want you more than I should."

Before she could overthink those words, he was kissing her, his tongue hitting hers in passion. They fell back, his body moving over hers.

Charlie let her mind stop. She let herself do something she never did—just *feel*. No thinking, no processing, no picking apart a moment or a feeling. She went with her gut. She moved with her body, letting his groans and gasps guide her.

He moved over her, his hips meeting hers, his body moving inside her, and she let out a moan, pulling his face to hers for a kiss.

"God, you feel so good," he groaned into her mouth. "Lift your hips up for me." He gripped them, and she moved to help him. "Good girl," he said, capturing her lips in a heated kiss, capturing her moan.

He started to move, his eyes meeting hers, and she didn't question their intensity as he hit the right place, her hips moving up to meet his.

It had been way too long. Too long since she'd felt this way, too long since she'd had a partner who made her want this much. But she shouldn't be surprised. Every moment since he'd arrived seemed to be leading up to this, building and building, until they'd had no choice but to crash together. His hands gripped her wrists, dragging her hands up and over her head, holding her hands there as his head bowed, dragging her nipple into his mouth, grazing with his teeth. "Page," she pleaded.

"Tell me what you want," he said, his head coming up to kiss her chest, her neck, as he shifted his hips, thrusting into her harder this time. She opened her mouth but gasped—

"There, just there—"

As they both moved closer, their bodies in sync, she let herself go completely and let herself feel.

Chapter 24
Page

Page wouldn't say he had been imagining this moment for long, but he had been *wanting it*. He had been wanting her for weeks, and a part of him couldn't quite believe she was in his arms right now. That he was kissing her. He knew this wasn't the best idea—hell, it was probably the worst idea he'd had in years.

But when his mouth brushed her skin. When her hands caressed him. When his tongue touched hers. When he seated himself inside of her, her body enveloping him—

He didn't care about why this wasn't a good idea. All he could think about was her.

Charlie.

He wanted to remember all of this. The moment she gasped when he moved inside of her for the first time. When she pulled him close. The sound she made when she came. The feeling of her coming undone around him. He came a few moments later, pulling her as close as possible, falling half on top of her and half onto the bed beside her.

Just sex. That was what they'd agreed to.

Just sex.

But then, why was his heart beating this fast?

He had been in relationships before—a few girlfriends in secondary school and Julliard, and since getting the show, a few women he had been with for one-night stands after going to clubs Theo and Sandhya had pulled him to when they weren't on set. He knew what just sex felt like.

This was not it.

He rolled over to lie beside her on his back. He got up a few seconds later to clean himself up and throw out the condom. But he found himself hurrying back to her. He brought back a damp washcloth, brought it to her skin. When he was done, he fell back into the bed beside her. He pointedly looked up at the ceiling, his arm coming over his head.

They were both still catching their breath. He could see her chest moving up and down out of the corner of his eyes, and he made sure not to look at her.

If he looked at her, he might do something, say something, stupid.

Something very, *very* stupid.

Just sex.

"Well," Charlie said, speaking first after a few moments. "That was not completely unexpected. But it was better than I thought it'd be."

The laugh jumped out of his chest before he could stop it. This woman.

"Better than you thought it would be, huh?" he asked, perching himself up on one elbow to look down at her. Her cheeks were flushed, one arm above her head. She made no move to cover herself as he looked at her, and at her small smirk, he had the urge to lean forward and kiss her again.

"I mean, you are very hot."

"Why, thank you."

She rolled her eyes, pushing him lightly with her elbow. "But you sometimes come off a bit uptight. I mean, I did call missionary, which might be considered uptight—"

He could not believe this woman. This smart, snarky, truthful, fiery woman.

"Uptight?" he said, rolling onto her, moving their hips flushed against one another. He met her eyes, loving the way they widened with her gasp as she felt how hard he was again. "I am not uptight," he said, his voice a growl as he bent down, catching her breast in his mouth and biting down slightly.

"You might have to prove me wrong then," she said through another gasp, and even though he didn't look up to see her mischievous grin, he knew it was there.

So, he did. He proved her wrong again, again and again.

Excerpt from *STARVERSE*: Season 3, Episode 6

THOREN'S ROOM — NIGHT

THOREN and CAR sit beside each other, drinking.

> CAR
> I know it's not smart.

> THOREN
> I didn't say anything, captain.

> CAR
> You didn't have to.

> THOREN
> Is it worth it?

> CAR
> I think so.

Chapter 25
Charlie

The next week was a blur.

A sexy blur. With lots of orgasms.

But a blur, nonetheless.

Charlie had taken a few days off work, and Page had taken some time off helping with the house on the beach. They had decided to burrow into their apartment together. It was the perfect start to their plan of keeping this—whatever it was—a secret. It was just fine with her. It meant she had more time to kiss him. And do... other things.

Other things in their rooms. In their bathrooms. In the kitchen. Against the wall.

All of their pent-up feelings, lust, and hidden looks had built up, and now it was all spilling over. They couldn't seem to get enough of each other.

"You have to be sick of me," Charlie let out a breath as she sank back against the couch, pulling one of the cozy blankets to cover her nakedness. She raised her arms to throw the blanket over them both. Page, sweat still covering his brow, collapsed on top of her, and she giggled at the delicious feeling of his body against hers. Today had been her first day back to work and he'd ambushed her when she'd stumbled in at the end of the day, murmuring how he'd been thinking of her all day, and then had proceeded to fuck her brains out over the couch.

He propped himself up on his arms, one on either side of her chest, bracketing her in. She had thought she would need space from him after, but she had found that this feeling of being around him, close to him, made her feel calm... safe.

"You say that as if it is a well-known fact," he said, kissing her nose lightly. She glared. "To my knowledge, you have no proof to go with that argument." He buried his head in her neck, and she tried not to mewl like a cat.

"It happens," she said, trying not to sound insecure. "It always happens." The words were out before she could stop them.

He lifted his head, his green eyes slightly darkening. "What do you mean?"

Charlie sighed, shifting her body so that she was sitting up a bit straighter against the arm of the couch. To her disappointment, Page moved as well, her legs across his lap but still close enough to where they could share the blanket and keep themselves warm. It made a cocoon of heat from their bodies and the warmth of the material. They had yet to fix the heater in the living room. Page insisted it wasn't needed until autumn, and Charlie was too happy getting warmth from his body instead.

"I mean," she said, clearing her throat, her awkwardness rising in her chest. "I've never done *this*," she admitted, waving a hand between them. At his raised brows, she fought back a smile. "You know what I mean. In the past, it's only taken a few weeks for someone I'm with to realize that I'm too much work or too hard to deal with, and that's when they leave. If it isn't after a few weeks, it happens eventually. Even with friends."

Page was frowning now. It was the same frown she'd seen

him wear when she'd mentioned her family. It was soft, hiding all the emotions plaguing him, but she could see those feelings briefly as if they were imprisoned and trying to be set free. Sometimes, she wished he would just let them. His anger never seemed directed at her or tainted with disdain. It seemed more like a righteous sort of anger.

It was, honestly, quite sexy.

All this sex was starting to rot her brain a bit.

"I—"

He cut her off with a kiss. It was slow, languid, his tongue caressing her lips until she opened for him. She was still learning all the different ways Page could kiss her, her mind cataloguing them for future reference. There was this kiss, the one he gave her when he was heated, in the moment. The kiss up against the wall that made her body feel like it was on fire. The soft one he gave her when they were finished and barely had any energy left. There was the one he gave her on the side of her head or her forehead while they read next to each other after a long day. And even though they both insisted that there weren't any feelings between them other than friendship and pure lust, she could have sworn that this kiss, though small, seemed to hold a bit more *something* than others.

"I know there really isn't much I can say to make you think differently," he said, his voice deep. She'd discovered how much she loved the sound of his voice. Especially in the morning, whispering dirty things into her ear. "I can't really compete with years' worth of trauma." She tried to open her mouth to say something, but he cut her off with another kiss. This one was short and chaste. When he pulled away, she was frowning at him. But when he grinned, she knew he saw how the frown lacked any real anger. "So, you will just have to see how you're wrong when I don't leave."

His words sounded like something more. They sounded like a promise meant for someone he cared about. They hung in the air between them, and she saw the moment they both decided not to acknowledge them. The moment they both turned away.

"Even when *this*," he said, motioning to her and their current, naked state, "changes, I would still consider you a friend."

She forced a small smile. She didn't want to know why the words made her a little bit queasy. She might not understand how to navigate what they had, but it wasn't giving her anxiety. Somehow, it felt natural, even though she knew she should be second-guessing everything. If someone had told her a few weeks ago that this would be where they were at, she would have scoffed.

A high-pitched ringing sounded from the coffee table, and she winced. Page caught the movement and grabbed his phone to turn the sound off. "Sorry," she said, and Page shook his head.

"If you don't like the sound, I'll change it."

He made it seem that easy. He had been saying and doing similar things for the past week. It still shocked her a bit. Other than Ripley, no one had noticed the things that made her senses scream. They had definitely not done anything to change them.

That reminded her that she needed to call Ripley.

Damn.

Her friend had been messaging her all week, and Charlie hadn't been the best at responding. It sometimes happened when she got overwhelmed or hyper-fixated on what was directly around her—answering the phone, taking off the blinders and talking with someone who wasn't directly with her could be a bit too much.

But that didn't mean she didn't feel guilty.

Page groaned.

That sound pulled her out of her own thoughts.

"What is it?" she asked, reaching for her own phone to check her messages.

"My agent," he said, his lips pursed. "She's reminding me of our next live interview, which is at the end of the week. She just sent me materials to review beforehand." His eyes darkened a bit.

Charlie tensed. It was a small gesture, but she knew that Page caught it. During this past week, they hadn't mentioned anything to do with their real lives. It seemed that both of them had needed to escape from reality, using each other to do so.

"This is your first interview since…"

He nodded. "Should be interesting."

Charlie snorted. "You could say that. Especially since you're fucking the woman who seems to have ruined the public image of *StarVerse*'s Handsome Rogue."

Page raised a brow. "I take offense to the fact that you aren't talking about me there."

"Didn't you know?" Charlie said humorously. "You're the Handsome Star Prince who decided to join the army. You are far from being a rogue."

Page winced. "Sometimes I hate that." At Charlie's confused expression, he continued. "Fans like to impose the characters onto us. Like we're the same person. Which is highly ironic since I've always been anti-royal and anti-military."

She snorted. "Same. That's why I never liked your character. Glass' character was always so much more interesting."

"Excuse you," he said indignantly, giving her an impressive glare. "How dare you." She giggled when he crawled over her, the blanket slipping. But it didn't matter because he was there, his body heat keeping her warm. His body was all muscle and smooth skin, and her finger came up to trace a freckle on his neck.

"I guess you'll just have to change my mind," she said, sending him a mischievous grin.

"I guess I shall," he replied and kissed her senseless. They forgot again, erasing everything else away with each other.

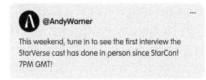

Chapter 26
Page

Page had a love-hate relationship with London.

He hated it because it was too big, too loud. But he loved it because Sandhya and Theo lived there.

Getting off the train at King's Cross, he grabbed a taxi, giving the driver Sandhya's address. He always stayed with her. It was better than staying at Theo's—he had a small studio flat barely big enough for him and Han Solo. Plus, Theo was always over at Sandhya's anyways. She lived in a beautiful two-bedroom flat in Notting Hill. She was far from her parents now, but he knew she liked living in London with its big city vibe, parks, loud nightlife, and large theater scene. She had started her acting career in theater while at university, before getting the *StarVerse* job, and still did a few smaller jobs here and there. He knew her parents' closest friends lived in London, and she liked to visit them during Diwali, Holi or Navaratri, and other family celebrations if she couldn't go home.

When he arrived, he found the key in the plant near the door and when inside, saw that her flat was empty, a small note sitting on Sandhya's kitchen counter.

Be back soon. Make your big ass comfortable whilst I grab some food. Theo is coming at 6.

-S.

So, Page did as he was told, moving his stuff into her guest room/office before making himself a cup of chamomile tea. Opening the fridge, he spotted a large jug of mango lassi with a sticky note saying, "Theo, if you drink all of this whilst I'm gone, I won't make any more for you, you dick" and let out a laugh. Sandhya's mango lassi was her mother's recipe that she'd made at home growing up, and it was one of Theo's favorite drinks in the entire world. She'd been making large pitchers of it to store in her fridge for friends when they came over since he had met her. He could bet money on the fact that, since it was summer, she had put some of it in the freezer as well for dessert. He grabbed an apple from the basket in the fridge, shutting the door. His tea in his hand, he settled himself at her kitchen counter on one of the high stools.

It had been a long train—seven hours, to be exact—and his muscles ached. He had been upgraded to first class by his manager, so he hadn't really had to worry about being randomly bothered, but it had still been lonely.

He'd had a book and his music on his phone, but he hadn't been able to read or let his mind wander.

It had been stuck on two things.

The upcoming interview and Charlie.

And, he conceded to himself, also how Charlie might have a chance of coming up in the interview.

Some part of him knew his agent would have warned him if the press had found out about her. He would have warned him and let him know that the questions had already been redacted in preparation. And yet, he still worried.

Then he got angry at himself and at the situation.

Because it wasn't bloody fair. The entire thing was doomed from the very beginning.

He had known from that first kiss that, whatever they had going on, it would not end well. And he had kissed her anyway. And now, stepping away from the town and from Charlie, common sense, his current arch-nemesis, had started to creep back in.

What was he doing?

They had both agreed this would only be sex, but he knew it was more. Maybe not something worth putting a name to quite yet, but the seed was there. He felt it in his chest, growing by the day.

He knew that their relationship, even if it was just sex, could ruin his standing with the show, possibly even his contract. But for some reason, on the train down, that hadn't been his worry. He had only been worried about what would happen to Charlie.

If the press and the show had been so hard on her for just being an angry fan, how harshly would they harass her when they found out they were together?

Not that they were together…

Were they together?

Page groaned. He had been so distracted by Charlie the past few days that he hadn't sat down with her to define anything. The only thing they had defined was this: just sex.

Page finished his tea, wishing it were a glass of whiskey instead, looking down at his phone with a glare. He'd been checking it every thirty minutes for any text from her like a lovesick puppy. He wondered if he should text her first. Was that something they were doing now? He had only really texted her before when he needed to.

At the sound of keys jangling, the door to the flat opened, and Sandhya walked in with her arms full of grocery bags, rapidly speaking Marathi into the phone pressed between her ear and shoulder. He didn't speak the language but recognized a few words here and there that Sandhya had taught him and Theo over the years. He knew that she spoke Hindi and Urdu as well, along with Spanish, Italian and French. She and Theo sometimes used French as a secret language whenever they wanted to annoy Page because he was horrible at it. She paused in the doorway when she saw him, smiling before saying goodbye on the phone.

"Ah! You got here already. I was hoping I would be home before you, but oh well." Her voice brought a sense of comfort and familiarity to him. Sandhya was like a second sister to him, though she liked to joke she was more of the lesbian aunt type.

He moved to help her gather the bags and put them onto the counter. "You know that it's my pleasure in life to disappoint you," he teased, and moved to kiss her cheek.

"It seems it is," she said before slugging him in the arm. He winced. She always had strong punches. He had learned that early on when they'd been in combat stunt training together in the first few months after being cast.

Other than Theo, Sandhya had been one of his first friends on set, and he was thankful for that first day when she had accidentally punched him in the face instead of faking it. It had been their first scene together, and afterwards, instead of getting angry, he had laughed his ass off, causing her to laugh as well and ruin the entire scene. They had gotten close, their characters romantic partners on and off during the first few seasons. But it had been their first sex scene, not long into the season, that had confirmed how much he adored Sandhya. She had looked him straight in the eyes before their Sex and Consent Training with the intimacy coordinator, her face serious and stern. Then she had said, "Look, we might be having sex on screen, but I'm gay, so we won't be those co-worker actors who fall in love and shit after they have sex on screen. So, keep it cool."

He had been so shocked at her straightforwardness that he had probably looked like a fish with his mouth opening and closing. Then he had taken a moment to collect himself and said, "No problem. But I also didn't assume this would happen going into this."

She had nodded. He had nodded back. And then they had gotten through the Sex and Consent Training and choreography with lots of humor, jokes, and contained laughter. Ever since, they had been friends off and on set.

Sandhya was now looking at him with one of her famous glares that rivaled his sister's.

"You haven't called me or Theo once since you've been home, you big oaf," she said. Her accent had changed softly over the past years, her time living in London affecting her cadence. He gulped, knowing he was in big trouble and would probably need to beg on his hands and knees for her forgiveness. But he was interrupted by Theo walking through the door.

More like falling through the doorway, his corgi pulling him in with a bound.

"Han Solo!" Sandhya said, falling to the ground and giving the dog a hug and kisses as it ran straight for her. Once, in the park, a stranger had instantly thought the dog belonged to Sandhya instead of Theo—that's how much the dog played favorites.

"Hello," Theo said, dropping the dog's leash and pushing the door shut behind him. He was dressed in his running gear, sweat shorts and a muscle tank that showed off the large muscles of his arms. His tan skin was covered in sweat. He must have just come from his run around the neighborhood.

"You, shower," she said, pointing at Theo. "You," she continued, pointing at Page, "are not off the hook, mister."

"I know," he sighed as Theo moved into the room he was staying in to shower and change. He stayed over so often that he kept some of his clothes in Sandhya's spare room. Early on, there had been rumors about the two of them dating, but Sandhya had put those to bed quickly when she'd started dating her girlfriend, Ray, right after the beginning of the first season's premiere. Ray was currently living in New York, studying for a master's in film makeup and special effects. They were disgustingly adorable together.

Theo, on the other hand, was like Page and tried his best to keep any romantic entanglements out of the press. He always got the same questions as Page—was he dating? Which lucky girl would he choose to date next? Was he with anyone special? But Page always felt worse for Theo because they just assumed his friend was straight. Theo had ranted about it plenty of times to Page and Sandhya, which always turned into a drunken discussion of how fucked up the heteronormative patriarchal capitalist society they lived in was. Those discussions usually ended with them getting drunk on Sandhya's couch and ranting about the monarchy or other politics until they were too pissed to walk.

Page moved to help Sandhya put the food away, and it wasn't long before they had dinner ready and were sitting around Sandhya's kitchen counter, wine in their hands and pasta in their stomachs.

"So," Sandhya said, her eyes narrowing on Page. "What have you been so busy with that you can't even call your friends to say hello?"

Page swallowed and winced. "I'm sorry about that. Things at home have been...something."

Theo nodded but stayed quiet, his gaze fixed on Page. There was no way he was getting out of this. "And I might have called Theo," he said, already preparing for the yell. "I needed some advice. But I wanted to tell you in person," he said.

"Advice on what?" Page felt the tension in his shoulders loosen as he heard the concern in Sandhya's voice. He should've known she would be understanding. He did his best to shove the guilt he felt at not calling her down.

"Do you remember that woman, Charlie James?" When her mouth dropped open, he continued and told her everything. Just like he always had. They had been his rock in so many ways since the start of filming, and he knew that, if he could trust anyone, it was them. When he was done, he was met with pure silence. Sandhya opened her mouth as if to say something and then shut it promptly, taking a large swig of wine and draining her glass instead.

Sandhya cocked her head. "So, you've been shacking up with the one woman on this planet you absolutely needed to not get involved with, who also seems to be working at your sister's store *and* living in the flat you have to stay in. Then you promptly decided to fuck her, and now you are what?" Page frowned at his friend's crassness. "Going to ride off into the sunset with her?"

"If I remember correctly, you two were teasing me about getting together with her a few months ago."

"Yeah, teasing," Theo said, rolling his eyes. "Not expecting her to be in Scotland when you got home."

"To be fair, neither was I."

Sandhya snorted. "I can't believe she knocked you out with a golf club. Priceless."

He sent a mock glare her way. "I still have the lump on my shoulders to prove it."

She let out another undignified snort. "I'll have to thank her when I meet her."

Page shook his head. "No, you two are not meeting her." At both of their protests, he continued. "I told you; it is just sex." At their skepticism, he groaned. "It is!"

"Yep," Theo said before taking a sip of his beer. "Totally believe you."

"Are you at least being safe?" Sandhya asked, her voice getting serious.

Page stiffened and tried to lighten the mood. "Yes, mom, we're using condoms."

She rolled her eyes. "Not what I meant, idiot. I meant, are you being safe from the press."

They all knew he had known what she meant and had purposely not responded. "Aye," he said, and at her look, he nodded. "I am. But—"

"It's a lot," she said, reading his mind. He didn't need to tell them how he was feeling. They knew his past, knew what anxieties were plaguing him.

"Yeah."

At that, Sandhya grabbed a few more beers and a bottle of wine from her fridge. "Well, then. I say we get raging drunk. Our interview is in the afternoon, so we have time to sleep it off tomorrow morning."

So, they did just that. He tried to forget about his anxieties. And failed.

@TurnThePageBookshop

We are now open from 10-17:00 during the weekdays. Make sure to visit before our end -of-the-summer sale is over.

Chapter 27

Charlie

The next day, at work, Charlie had a hard time focusing, which was nothing new; she found her mind always wandering when the store's business was slow. Page had left early that morning, taking the train down to London. And for some reason, his absence hit her more than she'd expected. A part of her had expected herself to be able to just jump back into what it had been like before him.

But she started noticing things the moment the door shut behind him.

She noticed every time she opened her mouth to say something to him, stopping when she remembered he wasn't in the next room. Or when she looked down at her phone, expecting him to ask what she wanted from the grocery store on his way home from working on the house.

Charlie knew quite soon and abruptly that she didn't like how much she was suddenly relying on him. She had never needed someone before. This feeling of needing him was starting to eat at her, and she didn't like it one bit.

Did she need him? Or just need the feeling that came along with him? Maybe she just needed the orgasms.

"Are you okay?" Layla asked, dumping a stack of books on the counter Charlie was sitting behind. Charlie looked up from where she had been glaring at the happy-face sticker on the back of their counter.

"Yeah, why?" she asked, starting to put the stickers she had been rubbing between her fingers onto the books in front of her.

"You've been glaring at the counter for the past thirty minutes, and before I set the books down, you didn't hear me calling your name." Layla sent her a small smile. "Need to talk?"

It was late in the day, and the bookstore was empty. They usually got a few stragglers who ran in right before closing time, but that wasn't for another hour.

"I was thinking—"

"About Page," Layla finished, a smirk covering her face at Charlie's annoyed look.

"Maybe."

Layla sighed, leaning on the counter in front of her. "So, what about our famous actor friend were you thinking about? Maybe his talent with his tongue?" At Charlie's blush, Layla gasped. "Wait. Do you know about his talent with his tongue?"

"Do you?" Charlie asked, a feeling rising inside of her that was not jealousy. It wasn't. It couldn't be.

Layla let out a deep laugh. "No, I don't. But my friend Louise dated him when they were seventeen and said that he was very talented at," she glanced down, smiling, "you know."

"He is," Charlie said, causing Layla to let out another squeal mixed with a shriek.

"You guys had sex."

"You could say that," Charlie admitted, moving to grab the stack of books and take them back to where they needed to be shelved.

"Oh, no, you don't. You do not get to act like nothing has happened," Layla said, following behind her.

"But it is nothing. Just sex," Charlie said, and at Layla's skeptical look, she groaned. "It is. We have a rule."

"A rule?" Layla asked, her voice filled with a bit of laughter.

"Yes. It is on the fridge and everything. Just sex. No falling for the flatmate."

Layla couldn't seem to hold in her laughter any longer, and Charlie glared at her. "Oh, that is priceless. What are you guys, twelve?"

"No, we're just two adults who know that nothing good will come from us getting attached," she said, putting the last book into place and turning to look at the woman who had become a close friend in the short span of time she'd been in Scotland. "You know it would be a disaster. It could even ruin his career. It's just sex."

Layla puckered her lips, taking a moment before she spoke again. "I get what you are saying, but Char, you know how this works." She set a light hand on her shoulder, sending Charlie a look that made her want to hide in the corner and rock back and forth. "It never ends up being just sex."

"It has to be," she said firmly.

Layla nodded. "Where is he, anyway?"

"London." She went to grab a bottle of water from the mini fridge in the back room. "He has a press interview with the other cast members for the new season."

"We can watch it together if you want." Layla shrugged at Charlie's look of shock. "I love *StarVerse*. I started watching it for Page, like everyone else in this small town, but you know I love myself a great Sci-Fi show. Plus, they have a diverse cast, which is pretty cool."

Charlie nodded slowly. How she hadn't known Layla watched *StarVerse* until now, she couldn't say. No, actually, she could.

It was easy for Charlie to get stuck in her own head at times, anxiety making it hard for her to ask people about their own hobbies and more about themselves. And with how she had been so caught up in Page...

She hadn't been a good friend to Layla at all.

"Come over for dinner tonight? I have wine," Charlie said and grinned when Layla smiled.

"Sounds amazing. I will bring bread and cheese."

"The holy trinity," Charlie said.

"And that's the truth," Layla agreed, and Charlie chuckled.

Charlie sometimes felt like friends were one of the hardest things for her to understand. She never knew if someone considered her a close friend or if they were just acquaintances. But right now, she felt like something had shifted between her and Layla. Even if she second-guessed it, she somehow knew she had just made a friend. And she was pretty set on making sure she didn't lose her.

Excerpt from *STARVERSE*: Season 1, Episode 2

TRAINING ROOM — DAY

CAR walks into the training room and takes a moment to look around. He walks up to the boy he saw the other day, hesitates a moment. The young man is THOREN.

> CAR
> Car Brandon.

> THOREN
> I think everyone here knows that. We all know you… Your Highness.

> CAR
> If you knew me, you would know not to call me Your Highness.

> THOREN
> Touché.

> CAR
> (Extends his hand)
> Car Brandon. Nice to meet you.

> THOREN
> Thoren Day. Nice to meet you too… Brandon.

A woman walks over, looks them up and down and nods to Thoren.

> VALERI
> I thought we were going to stay away from the royal prick?

> THOREN
> Val—

> CAR
> If you want to stay away from the royal prick, I recommend making sure you're never in a room with my brother.

> VALERI
> I'll make sure to do that. Valeri.

> CAR
> Car Brandon.

VALERI
Well, Brandon, maybe we'll give you a chance to
prove how you're not like your brother...

Chapter 28

Page

Page had drunk way too much last night.

The thought kept banging around in his head as he got dressed, and the three of them made their way to the hotel where their stylists were staying.

He was just glad he hadn't done anything stupid last night, like drunk dial Charlie.

That would have been bad.

"Ah, good, you're here," Jake said, standing from where he had been sitting and chatting with Page's makeup stylist, Anya, in the corner of the room. The moment they'd arrived, the three of them had split up and gone to their own designated hotel room with their own managers, agents and stylists.

Jake, who was Page's manager, was a white man just hitting the age of thirty. He was a bit older than Page and reminded him of the actor who played Mr. Darcy in the early two-thousands film version of *Pride and Prejudice*.

"I said I would be," Page said, sending a small grin his way. He liked Jake. He had always been calm and real with Page. Plus, he had always kept his word with Page, had always respected his decisions and space. Jake was one of the reasons why he felt safe in his job. He had helped him create a safe and trustworthy team around him alongside his agent, Angela. Speaking of Angela.

"Is Angie coming?" he asked. It wasn't a priority for people's managers and agents to come to every event, but since Page was one of their top clients and they were both based in London, they sometimes showed up for support if the event was in town. Angie was like a second mother. She was an older white woman from Oxfordshire with a blond bob that reminded him of Anna

Wintour. She was all no-funny-business and would scold him if she needed to. She was a bloody good agent, and he didn't really know where he would be without her. Without anyone in this room, to be honest.

"No, love," Anya said, their thick Australian accent filling the room with a sunny feeling. They were a Black non-binary artist in their twenties, their dark brown skin highlighted and accented with golden sparkles around their eyes. They were a makeup genius, but he knew that they also sold their paintings at galleries in Australia and London. He was damn lucky to have them on his team. He had met Anya through Sandhya, who was also a client of theirs, and he thanked his lucky stars every time he had them for makeup before an event. "It's her grandkid's play today. But she sends her love." Anya and Angie had formed a close friendship since working together with Page, and it slightly scared him at times.

He sat down quickly, knowing they needed to get done so they could move on to Sandhya a few doors down. When his makeup was done—a bit of concealer and contouring to make sure he didn't fade away on camera, they packed up their bags quickly, smacked a kiss on his cheek and brushed out the door. He instantly missed their energy.

"Clark dropped off your suit before you got here and rushed off to help Sandhya. Then he mumbled something about Theo being a baby," Jake said, pulling Page's outfit for the day out of the small closet in the hotel room. Clark was the stylist for all three of them. He was a twenty-eight-year-old Japanese American man who had grown up in Hollywood and now lived between his Malibu condo and a flat in New York. He was tall, graceful, could party like no other, and had a wicked fashion sense that always matched each of their styles while making them look a hundred percent better than they could have on their own. It was normal for him to move on from Page quickly since he was a no-fuss client and the other two always took a bit longer.

Today, Clark had given him a burgundy velvet suit to wear. It was old-fashioned and hinted at a fifties-style suit while still making him look modern. Paired with an off-white button-up that he kept slightly unbuttoned, and black flats, he looked like he was walking straight out of a James Bond movie.

"How are you feeling about it all today?" Jake asked him, holding his jacket out for Page. Page turned his back to his manager, sticking his arms behind him before shrugging the jacket on.

"Nervous," he admitted, his lips pressing together into a thin line. He caught Jake's gaze in the mirror in front of him. "But that isn't anything new."

Jake nodded and then moved to his briefcase before pulling out a few papers. "Like always, I looked over their questions with the show managers beforehand. You might not be happy about a few of the things that Jim and Mark wanted to okay for the interview."

Page held back a groan, not knowing what to expect. He sat on the edge of the bed, trying his best to button his sleeve cuffs. "Hit me."

"To no one's surprise, since it's the first interview since StarCon, there were questions about the panel." Page frowned. He should've known it was going to come up. "I was able to get rid of any questions relating to your personal life, as per usual, but you should be prepared for them to ask them anyway. You know how they get." Page nodded, knowing all too well. It was starting to get harder and harder for Jake and Angie to keep the questions at bay, and he would have to get better at deflecting them. He knew he was good; he'd had practice at it before when interviewers had ignored the pointers from Jake and asked the questions anyway, but he hated having to always be on edge.

"Unfortunately," Jake said, cutting into Page's downward spiral of anxiety, "I couldn't get them to drop the questions about the other topic."

Page's stomach dropped. A few days ago, before he had set out, he had known two things: he needed to call Angie and Jake to check in about the protocol for the interview, and he needed to ask them a favor. The favor was to get rid of any questions relating to Charlie and her speech at the StarCon panel.

He didn't really know why he did it.

That is a flat-out lie, a voice that sounded a lot like Sandhya's said to him in his head. He knew it was true. He had asked them to do so for a couple reasons. But mainly it was because he wanted to protect Charlie as much as possible…And he was pretty sure he would not be able to keep his cool if he had to listen to Jim, Mark, and Killian talk shit about Charlie. Not after everything.

Not ever again.

He didn't think he could do it. But also, he wouldn't let himself stay calm and quiet anymore. What they had been doing was bullshit, and he couldn't just stand by and let them demean her on television for speaking the truth.

Page tried his best to school his expression before answering. "They're still obsessed with that woman?" he asked, wincing to himself for referring to Charlie that way. He could only picture her scowling at him.

Jake nodded, looking tired. "The interviewer seemed eager to talk about it, especially because Killian hasn't done an interview since the con either. Both Jim and Mark refused to get rid of any questions about her." He looked at Page then, meeting his eyes with serious professionalism. He seemed to think about his next words carefully before he spoke. "I don't know why you asked me to try and get rid of those questions." When Page opened his mouth to respond, not really knowing what he would say, he stopped when Jake raised a hand. "And I don't want you to tell me unless you think it is truly necessary for me or Angie to know. I just want to make sure you are prepared for invasive questions on that front. We need you to keep your cool."

Page grumbled under his breath. He probably should have told Angie and Jake about Charlie. They knew almost everything else, even his past, needing to know what to look for in the press in case they had to bury a story he didn't want out. But he hadn't been able to.

He wanted to keep Charlie to himself. He wanted to feel her skin against his again, feel her coming around him, under him.

He wanted to make her laugh, make her smile. He just… wanted *her.* Just for a bit longer… as long as he could before this all blew up in their faces.

He let out a sigh and nodded. "I'll do my best. But I won't stay quiet if they start ranting offensive things again. I should have said something at StarCon. But with my anxiety and the shock of what happened, I failed to step up. I won't again." It wasn't an excuse. He owed it to Charlie, to all the other people and kids out there who would be watching. He needed to do better. And he would.

At Jake's short nod, he stood, knowing that was all they needed to talk about. Jake set a hand on his shoulder and raised a brow. "See you after, mate. Have fun." The last bit was laced with sarcasm as he left the room.

Have fun.

Page scrunched up his face in the mirror. He was not looking forward to this.

He rolled his shoulders, taking in a few deep breaths before he slid on the mask he showed the world. He felt his shoulders push back slightly. His body relaxed into compliance as he urged it to move with graceful, relaxed confidence. When he looked in the mirror again, it wasn't Page McAllister who stood in front of him but Jamie Mahone.

And they were both done with being silent.

"Why do I feel like this interview is going to be a mess?" Theo whispered to him and Sandhya as they made their way from their rooms and down into the lobby to grab the car that would take them to where the interview was being filmed. Clark had styled him in a dark blue suit that enhanced his blue eyes, and Sandhya was fitted in a dark green dress, the emerald complimenting her deep brown skin and dark hair. She wore gold jewelry, two gold bangles on her left wrist belonging to her grandmother, whom he knew still lived in India and had passed them down to her.

She always wore them to special occasions.

In Page's opinion, they all looked sexy and classy.

Page waited until they were in the car before deciding they should know everything Jake had said to him. He told them quietly, aware of the driver a few rows forward.

"Ugh," Sandhya said, her face scrunching up in disgust. "I'm not looking forward to seeing Killian or Jim and Mark. They deserve to be fired for how they've been acting online."

"I knew it was going to come up," Theo sighed, his hands massaging his temples. "Are you going to be alright?" he asked, eyeing Page.

"I told Jake I'm not staying silent if they say something bad."

"I think he meant more about them mentioning… Charlie."

Page had known what his friend meant. But he didn't really have an answer, so he stayed silent, ignoring Theo's worried glances.

It didn't take them long to get to the sound stage. It was set up like a normal talk-show stage, with a chair and couches that looked both comfortable and way too hard, everything set up in front of a bright blue background. He had watched the show growing up, and if he hadn't been so ridden with anxiety, he might have been a bit excited. He knew his mum and sister would be watching it live tonight.

A small part of him wondered if Charlie would be too.

He shook the thought from his head. He couldn't focus on her right now. He needed to focus on the show. He needed to focus on being Jamie Mahone.

"Well, if it isn't the three musketeers," a voice drawled from behind them. Page didn't let his shoulders tense, not giving any power to the man behind them. Instead, he turned, pasting on a relaxed smirk, and ignored Theo and Sandhya's slightly worried glances his way.

"Glass," he said, nodding at the man. Killian Glass looked like he always did. He had always reminded Page of someone who was way too comfortable in the spotlight. His dark hair was gelled into an effortlessly messy style. He wore a black suit with a navy-blue shirt, and his hands were in his pockets as he stood in front of them. The look on his face changed to annoyance at not having successfully ruffled Page before slipping back into its usual relaxed smirk. It had been his biggest regret telling this man, whom he had thought to be a friend at the beginning of filming, that he had anxiety. It hadn't been long before Page had realized that the only things Killian cared about were himself and fame.

"Mahone," he said and then nodded to Theo and Sandhya. "You guys look cozy. Excited for the show?"

"Ready to get it over with is more like it," Sandhya said, glaring furiously at Glass. She had always hated him. She hadn't told Page exactly why, but it had been like this since their first day of filming.

Before he or Theo could say anything, a PA announced quiet on set and motioned for them all to take their spots. He saw Jim and Mark move to stand with them, and he nodded their way before the lights dimmed.

The talk show host, Andie Warner, chatted to his viewers for a few minutes before he announced them. And then they were walking up, the cheering and the lights overwhelming his senses before they sat down. He was nearest to Sandhya, Theo on his other side. Killian and then Jim and Mark followed. It was almost as if they had teamed up, one team against the other. He knew that Bodega was supposed to be here while Carmen was stuck with her family in Ireland, but Bodega hadn't shown up, and Page hadn't had the time to check in with Mark and Jim before the show started. Usually, they all did the cast interviews together, but every now and then, Carmen and Bodega would do their own interviews separately since their characters had a separate story arc on the show.

"Thank you all for being here. We are so excited to have the cast of *StarVerse* on the show." They all smiled and nodded. It was an act. All of it. A character Page had constantly been playing since he had joined the cast.

He was glad that they didn't start with him. Instead, Warner asked Jim and Mark what they could expect from the new season, then moved on to Theo and Sandhya, first questioning Sandhya about her dating life. He saw her hold back from rolling her eyes as they made a big deal over her girlfriend and then asked Theo a serious question about the show instead of focusing on his dating life. They never asked her about the show, focusing on her personal life, men—that had changed when she'd come out— and her costumes on the show. Page knew that she was good at turning the question back onto the interviewer, always calling them out for their bullshit.

When Andie Warner's gaze moved to him, he tried not to flinch. "And now our rising star." They all laughed, but Page just smiled.

"Hiya, Andie."

"Jamie, thank you for coming. We all know how you never do interviews, but we hope to maybe get a bit out of you today." He laughed as if it were a private joke they were all in on. Page forced a smile. He saw Sandhya shift next to him, moving her body to face them as if she could jump and protect him. He wished he could send her a small smile of thanks.

"I don't know about that, but ask away," he said, grinning at the crowd. He heard them cheer.

"Well, I know you get asked this a lot, but since you started on *StarVerse*, the public has never seen you with someone on your arm. We are all starting to wonder if it will ever happen. So, I must ask. Is there someone special in your life?"

Page had known what he'd planned to say, but instead of answering right away, he paused because he instantly thought of Charlie, her in bed, the morning light shining on her freckled skin. He pushed it out of his mind.

He shook his head. "No, unfortunately, there is no lucky lass in my life."

"Oh well, I guess that means that a lucky lass," Andie faked a Scottish accent to tease him slightly, obviously playing into the international demographic of his audience, and Page tried not to wince, "still has a chance to steal this Scottish actor for herself."

That seemed to make the crowd cheer more. He lifted a hand, playing into the crowd a bit.

Andie went on to ask him about the new season, and he followed the script of what they were allowed to say to the T. Jim and Mark had sent it by email so they could all prepare.

After he was done focusing on Page, Andie moved straight to Killian, and the moment they had all been waiting for was upon them.

"Killian," Andie said, emphasizing the man's name.

"Yes, Andie," Killian drawled, and grinned at the crowd when they cheered. He blew a kiss their way, and Page had to stifle a growl. He hated how people still fawned over him.

"The last time everyone saw you, you were not having the best of days," he said, with a look that seemed to say they all were sharing a secret. It was not a secret Page wanted to be a part of. "We saw a bright young woman verbally attack you in public at StarCon."

Verbally attack?

He saw Sandhya and Theo stiffen slightly beside him. Not enough for people to notice, but enough for him to know he wasn't alone in his discomfort.

"... how you were fairing after that debacle," Andie continued.

Page felt his anger rising.

"Well, Andie, I have to say it was a surprise. But as we now know, the woman was unstable. As we've all seen in the press, she has had trouble with her mental health before. Even her own brother came out publicly to support me—"

That made Page freeze. Her brother had done what?

Did Charlie know?

He didn't think she did. She would have said something.

Or would she?

"... I just feel bad for her at this point." Page's hands clenched into fists. "I didn't say anything wrong that day at all."

Andie nodded and then turned towards them all. "And all of you?"

There was a pause. It was as if they were all waiting for the ball to drop. Jim and Mark were looking at the three of them expectantly.

"All of us?" Theo asked, the muscles in his jaw tensing.

Andie laughed, and Page could see the man sensed their tension. "You three have been silent on the matter. Public opinion has been quite split in either support for Killian or that woman—"

"I believe her name is Charlie James."

Everyone paused when Page spoke. Andie's face froze in a smile, and he saw Jim and Mark's bodies tense. Even Killian's smile slipped.

"Yes," Andie said, nodding towards Page and gesturing to him with the notecards in his hands. "Her name is Charlie James." They were all looking at him now. Mark was narrowing his eyes at him. "You don't have any social media to check up on, Jamie, so I know we are all wondering what you are thinking of the matter."

He took in a deep breath before speaking. "I wouldn't call Miss James unhinged at all. She was seemingly angry, and we all know that the press doesn't really know the full truth sometimes, let alone sympathize with an angry woman." He looked at Sandhya and she nodded.

"I mean, they all said I was dating Theo," she said, and he heard Theo try to hide a snort.

He smiled at his friends. He needed them right now.

"So, are you saying you disagree with what the show has been putting out? Do you not agree and stand by Killian's side?"

Page sucked in a breath and let it go. It was time to share just a bit. "No, I don't," he admitted, leaning back in his chair as everyone seemed to suck in their breaths.

"Do you care to expand?"

Did he?

He didn't, really. But he had to.

"My cousin has ADHD," he said, leaning his elbows on his knees. "Now, it isn't the same as being on the autism spectrum, but he is neurodivergent, and many ADHD traits line up with traits of autistic people. I've heard people say the same things about him that they were saying about Charlie James online, and I don't agree with what is being said about her. Plus," he looked to Killian and saw the fury clear in his co-star's eyes. "I do not agree with what Killian said that day. We've talked about it privately," they really hadn't, "and I think the situation, like many other situations with autistic and neurodivergent and/or disabled people in film and other fields, was not handled well at all."

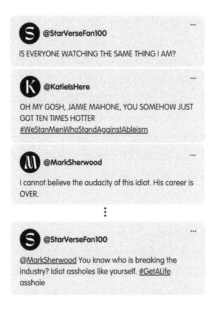

@StarVerseFan100

IS EVERYONE WATCHING THE SAME THING I AM?

@KatieIsHere

OH MY GOSH, JAMIE MAHONE, YOU SOMEHOW JUST GOT TEN TIMES HOTTER #WeStanMenWhoStandAgainstableism

@MarkSherwood

I cannot believe the audacity of this idiot. His career is OVER.

@StarVerseFan100

@MarkSherwood You know who is breaking the industry? Idiot assholes like yourself. #GetALife asshole

Chapter 29

Charlie

Layla came over as planned, an extra bottle of wine in her hands as she walked through the door.

"God, I haven't been here in ages," she said, shutting the door behind her. She hung her coat by the door, her body overwhelmed by a light blue fluffy sweater.

"Did Lilian not invite you over that much?"

Layla shrugged. "She did. She's a friend, but she's more my boss these days. We were friends in secondary school, but you will learn if you ever hang out with her that she can pull away a lot."

She didn't say more. She didn't need to. Charlie had a feeling she understood, as someone who usually was the friend who "pulled away a lot." There was no judgment in Layla's voice, just a little bit of disappointment.

A few glasses of wine in, fried rice eaten, bread and cheese splayed out in front of them, and they were ready for the talk show. Layla and she had been discussing fan theories for *StarVerse*, and to Charlie's delight, she discovered that Layla was more of a nerd than she first let on.

The show was going live at 8 pm, and Charlie was thankful to have Layla with her, as she seemed to know exactly what channel it would be airing on. Since her arrival in Scotland, she hadn't touched the TV, not really knowing which channels she would want to watch and not having the time to channel surf with no direction in mind. Instead, she had been watching Netflix romcoms and had invested in a good VPN to watch shows on her other streaming services.

They turned the TV on, and when they started announcing the show, her heart sped up. She wasn't sure what to expect from this. She had seen the cast and producers do plenty of interviews back when she was still a fan. But now, it felt different.

Of course, it was different. She was fucking the lead actor.

She snorted to herself and waved off the look of confusion that Layla sent her way.

"Tonight should be interesting," Layla said, pointing to the TV as the cast walked onto the set. "Isn't this the first interview they've done since StarCon?"

Charlie nodded, not really trusting her voice in the moment. Page had walked on screen, and he looked… He looked delicious. Whoever had dressed him deserved an Oscar. Layla chuckled beside her, and she found herself nudging her. Layla just chuckled harder, and then they both quieted for the interview, Layla grabbing the remote to turn up the volume.

The interview went smoothly at first, and when they got to Page, Charlie felt herself holding her breath.

"No, unfortunately, there is no lucky lass in my life."

Charlie felt something then. She wasn't sure what it was and didn't want to isolate and understand the feeling. She knew Layla was looking at her, but she ignored it, keeping her gaze on the screen instead and sipping her wine.

Not sipping. She took a large gulp.

She knew it was what he had to say. What she wanted him to say. What she needed him to say. If he had hinted that he was dating someone, the press would be as wild as a bad storm. It would make everything a million times harder.

But still… There was a part of her, a small part, that broke a bit. She knew what they had was just sex, but it still hurt to hear him say he had no one.

But she guessed it was something she had to get used to. He would never come out with their relationship. Why would he? It wasn't serious. It would never be.

Her mood soured when they moved on to Killian Glass. She had known it was coming. Of course, they would ask something. But when he spoke, all she felt was unbridled rage.

"Fucking asshole," Layla muttered, sipping her wine. "No wonder Page hates his guts."

Charlie hummed to herself.

"… As we've all seen in the press, she has had trouble with her mental health before. Even her own brother came out publicly to support me—"

Charlie's body seemed to freeze over.

Her brother had done what?

"Excuse me?" She wasn't sure if it was her or Layla who had said the words. Shock riddled her body. She had known her family would be asked to comment, of course, they would. She wasn't stupid. But she guessed she was naive to think they would respect her wishes when she had asked them not to comment.

"Charlie, love, are you okay?" Layla asked, scooting closer to her.

"I didn't know."

"I see that," Layla said, curling into her side and laying her head on Charlie's shoulder. "You aren't close?"

Charlie just shook her head.

"Well, he's a fucking piece of shit," she said and then pointed to the screen. "Look at Page."

Charlie pushed away the haze from her mind. The camera panned to take in the entire cast, and she looked closely at him. He was tense, the calm demeanor gone. He still had the mask on—the small, quiet smile that showed he was not angry—but the rest of his body told a different story.

God. He was pissed.

She didn't know when it had changed exactly. Maybe it was after they had started having sex, but she thought it was before that—when she had started to be able to read him a bit better. He hadn't been a stranger for a while. Now, she knew that look. He'd had the same look when she had told him about her brother at the beach. Or when he'd talked about his experience with Killian Glass before. He always had it when he mentioned the show.

His hands were fisted on his lap.

Don't do something stupid, Page, she thought to herself silently. Yes, Charlie knew it wasn't good to ask him to stay silent. It would hurt other people, more people than her. But she didn't want him—couldn't ask him—to jeopardize his career, the way he was caring for his family, because of her.

She couldn't.

She was pulled out of her panic when he said her name.

"I believe her name is Charlie James."

In fact, she almost jumped in her seat.

Layla looked between the screen and her. A look of pure glee lit up her face, her cheeks flushed with excitement. "Here we go, love. I knew he wouldn't be able to not say something."

"I knew as well. But I hoped he wouldn't."

"My cousin has ADHD," he said, leaning his elbows on his knees. Charlie's breath caught in her throat. She knew he never talked about his family. Ever. But here he was, mentioning his cousin, opening up—for her. For his cousin. For people like them. "Now, it isn't the same as being on the autism spectrum, but he is neurodivergent, and many ADHD traits line up with traits of autistic people. I've heard people say the same things about him that they were saying about Charlie James online, and I don't agree with what is being said about her. Plus, I do not agree with what Killian said that day. We've talked about it privately and I think the situation, like many other situations with autistic and neurodivergent and/or disabled people in film and other fields, was not handled well at all."

"Yes!" Layla said, breaking Charlie from her shock once again. "You go, Page!"

Charlie laughed, hugging her friend close. She needed the physical touch right now. She needed to know she had support right beside her because her brain was a million miles away. She couldn't believe what she was watching—what she was hearing.

Neither could anyone on the screen of their small TV.

There was a pause. A silent pause. A few people from the crowd of the live viewing had cheered. But for the most part, the interviewer, Andie Warner, seemed to be just as surprised as Killian and the producers.

"Well, thank you for telling us how you feel. Does the rest of the cast feel this way?" Warner asked.

"He couldn't have said it in a better way," Theo responded, and Sandhya nodded beside him.

Andie Warner looked to the producers, and there seemed to be a silent conversation between them. The next question, directed at them, changed the subject drastically.

"Damn," Layla said, pulling Charlie's attention away from the screen when the cast interview ended. "Well, that was entertaining."

All Charlie felt was pure panic. "What did he do? They're going to be so mad at him."

Layla looked over at her, both shocked and worried. "And who cares, Charlie? What he said needed to be said."

"Yes, but he needs the money. To help Lilian and the store and his parents. What have I done—"

"Charlie. Hey," Layla said, grabbing her arms and forcing her to face her. "Page made his choice on his own. On his own," she said with more conviction. "You couldn't make that boy do anything he didn't want to. Trust me, I've practically grown up with him and his family." Charlie's breaths were coming a bit slower now. "And what he did needed to be done." Charlie nodded. "It did. That film crew and set are obviously unhealthy. It needs to be changed for the better, and those ableist assholes need to be put in their place. And I love Page with everything, he is a kind soul, but he will be fine. For fuck's sake, he will be more than fine. He is a straight, cis, white guy, and even if he weren't, they would be idiots to fire him after that declaration because then, everyone would know how fucked up and discriminatory they are." At Charlie's raised brows, she shook her head. "Okay, not that everyone doesn't already know. But it would prove it even more."

Charlie nodded, letting Layla's words settle in her brain. "But—"

"He will be fine, Charlie," Layla said, giving her a look that told her to calm down. So, she took deep breaths and pushed the fear that had swelled up in her away.

"He really just did that, didn't he?"

"Yes, he did," Layla said, giving her a raised-brow smirk. "Just sex, my arse."

Charlie pushed her shoulder; a laugh being pulled out of her. "It is just sex."

"Charlie, love." Layla hugged her and settled her head on her shoulder. Charlie poured them more wine. "That was not the speech of a man who didn't care. That was the speech of a man standing up for the woman he has feelings for."

Charlie shook her head, not letting Layla's words get past her emotional armor. She couldn't listen to her. Because if she did, and if she hoped, she would have to acknowledge the feelings that had been building inside her as well.

And that was just asking for her to get hurt when all of this was over.

Gossip Headlines Following Andie Warner *StarVerse* Interview

STAR VERSE ACTOR ROCKS THE BOAT

JAMIE MAHONE STARTS RIVALRY WITH CO-STAR KILLIAN GLASS

JAMIE MAHONE FINALLY BREAKS HIS SILENCE

STAR OBSESSED WITH UNHINGED FAN?

JAMIE MAHONE SPEAKS UP AGAINST ABLEISM

Chapter 30

Page

To say the rest of the day was a nightmare would be an understatement.

"Are you out of your goddamn mind?" Mark yelled at him. They were all holed up in Mark's hotel room. They had been forced there after the show, not even being allowed to get some food in their own rooms before Mark and Jim had called an "emergency meeting".

"Mark," Jim said, standing up to console his business colleague. Jim had always been the more levelheaded of the two, and that could not be more apparent than right now. He whispered something into Mark's ear, likely telling him to be careful of how angry he got, in case Page felt unsafe enough to sue them or something, before he pulled back, sending the three of them a glare. Killian was leaning against a wall while Sandhya and Theo sat around Page on the bed nearest the exit.

Killian drank from the glass he had quickly filled when they'd walked into the room. Mark's mini fridge was filled with alcohol, and Page was even starting to consider opening a small bottle of whisky.

"I don't know what made you say that shit—"

"Let's be real for a second here," Theo stopped him. He

was just as furious with them as Sandhya and Page were. His blue eyes were cold as ice. "What Page said was nothing. All he did was support a marginalized community that you three are determined to insult every chance you get. What you've done to Charlie James, along with the shit you've pulled to not only silence her but the disabled community as well since StarCon, is disgusting. We've been silent because of your threat to pull our contracts, but after today, all three of us are done. We should have been done months ago when all of this started."

"Now listen here—"

"Actually, no," Sandhya said. "You should listen to us. It won't look good for you if the three of us leave the show."

"Leave the show?" Jim asked, the shock clear on his face clear.

"That's what you were threatening. Wasn't it?" Page asked, finally speaking up. They glared at him. "You were going to bring our contracts into the conversation, once again. Or threaten to cut our pay. But if you do, we will say something. We will leave. And then you won't have three of your leads for the next season of the show." He gave them a solemn smile. "You need us just like we," he held up his fingers for quotation marks, "*need you.*"

Mark sneered at him. "This shit wouldn't fly on any other set. You want to work in this industry? You better listen closely. You leave, and we will blacklist you in Hollywood. You won't fucking work again." With that, he opened his door and stepped aside. "I suggest you all take some time to think about that before the premiere in a few months. Because if we see this behavior again, you're cut from the show."

"See, this is what happens when white, straight, cis men are put in positions of power," Sandhya said, falling onto the couch the moment they all stepped into her flat. It had been a long drive home from the hotel, traffic making it even longer. "They throw a tantrum when they don't get their way."

Page had been silent most of the ride, stewing in his own

brain the entire way back.

He looked at his two friends and sighed.

"I'm sorry," he finally said, and when they both looked up at him, he ran a hand over his face before moving to sit on one of the chairs facing the couch. "I should have talked to you two before the interview. I shouldn't have brought you into this mess." Before either of them could say something back, he continued. "We all know that if something happens now, they aren't going to fire me first with my character being the lead. I put you and your careers in jeopardy, and it isn't—"

"Page," Theo said, sitting on the edge of the coffee table between them. "Shut up for a second." When Page stopped talking, he went on. "Yes, it is true they will both target Sandhya and me first. One, because Sandhya is a woman of color, and two, because we are both queer, though I guess that won't apply to me since they don't know about my sexuality. But you're right. My character isn't as important to the show, and they are discriminatory assholes. But that doesn't mean we don't want to stand beside you on something that is extremely important."

"I mean, I would have liked to know beforehand," Sandhya cut in and Page winced. "But mainly so that I could have thought up something better to say." She sat up, looking at Page directly. "We're not unfamiliar with how this industry, *any* industry, can be homophobic and racist. We have to deal with it every day. And yeah, you'll get a lot less of their fury because of your privileges. Just like Theo will get a lot less because he is a white, cis man. But what they said was wrong. What they've been saying is wrong. If you hadn't said this today, I probably would've eventually. Or at least, I hope I would have." She looked at them both then. "All three of us are perceived as abled." Page didn't pretend to notice how Theo had zoned out, looking out the window like he was a bit lost in the conversation. Both Page and Sandhya knew he had been diagnosed with intense anxiety as a kid. And even though Theo never talked about it, they knew he had also been diagnosed with ADHD in secondary school. But where Page was comfortable talking about his feelings, Theo... wasn't.

He didn't talk about his diagnosis—rarely even mentioned it. Sandhya continued, "We all needed to look at our own privileges in this situation. So, what you did, even if it did come out of nowhere, was good. And *if* they do shitty things, you're not to blame. It's on them. Because you were just standing up for what was right."

"And defending your girlfriend," Theo joined in, grinning.

"She's not my girlfriend," Page groaned. "I don't know what we are."

Sandhya fell back on the couch. "I think it might be time to DTR, my friend."

"What are we, thirteen?" Theo asked.

Page's phone pinged. And he looked down to see a bunch of messages he hadn't noticed. There were a few from his sister and his mom. Mainly a mix of "We're proud", "Good for you", and "Go Page!" Then there was one from his cousin that was a paragraph he needed to read through, and then—

He paused when he saw the text from Charlie.

Charlie
Thank you.

That was all it said. Two words.

Page felt his lips pick up in a smile.

"Oh, looks like someone is getting laid when they get back to Scotland."

"Oh, shut it, you fucker," Page said, setting down his phone. He would respond to Charlie when he had time to call her later. For now, he tackled Theo. He would spend some time with his friends first. Because he was lucky to have them.

Chapter 31
Charlie

Page

You're welcome. I should have said something sooner. I hope what I said was okay.

Charlie

What you said was great.

Charlie

When will you be back?

Page

Tomorrow night. S, T and I plan on getting drunk to block out our showrunner's scolding.

Charlie

Were they angry?

Page

...

Page

You could say that.

Charlie

Will you, S and T be ok?

Page

We'll be fine. T put them in their place after the show. You would've loved it.

Page

... you would like them.

Charlie

Oh, are we at the meeting the friends stage?

Page
Maybe.

Page
 This is Sandhya. What Page meant to say is that he will stop being a vague fucker, and when he gets home, he will DTR with you and then have his dirty way with you.

Page
If you want that.

Page
Fuck, sorry S took my phone.

Page
She is right, though. I do plan on having my dirty way with you when I get home. If you want that.

Charlie

Depends on what it entails.

Page
Well... see, I have this image.

Charlie

An image, huh?

Page
You. Naked. On my bed.

Charlie

Continue...

Page
Maybe some whipped cream?

Charlie

Whipped cream, huh?

Page
 Whipped cream is a masterpiece in a bottle.

Charlie

Seems fitting since you call it
squirty cream here.

Page

Now that you said it, I can't unsee
it.

Charlie

You're welcome.

Charlie

I think your plan sounds fun. But I
would insist you be naked and join
me in your bed. Maybe the
shower as well?

Page

Fuck.

Page

I'll be home soon.

The first week of July meant it officially felt like summer.

Or what the Scots called summer. Charlie wasn't so sure this weather qualified. But, to her astonishment, people wore shorts and T-shirts instead of leggings, sweaters and jackets. It was as if this new month had suddenly called for an outfit change, even though the weather hadn't improved that much.

Charlie had been here for a month, and suddenly, she realized she had become settled. Or as much as she could be for someone who would be leaving in a month. She was settled; and she was… happy.

Really happy.

With Page gone, she had decided to explore the town more. He was only away for a couple of days, but without his presence calling her back to the apartment, she found herself meeting Layla for fish and chips at the famous place down by the wharf, or grabbing ice cream at the delicious ice cream parlor after work.

And work…

Work was amazing. Charlie had known she would love working at the bookstore. But she still hadn't expected to love it this much. She didn't *not* look forward to going to work. She had soon become friendly with their regulars. Mrs. Tara, who came in after she closed the knitting shop for a new bodice ripper historical romance. John Hart, an old man whose grandson was coming home from school in France this week. He loved their crime and thriller section. Even Callum, who had come in with his daughter a few times to pick out books for her and himself. She seemed to love any book about fairies, and he liked non-fiction though she'd spotted him eyeing the romance section warily.

She didn't know if she was in love with the idea of small-town living or if she was just in love with this specific small town. But it had captured her heart before she had realized it.

Today, she was setting up shop when she heard the bell ring behind her. "I'll be right there!" she called, shuffling the new incoming books they had received yesterday into a corner in the back. She would unpack them once Layla arrived in the afternoon.

When she moved out from behind the stack of boxes and into the front of the store, she paused. A white woman in her mid-forties stood in the shop, perusing a table of books. She wasn't sure what made her pause and look at her a bit closer, but there was something about the way she held herself that told Charlie she wasn't from around town. She was dressed in a purple pantsuit, her brown hair pulled into a low ponytail. A camera bag hung around one shoulder.

Press?

Charlie's stomach dropped.

"Can I help you?" she asked, moving around the counter to see if the woman needed anything.

She looked up, and something in her eyes made Charlie tense. "The store is adorable," the woman said, tapping a manicured fingernail against the cover of a new thriller Charlie had just placed on one of their many display tables.

"Yes, it has the beautiful charm many independent bookstores have." Charlie forced a smile. "Is there anything I can help you with?"

"Oh, I'm just looking. I'm actually here to scout properties," she said, and Charlie's heart dropped. A developer? "My company takes smaller stores and develops them into our larger chain bookstores. We're based in the US and are looking to expand into the UK."

Charlie tried to stay polite. "Oh, interesting."

Charlie could tell the woman was lying. Maybe it was the way she held her camera close. Or the way she studied Charlie intently, waiting for a movement or a sign.

"Are you the owner?"

"Nope," Charlie said, folding her hands in her lap. "I just work here." She could tell her smile was fake, and she knew the woman would also be able to tell. But she didn't care.

"Dear, you look so familiar. Have we met?"

Charlie's jaw tensed. "I doubt it."

"Forgive me," she said, faking a laugh. Charlie forced another smile. "Ah, well, I must be going." She extended her hand, a small card between her fingers. When Charlie took it, she smiled. "Here is my card. Will you pass it on to your boss?" At Charlie's small nod, she looked around the store once more. "Your store is so *cute*."

With that, she left, and Charlie tried to ignore the tense feeling in her chest for the rest of the day.

IS JAMIE MAHONE'S CAREER AT RISK?
Written by Carrie Goode

As I am sure we all saw in the groundbreaking interview just a few days ago, Jamie Mahone, best known for his role on the new hit show *StarVerse*, rocked the boat when he decided to publicly support Charlie James. After the heated interaction between James and Mahone's co-star, Killian Glass, a few months prior at StarCon, many were surprised to see the Scottish actor defend the woman in question, especially when the show's policy has been ' no comment' or in full defense of Killian Glass. Now, as fans are divided by his actions, people are wondering if his choice will possibly impact his position on the show…

Chapter 32

Page

Charlie
> Don't come back to the store.
> When you're here, use the back
> door for the apartment.

Page stared at the message as he sat on the train back from London. It was vague, but he could read the worry in her text as plain as day. He had been in the middle of writing a new scene when he'd gotten the text, and now, all he could do was stare at his phone's screen.

Page
Is everything okay?

Charlie
> I think so? A woman came by the
> store today. She seemed off. She
> had a camera with her.

Page felt the anxiety that had left him after he had left London return.

Could this woman be press?

He dialed Charlie's number without thinking.

"Page?" she asked on the other side of the line. He felt his body relax at the sound of her voice. God, he was so screwed. Going away had made him look at their relationship more closely, and after the teasing from Theo and Sandhya, he knew they needed to talk. This couldn't go on forever.

Or it could. But both he and Charlie weren't people who could make friends with benefits and *no* feelings work.

"Hi," he said and winced when he heard his voice crack a bit. He grabbed his water from where it was sitting on the table in front of him and took a sip. "Talk to me."

She seemed to instantly understand what he meant.

"I don't have much else to add. It might just be my anxiety, but something seemed off. She asked me if we'd met before, almost as if she were trying to trick me into giving her my name. She also seemed to be guarding her camera and just came in, asked me questions, and then left." She sighed on the other side of the phone, and he wished he were there to pull her into his arms. "It just gave me weird vibes."

"Is there any way you can get Layla to come in and cover for you?" he asked. His hand tensed around his phone.

"Yeah, but do you think she'll be more suspicious if I stop working?"

Page understood what she was asking. But right now, he was more worried about her. "No, take the day off."

He needed to think. He needed to protect her from the craziness that was his life.

"I'll be home soon," he said, his voice rough, and then hung up.

It wasn't long before he realized he had called their flat *home*.

When he got back, the first thing he did was text his sister. Charlie was asleep. The train from London was around seven hours, and he had left in the latter part of the day. When he arrived, all the lights had been off, and when he'd opened her door to check if she was asleep, Charlie had been curled up in her duvet, her arms thrown up over her head.

He had to fight the urge to join her.

Instead, he moved to his room, dropping his bag by the laundry machine near the hallway. He would wash his clothes in the morning.

And no matter how hard he tried, he couldn't get his mind off where she was in the other room. Sleeping together had been the only thing they hadn't done. Ironically enough. They might enjoy time together in their beds, but the moment they got tired, they retired to their own rooms. It had been an unspoken agreement from the beginning. And even though everything in him wanted to go curl up beside her, he knew he couldn't. Not without discussing it with her first.

He looked at his own bed longingly, but before he could crash, his phone rang.

The screen lit up his dark room, his sister's photo and name popping up. He answered, falling back onto the bed.

"So, the interview."

"Yeah," he responded, looking up at the ceiling of his bedroom. Or Lilian's bedroom really.

"I'm proud of you," she said, her voice soft for a moment. She spoke again before he could say anything else. "I didn't really call to talk about your boring-ass interview. I wanted to know what you were planning for your birthday."

Page groaned. "I don't want to do anything. You know me, Lil."

"Page, you're turning twenty-six. It's not every day you're turning a year older than a quarter of a century, and we will celebrate."

He knew there was no way he was getting out of this one.

"Fine," he said, rubbing a hand over his face.

"I expect you to come up to the house and visit mum and dad on the day. I'll invite Sandhya and Theo."

"Callum as well," he said, and heard his sister's pause.

"Fine," she accepted, and he knew better than to ask her what was up. Maybe he needed to have a talk with Callum instead. He grimaced at that. He liked talking to Callum just fine, but the man was a vault when it came to his love life or anything he considered private. He and Lilian were too similar for their own good. They would come to him when they were ready, but trying to get anything out of them before they wanted to share would only result in them pulling away from him. Which was the last thing he wanted. "But you have to bring Charlie."

"Who will watch the store?" he asked, his heart beating fast. Bringing Charlie to meet his family? Wasn't that a bit fast?

Then again, wasn't that something you only did with a girlfriend?

Fuck.

"Layla said she wanted to attend but her brother is coming to town, so she'll stay and watch the store." Lilian sounded tired. He wondered then how she was faring up at their parents' and felt the guilt rise inside him. He hadn't been great at calling since he had gotten home, and before that…

"Tell mum I'll come up with Callum and Charlie. Hopefully, we'll have all the room we need for everyone. Give them my love."

"You know I will."

And with that, his sister hung up. Page let out a breath got up to turn off the lights in the flat, slowly moving to the room Charlie was asleep in. The image of her in bed made him pause in the doorway. She was wearing nothing but her underwear and a large *StarVerse* crew T-shirt of his, her body spread across the mattress, the blankets caught up in her legs.

"Page?" she asked, her voice sleepy. She didn't even open her eyes. He froze.

"I didn't want to wake you up," he said softly. She smiled, her eyes still closed, but her body shifted over.

"Come on, it's late."

His hand came up to his chest, and he rubbed the muscle there, moving to close the door behind him. It took him a few seconds before his eyes adjusted to the darkness, the only light coming in from the street outside the window.

It didn't take him long before he was ready for bed, climbing in beside her. He chuckled as her forehead scrunched up a bit as he moved her over.

He realized then just how much had changed… just how much trust had grown between them in such a short time.

"You're home," she said, and he tried his hardest to ignore what those words did to him.

"Yeah," he said, pulling her to him, her head falling on his chest. Her arms came to wrap around him, his hand tangling into her dark curls. "I'm here."

He fell asleep faster than he ever had before.

Excerpt from *STARVERSE*: Season 2, Episode 8

VALERI'S ROOM — DAY

VALERI storms into her room, Car behind her. The door shuts behind him, and silence falls over the room.

> CAR
> Val—

> VALERI
> You don't get it, do you?

> CAR
> Get what?

> VALERI
> That is exactly what I mean. You're a prince, Car. A prince. And I am just a first mate of a star cruiser. A first mate who has barely made a name for herself in the fleet. I am just a woman—

> CAR
> Whom I am irrevocably in love with.

> VALERI
> … What? You're what?

Chapter 33
Charlie

Charlie blinked at Page. He was sitting in one of the chairs at the kitchen counter, a bowl of cereal and a glass of orange juice in front of him.

"It's your birthday?" she asked, before narrowing her eyes at him when he winced. "And when were you going to tell me?"

She instantly regretted the words.

Did she have a right to know? It wasn't as if she were his girlfriend.

"It's not soon. A couple of weeks from now," he said, pushing his blond hair away from his face. She briefly wondered if he got it cut at a barber or had a family member do it.

She must be kidding herself. Of course, he went to someone. He was a movie star. Something she needed to stop forgetting. Movie stars didn't cut their hair at home.

"Lilian is throwing me a small party up at our parents' house." His hand came to scratch the back of his neck. Charlie could have sworn he looked a bit nervous. "And uh, I was wondering if you wanted to join us all?" Before she could respond, he spoke. "Layla's going to stay and take care of the store. Her brother's in town. You could stay and hang out with them or come up and hang out with Lilian." He laughed awkwardly. "She insisted I bring you."

Lilian insisted he bring her.

But did Page want her there?

"I don't want to intrude…"

Page looked her in the eyes, a small smile appearing on his lips. A knowing smile. He seemed to read her so perfectly. "You won't be. I don't like celebrating my birthday…" She waited for him to expand, but he didn't. She realized then just how much they didn't know about one another. For some reason, she felt as if she knew him better than anyone else. But there was so much about his life, about her life, that they hadn't shared. Because it meant popping their little bubble. "It would be nice to have you there with us." He cleared his throat. "I want you there."

She nodded and sent him a small, cautious smile. It wasn't like she would be able to say no.

Two weeks later, Charlie found herself and her overnight bag stuffed into Callum's small car. It was packed full—Charlie and Flora, her bright blonde curly hair in pigtails, sitting in the back, their bags behind them in the trunk, and Page in the passenger seat. It was about over an hour's drive to where Page's parents lived. They had a house right above Aberdeen.

She didn't know much about the area other than what she had

seen on the drive up, but Page had told her there was a seal beach nearby. Since they were here for the weekend, she would have to make him take her.

I don't even know why I'm here, she thought to herself as they pulled off the highway and onto a single-lane, winding road. They were surrounded by green pastures, sheep and cows sliding past them as they drove by. The beach was to their right as they swerved closer and then away from the coast. After driving through another small town, Callum finally pulled off the road, turning onto a long driveway that led to the beach.

Charlie tried her hardest not to gape at the house that came into view. It was beautiful, the grey stone covered with ivy. It was big enough to hold a four-person family, looking like it belonged in a historical drama. It wasn't obnoxiously large but just picturesque enough to remind her, once again, that she was not in California anymore. When they parked, she spotted a small garden to their left and the fenced in areas for ducks and chickens. It was literally right out of a Jane Austen book.

"They have sheep!" Flora said, her smile wide. And even though Charlie wouldn't necessarily call herself a kid person, she had to admit that Flora Ferguson was adorable. Charlie had been an instant fan when the girl had gone on her own rant about how amazing *Avatar: The Last Airbender* was. Charlie had proceeded to get lost in the flowing conversation for the entire drive. She didn't know the full story behind Flora's family, but Callum seemed to be a single dad. Flora hadn't mentioned her mother once. It was adorable how Callum, a tall, brooding, silent man, softened when he looked at Flora, who barely came up to his mid-thigh. Their relationship was relaxed, but she noticed that he always seemed to have an eye on her from where he sat in the front of the car.

"Do they?" Charlie asked, raising a brow and moving to grab her bag from the back of the car. Page and Callum were already there, getting the bags out.

"You're here!" came a call, the voice high and filled with energy. And the next thing Charlie knew, Page was being tackled

273

by a woman. She was all curves and bright red curls, her head barely reaching Page's chest. She was wearing a bright yellow sundress that accented her wide hips and fuller breasts, and her hair was tied up in a yellow bandana that matched the dress.

Lilian, Charlie thought to herself. She had talked to her a few times on the phone before she had come, and they had texted back and forth, but she had never met her in person. She was honestly a bit terrified. Not only had she been living in this woman's apartment, but she'd been…Well, fucking her brother.

"Lili!" Flora squealed. Page grunted as the little girl tackled him around the knees, her arms hugging him and Lilian. Lilian reached down to wrap the small girl in a large hug, her face filling with joy.

"Hello, my flower. How are you today?"

"Good," Flora responded and promptly decided to show Lilian her teddy. His name was Hopper.

Page extracted himself from the pile of hugs and laid a hand on his sister's shoulder. "Is everyone home?"

"Everyone's inside," she said and then seemed to remember that Charlie and Callum were there. Her green eyes, the same shade as Page's, landed on Charlie and widened. "You made it!"

Before she knew it, she was being pulled into one of the strongest hugs she'd ever experienced. Her arms moved a bit slower, but she hugged Lilian back.

"Hi," she said, chuckling a bit. "Thanks for having me."

"Oh, we wouldn't want it any other way! Page hates celebrating his birthday, so we usually just make a large family gathering out of it." She turned her head, speaking to Page. "T and S are on their way. Their train just got to Aberdeen, so they should be on the bus now."

Charlie felt her nerves quicken. She was so out of her element.

Lilian grabbed Charlie's bag out of her hands and headed off into the house before she could protest.

Charlie stood there, a bit overwhelmed, and then froze when she spotted Callum across from her. He and Page were watching Lilian as she made her way inside. But where Page looked happy and calm, Callum's face was blank, his eyes almost... sad as he watched Lilian head inside with Flora running after her, calling her name.

"So," Charlie said, smiling a bit at Page's chuckle. "That's Lilian."

"She grows on you," he said, lifting a shoulder in a shrug.

"She reminds me of Ri."

"Ah, the infamous Ripley. I still have to meet her."

The words made her freeze. He wanted to meet her. But if he did, that meant he would come to the States... that what they had, what they were doing, went further than a couple of weeks. He seemed to realize his own words the same moment she did, a flush covering his cheeks. She decided, then and there, that one of her favorite things was to make Page McAllister blush.

Charlie cleared her throat. "So, Lilian knows?" she asked, her voice lowering as they walked to the house, Callum trailing behind them. He seemed to be lost in his own head.

Page nodded.

"And your parents?"

He shrugged. "I don't know."

"So, everyone knows?" she pushed, and she could hear her own voice getting higher with nerves.

"Maybe," he admitted, his voice low and filled with laughter. His free hand came to rest at the small of her back, and the touch made her shoulders relax.

What was she doing here? She was meeting his family. This was all happening too fast. This was supposed to be a family gathering and—

"Stop," he said before shaking his head with a small smile when she glared at him. "My parents are going to like you. And they don't have to know about us if you don't want them to."

"It's not like I'm ashamed," she said and looked away from him, embarrassed. "But I just don't know if I'm ready for what it would mean," she added, her voice getting smaller.

His hand reached out, his fingers tipping her chin up so she could see his face. "I get it, Charlie. It's okay," he smiled. "I will say, though, that you'd better be ready for questions from Lilian. Because she definitely knows."

Charlie groaned and Page laughed. "Come on," he smiled, his head tilting towards the house. "Let me show you around."

The house was not only beautiful on the outside but on the inside as well. The interior was understated, reminding her of a cottage. There were pictures littering the walls, a few paintings depicting the Scottish landscape scattered between smiling faces and awkward group photos. The walls were a light yellow that radiated warmth and comfort. Page led her from the entryway into another room that had big leather couches, a piano, and a large hearth. Seated in the room were Flora and Callum, Lilian, and an older white man. An older white woman was taking in Flora's words, her hands reaching out to pet Flora's bear.

"Mum, Da," Page said, dropping their bags by the door.

"Page!" The woman near Flora, who Charlie assumed was his mother, stood up and tackled Page in a hug. She was short, around Lilian's height, but she had Page's blond hair and green eyes, her body lithe and small. But as she hugged Page, rocking him back and forth, Charlie could almost see the energy bouncing off her. The woman's smile was infectious. She was the perfect mix of both Page and Lilian.

"Oh, you must be Charlie!" Before Charlie knew it, the woman was hugging her. Page's family was obviously big on hugging. It made Charlie want to both relax and curl up into a ball at the same time. It was nice, a feeling she wasn't quite used to—being from a family that was never this affectionate. She and her parents said they loved one another, but the hugging, the light kiss Page put on his mother's cheek, the way his stepdad patted his shoulder... It was all so new. "I'm so glad you were able to make it. I miss being able to meet the people participating in the bookseller's abroad program we made."

"Thank you for having me."

"Laura wouldn't have anything else." Page's dad walked forward to shake Charlie's hand. He was a tall, bulky man with broad shoulders, his red hair matching Lilian's. He wore a white button-down covered by a sleeveless, brown, woolen vest and had a kind smile that made the skin at the corners of his eyes crease. "Plus, Lilian mentioned that you and Page have been sharing the flat. I'm Steve. I hope everything has been working out okay."

"Yeah," she said, her eyes glancing around the room, looking everywhere and then focusing on the wrinkles on Steve's forehead. "It's been fine."

"Fine," Lilian said, her eyes gleaming. "Hear that, Page? You're fine."

Charlie tried not to blush, but the look Page gave her when his parents turned away said she'd failed.

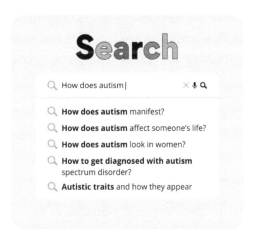

Chapter 34
Page

Page didn't get overwhelmed easily. But he could tell Charlie did.

He noticed it in the small things. Near the beginning of conversations, she would participate fully, but then, as they moved on, she would become quieter—as if her brain were too tired to continue. The other day, in preparation for coming, he had done his own research—turning to the Internet instead of asking Charlie because he didn't want to bother her. He had listened to her enough to look for key phrases or words that told him a source was good or bad. But he had wanted to learn, not only for himself but also so he could help her if she needed any support at his parents' house. There were so many people coming, and he didn't want her to feel like she had to hide.

Not that Charlie would hide… he had just wanted to be able to help.

Because he cared. More than he knew he should.

When they'd arrived earlier, his parents had just been finishing up lunch, and after they put everything away, the rest of the day had been a whirlwind. The next few hours were full of showing

Charlie her room—in the guesthouse that Callum and his family had built after Page's parents moved in. It had three bedrooms for weekends just like this—when his extended family or friends joined them in bulk. He was glad his extended family wouldn't be coming this weekend, though. His mum always knew what he needed on his birthday and this weekend, he needed friends, the people he was closest to. He loved his extended family, but sometimes they didn't understand boundaries.

Boundaries like not mentioning Anna at all.

He loved coming home. But sometimes it was… hard.

He had remembered in therapy how, right after the accident, his mother had taken down all the photos containing his father, Adam, and Page's twin. How she had tried her best to simply erase them because the memory of them was too hurtful.

But once she had met Steve, married him, and brought Lilian into the family, she had started to heal. And the photos had reappeared.

It's not like he wasn't glad. He had been so small back then he hadn't really understood her pain. But as he had gotten older, as he had grown into his own pain of missing his sister and father—he had started understanding why she had hidden those pictures.

"Hello?" Page, who had been in the hallway that connected the living room to the kitchen, heard the front door close. He quickly went to check and was instantly invaded by Sandhya's hug, her honeysuckle perfume filling the space.

"Happy birthday, mate!" Theo said, slapping his back before dropping their bags in the foyer—Sandhya would only carry her own bag if hell was freezing over.

"Thanks for coming," he said, his voice still tired.

Sandhya gave him a knowing smile and gestured to the bags. She lifted a large ceramic casserole dish in her hands. "I brought kheer for dessert because I know you love it. Where should we put it and the bags?"

"You are a goddess." Page kissed her cheek, gesturing into the house. "The kheer can go in the kitchen. You two are in the guesthouse with Charlie. You can take the bags out back."

"Charlie is here?" Sandhya's eyes widened with pure glee. Before he could respond, she was bounding past him and into the house.

"I have a feeling this friendship is going to bite us in the ass," Theo said, giving Page a look.

Page chuckled, grabbing one of the bags from his friend. "Come on, let's go back there before they burn the house down."

Charlie

"Oh my God, it's really you."

Charlie, who had been in the process of unpacking her backpack full of clothes into one of the small wardrobes in the guesthouse's two bedrooms, quickly stood up and turned at the sound of the smokey voice behind her. She froze when she spotted none other than Sandhya Vaughn standing in the doorway to her room. Her long legs and graceful body looked like someone had placed a Greek statue in the middle of a cozy coffee shop. Out of place, yet somehow adjusting the space, molding it to her.

Charlie suddenly felt very plain in her cutoff jeans and sweater. Pulling her sleeves over her hands, she awkwardly waved. "Uh, hello."

"Hello?" Sandhya crossed her arms, narrowing her eyes at Charlie. Her nerves had been simmering since Page had told her Sandhya and Theo would be present, and she could now feel them boil and start to steam. Charlie felt her chin rise and her arms cross over her chest. Maybe she didn't have as much of a right to be here as Sandhya and Theo did, but... well, Page had said he wanted her here... and... she just wanted them to like her.

Sandhya's narrowed eyes softened, her lips tipping up in a grin that widened the longer they stared at one another. Then,

"You are the talk of the town, Charlie James. Got to say, I never really thought we'd see you again and didn't quite believe it when Page told us about... well."

"Yeah, uh..." Charlie winced. "I wouldn't believe me if I told someone either."

Sandhya nodded, walking into the room as if she had lived there for years. Charlie realized she'd most likely been to Page's parents' house before and wondered if this was her usual room. The two twin beds were against the far wall, a small window letting the summer sun in. Even though it was late already, orange and yellow light fell over the room and the yellow comforters. Sandhya moved to sit on the farthest bed, crossed her legs, and leaned back on her hands. She closed her eyes, her head falling back for a moment, and then sat up and looked at Charlie.

"How are you?"

"Me?" Charlie asked after a moment of confusion.

Sandhya let out a small laugh. "Yes, you, Charlie James. How are you doing?"

Charlie knew then that she would like Sandhya. She just hoped the woman would like her back. She hadn't had anyone other than Ripley and Page ask her that question since StarCon. Charlie leaned back against the dresser.

"Better," she finally answered.

Sandhya didn't ask for more and just nodded before adjusting her hair, which was pulled back in a long French braid, behind her shoulder. Then she smiled. Sandhya Vaughn's smiles were bright rays of sunshine that filled the space, Charlie thought to herself. She'd almost felt the room warm up around her since she'd walked in. "This is weird, isn't it?" When they both laughed, Charlie felt the tension seep from her shoulders.

"Sandhya Vaughn," she said, reaching her hand out for Charlie to shake. Charlie did.

"Charlie."

The silence that followed didn't last as the doorway was filled again with noise, heavy breaths, and the sound of feet on the steps. Charlie turned when Theodore Marcus slumped against the door and dropped three bags at his feet, blowing out a breath. His shoulder-length brown hair was pulled back in a bun at the nape of his neck, his tan skin scattered with freckles. A strong jaw, covered with a five-o'clock shadow, dark brows over bright blue eyes, and lips twisted into a scowl made him look like young Harrison Ford.

"Fuck you, Sandhya."

"Fuck you too, Theo."

Then Theo looked up. "Well, look who it is," he said with a wolfish smile. He walked forward, and before Charlie knew what was happening, she was being wrapped in a bear hug, her body lifted off the ground and twirled. "Charlie James, if I live and breathe."

"Um," Charlie froze in his arms, unsure of her next steps. "Hi?"

"Put her down, Theo." At the sound of his voice, Charlie saw Page walk in, frown at where Theo held her in his arms, and lean against the doorway.

"You're right, mate. She might end up liking it too much and realize she could have a better time with me than you."

Charlie wasn't quite sure if she should be offended, but the teasing look in his eyes when he glanced at Page and Page's scowl almost made Charlie laugh. Theo put her down, and she pulled away. A hand grabbed her wrist, pulling her body towards Page's, and she frowned at him.

"Stop treating me like a pillow you can throw around."

His arms wrapped around her, his head falling into the space between her neck and shoulder. She felt him place a small kiss there. Charlie flushed, very aware that he was being affectionate in front of his friends. Of course, even though they should have discussed how they would act around everyone, they hadn't. But that was what they were good at—ignoring everything outside of the apartment. And she couldn't complain. She liked the feeling that filled her chest whenever he had his arms around her.

"Then why are you so cuddly like one," he whispered into her ear.

"You're so lovely, Charlie," Charlie heard Sandhya say in a whiny, low, fake Scottish accent.

"I just want to hold you all day, Charlie," Theo responded in a similar voice.

"But, Sandhya, I don't know how to express my manly feelings. Can you teach me your ways?"

"I just want to be around her *all* da—"

"Shut up." Page finally said, hugging her tighter as she laughed.

"No, please continue," she laughed, grinning over her shoulder at him and then at Theo and Sandhya.

"I'm going to regret introducing you all, aren't I?" he asked. But Charlie knew he didn't mean it.

Falling for You
StarVerseIsAwesome

I saw someone on twitter ask if there was any fanfiction about Charlie James and Jamie Mahone... and well, I just had to write one! So here it is! Finally! I will be uploading a chapter a week (hopefully, that is if school doesn't get in the way. My AP Gov course is kicking my ass at the moment). For now, please enjoy.
Please note that these are real people. Anything that happens in my fanfic is based on a few actual events, but everything else is fiction. Be respectful in the comments, thanks!

 Jamie Mahone could not get Charlie James out of his head.
 He knew he was being an idiot but couldn't care less. A Scottish man turned famed actor because of Star Verse, Jamie hadn't been in the spotlight long, but loved the fame. But now, he wished he could take his fame and shove it out the window because all he wanted was some perfectly normal anonymity.
 As he walked out of the convention hall, all he wanted to do was run and find her—but no, he couldn't, because if he walked away from the security at his side, he would be mobbed in an instant—especially after the shit that had just gone down.
 All he knew was that he needed to find her. And soon. Because he just had to make sure she was okay.

Chapter 35
Charlie

Charlie hadn't seen a house so full of love in a long time. Probably since the last time she'd visited Ripley's family up in Santa Barbara.

Page's parents were lovely, and his friends and sister... well, they were incredible. They all seemed to have a tight bond, inside jokes and looks that didn't need words to go along with them. It was perfect. It was what she imagined a family should be.

At the same time, though, it was hard to be in her position—looking in and passing through. Because she was passing through. She would be leaving in a few weeks. Something that she and Page had yet to talk about.

After a boisterous dinner, Charlie offered to help with the cleanup, taking up dish duty. She weirdly didn't mind. It gave her something to do with her hands while everyone else talked around her. She joined in every now and then, but she found participating fully in their conversations hard. Sometimes, when there were more than three people in the room, all talking together, her brain had trouble staying present. It happened more often when she was tired or in a new space with new people. It had been a long day—she didn't know why, but car rides always made her exhausted—and now she was just glad to step back and observe. She spoke enough that they didn't think she was rude... or at least she hoped they didn't.

"I'm so glad you're here," Lilian said, moving into the kitchen and dumping another stack of dishes beside Charlie. Charlie could hear Theo playing the piano softly in the living room. The music wafted through the rest of the house, fading in and out between snippets of conversation. Lilian rolled up the sleeves of her bright green cardigan and stepped up next to Charlie to help dry the clean dishes. It took Charlie a moment to realize Lilian was talking to her.

"Thanks for inviting me," Charlie said, glancing at her. It was a bit surreal to be standing next to the woman in person. Seeing her and talking with her over email, call, and text was so different from talking to her in person. Lilian had a presence—an aura around her that demanded attention.

Her smile was bright. "I insisted. Page has always hated his birthday, and I knew you would help make it better for him."

Charlie didn't know what to say, so she didn't respond. She had picked up on little hints here and there, people mentioning how Page didn't like this specific day or when she heard Steve ask his wife if she was doing okay, but she didn't know what they all meant. She also didn't know if she had the right to ask.

And she doubted that Page was better off with her here. Maybe it was nothing, but ever since the woman had shown up at the store, a negative feeling had been simmering in her chest. She worried. Worried that what they had wasn't worth all the pain it would cause them both if the press found out. Worried that Page was better off not having to deal with Charlie and what she brought with her.

When the press found out. Charlie frowned down at the dish she was washing. It was bound to happen if everything stayed like this. Especially if they stayed together when she went home.

But she was looking too far into the future. Ever since she was little, looking forward like that, even in hope, had made her anxious. She felt that if she planned too far ahead, she would start worrying more. And if things happened differently than she wanted or planned, it really messed with her head. She learned early on that taking everything day by day or week by week was easier for her to take in.

Charlie and Lilian switched jobs, Charlie taking over the drying part while Lilian dove her hands into the soapy water.

"How has working at the store been?" Lilian asked. Her red curls were pulled away from her face in a low bun, her cheeks flushed.

"It's been good. I mean..." Charlie sighed. "Better than good. I've always wanted to own a store like yours, so it's been a real dream."

"You leave soon, right?"

Charlie nodded. "On the twenty-second."

Lilian hummed under her breath. They fell into a comfortable silence and then—

"I can see how he loves you; you know. I'm happy he found you."

The words shocked Charlie out of her own mind and into the present. She almost dropped the plate she was holding. "Wha—What?"

Lilian chuckled, pushing a piece of her red hair out of her face with the back of her hand. Soap was sticking to her arms.

"Just... go easy on him when you leave, okay?" Lilian looked straight at her now, meeting Charlie's eyes. "He's been through a lot. A lot he doesn't even talk about. It'll be harder on him when you leave than he lets on."

Before she could say anything back, Page's mom came into the kitchen, smiling at them. Her eyes were teary. Lilian instantly pulled away from where she was standing and went to her mother. They exchanged a few hushed words, Lilian pulling her into a tight hug.

Charlie turned to leave the room, but she stopped when she saw Page in the kitchen entryway. He was looking at his mother and sister, huddled in the middle of the kitchen, his face—

He looked devastated. The mask he usually slipped on was gone, and Charlie wanted nothing more than to go to him, even though she had no idea what was happening. But before she could move, he was gone.

"He'll be on the roof," Lilian said, her head lifting from talking with her mom. Laura had turned, leaning her hands on the counter, her head bent. "Just take the main stairs and go up the first stairwell on the right. It leads to the rooftop." With that, she turned away.

Charlie stood still for a second and then glanced back at Lilian. But instead of questioning everything, she left the room to go after Page, Lilian's words from a few seconds before still resounding in her head.

I can see how he loves you; you know.

Chapter 36

Page

Page was surprised when Charlie found him on the roof.

Even though his parents had lived in Stonehaven, they had bought this house to renovate when he was in secondary school. On holidays, they would all come up to the house, spending Christmas or New Year's and Hogmanay here. Or Page's birthday. They had spent it up here a lot. It had always been easier for his mother to escape the town during this week.

He turned at the sound of the window pushing open and watched as Charlie climbed out of it, a blanket draped around her shoulders. She padded her way across the flat portion of the roof and sat beside him on the edge.

Her hair was tied back in a ponytail, a bit of soap stuck to the curls that fell around her face. He reached up and brushed them out of her hair, smiling a bit when she scrunched up her nose at him playfully.

"Do you want to talk about it?" she asked, her voice drifting around him in the wind. He shouldn't have been surprised by her straight forwardness. But in this moment, he was, though he wasn't bothered by it.

"I mean, you've probably heard a bit of it," he said, not ready to look at her yet.

"No," she said, nodding softly. "I don't know what's going on. But I don't need to understand to be here for you. If you want to share or talk about it, I'm here. Or... even if you don't want to talk."

Page didn't think he was going to tell her, but before he knew it, he started talking.

"Anna was my twin." He thought that Charlie might say something, but she stayed quiet, giving him space even as she scooted a bit closer to him. "When we were four, turning five that month, our mum and dad had an argument. Mum said they were close to getting a divorce, and when she brought it up, Dad kind of lost it. He grabbed Anna in the middle of the night, packed bags, and decided to leave." Charlie was looking at him. He could feel the weight of her gaze like it was a weighted blanket. "They made it about an hour outside of town. Dad must have been drinking because he swerved in the rain, and their car flipped. Both he and Anna died on impact. I wish I could say the worst part was the accident, but it wasn't. The worst part was the media afterwards. Later in therapy, I discovered they'd hounded us for a year. I was scared of cameras and flashes for years after, and I had a huge problem with agoraphobia when I was growing up. It took a lot of therapy to work through all of it."

"That's why you have your false identity," she said, her voice softening. He looked at her then, taking in her profile. There was very little light where they were on the roof. It allowed the stars to shine above them, the sky clear of clouds for the first time in weeks. He had been up here long enough that his eyes had adjusted to the darkness, now able to pick up on the small freckles spilling off her cheeks and down onto her neck. "It's why you're always so worried about the press."

"Yeah." His voice was shaking as he spoke.

"I understand." Her words didn't shock him, but they weren't what he'd expected to hear. He didn't know how, but this woman beside him continued to surprise him. "I mean, I didn't go through anything like you did, but after the con, it was hard to even go outside. I came here to get away from all of it. But I'm not sure I could function if I were in a situation like yours. My anonymity protects me. You lack that."

Page's hand, resting on the edge of the rooftop, moved to cover hers, lying next to his own. His hand was much larger, his palm engulfing hers as he turned their hands over and knitted their fingers together. Her hand was cold. He pulled her closer, her shoulder hitting his and her head falling into the crook of his neck.

"I think what hurts is that I still don't understand why he grabbed Anna." He felt Charlie still, pulling back to look at him. He shrugged, focusing on their hands instead of her. "Why did he take Anna with him and not me?" He let out a breath. "It's a stupid question, I know, but—"

"Hey," she said, her hand coming to his cheek, pulling his face towards hers and dipping her head down so their eyes met. "Your thoughts aren't stupid. They aren't."

"I just wish he were here so I could ask him… move on."

Charlie nodded. Then, instead of saying anything, laid her head on his shoulder. The silence was too much, though.

"Talk to me?" She lifted her head at his words, a confused look on her face. He felt himself blush a little bit. Maybe he was being stupid, but he couldn't care less right now. "About anything. Something you love… I just… need the distraction."

Charlie frowned, concentrating. "Did you know that manatees are the cows of the sea?"

He raised a brow.

She shrugged. "You said anything."

"Tell me about manatees," He almost laughed when she gasped with excitement. It was… adorable. Before he could say anything, she launched into a million facts about manatees—

Well, he *was* listening. Truly. He just couldn't stop staring at her. There was so much sudden, unfiltered joy on her face that it knocked the breath out of him. Her face lit up, her eyes shining, even in the darkness surrounding them. And even though he could feel his body start to chill because of the wind, her energy made his bones warm up again.

He opened his mouth, the words almost falling out.

I lo—

He closed his mouth, her past words playing through his head, cutting him off.

But I'm not sure I could function if I were in a situation like yours. My anonymity protects me.

So instead, laughing softly, he pulled her closer, pressing a kiss to her head and letting his body express the words he couldn't say out loud.

@TurnThePageBookshop

Have you read Katie Jones' latest romance? The Lust Inside You is now on our shelves and ready for all of you romance readers to pick up!

Chapter 37

Charlie

Charlie stared at the paper on the fridge. CHARLIE AND PAGE/JAMIE'S FLATMATE RULES glared at her in the bright red pen they had written it in that first night they'd had a conversation. Her knuckles were white as she gripped the coffee cup in her hands. At any other moment, she might have been afraid she was gripping the coffee cup so tightly it might shatter—was that even possible? To shatter ceramic with her bare hands? But right now, all she could think of were Lilian's words.

I can see how he loves you; you know. I'm happy he found you.

Loves you.

Loves.

"Charlie?" She startled at her name, turning as if she'd been caught doing something she shouldn't just to find Page walking into the kitchen.

They had left his parents' house two days ago. The travel hadn't been bad, especially borrowing Callum's car, though the big Scot had been particularly silent on the drive back down. She wasn't oblivious. Callum and Lilian had been ignoring each other for the entire trip. Callum had been like a puppy, sending her long, lingering looks, but had never approached her. There was obviously something there, but Charlie knew better than to pry.

Instead, she had been stuck in her own head these past two days, Lilian's words replaying again and again until she was sick of them. She didn't know how one could get physically and metaphorically sick of words themselves, but here she was.

Their small vacation was over and, once again, they needed to get back to their lives.

But that was a lie. Charlie wasn't living her normal life right now. She was still on vacation from reality. No matter how much she loved the small life she'd made here in Stonehaven alongside the bookstore, Layla, and even Page, it wasn't hers.

She only had a few more weeks.

"Are you okay?" Page asked her, moving to wrap his arms around her. She set her coffee on the counter, letting her now free hands move up and wrap around his neck, her fingers falling into his hair at the nape of his neck. His eyes closed at the contact, and she smiled slightly at the fact she knew he loved it when she played with his hair there.

"Yeah," she replied. Because in this moment, right now, she was fine. In his arms, she was. But in a few weeks?

She wasn't sure if she would be.

Page opened his eyes, his gaze hitting her like a ton of bricks. There was so much weight in that look, settling on her shoulders and on her heart. He opened his mouth as if to say something but then thought better of it. Instead, he moved to kiss her, his lips lingering on hers.

She didn't want to give this up. Whatever it was turning into.

He pulled back, looking her up and down. She was wearing short pajama shorts and a see-through tank. "Do you have plans for the day?"

Something about the way he said the words made her think that he'd just made the plans. It was Sunday, and neither of them had work until tomorrow. Not that Page had to work. But he'd been writing more and more, and she knew he wanted to help Callum with the house this week.

"I don't know. It depends."

"Depends on what?" he asked, his eyes darkening as he leaned in closer.

"Did you get whipped cream from the store?"

Page laughed and pulled her in for another kiss—a kiss that made her knees turn weak.

There was no way this wasn't going to hurt when she left. Because Charlie knew then that she was all the way in—her heart and her body already swimming in deep waters.

Callum
Let me know when you want us to
leave for the day.

Page

Leave the key where you usually
do? And maybe a few hours
early? I'd like to look around the
place by myself.

Callum
Does "by myself" mean with
Charlie?

Page

Maybe...

Callum
Just make sure to clean up after
yourselves.

Page

Mate...

Chapter 38
Page

Page knew that something had shifted after his birthday. He wasn't an idiot.

It wasn't a bad shift. It just... happened.

He and Charlie had gotten even closer, and with the date of her leaving coming up, they hadn't left each other's sides.

"I can't believe you haven't taken me to the house," she said, pulling him along, his hand in hers, their feet walking in tandem on the sandy beach. It was the end of the day, the sun low on the horizon. This was his favorite time of day, golden hour, the entire landscape blanketed in golden light. He also loved how it made Charlie's hair and eyes shine.

"It's just a construction site," he reminded her. They had just grabbed ice cream and were walking along the south side of the beach. "But if you really want to, I can show you," he added as if that hadn't been his plan. And when her eyes lit up in curiosity and excitement, he knew he was lost.

Totally and completely lost.

The house was at the very end of the beach. From the outside, it didn't look that spectacular. When he'd bought it, it was a semi-detached house, but he'd gotten both houses to change the inside to flow into one cohesive home. Like all the other homes in the area, it had the usual grey brick and white-rimmed windows, which looked out onto the beach and sunrise. Once they had their shoes on, he led her through the small walled garden, around the construction tools that had been left outside under tarps, and up to the front door.

Rummaging around behind one of the outdoor lamps, he found the key and pushed open the front door to lead her inside. There was still a lot to do; the floors were ripped up downstairs, the only thing left being plywood. But they had just finished knocking down and sealing all the walls, so the layout was exactly what it would be when they finished. There was a large living room opening onto a kitchen with an island and the white marble countertops he had chosen—a kitchen big enough for his entire family. Two rooms sat to their left, what would be a dining room and a library, and in the middle were the stairs leading up to the second floor.

"There's more upstairs and a loft," he said, moving them into the room that would be the library. They had just finished putting in the floor-to-ceiling built-in shelves. He hadn't been here in a few days, and it surprised him to see that every surface had been dusted. Even though he ran a construction site, Callum always loved his spaces to stay as clean as possible. He had been that way since secondary school.

He saw the moment her eyes lit up, and he chuckled when she looked at him. "I do read, you know. My mother owned the bookstore before Lil, and I worked there as a teen." He shrugged. "I can't really imagine a house that doesn't have a space for books."

"This is amazing," she said, running her hands over one of

the wooden shelves. "And you're creating the house yourself?"

He nodded, "Yeah, I mean with the help of Callum and his team. His brother is an architect, and they have an interior designer who works from Edinburgh with his team whenever they take on a project like this. They helped with the minute details, but the general idea was mine."

He didn't know why he suddenly felt so nervous. But having her here, in this space that he was building, made him want to say stupid things.

Things that he couldn't say... couldn't promise.

Charlie moved to lean back against one of the worktables. It had obviously been where Callum set up his on-site desk. It was empty, but a clean tablecloth had been laid on top. She leaned against it, her arms crossing on her chest as she looked out at the room.

Then her gaze met his.

She let out a small laugh. "What?"

He shook his head, moving towards her. "Nothing, you just look sexy."

She looked down, taking in the jeans and sweatshirt she had pulled on. "You think that, right now, I look sexy?"

"Mmhm," he said, moving closer, his body bracketing hers against the table. She chuckled when he moved to kiss her neck, pushing her hair over her shoulder.

"Page, we are in public."

"I own this house."

"A house that is a busy construction site."

He lifted his head, raising his brows. "Does it look busy to you?"

"Someone might be here—"

"Hello?" he yelled, his voice carrying throughout the house. Charlie started laughing. "Is anyone here?"

The house's silence carried back to them. Charlie was laughing, her head leaning against his chest. His hands came to her waist, his fingers tightening on her hips. He let his hand come up, tipping her chin up so he could look into her face.

"What are we doing?" she asked. The words hung in the air,

her smile falling a bit.

He didn't know what they were doing. He just knew he didn't want this moment to end.

"I don't know," he said, his voice low, before cupping her cheek in his hand. She closed her eyes, leaning into the gesture. "I just know that I—"

He leaned down, catching her lips with his. Page felt it then, the connection. Whenever he wasn't around her, a part of him doubted that it existed, wondering if he had imagined it. But in moments like this, he knew. Deep down, he knew.

Three words he had almost said to her on the roof. Three words he knew were the truth—but he was scared to say. Because it was too soon. It had to be too soon. A part of him knew, too, that if he said them, things would change, and this was the last thing he wanted.

Instead, he kissed her, his hands moving up her waist. He showed her with his body, with his hips, with his hands. And he could feel that connection between them strengthen as her hands touched him, as her breath caught, as her skin warmed, as she let go, her head falling back as she came around him.

Her hands roamed over his shoulders, up and down his back. He had to hold in a groan when her nails dug into his upper back, when her hands slid under his shirt. He pulled away, shedding his jacket between kisses. Her hands dug into his hair, and he pulled away again as he took his shirt off, dropping it on the ground.

"The sawdust—"

"Don't care," he said, pulling her in again. She removed her jacket, bringing him back to her. Page decided then and there that he was addicted to her. Her kisses, the noises she made when he ran his tongue over hers, the way her body moved with him as he grabbed her thighs and lifted. Her legs wrapped around his waist, bringing them closer as he almost fell sideways. He caught them, both laughing as he pulled away. One hand supported her as his other found purchase on one of the built-in bookshelves. She lowered herself, her hands running from his chest, over his shoulders, then up to cup his face.

"Sometimes, I wish I could capture every moment with my camera," she whispered as he leaned down, pulling her shirt down slightly and dragging his mouth over her shoulder.

"Maybe one of these days, I'll let you." He said, nipping at the skin above her breasts. She moaned. He grinned up at her. "That turns you on, doesn't it?" He chuckled when she blushed bright red. "What else turns you on, Charlie?" When she didn't answer, he gripped her hips in his hands a little tighter. "What in those steamy romance books of yours makes you wet?" His hand came up and brushed her breast, right where it was covered by her bra. He felt her hips move towards his.

"When they get on their knees." He almost grinned when she said the words. A part of him was shocked she'd said anything back because, so far, Charlie hadn't been the most vocal in bed. He was testing the waters. But he also knew she wasn't ever afraid to ask for what she wanted or voice her opinions.

He kneeled. "And then what?" he asked, his voice hoarse. His blood was pumping loudly in his ears. All his senses were focused on one thing—her.

"Then—" He unbuttoned the top of her jeans, one hand running up and down the outside of her thigh. He pulled her zipper down. "Then—" Leaning to kiss above her panty line, he grinned at her gasp.

"Then?"

"Then—kiss me, Page, please. Make me come."

"You're beautiful when you beg," he pulled her jeans down over her legs, barely waiting for her to step out of them before he gripped her hips, pulling her to him and kissing her hip. He pulled her underwear to the side, kissing her inner thigh before settling over her clit. He knew her now, knew what made her gasp, and it wasn't long before she was trembling in his hands. She moaned out his name, her hands gripping his hair as she came a few moments later. He kissed her through it as her body shook, and when she stilled, he stood, his fingers gripping her chin as he leaned forward to kiss her, his tongue slipping into her mouth.

"I need you inside me," she said, her hands at his pants,

pulling them down. He pulled out a condom from his wallet, slipped it on and gripped her hips as she jumped up, wrapping them around his hips. He pushed her against the shelves, kissing away her moan as he slid into her. This, *this* moment. He wanted to document, write, photograph, remember this moment. He wanted to *remember* the way she felt, the way she sounded, the way she gripped his hair and shoulders as she came around him again, him following a second later.

They were both breathing heavily, her arms still wrapped around him a few minutes later. His legs shook—his whole body seemed to be shaking. But he pulled her closer to him, needing her warmth.

A few minutes later, after their sweat had dried, they cleaned up as best they could and dressed. He felt it when she pulled away slightly.

"People always leave," she said, her voice small.

The words made his shoulders stiffen. He pulled back far enough so he could look at her. But before he could say anything, she put a finger to his lips.

"They do. Or they go silent, and I realize too late that I did something or said something that made them pull away. I've always been too honest, or harsh, or straightforward."

"You aren't *too* much of anything." Page tucked a piece of hair behind her ear. "I like your honesty. I like your weird love for romance. I like how you're an intense nerd, even if you like to hide it. I like the way you bite your lip when you're thinking or that you named your vibrator after a superhero." He chuckled at her blush, but he looked at her, trying to convey his seriousness. "I like your body, your mind, your everything, Charlie. I like *your* truth."

He loved it.

So much of his life was a lie. So much was crafted, was false personas or was a job he had to perform. Everything but her. With her, he could just... be.

She looked at him, studying his face so intensely. He hoped she saw the truth in what he said, how much he cared, even if he was scared to say the words. Finally, she nodded.

Chapter 39

Charlie

Charlie was working when she got the phone call. It was early in the day, so she frowned when she saw Ripley's name on her phone.

"Aren't you supposed to be in bed?" she said, shelving one of the books.

"Charlie." At her friend's worried, almost scared tone, she froze.

"Ri? Are you okay?"

"Charlie, you need to check the news," Ripley said, her voice hard. "You and Page need to check the news."

Charlie's heart dropped in her chest.

"I'll call you back," she said and then found Layla's gaze across the store.

Layla sent her a concerned look. Charlie didn't realize she was shaking until Layla put her hands on her arms comfortingly. "Call him and head upstairs," she said. "If it's what I think it is, then you need to not be in the store today."

Charlie grabbed her stuff, headed up the back stairs and dialed Page once she got in the door.

"Charlie," Page's voice sounded pained. "Are you inside? Are you safe?"

"Yeah," she said, her brain filled with clouds. "What's going on?"

"The press. I don't know how, but they got a photo of us on the beach. They did an article. I need you to stay inside. It dropped this morning, and I don't know what's going to happen, but my agent called and—"

"Just get home, okay?" Charlie asked, cutting him off. She could hear the panic in his voice.

"Okay," he said, the word more of a deep sigh.

Then he disconnected.

Charlie spent the next twenty minutes doing the one thing she had told herself she wouldn't do on this trip—checking the news surrounding her name.

Even though the first story had dropped three hours ago, there were headlines all around. Charlie counted ten in total, all major news outlets for film, gossip, and celebrity news.

Jamie Mahone, or someone else? Sex Scandal, Small Business and Family Revealed.

Fuck.

She paused when she saw a new headline, instantly feeling sick.

Movie Star Dates Unstable Fan.

Angry Charlie Is at It Again

God, this was all a mess.

What had she done?

@FangirlsAreAwesome

Well, now his defense of her a few weeks ago makes sense…

@StarVerseFandom

Where are all of our Charlie and Jamie Stans at? Our fan fiction dreams are coming true!

@StarVerseIsAwesome

Am I an oracle? Did I predict the future with my fan fiction? I feel like I must have some power over the universe at this point. #Jarlie for life y'all.

Chapter 40

Page

Jake called him around lunch and seeing his name on his phone had made his stomach drop.

"You're going to need to sit down," had been the first thing his manager had said when he'd answered.

Apparently, the woman Charlie had seen in the shop the other day was a journalist from one of the top gossip sites in the UK. She had been living out of an Airbnb in town since she had arrived. Without his knowledge, she had gotten a few condemning photos of him and Charlie. A few of them on the beach—he could tell they were from the day he'd shown her the house—and one of them kissing in the window of the bookstore.

It was blurry, but still obvious that it was him. And in conjunction with her research of Charlie and the photo of them on the beach, it was clear who Charlie was as well.

Jake had told him about the first article, had mentioned there were others, and then had forwarded them to Page's email. Callum had seen the look on his face, ushering Page to sit on the workbench upstairs while he pulled up the stories on his phone.

That was when the messages had started coming in.

Theo
> You need to check the news.

Theo
> Nvm. Don't check the news. I don't
> think you want to read these.

Sandhya
> You ok? Is Charlie ok? Let us
> know if we can help.

Lilian
> Hey. Call me when you can? Mum
> is worried.

That one had made him want to throw up. That and the story about his family that had leaked not thirty minutes earlier.

Page let out a deep breath, his head falling into his hands.

"What can I do?" Callum asked. He had told his crew to head home for the day and had come in to sit by him. Out of all the people who were working on the house—all of them locals— Callum was the only one who really knew what Page had gone through as a kid. Of course, most people in Stonehaven had been there for the accident and the aftermath, but Callum had been his friend. Even if they had drifted apart for a bit, what Page had gone through was an experience that still bound them.

"I have no idea. There's no way to refute the photos. It blew up within an hour before our media team could shut it down. It's out. It's all out. Charlie and my family's story. They even talk about the bookstore." He let out a dark chuckle. "Lilian will be happy about that, at least. The store should be getting a lot of press in the next few weeks."

Callum shook his head. "She wouldn't have wanted it this way, though, mate," he said. "You know that."

Jake
> P, I hate to be the one to say this,
> but you are going to need to make
> a statement.

Angie

He's right. Also, I've already been contacted by the show. It doesn't look good. I don't really know what I recommend there. They can't legally fire you or sue you, but they aren't going to be nice.

That was his worst fear. To others, he could see how this didn't seem like a big deal. How they could just move on, knowing that their relationship meant more than what the press said. But Page knew how damaging the press could be. He had dealt with it as a kid and as an actor. He couldn't put his mother through this again, and Charlie...

She didn't deserve this.

Page nodded to Callum, his breath coming in short bursts. He was trying to hold in the panic attack that was waging itself in his mind. He couldn't let that out. Not here. Not now. He needed—

His phone rang, and when he saw the name on it, he closed his eyes. Then he answered.

"Charlie. Are you inside? Are you safe?"

"Yeah," she said. Her voice was so small. He could hear her worry. Her fear. God, he didn't even know what to do. "What's going on?"

"The press. I don't know how, but they got a photo of us on the beach. They did an article. I need you to stay inside. It dropped this morning, and I don't know what's going to happen, but my agent called and—"

"Just get home, okay?" Charlie asked.

"Okay," he said. He disconnected, ignoring Callum's worried look, and stood.

"What are you going to do?" Callum asked, and Page shrugged.

"Whatever I have to in order to keep everyone the safest."

He just had a feeling that he wouldn't like what that was.

When Page got home, the lights in the flat were turned off. But that didn't stop him from spotting the two news vans parked outside or the click and flash of their cameras as he walked up the walkway and up to the flat from the back entrance. He was lucky all they wanted were pictures right now. If they had tried to talk to him...

He didn't know what he would do. But he was sure Angie and Jake would not have liked the outcome. His heart beat loudly in his chest, dread filling his stomach as he pushed open the door to the flat.

"Charlie?" he called, closing the door. The blinds were drawn, all the lights off, and he almost thought the flat was empty until a ball of blankets moved on the couch.

"Page?" Her voice was rough, as if she'd been crying.

"Hey," he said, moving to sit on the edge of the couch. His hand came to rest on her hip. His hands were sweaty, the weight of what needed to be done falling in his chest. He chose to do the one thing he shouldn't—he pulled her to his chest.

"I didn't—I shouldn't have—"

"Hey," he said, his hand cupping the back of her head. "This isn't your fault. It's mine."

"But—I'm scared, Page. I know it's stupid, but I'm scared." He could feel her shaking. But he wasn't surprised. The aftermath of the convention had been so intense for her that he wasn't surprised she was panicking now.

"It's not stupid. Look, Charlie," he swallowed, and he felt her stiffen as he pulled away. "I'm not sure how, but they found out about my sister and dad, and they're targeting you. Jake and Angie said they got a statement from your brother again, and it won't be safe for you to stay here."

He could already imagine all the ways things could go wrong if she stayed. The flat was small, and it barely had any security. And after the way the Internet had leaked her address after the convention... he didn't want to risk her safety. The last option he had was to take her home.

He couldn't bring this attention back to his mum. Page wouldn't be responsible for putting her through that again.

Maybe some would think he was overreacting. They'd say his anxiety, the panic he felt, was not needed. He had friends who didn't give a shit what the press said or did, friends who didn't care about themselves making the gossip news sites. But he did. He had seen what it did to his mum; he couldn't let it happen to Charlie. Not again. He wouldn't let this happen again.

Charlie's face was shadowed in the dark light of the flat. He saw her frown. "What are you saying?"

"I—" he broke off, pushing to a stand. He paced, his hands coming up to lace behind his head.

"Page," she said, her voice firm. "What are you saying?"

He winced. He didn't want to say this. He didn't want to do this. But on the way over, his mind had been moving like a whirlwind, all the bad situations floating around in his head over and over again.

When they had been just the two of them, without his past, without his job—they'd been fine. But with all of it? They wouldn't last. The press would be too much. He wasn't even sure what his job would look like now. And Charlie... She had told him that she was scared. She had said she didn't want—didn't like—the spotlight. And the selfish part of him, the part that wanted the memories of them to stay good, to stay untainted from the rest of his life... won.

"I think it would be best if you went back to LA. If you stayed away from the store, from me."

Charlie stood slowly, the blanket falling from her grip. "Why?" she asked, her voice sounding a bit strangled. "How would that help? There are going to be stories as long as we—" Her eyes widened. "Oh."

"I can't do this," Page finally said, his hands coming up over his eyes, dragging over his face. "I can't. This is the only thing that is going to stop it all. Maybe if you go home, the press will get better and—"

"I get it." Her voice was harsh. Cold. The words felt like she was stabbing him. He could normally see all her emotions on her face, but right now, she felt far away. Her expression was stone cold. Not angry, not sad, not… anything.

Did she even care?

"No, you don't. This isn't about us or you—"

"How is this not about us? Or me?" she said, her voice rising. "This is *all* about us, Page!" Emotion broke through her stone façade for a moment before it shut down again.

"They're hounding my family!" he said, his voice rising to meet hers. "Lilian said there are reporters outside the house and—They're outside of this damn flat!" He set his hands on the edge of the counter, leaning against it, his head falling to his chest. "I have to worry about my family, Charlie. My mum can't take this type of pressure, not again. If you go home, if we refute what they are saying, say it isn't true, then maybe it will all stop."

"But it is true," she said. He couldn't look at her. "It is fucking true."

When he didn't say anything, he heard her move to stand next to him. But he didn't look up. He couldn't.

"If I leave, we're done, Page. I deserve more. I deserve someone who isn't ashamed to be with me. Who wants to fight for me," she said, and he could hear her tears. Whatever numbness had been on her face before had broken. He felt tears in his own eyes. He wanted to tell her he wasn't ashamed, that he did want her just as she was. But when he opened his mouth, he couldn't get the words out, anxiety pulsing through his body. "I understand your trauma. I *get it*. I do. I have my own. But I guess I thought that we both—that we could help each other. What happened was years ago. This is right now. Right now."

Panic filled his chest. Panic mixed with hope. But in the end, panic won.

"I'm sorry, Charlie." He stood and turned, moving away from

her, going into his sister's room. He shut the door, the sound loud in the silent flat.

It was the only thing he could do to keep her away from everything, from the press, from the show. She was right. She deserved so much better.

Now, with him out of her life, she would be able to find that.

Chapter 41

Charlie

The next week was a blur.

Once Page had gone into his room, the door solid and closed behind him, Charlie had collapsed, all the emotions, anger, fear, hurt, spilling out. She'd instantly called Ripley, who had helped her book an immediate flight home to LA.

She left the next morning. A week before she was originally supposed to.

Charlie had been imagining leaving Scotland since she'd arrived. She had hated how soon she would have to go, but she had never imagined it would be like this. Lilian had understood, of course. She'd told Charlie to take the time for herself, to recover, to rest. After that, Charlie hadn't been able to check her texts anymore.

When she'd arrived in LA, Ripley had been waiting for her. Charlie's own family was staying in Northern California for the summer and could not be bothered to meet her at the airport. Her mother's exact words were: *We don't need that attention as your father is getting reelected to the community board.*

It didn't matter to her. If Charlie was being honest with

self, it was probably better if she didn't see them anytime soon. She already knew too well what would happen. Her brother wouldn't apologize, and her parents would make up excuses for his behavior. Just like they'd always done. And just like they always would.

Charlie had purposely chosen a redeye flight to arrive back in LA in the middle of the night. Ripley would be awake anyway, and that way, she had hoped they would be able to get away with not seeing any press.

She was thankfully right.

"Come on," Ripley, with her bright pink hair tied back in pigtails, pulled her against her in a fierce hug. "Let's get you home."

But they didn't go home. Charlie had left LA because the press had known about their apartment. Instead of going there, Ripley took Charlie to her parents' house up in Santa Barbara. They had a house in the hills, a few minutes' drive from the beach.

It was another escape. Another chapter added to Charlie's saga of running away.

She was so tired of escaping. She just didn't know how to stop.

Excerpt from Talk Show

Host #1: Well, the new hit news of the week is the Jamie Mahone Scandal. Or should we now call him Page Jamie McAllister?

Chapter 42

Page

When he woke up the following morning to find Charlie gone, all her stuff packed, he had frozen. He had stood there, staring at the paper still magnetized to the fridge, reading the rules repeatedly.

1. The apartment stays clean, and we stay out of each other's respective rooms.
2. If one of us feels uncomfortable, we need to tell each other.
3. Flatmates don't fall for flatmates.

Then his eyes fell on the title. CHARLIE AND PAGE/ JAMIE'S FLATMATE RULES. He stared at the words until his eyes hurt. Then he ripped the list off the fridge. But when he went to throw it in the trash, he stopped. He gripped it in his hand, the side of the paper crinkling in his grasp.

They had broken every single rule on the list. They hadn't stayed out of each other's rooms. In fact, they had done the opposite. They had been the worst at open communication. This moment was proof of that. And—

Page scoffed, his other hand coming to cover his face.

He had fallen in love with her. He had fallen head over heels in love with her. And instead of pulling her closer, he had pushed her away. And then she'd left.

He folded the paper, setting it on the counter in front of him, where the mail also sat. He lifted it, stopping when he saw the ck envelope.

The photos. After their day at the castle, Page had helped her find the nearest camera store to get the film developed. She'd ordered the prints to be sent here because she hadn't planned to leave.

She hadn't planned to leave...

He gripped the envelope hesitantly, not wanting to bend the photos but not able to let them go from his grip.

GW, his nickname for Gandalf the White, jumped up onto the counter. He stared at the cat. His smushed face seemed to look angrier than usual as he sat and stared back at him.

"I know buddy, I know."

He stuffed the photos in his inner jacket pocket and grabbed his overnight bag. He would only be gone for a few days, Layla already agreeing to check up on GW.

It was all for the best. It had to be. Otherwise, he'd just made the biggest mistake of his life. Page went home. Not Stonehaven. Not London. But home.

lly, Yours

@Fangirl200

Did everyone see the article? I guess #Jarlie was
never really a thing, y'all. *sobs*

Chapter 43
Charlie

It was a week from the day she'd left when the article was released. Charlie had been hiding out in the guest room in peak breakup fashion—her hair tied up in a bun on the top of her head, her body smelling from lack of a shower and stuffed in the most comfortable pajamas she had. Her bedside was littered with used cups of tea—she had annoyingly become addicted to the stuff in Scotland and had a hard time moving back to coffee—and now empty bowls of cereal. Curled into a ball on her side, her headphones over her head, she was rewatching Gilmore Girls, skipping all the parts except for Jess and Rory moments.

Because why the fuck not?

The burnout that came after an autistic meltdown was bad. And she knew that's what she was experiencing. She had gone through one the summer after her junior year of college. Autistic burnout—burnout on steroids that seemed to consume her body and mind and soul and… well, consume pretty much everything—was the bane of her existence. She just wasn't sure if she was in a burnout or if it was an extended autistic meltdown. Whatever it was… She wasn't functioning.

It made her angry.

Her new bubble had been fully impenetrable. At least until today, when she heard the voices outside her room. She pulled her headphones off all the way and stopped the show, listening closely. It was Ripley and her mom.

"She doesn't need to see that, Mom," Ripley said, her voice tired.

"Th... ...an... ...I can't believe he said it was all a lie. The
...ticl...

"...h... ...pley interrupted. "She might hear."

...t... when Charlie did the one thing she knew she
...ur... She went to find the article they were talking about.
...um...of her, yes, but... fuck it. She was already in a bad mood.

Page McAllister Tells All: Says the Relationship Was Fake

In a recent interview given to our source, actor Page McAllister tells all, saying, "I knew Charlie James very briefly. She worked at our bookshop, and the photo and story of us being together is false. I wish her well, but she's of no importance to me or my family." When asked why he was friendly with her, he answered, "I thought if I befriended her, all of the conflict could stop."

Charlie stared at the words in shock.

Absolute shock.

"Charlie?" Ripley had opened the door and was looking in to check on her. She seemed to register the look on Charlie's face with resigned anger. "You saw it."

Charlie nodded. And then promptly burst into tears for the first time since coming home. Ripley rushed into the room, wrapping her in a tight hug.

"Shh. Just let it out. I'm here. Let it all out."

She did. Once again, she hadn't read the room. Once again, what she had believed to be true hadn't been true at all.

Page's Phone

Theo
Hey mate, are you doing okay?

Theo
WTF is that article?

Theo
Page, did you say this?

Theo
There's no way you said this, wtf

Sandhya
WTF PAGE

Sandhya
There's no way you said those
things. Text me back right now.

Sandhya
PAGE????

Chapter 44
Page

Page was angry.

Actually, no. He was furious.

"They did what?" he asked, his voice rising. He could see his agent and manager wince from where their heads were sitting on his tiny phone screen.

"They put out an article," Jake sighed, rubbing his temples. "They put in some quote from you saying that the relationship and photos weren't real and that you befriended her so she would stop shit-talking the show—"

"But I never said any of this," he said, panic breaking into his voice. Panic. All-consuming anger. He didn't even know what he was feeling anymore.

...r he'd reached his parents' home, he had broken. Lilian ...arrived later that night, saying she'd gotten a text from ...arlie ab...t leaving, and she had held him while everything had hit him at once. All the pressure. All the pain.

He had cracked.

Page didn't remember the last time he had broken down like that. It had to be after his sister and dad had died. Or when he had started dealing with the grief when he was in secondary school. But he hadn't allowed himself to really feel like that since then. He had always needed to be strong—to be the one his mother could rely on. She had been such a mess after Anna had died that *she* had needed him. Even as a toddler, a part of him had always known. He was their rock. They relied on him.

But now, looking back, he saw how that was all just his own anxiety and depression hurting him.

Lilian had taken him back to his room, shutting all the blinds to shield him from the press. They weren't allowed anywhere near his parents' private property, but they all knew how tricky they could get. At least, there, he could pretend he was hiding without them a few feet outside his house, waiting for his next move. His mum and stepdad had left before he'd gotten there, taking a small trip to the Isle of Skye. Lilian had decided to stay, and Page was just thankful he wasn't alone.

To say he had been in a dark mood the next few days would be an understatement.

It was on the fourth day that he got the call from Jake. About this damned article.

"If you never said that or gave them a statement, it isn't legal," Angie said, her voice heavy with a sigh. She looked exhausted. In fact, they all did. "I don't even think the fault is on the reporter or writer of the article. It says the statement was provided by the showrunners on your behalf. You're supposed to be recovering with your family from the trauma."

Page's mouth dropped open. "Fuck," he said, blowing out a breath. "Fuck! We need to do something. Angie... this article can't—" he cut off, horror filling him. God, what if Charlie saw this? Of course, she'd probably seen it already. He knew they were over—she probably never wanted to see him again—but there was something wrong about her thinking or possibly believing those lies.

… and I realize too late that I did something or said something that made them pull away. I've always been too honest, or harsh, or straightforward…

"What do you recommend?" he asked, his voice falling into a flat anger.

Angie chewed on a ballpoint pen, taking her time before responding. "You said you broke up with her?" she asked, and her lips quirked up a bit at his solemn nod. "I know and hear your anxieties, Page. I get them, but this is what comes with the life you live. And I think it's time to change." Before he could speak, she continued. "Do you love her?"

The question stopped him. He looked down at the envelope of photos in front of him. He hadn't opened them yet, but he'd been carrying them everywhere. The word was out of his mouth before he could think it through. "Yes."

She nodded. "Then here's what I suggest we do."

After the call, he opened the envelope.

Page's parents came home later that day. He hadn't known they were coming back until he heard them walk in. When he found them in the living room talking to Lilian, he stopped in the doorway.

Because his mother looked… okay.

It was late in the afternoon, and with the blinds drawn, their living room was bathed in darkness, the only light coming from the overhead lamp. Page didn't know what he was expecting. Maybe it was the flashbacks to what she had been like when he was young, but for some reason, he hadn't expected her to be standing and looking like she could take on the world.

Which embarrassed him because, if anyone could take on the world, he had always thought it would be her. It wasn't that

Page didn't think his mother was strong… She was the strongest woman he knew. But for some reason, he had expected this to affect her as much as it was him.

"Page," his mother said, moving to the couch. His stepfather and Lilian left the room, giving them space. "Love, talk to me."

"I thought you were going to be gone longer," he admitted, moving to sit next to her.

"Yes, I know." She let out a breath, her hand coming up to touch his shoulder. "And I'm not going to lie, I needed a few days. But then I realized that this wasn't about me." Her gaze moved from his to where the photos Charlie had taken were spread over their coffee table. She picked up the photo he had been unable to put down, the one the woman had taken of the two of them, Charlie smiling at the camera, and he was smiling… at her. He looked up at his mom and tried to say something, but she spoke before he could. "Love, it's okay to need time," she said and then urged him to look at her. "But it is time to work through all of this. Lilian told me what you did."

"It needed to be done," he said, his voice tired.

His mother sighed. "No, what needed to be done was for your mother to realize that you need her." Page looked at his mother then. She looked tired but determined. "We should have had this conversation years ago. Steve made me realize over the last few days how you are still holding on to my trauma, Page," she said, not letting him speak when he opened his mouth, "you need to stop protecting me and live your own life."

"But mu—"

"No buts, Jamie Page," she said sternly. She only used this voice when she was serious. He almost winced. "Your father and Anna died years ago. And we will always carry that pain. But you do not need to keep on actively protecting me, especially when it hurts you." Her eyes filled with tears. His breath was stuck in his chest. "I have Steve to be there for me, and I can protect myself, too. It all might still hurt but I have healed from it. I don't want you sacrificing anything else out of fear. And," she added, holding up her hand when he went to speak, "I don't need you to protect me. Lilian and I are grown women, Page. We will have the support we need, but we can stand on our own."

"I didn't just do this to protect you."

"I know," she said finally. "And I know you want to protect Charlie, too. But sometimes, in our protecting the ones we love, we get so single-minded that we don't see when we are hurting them."

The words were like a punch to his gut.

Page let out a deep breath, his shoulders sagging. His mum pulled him into a hug. "She deserves to be able to choose you just as much as you do her." She swept his hair back, placing a kiss on his forehead. "I know you think being with you won't be worth what comes with your life. But you're wrong. You are worth it." She placed the photo in his hand, her hand cupping his cheek softly. "Now, make sure she knows she's worth it as well."

Page looked at his mum, the woman who had been there for him through everything. He hugged her back and tried to soak up some of her strength. He would need it in the next couple of weeks if wanted to fix everything.

3 weeks later...

Chapter 45
Charlie

"I think you need to watch this."

"Ripley," Charlie said, letting out a long breath. She was too tired for this. These last three weeks, she had just been trying her best to forget. She wasn't quite ready for the move-on portion of her plan, her chest still hurting when she was reminded of that article, but she was good at trying to forget. "I don't want to—"

"Charlie. Just click the link and shut the fuck up."

Charlie, stunned, glared at her best friend. But Ripley didn't budge, so she grabbed her computer and opened the link Ripley had sent her. It opened to a YouTube tab, and she frowned when she saw the name. It was a channel for the same talk show that Page had gone on when he was in London. It was a live stream, and when she saw the title, she tensed.

PAGE MACCALISTER TELLS ALL.

"Ripley, why—"

"Shhh," she said, cutting Charlie off.

She shut up and pressed play.

"Welcome back to the show, everyone! Today is a special day. We have our very own space prince on today's show, the infamous Jamie Mahone, otherwise now known by his real name now as Page McAllister."

Charlie knew what was coming next, but she wasn't prepared for the camera to pan onto him when it did. He looked—

He looked terrible. Not in a literal sense. Page looked put together in dark blue slacks and a white button-down shirt. He had gotten his hair cut, the strands no longer falling into his eyes. He had a small smile on his face.

But she saw through all of that. How could she not?

Bags were under his eyes, his shoulders tense. And his eyes—

He looked sad.

She took in a deep breath.

"I thought you said he never does interviews," Ripley said. She was smooshed on the couch next to Charlie, their shoulders pressed against one another—a silent reminder she wasn't alone. Ripley had barely left her side in the past three weeks. And Charlie... Charlie knew that Ripley would hate for her to say she owed her... but she did.

"He doesn't."

"Now, this is a special interview because I am very lucky to say I am the first person to ever interview you one-on-one," Andie said, his eyes gleaming.

Page nodded. *"That's true, Andie."*

"Why is that?"

Page leaned forward, his forearms on his knees. *"Well, soon after getting cast on StarVerse, I decided I wanted to keep my private life out of the press. As most people now know, my twin sister and father passed away when I was young. The story was pretty sensational where I live, and I had a great deal of trauma from that experience. I thought that keeping my life and the lives of my family out of the press was for the best."*

"*I know it was a long time ago, but I am sorry for your loss,*" Andie said, his tone somber.

"*Thank you. Unfortunately, I do still deal with anxiety attacks if I get overwhelmed by the press. I had a lot of trouble with public speaking in secondary school and still do. Coming up with my acting name and the persona of Jamie Mahone helped me cope with all of that. Not that the persona wasn't me.*" Page seemed to pause and then continued a few moments later. "*We are the same person, but it was a front to hide what I was dealing with.*"

"*Now, all of this didn't necessarily come out willingly,*" Andie said next, his statement not a question.

"*No, it didn't,*" Page agreed, a small smile hitting his face. It didn't reach his eyes. "*But even if it hadn't, I think a part of me knew it would eventually.*"

"*There's been a lot of debate recently online about whether your fans can trust that they know who you are. What do you say to that?*"

Page leaned back, raising a brow. "*I would say that's not true. What people have seen isn't a lie but more a coping mechanism. Also, I'd like to point out that I love my fans and the people who support my work, but none of them truly know me. You won't unless you're a close friend of mine. That's just the honest truth about being a person in the spotlight. I appreciate their support, but I don't think I would want millions to know every detail about my life. I don't think anyone would want that.*"

"*But you had to know that would come with your job.*"

Page sighed. "*I wanted to act because I loved acting. Not because I liked the spotlight and fame. I understand why people want to know everything about a person they look up to, but I also think it's okay to ask people to still respect my privacy.*"

"*Speaking of privacy,*" Andie said. Charlie almost groaned, knowing exactly what was going to come up.

"Ri, I don't want to listen to this."

"Charlie. I already watched it. This isn't live. It aired hours ago. You need to watch it."

"*With all of this personal information that has been revealed came a delightful story about you and a young woman by the name of Charlie James.*"

She looked to Page's face, but he seemed to be playing it cool and collected. He nodded, letting Andie continue.

"Recently, an article came out with a statement from you saying that the photos were false and that you only befriended her to stop the tension between the show and herself. Is that true?"

Page didn't take long to answer. He responded clearly and distinctly. *"No."*

"No?"

"No?" Charlie asked, the question jumping out of her. All she could hear was Page's voice, static, Page's voice again. She couldn't feel her toes. "What the fuck?"

"Just what I said. I want to be clear, Andie. I can't say much for legal purposes, but I am pursuing legal action against the showrunners for releasing a statement to the press that I never made. I never befriended Charlie for the show. In fact, we were explicitly told to avoid her or any questions pertaining to her after StarCon. And the photos are not fake. I know Photoshop has gotten pretty good, but I don't think it's good enough to fake those photos. It's obvious that the two people in the pictures are us."

"So, are you saying that you were indeed in a relationship with Miss James?"

"Oh, Miss James. He makes you sound so distinguished. Or maybe that's just his accent—"

"Shut up, Ri."

"Yes. Charlie and I met shortly after StarCon when she started working and living above my sister's bookshop in Stonehaven. To say I was shocked to see the woman who had been at the convention would be an understatement. We became friends and shortly after started seeing each other."

"So, you were seeing her back when you did the show with us earlier in the summer?"

"Yes," Page said, his voice calm. *"I was."*

"And are you and Miss James still together?"

Charlie wasn't breathing. She. Was. Not. Breathing.

"No. I broke things off."

"Why would that be, if I may ask?"

"Exactly my question, dude," Ripley said, her voice laced with amusement.

"Ri."

Page ran a hand over his hair and smiled sheepishly. He smiled. Sheepishly. God, she missed him.

No. She was still angry. She had to be angry. Otherwise...

"I wanted to protect her. I knew the media would attack her if we were still together. I broke it off when the first story was released. Now, looking back, I realize how stupid it was. I pushed away the woman I love to protect her."

Charlie's world stopped.

The woman I love.

The woman he loves.

He loves.

Her.

"What would you say to Charlie now if she were watching?" A part of her wanted to laugh at the question. It was so stupid, so stereotypical. So cheesy.

But the audience was cheering. She was holding her breath. She felt like she was going to pass out.

"God," Page said, his eyes widening a bit. *"I mean, I owe her an apology, though I don't deserve a response. I was stupid. I acted out of fear, pushing her away when the one thing I needed was for her to stay close. I didn't get to tell her how much I loved her before she left. I just wish I could go back and change how I reacted in the moment."*

It was 5 in the morning, and Charlie was awake. In fact, she had never gone to bed. Her brain hadn't been able to stop thinking since she'd watched the clip of the show.

She hadn't been able to think clearly since the text had come through.

Page

> I'm sorry. I should be saying this
> in person, but I know you don't
> want to see me. I'm so sorry,
> Charlie. I will prove it, I promise.

The text had been sent at 2 am her time the night before. Right before the show had aired that day. She'd been in such a haze she hadn't seen it before Ripley had forced her to watch the clip.

God, what was she doing?

Charlie groaned, her hands coming up to rub her eyes. He had done this to them. She hadn't wanted to leave him. She hadn't wanted to give up. He had left her. He had pushed her away.

But she also hadn't fought for them. She had just grabbed her stuff and ran.

They had both run from each other.

"...I just wish I could go back and change how I reacted in the moment."

Page's words were a broken record playing in her head.

She wished she could go back in time and change everything, too.

If only a time machine existed.

But she couldn't. She could only move forward.

Charlie stared up at her bedroom ceiling, her hand fumbling for where her phone lay at her side. She dialed Ripley without thinking.

"Could you possibly drive me to the airport?" she asked, her voice tired. She hadn't given Ripley a moment to say hello.

"Are you going after him? Or running away again?" Ripley asked, her voice serious but loving. She could picture her friend's conspiratorial look of mischief on the other end of the phone.

"No more running," she said.

Your friend Charlie James tweeted for the first time in a while!

@CharliesWorld
Wish me luck, world. I'm going to need it.

@Sarahthefangirl
HOLY SHIT, SHE'S BACK

@Sarahthefangirl
What does this mean???

@Sarahthefangirl
SHE'S BACK, WORLD! GOODLUCK, CHARLIE! #Jarlie

Chapter 46

Charlie

Growing up in Los Angeles, Charlie learned from an early age that LAX airport was its own circle of hell. It took her and Ripley almost an hour to find a parking spot, another half hour to get her bags checked, and forty-five minutes to go through security in the international terminal. By the time Charlie was speed-walking through the terminal and to her gate, she was running behind.

She had five minutes until boarding.

Fuck.

She picked up her pace, her backpack falling off her shoulders and catching on her arm. She just needed to get on this flight. If she could make it to Edinburgh, then she could go back to the store. Someone there had to know where he was staying. Layla would help her. Wouldn't she?

Since deciding to fly back to Edinburgh, Charlie had been looking back on the past couple of weeks with pure guilt. Because she hadn't just left Page behind in Scotland.

She had left Lilian.

Layla.

Callum and Flora.

She had even left that damn cat, Gandalf the White.

She had multiple texts from Layla and Lilian that had been sitting unopened on her phone. She hadn't been able to open and read them—her brain immediately thinking they would be furious, angry, or disappointed in how she had left. She had assumed the worst.

But she had read them on the way to the airport. She had read them and tried not to cry. Because despite her thinking they would instantly take a side against her, they hadn't.

Layla
> Hey, I heard what happened?
> Lilian said you left. Are you okay?

Layla
> I hope you're okay.

Layla
> I understand if you need space.
> But don't forget you have friends.

Layla
> The bookshop does miss you btw.

Lilian
> My brother is an idiot and will regret letting you leave one day. I hope it's soon.

Lilian
> I know you need space. But he was scared, Charlie. He loves you. Please, don't give up on him.

That last text had made the tears start. Because it was true, she had given up on him—on them. They both had. In fact, thinking about it now, the idea of sides was completely stupid. Page and Charlie had left, had dissolved what they had and ran

332

away. Both of them had been wrong.

But she was going to try and fix it.

When she rounded the corner, she almost groaned in relief when she saw her plane wasn't boarding yet. In fact, they were disembarking from the plane before. She scanned the sign and saw it had come from New York—

Charlie stopped dead in her tracks.

He was wearing a faded blue flannel and jeans, an LA Dodgers baseball hat—*her* baseball hat—pulled over his hair, a pair of sunglasses sitting on his nose. But where others didn't seem to realize who he was, Charlie recognized him instantly.

She would always be able to spot him.

He saw her a few seconds later. He adjusted his bag on his shoulder, his hand coming up to push up his glasses, and he froze. Page lowered his hand, his glasses clenched in his fist. Their eyes met.

Charlie had always watched movies growing up—she had grown up in Los Angeles, for God's sake. You couldn't avoid the film industry here. She'd always hated how, in rom coms, there always seemed to be a moment where they saw one another and everything else faded away. It had always seemed unrealistic to her. How could everything else fade away? The sounds, the people, the colors—everything was always so overstimulating that she never got that feeling unless she had her headphones on and closed her eyes.

But as their eyes met, she only saw him.

He was the first to move. He walked towards her, to where she was standing, frozen in the middle of the hallway.

"Charlie," he said, and the sound of his voice, the sound of him saying her name, broke her out of her frozen state.

"What the fuck are you doing here?" she asked, her hands tightening on the straps of her bag. He caught the movement and nodded towards her bag.

"I could ask the same thing."

"I'm going to Scotland," she said, and at his raised brow, she cleared her throat. She knew her tone was angry, annoyed. "Or

I was going to Scotland. I—I had to talk to you. I was coming *to you*." She was going to apologize to him. But he was here, once again throwing a wrench into her perfectly laid-out plans.

"You saw the interview." It was more of a statement than a question. "You know, you could have picked up the phone to call me," he said with a small grin.

"So could you."

He lifted his shoulder in a small shrug. "Maybe I'm here for work."

Her stomach fell a bit, and she tried her hardest to keep her expression neutral. But her voice shook when she spoke. "Are you here for work?"

He shook his head. "No," he said softly.

"Oh," she said, her voice low.

"I—" he paused, and before he continued, Charlie cut in.

"I heard what you said. And before you say anything, I need to say something." She didn't miss how his shoulders slumped a bit. But he nodded, and she kept going. "That night was a mess. We were both angry and confused. We were both scared. I'm sorry that I didn't even think about how you were feeling, dealing with the trauma of what had happened when Anna died. I should have seen how scared you were, but I was so upset myself. So much that I was—"

"Charlie," he said, his hand raising as if to touch her arm, to pull her closer. But he dropped it before he touched her. "Like you said, we both fucked up. I realized the moment you left that it was a mistake. But I was still so worried that I thought you would be safer if you went home and didn't have me in your life." He shook his head. "I thought you were better off without me. And I'm not saying that I still don't think those things every now and then—it's going to be hard for me not to worry about that. But I should have respected that you could make those decisions on your own instead of forcing you away. But Charlie… you came into my life unexpectedly, yes, and I kind of wish we hadn't met the way we did—"

"It will be a funny story to tell the grandkids—"

"—but I could not be happier than I am that you knocked me unconscious. You came in, disrupted my life, made me rethink things I wanted, made me look up from the ground I had been staring at to get away from everything. And…" His hands came up to grasp her arms, but they fell before he touched her. She wanted to scream at him to touch her, to hold her. "I want you. I want your truth, because I love the way you scrunch up your nose when you're annoyed, or when your eyes light up with joy when you're talking about something you love. I love your truth. All of you."

They both stood there, staring at each other. Charlie moved first, her hand catching his. His skin was warm and calloused, his hand engulfing hers in his grip. When she looked up, she caught him looking at their hands. He looked exhausted, but she saw the glimmer of hope, how at their touch his shoulders relaxed.

She reached up with her other hand, punching him lightly in the shoulder.

"Oof," he said, his hand coming up to capture hers before she could hit him again. "What was that for?"

"That," she said, trying to keep her voice steady as he pulled her closer, "was for saying you loved me on national television before you told me yourself in person."

He winced and opened his mouth, but she beat him to it.

"I love you," she said, her voice clear. She met his eyes with her own, stepping into his warmth. "I was scared and stupid. When I landed in Stonehaven, I was running away from everything. And I ran into you. I didn't know it at the time, but I do now. And I want, am ready, to stop running." She felt butterflies flapping around in her stomach. She took a breath. "I love you."

His arms wrapped around her waist, his hands settling on her lower back. A part of her could hear the whispers around them and noticed how a girl to their right had her phone out. How another man was whispering to his wife and pointing at them. But she didn't care. Not anymore.

"Are we going to do this?" he asked, his lips tilting up into a grin. As if in a challenge. A challenge she accepted with everything in her.

"I'm all in if you are."

"Are you going to insist that we have rules this time?" he asked cheekily, chuckling at her narrowed eyes.

"Just one." She grinned. "You have to kiss me right now."

So, he did. And between kisses, he told her he loved her. She said it back. And they didn't care if anyone saw.

@CharliesWorld

Gandalf the White needed to make an appearance. I think he's finally team #AngryCharlie 😊

8 months later

Epilogue

Page paced as he waited for Charlie to finish reading. When he had given her the script, she had insisted on reading it right away. He had been the one to insist she read it in the other room. He was now regretting that. He wished he could see how she was reacting.

Was she liking it?

But before he moved to barge into her room, the door opened, and Charlie stepped out. They'd been in LA for the past five months, taking a mini break for just the two of them after the holidays and staying in Charlie's LA apartment while Page had started filming season three of *StarVerse*. After he had done his interview and the lawsuit had gone through, he hadn't been shocked when the entire cast had gotten the notification that, not only would filming for season three be pushed by a few months, but that Jim and Mark had "taken a leave of absence". It had been a few weeks after when they'd all been introduced to their new showrunner, a woman named Kerry Jameson. His lawsuit hadn't even gone to court, the two assholes not wanting their shit to be aired publicly and agreeing to the settlement. Even though it had almost been a year since his interview, he still got asked about it in new ones he did for the show, which had just finished filming season three a few weeks ago. But he hadn't let it overshadow anything. Not with Charlie by his side, and his friends finally able to feel more comfortable on their sets.

And Killian Glass? He was on probation with the new showrunner, and if he stepped out of line… well, he wouldn't have any more scenes in the show and the writing room had announced they had a great, dramatic death planned in the works for Asmor. Their time in LA had not been relaxing… just different. A good different.

A week ago, after Page had met Ripley and they'd gone up north to meet Charlie's parents, they had decided to head back to Scotland. Lilian had helped them with everything, giving Charlie her position back at the store, helping her with the work visa, and making sure everything would be in place for them when they arrived. With Lilian now busy with… other things, the apartment stood empty. So, instead of staying at a hotel, they were back in the flat. Just like they had been during last summer.

"So?" Page asked, moving away from the door. Lilian had given them free rein with the flat, and they had decided to move into Charlie's bedroom. They'd been living together since, falling back into their old patterns. It was strange being back in the place that had felt so safe, but looking back, had almost been a cage—allowing them to hide away. Now that they weren't hiding anymore, the flat felt different. The weight, the anxiety, was gone.

He loved how, every day, he seemed to learn more about Charlie. He learned how she hid her hatred of tomatoes when he cooked. So, he stopped putting them in her food. He loved how he learned about her love for Star Wars, and they proceeded to consume all four seasons of Star Wars Rebels, their debates filling the flat until midnight. He loved how, even after almost a year, he still caught his breath every time he woke up and saw her next to him.

"What did you think?" Page rested his hands at his side, his nerves twitching as he stared down at her.

"Page," she let out a breath. "It was amazing."

Page let out a breath he didn't know he had been holding in. He cracked his neck, trying to get rid of the tension. "Really?"

She moved, setting the printed script on the kitchen counter before heading back to stand in the circle of his arms. "Really. Promise me you'll send this to Angie? It deserves to be read, Page."

He nodded. "I'm just glad you liked it." He had been working on the script since he had arrived in LA. It seemed that everything over the summer had unfurled inside of him, and he had needed the written words to let out everything that had been piling up. He knew it wasn't perfect—not yet. But he was glad Charlie thought it was good enough to show Angie. He had been thinking of sending it to her for the past couple of weeks, but he had wanted to give it to Charlie first.

Because it wouldn't have been written without her. The story wasn't about him or even them. But it did deal with his trauma. It dealt with anxiety. It was a love letter to mental health. To surviving. To falling in love.

Charlie stood on her toes, fitting her mouth to his. His hands tightened on her waist, but instead of pulling her into the bedroom like he wanted, he pulled back.

"Come on," he said, moving to the door and grabbing his jacket. "I want to show you one more thing."

Charlie looked up at the house on the beach, her gaze moving quickly between Page and the front door. The last time she'd

339

been here was before she went back to LA. Since then, she'd been so busy with the store that she'd yet to see how the project had progressed. The tools had been cleared, and a small garden was now planted in the front yard. The door, once rough wood, was painted a deep forest green, along with the rest of the windowsills.

"What are we doing here?" she asked, laughing a bit as Page pulled her from the small gate, through the walkway, and up to the front door.

"I told you. I want to show you something," he said, grinning at her. She couldn't help but smile back. The last eight months had been healing for them both. Yes, being out in the spotlight had been rough. But so was life… and she had come to the conclusion that a life with him was worth the stupid gossip, the stories, and the press. Especially when they were able to escape most of it here in Stonehaven. They had dealt with a few reporters showing up at the store, but so far, nothing bad had happened. Back in LA, it had been a bit worse, but here—here, they had their own haven, the small town protecting them from the rest of the world.

Page reached into his pocket, pulled out a key, and unlocked the door, stepping aside so that she could step in first. Charlie sent him a suspicious glance but then froze when she walked over the threshold.

The house… was finished.

The last time she'd been here, the flooring hadn't even been done. But now, a deep, rich hardwood ran beneath her feet, the walls bare, yet to be given life. But everything else—everything else was finished. She moved through the living room, into the kitchen, through the dining room and finally, stopped in the library.

It was full of books. She studied their spines, her eyes glossing over the different covers—

Wait a minute.

"These are my books," she said, turning to find Page standing in the doorway to the library.

"I had Ripley ship them ahead of us from the US."

"Yes, I can see that. But why?" She opened her mouth, froze, and then chose her next words carefully. "Why are they here?"

Page moved into the room, raising a brow at her. His hands were in his pockets, his hair falling in front of his glasses and into his eyes. He stopped right in front of her. "I thought that was obvious."

"You know that sometimes what seems obvious to you might not be to me. Spell it out."

He took his hand out of his pocket and opened his closed fist. In it was a silver key. "This place is done. Even the upstairs. And when Callum told me it was ready to move into, I— I knew I couldn't do it without you." He held the key in front of her. "So, this is me," he chuckled and rubbed the back of his neck with his other hand. "This is me asking you to move in with me."

"I already live with you."

He coughed. "Well, yes, I suppose you do but—"

She cut off his words by kissing him. Her hand closed over his, wrapping the key in their entwined grip. "Yes, I would love to move in with you," she said, grinning as she pulled away. "I mean, GW would have a fit if I left again."

At Page's mock glare, she giggled. He gripped her by the waist, grinning. "That is true. We can't have that."

"And you'll need help editing that script. It might be good to have someone with a writing degree living in the same house."

"True again," he said, kissing her cheek. Her nose. Her neck.

"And," she added, her breath catching, "you did already move my books in."

He pulled back, grinning even more. "I knew that was how I could get you to say yes."

She laughed, and he kissed her, bringing her closer to him, her hands wrapping around his neck. "I would have said yes, regardless," she said and pulled him in for another kiss.

The End

Acknowledgements

This book is a passion project that could not have been published without the help of some truly incredible people. So please, sit back and grab yourself a coffee because I have a lot of amazing people to thank.

First, thank you to you, my wonderful reader, for picking up this book and giving my little nerdy, queer, neurodivergent love story a chance. When writing this book, I knew it would not be for everyone—it was written at a very specific moment in my life where I was feeling a lot of rage at the world after my diagnoses. Writing Charlie and Page's story was one I found myself needing to write. And I hope you loved my "autistic rage romance" as much as I loved writing it.

Second, thank you to my wonderful editor, Romie Nguyen, without whom this book would be a pile of words with many grammar mistakes. You are not only my friend but also an absolute wonder to work with. I am always in awe of your ability to take a story and polish it to the best it can be.

Thank you to my wonderful sensitivity readers: Joel, Swati, Sukhi, Bethany, Chloe, Jess, and Theresa. This book would not be where it is without you all. Your work, dedication, and passion helped make this book possible and I am forever grateful.

Next, thank you to my wonderful cover artist, Yasemin Anders. Your talent and art always astound me, and I am still in awe of your ability to bring my book and characters to life with this beautiful cover.

To my beautiful writing mentor and friend, Romina Garber, I send a big hug and big thank you. You have believed in me ever since I started writing at the age of sixteen, and have continued to support and cheer for me through the highs and lows of writing and publishing. I would have stopped writing years ago if it weren't for you and I am so lucky to have you in my life as a mentor and big sister figure.

To the people who have supported me with their friendship

and guidance through this long but rewarding journey of writing so far: Nicole Maggi, Chloe Liese, Annabelle Lee, Emma Finnerty, Joel Rochester, Jess Lee, Swati Sudarsan, Theresa Fettes, Dilan Dyer, Elliot Fletcher, Rae Douglas, Sarah Underwood, Danielle Page, Bethany Lord, Jesy Elyse, and Kaitlyn Foster.

A special thanks to Michelle Grondine for being the first person I pitched this book to and who encouraged me to actually sit down and tell Charlie and Page's story.

To all the wonderful book bloggers who mentioned, discussed, and shared Charlie and Page's story, thank you. Your work and time dedicated to this book, as well as every comment and loving review about their story means the world to me.

To my best friend, Sukhi. Our friendship is one I hold very close to my heart, and every day I am so thankful that we had the most autistic interaction in the university lounge area and suddenly became friends. I truly don't know what I would do without you in my life.

To my partner, Jack, for supporting me by feeding me and giving me coffee during my highs and lows, and always saying my writing is amazing even though you haven't read the book yet. You have helped further my delusion that my writing is brilliant, and for that, I am forever grateful because it kept me writing. Where Page and Charlie's story is not autobiographical, your love showed me that I deserved to and could be loved. Therefore, this book, in part, is for you. I love you.

And finally, to my parents. Thank you for cultivating a childhood that celebrated the arts and for always supporting me no matter what I wanted to do with my life, even if that means writing smut. Your love and guidance have been with me since day one and I will forever be thankful.

Author bio

Caden Armstrong is a 23-year-old book nerd originally from sunny Los Angeles, California. At 18, she set off to explore the world, studying in Paris, France, for four years, and is now living out her dark academia dreams in Edinburgh, Scotland, with her partner.

She fills her days working at a bookshop and fangirling over whatever she is now obsessed with. As a disabled and queer author, she aims to write novels giving queer and disabled people their own love stories on the page.